D1533213

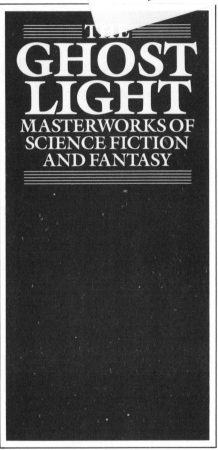

THE
GHOST
LIGHT

MASTERWORKS OF
SCIENCE FICTION
AND FANTASY

FRITZ LEIBER
THE
GHOST LIGHT

MASTERWORKS OF
SCIENCE FICTION
AND FANTASY

A BYRON PREISS
VISUAL PUBLICA-
TIONS, INC. BOOK

BOOK DESIGN BY ALEX JAY

BERKLEY BOOKS, NEW YORK

THE GHOST LIGHT
Masterworks of Science Fiction and Fantasy

A Berkley Book/published by arrangement with
Byron Preiss Visual Publications, Inc.

PRINTING HISTORY
Berkley trade paperback edition/April 1984

Book design by Alex Jay/Studio J.
Cover painting by John Jude Palencar.

Special thanks to John Silbersack for his help in making the selections for this collection. Additional thanks to the author's agent, Robert P. Mills; Ann Weil; Jim Gasperini; Roger Cooper, Susan Allison and Ony Ryzuk of Berkley Books; Joan Brandt; and Peter Glassman of Books of Wonder.

CONTENTS

•

Sculptures for the title pages
of this book were designed
by JoEllen Trilling.
All title page photographs
and frontispiece photograph
by Ben Asen.

THE GHOST LIGHT

MASTERWORKS OF SCIENCE FICTION AND FANTASY

AUTHOR'S INTRODUCTION

I**T'S VERY SUGGESTIVE HOW OFTEN A STORY,**
especially an adventure story, fantasy or mainstream, but
leaning toward fantasy, revolves around an *object*. Often
it's a very ordinary object, or seems to be so, at least at
the start of the story, but it gets involved in the lives of
the characters and draws their attention more and more,
eventually becoming a thing of significance and power, even magical.

Sometimes it's a treasure in itself (though the object may be
sinister, even deadly), perhaps a treasure in disguise, or points the
way toward treasure.

Often it gives the story its name. One thinks of Walter Scott's
novel of the Crusades, *The Talisman,* and Dashiell Hammett's detective story about another object from the Crusades, *The Maltese
Falcon,* an example of the treasure in disguise: seemingly just a dull
black statuette of a bird, but if you scrape away the black enam-
el...jewel-crusted gold!...or just lead? Which reminds me of
Shakespeare's *The Merchant of Venice,* with its three caskets (the
object becomes multiple) of gold, silver, and lead, among which
the hero must choose.

Or Dorothy Hughes' high Gothic thriller, *The So Blue Marble,* a
tiny turquoise sphere that seems to hold the whole earth in it. Which
recalls the supernally beautiful deep blue Chinese bowl called "The
Flower of Forgetfulness" in Heinlein's "We Also Walk Dogs."

Or de Maupassant's "The Diamond Necklace" (another ambig-
uous treasure), Jacobs' "The Monkey's Paw," Elizabeth Counsel-
man's "The Three Marked Pennies," Montague Rhodes James's
"Canon Alberic's Scrapbook," the grand piano (the object may be
big) of Bob Bloch's "Mr. Steinway," Poe's "The Cask of Amontil-
lado" (a parade of sinisters!), and Lewis Padgett's "Mimsy Were
the Borogroves" with its wonderful box of entrancing children's
toys time-traveled from the future.

All this isn't very surprising when you consider that magical
objects are the stuff of myth and legend. Swords like Excalibur,
Stormbringer, and Scalpel. Odin's spear Gungnir and ring Draup-
nir, which gives birth to nine like it each night (more multiple

objects). The ten rings of Susan Dexter's *The Ring of Allaire*. The twelve of Tolkien's *The Lord of the Rings*. Macbeth's bloody daggers, Alice's "Drink Me" bottle.

Such an object provides a crystallization point for the ideas swirling up from the writer's unconscious. And gives the reader something to focus on while the story's magic takes hold, very much like the twinkling object a person being hypnotized is directed to watch while getting dreamier and dreamier. And have you noticed how often, at least in stories and film, that's a watch swung on its chain? Which makes me think of John D. MacDonald's *The Girl, the Gold Watch, and Everything,* where the timekeeper controls time travel.

A while back I was talking about the stories we'd selected for this book with its producer, Byron Preiss. I'd already woven nine of them together in my "Interpretive Memoir," explaining where each came from in my life, where I got the ideas and characters, what drove or tickled me into writing each tale, how my childhood fears and interests and excitements and inhibitions left their mark on them, what writing them taught me, and all the odd and curious things that happened in the course of that writing.

Byron was pointing out how many of the chosen stories featured objects of the sort I've been talking about: the skull-faced dice in "Gonna Roll the Bones," the hardly larger cubical lioness talisman in "Black Glass," the steel finger-claws and mask of the girl in "Coming Attraction," and how two of the stories featured curio shops with whole collections of such objects, "The Bazaar of the Bizarre" with its spiders and girls in cages, and the elusive San Francisco boutique with its unique watch and chessmen in "Midnight by the Morphy Watch."

Which reminded us of similar hard-to-find stores in other fantasies and books: Dickens' *The Old Curiosity Shop*, Wells' "The Magic Toyshop," Sturgeon's "Shottle Bop," and the appearing and disappearing Weapon Shops in Van Vogt's series.

And then Byron flashed on the idea of illustrating the book by putting its stories on display, as it were, in the show window of just such a curio shop. Sculptress JoEllen Trilling was commissioned to build objects for all of the stories in this book and a search for the proper setting in which to photograph them was begun. A New York bookstore specializing in rare children's books, *Books of Wonder*, for one morning would become *Fritz Leiber's The Ghost Light*, a shop featuring "rare tales". I agreed to pose in front of this most curious of curio shops for the marvelous photograph by Ben Asen that appears in this book.

That left us with the new story to be decided on that would give the whole book its title. My "Interpretive Memoir" provided the answer. It ended with me getting the Christmas gift of a charming little night light with green and blue panes, which nevertheless had set my mind working in sinister and shivery ideas. What if there were a night light that *attracted* ghosts rather than holding them at bay? And so "The Ghost Light" came to be written.

The Ghost Light

AFTERWARDS WOLF AND TERRI COULDN'T
decide whether little Tommy's slightly off-beat request about the green and blue night light (that later came to be called the ghost light) had come before or after the first dinner table talk about ghosts with the white-haired old man (Wolf's widowed professor emeritus father, Cassius Kruger, a four-years reformed alcoholic) in the living room of the latter's dark, too big, rather spooky house on the steep wooded hillside of canyon-narrow Goodland Valley up in Marin County just north of San Francisco that was subject to mud slides during seasons of heavy rain.

For one thing, there'd been more than one such conversation, scattered over several evenings. And they'd been quite low key and unscary, at least at first, more about memorable literary ghost stories than real or purported ghosts, so that neither Terri nor Wolf had been particularly worried about Tommy being disturbed by them.

Little Tommy Kruger was a solemn, precocious four-year-old whose rather adult speech patterns hadn't yet been corrupted by school and the chatter of other kids. Although not particularly subject to night terrors, he'd always slept with a tiny light of some sort in the room, more his mother's idea than his. In his bedroom at his grandfather's this was a small, weak bulb plugged in at floor level and cased in tiny panes of dark green and deep blue glass set in tin edges crafted in Mexico.

When in the course of the putting-to-bed ritual on the second or third (or maybe fourth) night of their visit Wolf knelt to switch on the thing, Tommy said, "Don't do that, Pa. I don't want it tonight."

Wolf looked up at his tucked-in son questioningly.

Terri had a thought based on her own unspoken feeling about the light. "Don't you like the colors, Tommy?" she asked. "Wolf, there's a plug-in fixture like this one, only with milky white glass, under that strange old painting of your mother in the living room. I'm sure your father wouldn't mind if we changed—"

"No, don't do that," Tommy interrupted. "I don't mind these

colors at all, Ma, really. I just don't want a light tonight."

"Should I take this one away?" Wolf asked.

"No, don't do that, Pa, please. Leave it there, but don't turn it on. But leave the door to the hall open a little."

"Right," his father affirmed vigorously.

When good-night kisses were done and they were safely beyond Tommy's hearing, Wolf said, "I guess Tom's decided he's too grown up to need a light to sleep by."

"Maybe. Yes, I guess so," Terri agreed somewhat reluctantly. "But I'm glad it's off, anyhow. Loni said it gave the room a corpse look, and I thought so too." Loni Mills was Terri Kruger's attractive younger sister. She'd come with them on their visit to meet Wolf's father, but had decided the day before that she needed to get back to campus a couple of days before winter vacation ended at the Oregon college where she was a sophomore.

Terri added, frowning, "But why did he make a thing of your not taking the fixture away?"

"Obvious." Wolf grinned. "Little guy's keeping his options open. So if he should get scared, it's there to turn on. Good thinking. Also shows the colors don't bother him. Why'd Loni think of blue and green as corpse colors, I wonder?"

"You've seen a fresh drowned person, haven't you?" Terri responded lightly. "But why don't you ask Cassius that one? It's the sort of question gets him talking."

"Right," Wolf agreed without rancor. "Maybe I will."

And true enough, there'd been a couple of times during the visit (though not as many as Wolf had feared) when conversation had languished and they'd been grateful for any topic that would get it going again, such as oddities of psychology, Cassius' academic field, or ghost stories, in which they all seemed to share an interest. Matter of fact, the visit was for Wolf one of ultimate reconciliation with his father after a near-separation from both parents for a period of twenty years or so, while Terri was meeting her father-in-law, and Tommy his grandfather, for the first time.

The background for this was simply that the marriage of Wolf's father and mother, Cassius Kruger and Helen Hostelford, had progressively become, after Wolf's early childhood, a more and more unhappy, desperately quarrelsome, and alcoholic one, full of long, cold estrangements and fleeting reconciliations, yet neither partner had had the gumption to break it off and try something else. At the earliest teen age possible, Wolf (it was short for Wolfram, a fancy of his father) had wisely separated himself from them and

NOTES

Cheeref

Fritz Leiber

ATTITUDE = BOOKS · TAPES · SEMINARS · RALLIES

MY MONTHLY P.V. GOAL:

MY RALLY DATE THIS MONTH:

MY STP GOAL THIS MONTH ·   MEETINGS

JANUARY 1989

SUNDAY	MONDAY	TUESDAY	WEDNESDAY	THURSDAY	FRIDAY	SATURDAY
G, Downe 1 J. Addington	2	3	4	5	Charles 6	7
New Year's Day 8	9	Nathan year 10	11	David Anderson 12	13	Carl Tobey 14

largely gone it on his own, getting a degree in biology and working up a career in veterinary medicine and animal management, feeling his way through an unsuccessful early marriage and several living arrangements, until he'd met Terri. His mother's death several years back from a mixture of alcohol and barbiturate sleeping pills hadn't improved his relationship with his father—the opposite, rather, since he'd been somewhat closer to Helen and inclined to side with her in the unutterably wearisome marriage war—but then the old man, whom he'd expected to go downhill fast once he was alone, had surprised him by pulling out of his alcoholism (which had again and again threatened to end his academic career, another wearisomely repetitive series of crises) by the expedient of quitting drinking entirely and slowly rebuilding the wreckage of his body into at least a fairly good semblance of health.

Wolf had been able to keep tabs on his father's progress through letters he got from an old crony of his mother, a gossipy and humorous theatrical widow named Matilda "Tilly" Hoyt, who was also a Marin resident not far from Goodland Valley and kept in touch with the old man after Helen's death; and from infrequent, cold-bloodedly short hello-good-bye solo visits he paid Cassius to check up on him that came from a dim unwilling feeling of responsibility and from an incredulous and almost equally unwilling feeling of hope.

After several years, his father's repeated good showings, his own reawakening good memories from early childhood before the marriage war had started, the old man's seemingly sincere, even enthusiastic, interest in Wolf's profession and all his son's life, for that matter, plus some encouragement from Terri, worked a perhaps inevitable change in Wolf. He talked more with Cassius on his solo visits and found it good, and he began to think seriously of accepting the old man's repeated invitation to bring the new family to visit.

He talked it over first with Tilly Hoyt, though, calling on her at her sunny cottage nearer the beach and the thundering, chill, swift-currented Pacific than the treacherous brown hills which rains could tumble.

"Oh, yes, he's changed, all right," she assured Wolf, "and as far as the liquor goes, I don't think he's had a drop since two or three months after Helen died. He's got some guilt there, I think, which showed in odd ways after she died, like his bringing down from the attic that weird painting of her by that crazy French-Canadian— or was it Spanish-Mexican?—painter they used to have around." She searched Wolf's eyes unhappily, saying, "Cassius was pretty rough with Helen when he got very drunk, but I guess you know about that."

Wolf nodded darkly.

She went on, "God knows I got my share of black eyes from Pat when he was still around, the bum." She grimaced. "But I gave as good as I got, I sincerely hope, and somehow though we were fighting all the time, we were always making up a little more of the time. But with Helen and Cassius anything like that seemed to cut deeper, down to the bone, take longer to heal, they were both such nice, idealistic, goofy, perfectionist people in their ways, couldn't accept the violence that was in them. And the fault wasn't always on Cassius' side. Your mother wasn't the easiest person to get on with; she had a bitter streak, a cold-as-death witch thing, but I guess you know that too. Anyway, now Cassius is, well, what you might call...chastened." She curled her lip in humorous distaste at the word and went on briskly, "I know he wants to meet your new family, Wolf. Whenever I see him he talks a lot about Tommy— he's proud as anything to be a grandfather, and about Terri too, even Loni—he's always showing me their pictures—and he positively makes a hero of you."

So Wolf had accepted his father's invitation for himself and Terri and Tom and Loni, and everything had seemed to work out fine from the start. The days were spent in outings around the Bay, both north and south of the Golden Gate and east into the Napa wine country and Berkeley-Oakland, outings in which Cassius rarely joined and Wolf enjoyed playing tour guide, the evenings in talking about them and catching up on the lost years and comfortably growing a little closer. The old man had spread himself and not only had his cavernous place cleaned up but also had the Latino couple, the Martinezes, who looked after it part time, stay extra hours and cook dinners. In addition he had a couple of neighbors over from time to time, while Tilly was an almost constant dinner guest, and he insisted on serving liquor while not partaking of it himself, though he did nothing to call attention to the latter. This so touched Wolf that he hadn't the heart to say anything about his father's almost constant cigarette smoking, though the old man's occasional emphysemic coughing fits worried him. But the other old people smoked too, Tilly especially, and on the whole everything went so well that neither Loni's premature departure nor the occasional silences that fell on their host cast much of a damper.

The talk about ghost stories had started just after dinner at the big table in the living room with the masklike painting of Wolf's mother Helen with the little white light below it, looking down on them from the mantelpiece on which there also stood the half dozen bottles of sherry, Scotch, and other liquors Cassius kept for his guests. The conversation had begun with the mention of haunted paintings when Wolf brought up Montague Rhodes James' story, "The Mezzotint."

"That's the one, isn't it," Terri had said helpfully, "where an old engraving changes over a couple of days when several different people look at it at different times, and then they compare notes and realize they've been witnessing the re-enactment of some horror that happened long ago, just before or just after the print was engraved?"

"You know, that's so goddam complicated," Tilly objected, but "Yes, indeed!" Cassius took up enthusiastically. "At first the ghost is seen from the rear and you don't know it's one; it's just a figure in a black hood and robe crawling across the moonlit lawn toward a big house."

"And the next time someone sees the picture," Wolf said, picking up the account, "the figure is gone, but one of the first-floor windows of the house is shown as being open, so that someone looking at the picture then observes, 'He must have got in.'"

"And then the next to last time they look at the picture and it's changed," Terri continued, "the figure's back and striding away from the house, only you can't see much of its face because of the hood, except that it's fearfully thin, and cradled in its arms it's got this baby it's kidnapped..." She broke off abruptly and a little uncertainly, noticing that Tommy was listening intently.

"And then what, Ma?" he asked.

"The last time the picture changes," his father answered for her, his voice tranquil, "the figure's gone and whatever it might have been carrying. There's just the house in the moonlight, and the moon."

Tommy nodded and said, "The ghost stayed inside the picture really, just like a movie. Suppose he could come out, sort of off the picture, I mean?"

Cassius frowned, lighting a cigarette. "Ambrose Bierce got hold of that same idea, Tommy, and he wrote a story, a shorter one, about a picture that changed, only as in the James story no one ever saw it at the moment it changed. The picture was mostly calm ocean with the edge of a beach in the foreground. Out in the distance was a little boat with someone in it rowing toward shore.

As it got closer you could see that the rower was a Chinaman with long snaky moustaches—"

"Chinaperson," Loni corrected and bit her lip.

"Chinaperson," Cassius repeated with a nod and a lingering smile at her. "Anyhow as he beached the boat and came toward the front of the picture you could see he had a long knife. Next time someone looked at it, the picture was empty except for the boat in the edge of the wavelets. But the time after that the Chinaperson was back in the boat and rowing away. Only now lying in the stern of the boat was the corpse of the...person he'd killed. Now I suppose you could say he got out of the picture for a while."

Shaking his head a little, Tommy said, "That's good, but I don't mean that way 'zactly, Grandpa. I mean if you saw him step or float out of the picture, come *off* the picture like, same size and everything as in the picture."

"That would be something," Wolf said, catching his son's idea. "Mickey Mouse, say, mouse life-size—no, comic book size—waltzing around on the coffee table. That tiny, his squeak might be too high to hear."

"But Mickey Mouse isn't a ghost, Pa," Tommy objected.

"No," his grandfather agreed, "though I remember an early animation where he challenged a castle run by ghosts and fought a duel with a six-legged spider. But that surely is an interesting idea of yours, Tommy," he went on, his gaze roving around the room and coming to rest on the large reproduction of Picasso's "Guernica" that dominated one wall, "except that for some pictures," he said, "it wouldn't be so good if their figures came out of the frames and walked, or floated."

"I guess so," Tommy agreed, wrinkling his nose at the looming bull man and the other mad faces and somber patterns in Picasso's masterpiece.

Terri started to say something to him; then her eyes shifted to Cassius. Wolf was watching her.

Loni yielded to the natural impulse to look around at the other pictures, gauging their suitability for animation. She hesitated at the dark backgrounded one which showed the head only, all by itself like a Benda mask, of a rather young Helen Kruger with strange though striking flesh tones. She started to make a remark, but caught herself.

But Tommy had been watching her and, remembering something he'd overheard before dinner, guessed what she might have been going to say and popped out with, "I bet Grandma Helen would make a pretty green ghost if she came out of her frame."

"Tommy…" Terry began, while, "I didn't—" Loni started involuntarily to protest, when Cassius, whose eyes had flashed rekindling interest rather than hurt at Tommy's observation, cut in lightly and rapidly, yet with a strange joking or mocking intensity (hard to tell which) that soon had them all staring at him, "Yes, she would, wouldn't she? Tiny flakes of pink and green paint come crackling off the canvas without losing their configuration as a face.…Esteban always put a lot of, some said too much, green in his flesh—he said it gave it life.…Yes, a whole flight, or flock, or fester, or flutter, or flurry, yes *flurry* of greenish flakes floating off and round about in formation, swooping this way and that through the air, as though affixed to an invisible balloon responding to faintest air currents, a witches-sabbath swirling and swarming.…And then, who knows? Perhaps, their ghost venture done, settling rustlingly back onto the canvas so perfectly into their original position that not the slightest crack or faintest irregularity would be evidence of—"

He broke off suddenly as an inhalation changed into a coughing fit that bent him over, but before anyone had time to voice a remark or move to assist him, he had mastered it, and his strangely intent eyes searched them and he began to speak again, but in an altogether different voice and much more slowly.

"Excuse me, my dears. I let my imagination run away with me. You might call it the intoxication of the grotesque? I encouraged Tommy to indulge in it too, and I ask your pardons." He lit another cigarette as he went on speaking measuredly. "But let me say in extenuation of our behavior that Esteban Bernadorre was a very strange man and had some very strange ideas about color and light and pigments, strange even for a painter. Surely you must remember him, Wolf, though you weren't much older than Tommy here when that painting of Helen was executed."

"I remember Esteban," Wolf said, still studying his father uneasily and revolving in his mind the words the old man had poured out with such compulsive rapidity and then so calculatedly, as if reciting a speech, "though not so much about his being a painter as that he was able to fix a toy robot I'd broke, and that he rode a motorcycle, oh yes, and that I thought he must be terribly old because he had a few grey hairs."

Cassius chuckled. "That's right, Esteban had that mechanical knack so strange in an artist and always had some invention or other he was working on. In his spare time he panned for gold—oh, he was up to every sort of thing that might make him money—the gold-panning was partly what the motorcycle was for, to take him up into the little canyons where the little goldiferous streams are. I remember he talked about vibrations—vibes—before anyone else did. He used to say that all vibrations were one and that all colors were alive, only that red and yellow were the full life colors—blood and sunlight—while blue was the death, no, life-in-death color, the blue of empty sky, the indigo of outer space...." He chuckled again, reflectively. "You know," he said, "Esteban wasn't really much of a draftsman; he couldn't draw hardly anything worth a damn except faces; that's why he worked out that portrait technique of making faces like hanging Benda masks; that way he never got involved in hands or ears or other body parts he was apt to botch."

"That's strange," said Wolf, "because the only other one of his pictures I seem to remember now from those days—I think now that it had some influence on my life, my choice of profession—was one of a leopard."

Cassius' sudden laugh was excited. "You know, Wolf," he said, "I believe I've got that very picture up in the attic! Along with some other stuff Esteban asked me if he could store there. He was going to send for them or come back for them but he never did. In fact it was the last time I ever saw him, or heard from him for that matter. It's not a good picture, he never could sell it, the anatomy's all wrong and somehow a lot of green got into it that shouldn't have. I'll take you up and show it to you, Wolf, if you'd like. But tomorrow. It's too late tonight."

"That's right," Terri echoed somewhat eagerly. "Time for bed, Tommy. Time for bed long ago."

And later, when she and Wolf were alone in their bedroom, she confided in him, "You know, your father gave me a turn tonight. It was when he was talking about those dry flakes of green paint vibrating in the air in the shape of a face. He dwelt on them so! I think imagining them brought on his coughing fit."

"It could have," Wolf agreed thoughtfully.

The third-floor attic was as long as the house. Its front window seemed too high above the descending hillside, its rear one too close to it, shutting off the morning sunlight. Cassius piloted Wolf through the debris of an academic lifetime to where a half dozen canvases, some of them wrapped in brown paper, were stacked against the wall behind a kitchen chair on which rested a dust-filmed chunky black cylindrical object about the size and shape of a sealed-in electric generator.

"What's that?" Wolf asked.

"One of Esteban's crazy inventions," his father answered offhandedly, as he tipped the canvases forward one by one and peered down between them, hunting for the leopard painting, "some sort of ultrasonic generator that was supposed to pulverize crushed ore or, no, maybe agitate it when it was suspended in water and get the heavier gold flakes out that way, a mechanical catalyst for panning or placering, yes, that was it!" He paused in his peering search to look up at Wolf. "Esteban was much impressed by a wild claim of the aged Tesla (you know, Edison's rival, the inventor of alternating current) that he could build a small, portable device that could shake buildings to pieces, maybe set off local earthquakes, by sympathetic vibrations. That ultrasonic generator there, or whatever he called it, was Esteban's attempt in the same general direction, though with more modest aims—which is a sort of wonder in itself considering Esteban's temperament. Of course it never worked; none of Esteban's great inventions did." He shrugged.

"He fixed my robot," Wolf mused. Then, somewhat incredulously, his voice rising, "You mean he left it here with you, and the other stuff, and actually never came back for it, even wrote? And you didn't do anything about it either, write him at least?"

Cassius shrugged more broadly. "He was that sort of person. As for me, I think I tried to write him once or twice, but the letters came back. Or weren't answered." He smiled unhappily and said softly, "Alcohol's a great forgettery, you know, a great eraser, or at least blurrer, softener...." With a small gesture he indicated the shelves of books, the piled boxes of old files and papers between them and the ladder to the second floor. "Alcohol's washed through everything up here—the university, Helen, Esteban, all my past—and greyed it all. That's alcohol dust on the books." He chuckled and his voice briskened. "And now to things of today. Here's the picture I promised you."

He straightened himself, drew a canvas on which he'd been keeping his hand out of the stack with a flourish, wiped it off on his sleeve, and faced it to Wolf.

It was a medium-size oil painting, wider than high, of a golden leopard with black spots like tiny footprints, stretched out on a branch in a sea, a flood, of green leaves. You knew it was high in the tree because the branch was thin and the green sunlight the leaves transmitted was bright, so all-suffusingly bright that it gave a greenish cast to the leopard's sleek fur, Cassius had been right about that. And also about the bad anatomy too, for Wolf at once noted errors of muscle placement and underlying bony structure.

But the face! Or muzzle or mask, rather, that was as magnificent as memory had kept it for him, a wonderfully savage sensitive visage, watchful and wild, the quintessence of the feline. . . .

Cassius was saying, "You can see he's even got the eyes wrong, giving them circular pupils instead of slits."

"In that one point he happens to be right," Wolf said, happy to get in a word for the man who, he was beginning to remember, had been something of a childhood hero to him. "The leopard does not have slit eyes like a house cat, but pupils exactly like ours. It's that detail which gives him a human look."

"Ah so," Cassius conceded. "I didn't know that. Live and learn. He should have painted just that, used the mask trick he did with his pictures of people."

Wolf's gaze and mind returned to the black object. He looked it over more closely without handling it, except to brush off dust here and there. "How the devil was it supposed to be powered? I can't see any place for plugging in wires, just the one switch on top, which indicates it was run by electricity."

"Batteries, I think he told me," the old man said, and, bolder or less cautious than his son, reached over and pushed the switch.

It was, at first, to Wolf holding it, as if a very distant unsuspected ponderous beast had roused and begun to tramp toward them across unimagined miles or light years. Under his hands the black cylinder shook a little, then began to vibrate faster and faster, while in his ears a faint buzzing became a humming and then a higher and higher pitched whine.

The unexpectedness of it paralyzed Wolf for a moment, yet it was he rather than his father who thrust back the switch and turned off the thing.

Cassius was looking at it in mild surprise and with what seemed to be a shade of reproach. "Well, fancy that!" he said lightly. "Esteban returning to us through his works. I never dreamed— This seems to be my morning for misjudging things."

"Batteries that last *twenty* or more years—?" Wolf uttered incredulously and then didn't know how to go on.

His father shrugged, which was not the answer Wolf was looking for, and said, "Look, I'm going to take this picture downstairs. I agree it has possibilities. Could you carry that . . . er . . . thing? I know it's too heavy for me, but perhaps we should have a look at it later. Or something . . ." he trailed off vaguely.

Wolf nodded curtly, thinking, *Yes, and shut it away safely where neither Tommy nor anyone else can get their eager little unthinking hands on it.* He found himself strangely annoyed by his father's irresponsibility, or over-casualness, or whatever it was. Up to now the old man had seemed to him such a *normal* sort of reformed or arrested alcoholic. But now—? He hefted the black cylinder. It *was* heavy.

He found himself wondering, as he followed the slow-moving Cassius to the front of the attic, what other time bombs there might be, in the old man's mind as well as the house, waiting to be detonated.

But his thoughts were somewhat diverted when he glanced out the front attic window. A short way down the hillside and to the side of the house amongst the nearest trees and further fenced by tall shrubs was a grassy bower that was bathed in sunlight and into which he could look down from his vantage point. Sprawled supine at its center on a long black beach towel was Loni clad in black wraparound sunglasses, a quite splendid sight which somehow reminded Wolf of a certain wariness Terri had had of her then thirteen-year-old sister during their courtship and also reminded him perhaps to tell the girl a cautionary tale or two about the Trailside Murderer who had terrified Marin County some years back.

When he got the black cylinder downstairs he set it, at Cassius' direction, on the high mantelpiece, which would at least put it out of Tommy's reach, and as an extra precaution taped the switch in the off position with two short lengths of friction adhesive. The old man had propped the painting on a straight-backed chair standing against the wall nearby.

Wolf's speculations about Cassius and the house were further driven from his mind, or to its shadowy outer reaches at any rate, by the day's activities when he drove Terri and Tommy up into Sonoma County through the Valley of the Moon to the Jack London Museum and led them through the big trees to the fire-darkened gaunt stone ruins of London's Wolf House. (Tommy made a solemn joke of calling it "Pa House," while Wolf promised to show him some real wolves at Golden Gate Park tomorrow.)

That must have been the day, Wolf figured out later, of Loni's impulsive departure for her Oregon college, for she wasn't there the next morning to hear Cassius' dream of the giant spider and Esteban (though Tilly was, who'd come over early to share their late breakfast). It was also the day when Weather confirmed that the big storm front building up in the North Pacific had veered south and was headed for San Francisco.

Cassius prefaced his account of the night's somnial pageantry with some nervous and veering verbal flamboyancies. He seemed a bit hollow-eyed and overwrought, as if sleep hadn't rested him and he were clowning around and gallumphing to hide the fact, and for the first time Wolf found himself wondering whether their visit hadn't begun to tire the old man.

"Never dream these days," Cassius grumbled, "just feelings and flashes, as I think I've told you, Terri, but last night I sure had a doozie. You brought it on me, Wolf, by making me go up to the attic and look at that old stuff of Esteban's I'd forgotten was there." He nodded toward the black cylinder and green-flooded leopard painting. "Yes, sir, Tommy, your Pa gave me one doozie of a dream." He paused, wrinkled his nose, and looked comically sideways at Wolf. "No, that isn't true at all, is it? I was the one who told you about it and led you up there. I brought it all on myself! See, Tommy, never trust what your Grandpa says, his mind's slipping.

"Anyhow," he launched out, "I was standing in the front attic window, which had become French windows nine feet tall with yellow silk drapes, and I was working away on a big kirschwasser highball. I sometimes drink in my dreams," he explained to Terri. "It's one of my few surviving pleasures. Sometimes wake up dream-drunk for a blessed moment or two.

"Around me in my dream the whole house was jumping, first floor, second floor, attic turned ballroom. People, lights, music, the tintinnabulation of alcoholic crystal. Benighted Goodland Valley resounded with the racket from stem to stern. Even the darkness jumped. I realized that your Grandma, Tommy, was giving one of her huge parties, to which she invited everyone and which generally bored me stiff." He looked surprised and tapped himself on his mouth. "That's another lie," he said. "I enjoyed those parties more than she did. She gave them just to please me. Keep remembering what I told you about trusting your Grandpa, Tommy.

"Anyway," he went on, "there I was carousing on the edge of nothing, leaning against the friendly dark outside, for the French windows were pure ha-ha." He explained to Tommy, "That's a place in a British fancy garden where there should be a flight of steps, but isn't. You start down it and—boomp. Hence ha-ha. Very funny. The British have a wonderfully subtle sense of humor.

"But in my dream I was gifted with an exquisite sense of balance. I could easily have walked a tightwire from where I was to the opposite crest of the valley, balancing myself with sips of kirsch and soda, if my dream had only provided one. But just then I felt something tug at my trousers, trying to topple me forward.

"I looked down at my leg, and there was a naked baby no higher than my knee, a beautiful cherub straight out of Tiepolo or Titian, but with a nasty look on her cute little face, yanking ineffectually at my pant leg with both hands. I looked straight down the outside of the house and saw, just below me way down there, a new cellar door of the slanting flat kind thrown wide open, revealing a short flight of steps leading down into the basement, from which light was pouring, as if the party were going on there too.

"But a green tinge in that light telegraphed 'Danger!' to my brain, and that was no lie for suddenly there was rearing out of the cellar up toward me a huge green and yellow spider with eight glaring jet black eyes and terribly long legs, the first pair so super long, like the two tentacular arms of a squid, that they could reach the attic.

"At that moment I felt something that made me look back at my leg, and I saw that the cherub had let go of my pants and was starting to overbalance and fall (she had no wings as a proper cherub should).

"With one hand I steadied the baby-skinned creature and with the back of the other (oh, my balance was positively miraculous) I knocked aside the spider leg that was about to touch the cherub.

"At the same instant I saw that the monster was only a large pillow toy made of lustrous stuffed velvet, the eyes circles of black sequins, and that the whole buisiness was a put-on, a party joke on me."

Cassius took a swallow of cold coffee and lit another cigarette. "Well, that ended that part of the dream," he said, "and the next I knew I was standing on the dark hillside beside the house, the party still going on, and calculating how many inches the hill had shifted down and forward during the last rain (it never has, you know, not an iota) and wondering what the next rain was going to do to it—guess I was anticipating today's weather forecast—when I heard someone call my name softly.

"I looked down the hillside to the road and saw a small closed car, one of those early Austins or maybe a Hillman Minx, drawing up to park there. And, this is a funny part, although it was black night, I could see the driver silhouetted inside, as if by an impossibly belated sunset afterglow, and although he was wearing a big white motorcycle crash helmet I identified him at once—something about his posture, the way he held himself—as Esteban Bernadorre, whom I haven't seen for almost a quarter of a century.

"'Esteban?' I called hoarsely, and from the tiny car came the quiet, clipped, clearly enunciated response, 'Certainly, I will be happy to coffee with you, Cassius.'

"Next thing I knew I was walking uphill toward the house with Esteban close beside me. As we approached the open door, which was filled with a knot of animatedly conversing drinkers—a sort of overflow from the hubbub inside—I realized Esteban was still wearing his crash helmet, oversize gauntlets too, and that I still hadn't greeted him properly.

"Preparatory to introducing him to the others, I swung in front of him, offering my hand and trying to discern his face in the cavernous seeming helmet's depths. He drew off his gauntlet and shook hands. His hand was oversize, as its glove had been, and wet, gritty, and soft all at once. After shaking mine, he lifted his hand and made the motion of wiping the back of it across his eyes, and I saw it was composed of wet grey ashes except where the wiping motion had bared a narrow edge of pink flayed flesh. And at the same time I saw that his eyes were nothing but charred black holes, infinitely deep, and his whole face granular black char wet as the ashes.

"I swiftly turned to check how much, if anything, those in the door had seen, for we were now quite close to them. I saw that the centralmost carouser was Helen, my dear wife, looking very dashing in a silver lamé evening dress.

"She said to me, gesturing impatiently with her empty glass, 'Oh, we're *quite* familiar with Esteban's boundless self-pity and self-dramatizing tricks. You should know him by now. He's forever parading his little wounds and making a big production of them.'

"At that moment I remembered that Helen was really dead, and that woke me up, as it generally does."

And with that Cassius blew out his breath in a humorously intended sigh of achievement and looked around for applause. Instead he encountered something close to stony gazes from Terri and Tilly too, Wolf looked both doubtful and slightly embarrassed, while Tommy's face had lost the excited smile it had had during the cherub-spider part of the dream, and the child avoided his grandfather's gaze. The four faces, for that matter, were a study in varieties of avoidance.

"Well," the old man grumbled apologetically after a moment, "I guess I should have realized beforehand that that was an X-rated dream. Not on account of sex or violence, but the horrifics, you might say. I'm sorry, ladies, I got carried away. Tommy, Gramps is not only a liar, he never knows when to stop. I thought my dream was a pretty good show, but I guess it overdid on the unexplained horrifics. They can be tricky, not to everyone's taste."

"That's true enough," Wolf said with a placating little laugh as Cassius went off into the kitchen to raise mild hell with the Martinezes about something. Wolf was glad to turn his attention to getting the day's drive to Golden Gate Park under way. That boiled down to plans for Tom and himself, since Terri decided she was tired from yesterday and wanted to gossip with Tilly, maybe drive over to the older woman's place. This didn't exactly displease Wolf, as the thought had struck him that Terri might be as tired as his father of their visit, maybe more so, and a day with Tilly Hoyt might set that right, and in any case give him time to rethink his own thoughts.

Tommy was uncommonly silent during the drive down, but a rowboat ride on Stow Lake and a visit to the buffaloes got him cheerful and moderately talkative again. Wolf couldn't produce any live wolves but at least found the kid a group of stuffed ones at the Academy of Sciences, while both of them enjoyed the speeding, circling dolphins at the Steinhart Aquarium, the only seemingly simplistic Bufano animal sculptures in the court outside, and the even more simplified, positively sketchy food in the cafeteria below.

Emerging in the court again, their attention was captured by the hurrying hungry clouds, which devoured the red skeletal Sutro TV tower as they watched.

"Pa, are clouds alive?" Tommy asked.

"They act that way, don't they?" Wolf agreed. "But, no, they're no more alive than, say, the ocean is, or mountains."

"They're made of snowflakes, aren't they?"

"Some of them are, Tom. Mostly high, feathery ones called cirrus. Those're made of ice flakes, you could say, tiny needles of ice. But these we're looking at are just water, billions of billions of tiny drops of water that sail through the air together."

"But drops of water aren't white, Pa. Milk clouds would be white."

"That's true, Tom, but the drops of water are tremendously tiny, droplets you call them, and at a distance they do look white when sunlight or just a lot of sky light hits them."

"What about small clouds, Pa, are they alive? I mean clouds small enough to be indoors, like smoke clouds or paint clouds, clouds of smoke flakes or paint flakes. Grandpa can blow smoke clouds like rings. He showed me."

"No, those clouds aren't alive either, Tom. And you don't say smoke flakes or paint flakes, though there might be flakes of soot in heavy smoke and you could blow a sort of cloud of droplets— droplets, not flakes—from a spraypaint can, but I wouldn't advise it."

"But Grandpa told about a little cloud of paint flakes flying off a picture."

"That was just in a story, Tom, and an imaginary story at that. Pretend stuff. Come on, Tom, we've looked at the sky enough for now."

But the day, which had started in sunlight, continued to grow more and more lowering until, after their visit to the Japanese Tea Garden, whose miniaturized world appealed to Tom and where he found a little bridge almost steep enough to be a ha-ha, Wolf decided they'd best head for home.

The rain held off until they were halfway across the Golden Gate Bridge, where it struck in a great squally flurry that drenched and rocked the car, as if it were a wet black beast pouncing. And although they were happily ahead of thick traffic, the rain kept up all the way to Goodland Valley, so that Wolf was relieved to get his Volks into the sturdy garage next to Cassius' old Buick, and hurry up the pelting slippery hill with Tommy in his arms.

During their absence, things had smoothed out at the old man's place, at least superficially; and mostly by simplification—the Martinezes had both departed early to their home in the Mission after getting dinner into the oven, while Tilly, who'd been going to stay for it, had decided she had to get to her place to see to its storm defenses, so there were only the four of them that ate it.

By this time the rain had settled down to a steady beat considerably less violent than its first onset. Wolf could tell from Terri's manner that she had a lot she wanted to talk to him about, but only when they were alone, so he was glad the Golden Gate Park talk both lasted out the meal and trailed off quickly afterwards (while the black cylinder on the mantelpiece and the green leopard painting under it stood as mute signs of all the things they weren't talking about), so they could hurry Tommy, who was showing signs of great tiredness, off to bed, still without night light, say good-night to Cassius, who professed himself equally weary, and shut their bedroom door behind them.

Terri whipped off her dress and shoes and paced up and down in her slip.

"Boy, have I got a lot to tell you!" she said, eyeing Wolf excitedly, almost exultantly, somewhat frightenedly, and overall a bit dubiously.

"I take it this is mostly going to be stuff got from Tilly today?" he asked from where he sat half-reclining on the bed. "That's not to put it down. I've always trusted what she says, though she sure loves scandal."

Terri nodded. "Mostly," she said, "along with an important bit from Loni I've been keeping back from you, and some things I just worked out in my head."

"So tell," he said with more tranquility than he felt.

"I'll start with the least important thing," she said, approaching him and lowering her voice, "because in a way it's the most pressing, especially now that it's raining. Wolf, the hill under and back of this house—and all of Goodland Valley for that matter (they really should call it Goodland Canyon, it's so constricted and overhung!)—isn't anywhere near as stable as your father thinks it is, or keeps telling us it is. Why, every time a heavy rain keeps on, the residents are phoned warnings to get ready to evacuate, and sometimes the highway police come and make them, or try to. Wolf, there have been mudslides around the Bay that smashed through and buried whole houses, and people caught in them and their bodies never recovered. Right in places like this. There was a slide in Love Canyon, and in other places."

Wolf nodded earnestly, lips pressed together, eyeing his aroused wife. "That doesn't altogether surprise me. I've known about some of that and I certainly haven't believed everything Cassius has to say about the stability of this hillside, but there seemed no point in talking about it earlier."

She went on, "And Tilly says the last times there've been warnings, Cassius has gone down and stayed at her place. We've never heard a word about that. She says it looks like it might happen again, and we'll have to be ready to get out too."

"Of course. But the warnings haven't come yet and the rain seems to be tapering off. Oh, I guess Cassius is pretty much like the other residents in spots like this. Won't hear a word against their homes, they're safe as Gibraltar, anyone who says different is an alarmist from the city or the East or LA, an earthquake nut, but when the rains and warnings come, everything's different, no matter how quick they forget about it afterwards. Believe me, Terri, I could feel that myself when I drove back this afternoon and rushed up this soggy hill with Tom." He paused. "So what's the other stuff?"

She started to pace again, biting her lip, then stopped and eyed him defiantly. "Wolf," she said, "this is one of those things I can't talk about without cigarettes. And if you don't like it, too bad!"

"Go ahead and smoke," he directed her.

As she dug out a pack, ripped off its top, and lit up, she confessed, "I started smoking Tilly's when she was telling me things at her place, and when she drove me back here, I picked up a couple of packs on the way; I knew I'd be needing them.

"Well, look, Wolf, before Loni left she told me, after I'd agreed not to tell you, that one of the reasons she was leaving early was that your father had been...well...bothering her."

"You know, that doesn't altogether surprise me either," Wolf responded. "Depending, of course, on how far his bothering went and how she behaved." And he told Terri about seeing Loni sunbathing yesterday morning and how Cassius could have as easily seen her too, and probably did, finishing with "And, Terri, it was really a most stimulating sight: sweet black-masked nubility sprawled wide open to the wild winds and all that."

"The little fool!" Terri hissed, quickly supplementing that with, "Though why a woman in this day and age shouldn't be able to sunbathe where and whenever she wants to, I don't know. But Loni didn't, wouldn't, tell me exactly how far your father tried to go, though I got the impression there was something that really shook her. But she and I have never been terribly close, as I think you know. That's one reason why it became important what Tilly had to tell me on the subject."

"Which was?" Wolf prompted.

Lighting another cigarette and puffing furiously, Terri said, "When we got to talking over lunch at her place, the conversation somehow got around to your father and sex—I guess maybe I hinted at what Loni told me—and she came right out with (remember how rough she often talks), 'Cassius? He's an indefatigable old lecher!' and when I tactfully asked her if he'd made advances toward her, she whooped and said, 'Me? My dear, I'm much too ancient for him. Cassius, I'll have you know, is only turned on by the college freshman and *especially* high-school junior types.'"

Wolf scowled despondently. Somehow he'd not expected his own father to be so ordinary, so humdrum, in his psychology. You'd think a recovered alcoholic would have gained some mellowness, some dignity. He shrugged.

Terri went on, "Of course I asked for more. It turned out that Tilly knew a local girl in the latter (I mean, high-school) category. A tough, outspoken girl rather like she'd once been herself, I gather.

Well, it seems Cassius' advances were an old story to this girl and to another of her female classmates too—they'd compared notes. She made a sort of joke out of the old man's attempts at 'romance,' as she called them, though they sounded like more. She told Tilly, 'Mr. Kruger? First he reads poetry to you and talks about nature and tells you how beautiful and young and fresh you are, maybe offers you a drink. Then he carries on about his dead wife and how terribly lonely he is, life over for him and all that. Then if you're still listening he begins to hint about how he's been completely impotent for years and years, and how dreadful that is, but you're so wonderful and if you'd only deign to touch him, if you'd just be a little bit kind, it would only take the tiniest touch, that's all an old man needs—a tiny touch below the belt— Well, if you fall for that and begin thinking, "A good deed. Why not?" why, then you'll find him telling you he has to touch *you* just the tiniest bit to balance things out, to make them right, at the same time he's clamping down on you with kisses, cutting off your breath, and before you know it he's got one hand down your blouse...Now I won't say that all happened to me, Ms. Hoyt, but it's sure what Mr. Kruger has in mind when he gets romantic and recites poetry and begs for the slightest touch of your beeyootiful fingers.'"

"Oh God," Wolf sighed, drawing it out. "'To see ourselves as others see us.'" He shook his head from side to side. "What else? What next? There is something more?"

"There is," she confirmed, "and it's the most important part. But I want to get my mind straightened about it first, and that performance wore me out." And she did look a bit frazzled. "Oh hell," she said, stubbing out her cigarette and wetting her lips dry with talking, "Let's screw."

They did.

Considerably later she sat up in bed, seemed to think for a while, then with a dissatisfied sigh got up, slipped on her robe, lit another cigarette, and came back and sat on the side of the bed smiling at Wolf. The sound of the rain had sunk to a barely audible patter and the wind seemed to have died.

"You know," she said, "that should have made it easier for me to tell you the rest, but somehow it hasn't exactly.

"The thing was," she went on, her voice picking up as she began to reconstruct, "that I'd suddenly realized that repeating to you those things that girl told Tilly that Cassius did to her, or tried to do, was getting *me* excited, which made me ask myself how much of my indignation at your father was honest. That's what I wanted to straighten out in my mind, especially when Tilly (and the girl too apparently) seemed to treat it half as a joke, or one quarter at any rate, one of the grotesque indecencies you expect from practically all men, or at least all old men.

"Well, it's not too clear in my mind yet, the real reasons for my indignation, or at least my being upset. I'll try to keep it simple. It seems to boil down to two things, and one of them has nothing to do with sex at all. It's this, I just can't get out of my mind two or three of the horrible stories your father told in Tommy's presence. He made them so vivid, he seemed to gloat on them so, as if he were trying to infect that child—and all of us!—with dreads and superstitions. And the way he watched Tommy while he told them. That horrible dream of the burnt-to-ashes Esteban. And especially the way he described your mother's face coming off the painting and ghosting around the room as a cloud of green paint flakes. I'm sure Tommy's been thinking about that ever since."

"You know, that's true," Wolf said, sitting up, his face serious. And he told Terri the questions Tommy had asked him at the park about clouds being alive.

"You see," she said, nodding, as he finished, "Tommy's got flakes on his mind, that horrible vibrating cloud-face of pinky-green flakes. Ugh!" She shivered her revulsion.

"The other thing," she went on, "*is* about sex, or at least starts with sex. Now after Tilly told me about that girl, I naturally asked her how soon after your mother's death Cassius had started to hunt high-school girls, or younger women at any rate. She whooped a little again and told me he'd always been that way, that it sometimes got obvious at those big parties your mother gave, and that she thought Cassius had been attracted to your mother in the first place because she was such a small, slight woman and always stayed somewhat girlish looking. 'Helen knew about Cassius' chasing, of course,' Tilly said. 'It was one of the things we used to drink about. At first we had both our husbands to rake over the coals. I was the most outspoken, but Helen was more bitter. Then Pat died and there was only Cassius for us to gripe at, mostly for his drunken pawings at parties, his dumb little infatuations with whatever young stuff happened to be handy.' Wolf, I don't like to ask you about this, but does that fit at all with your memories of your father's behavior then?"

He winced but nodded. "Yes, during the last couple of years before I lit out on my own. God, it all seemed to me then so adult-dumb, so infantile and boring, adult garbage you wanted to get shut of."

Terri continued, "Tilly said that after you left, Cassius and Helen made up for a while, but then their battling got still more bitter and more depressing. Twice Helen took too many sleeping pills, or Cassius thought she did, and rushed her the morning after to the hospital to have her stomach pumped out, though Helen didn't recall overdosing those two times, just that she blacked out. But then there came this Sunday morning when Cassius called up Tilly about ten or so, sounding very small and frightened, but rational-seeming, and begging her to come over, because he thought that Helen was dead, but he wasn't absolutely sure, and—get this!—he didn't know either whether he had killed her, or not! Helen's doctor was coming, he'd already called him, but would Tilly come over?

"She did, of course, and of course got there before the doctor—Sunday mornings!—and found Helen lying peacefully in bed, cold to the touch, and the bedroom a minor mess with unfinished drinks and snacks set around and a couple of empty sleeping pill bottles with their contents, or some of their contents, scattered over the bed and floor, a snowfall of red-and-blue Tuinal capsules. And there was Cassius in bathrobe and slippers softly jittering around like an anxious ghost, keeping himself tranquilized with swallows of beer, and he was telling her over and over this story about how everything had been fine the night before and he'd taken two or three pills, enough with the drinks to knock him out, and then just as he was going under Helen had started this harangue while flourishing a bottle of sleeping pills, and he couldn't for the life of him remember whether she'd been threatening to commit suicide or just bawling him out, maybe for having taken the pills himself so as not to have to listen to her, and he'd tried to get up and argue with her, stop her from taking the pills if that was what she intended, but the pills he'd taken were too much for him and he simply blacked out.

"Next he remembered, or thought he remembered, waking in the dark in bed and talking and then sleeping with, and then arguing with Helen and shaking her by the shoulders (or maybe strangling her! he wasn't sure which) and then passing out again. But he wasn't too sure about any of that, and if there had been talk between them, he couldn't recall a word of it.

"When he next woke up it was fully light and he felt very tranquil and secure, altogether different. Helen seemed to be sleeping peacefully, and so he slipped out of bed and made himself some coffee and began to tidy up the rest of the house, returning at intervals to check if Helen had woke up yet and wanted coffee. The second time it struck him that she was sleeping too peacefully, he couldn't see her breathing, she didn't wake up to being called or shaken, and he tried the mirror and feather tests and they didn't work, so he'd called her doctor and then Tilly.

"Tilly was sick about Helen and coldly enraged with Cassius, his
pussyfooting around so coolly especially infuriated her, but on the other hand she couldn't see any bruises or signs of strangulation on Helen, or other form of violent death, and there were no signs of a struggle or any particular kind of commotion except for the scattered pills (she picked up some of those and stashed them in her bag with the thought that she might be needing them herself), and after a bit she found herself sympathizing with Cassius while still furious with him—he was being such a dumb ox!—and be-having toward him as she would have to her own husband Pat in a similar fix.

"For instance, she said to him, 'For God's sake don't talk about strangling Helen when the doctor comes unless you're really sure you did it! Don't tell him anything you're not sure of!' But she couldn't tell how much of this was really registering on him; he still seemed to be nursing a faint crazy hope that the doctor might be able to revive Helen, and muttering something about stories by Poe and Conan Doyle."

"'Premature Burial' and 'The Resident Patient,'" Wolf said ab-sently. "About catalepsy."

"About then Helen's doctor came, a very cautious-acting young man ('My God, another pussyfooter,' Tilly said to herself) but he pronounced Helen dead quickly enough, and soon after the doctor a couple of policemen arrived, from San Rafael, she thought, whom the doctor had called before starting out.

"Maybe the appearance of the cops threw a scare into Cassius, Tilly said, or at least convinced him of the seriousness of the situ-ation, for there wasn't any mention of strangling in what he told the three of them, nothing at all about maybe waking in the dark, it all sounded to Tilly more cut and dried, more under control. And when he mentioned the two previous times that Helen had over-dosed, the doctor casually confirmed that.

"The doctor had another look at Helen and they all poked around a bit. What seemed to bother the doctor most were the scattered sleeping pills, they seemed to offend his sense of propriety, though he didn't pick them up. And the two cops were quite respectful—

your father does have quite a presence, as Tilly says—although the younger one kept being startled by things, as though the like had never happened before, first by Cassius not realizing at once when he got up that Helen was dead, then by Tilly just being there (he gave her a very funny look that made her wonder if that was what being a murder suspect was like), things like that.

"About then the ambulance the doctor had called arrived to take off Helen's body and he and the cops drove off right afterwards."

She paused at last. Wolf said earnestly, "Cassius never told me any of that—nothing about his suspicions of himself, I mean, nor about the doctor calling in the police at first. Nor did Tilly tell me—but of course you know that."

Terri nodded. "She said she didn't want to rake up things long past just when you were getting reconciled to your father and after he'd managed to quit drinking."

"But what happened?" Wolf demanded. "I mean at the time? As I think you know, Cassius didn't write me about my mother's death until after the funeral, and then only the barest facts."

"Exactly nothing happened," Terri said. "That's what made it seem so strange, at least at the time, Tilly told me—as if that weird and frantic morning of Helen's death had never happened. The autopsy revealed a fatal dose of barbiturate without even figuring in the alcohol, Cassius did call and tell her that much. And she saw him briefly at the funeral. They weren't in touch again after that for almost a year, by which time he'd been six months sober. Their new friendship was on the basis of 'Forget the past.' They never spoke of the morning of Helen's death again, and in fact not often of Helen. Tilly told me she'd almost forgotten Helen in a sort of way and seldom thought of her, until about six months ago when Cassius brought Esteban's painting of Helen down from the attic and hung and lighted it—"

"He could have been anticipating our visit," Wolf said thoughtfully.

Terri nodded and continued, "—and a couple of times since when Tilly came calling and noticed he'd hung a towel over it, as if he didn't want it watching him, at least for a while—"

At that instant there was a great flash of white light that flooded the room through the window curtains and simultaneously a ripping *craaack!* of thunder that catapulted Terri across the bed into Wolf's arms. As their hearing returned, it was assaulted by the frying sound of thick rain.

Murmuring reassurances, Wolf disengaged himself, got up, and shouldered hurriedly into his robe. Terri had the same thought: *Tommy.*

The door opened and Tommy hurtled in, to stop and look back and forth between them desperately. His face was white, his eyes were huge.

He cried out, losing three years of vocabulary from whatever shock, "Ma take me! No, *Pa* take me! 'Fraid *Flakesma!*"

Wolf scooped him up, submitted to being grappled around the neck, speaking and cuddle-patting reassurances about as he would have to a frightened monkey. Terri started to take him from Wolf or at least add her embraces to his, but restrained herself, uneasily watching the open door.

White lightning washed the room again, followed after a second by another loud but lesser ripping *crack!*

As if the thunder had asked a question, Tommy drew his head back from Wolf's cheek a little and pronounced rapidly but coherently, regaining some vocabulary but continuing to coin new expressions under the pressure of fear: "I woke up. The ghost light was on! It made Grandma Flakesma come in after me, ceiling to floor! Pa, it brings her! Her green balloon face buzzed, Pa!"

Gathering her courage, which a new-sprouted anger reinforced, Terri moved toward the door. By the time she reached Tommy's room she was almost running.

The green and blue night light was on, just as Tommy'd said. Its deathly glow revealed a scattered trail of pillows, sheet, and blanket from the abandoned bed to her feet.

Behind her, footsteps competed with the pounding rain.

As she heard Cassius ask, "Where's Tommy? In Wolf's bedroom, Terri? Did the thunder scare him?" she stooped and switched off the offending globe with a vicious jab.

Then, as she hurried past the whitely tousle-headed old man mummy-wrapped in a faded long brown bathrobe, she snarled at him, "Your poisonous night light gave Tommy a terrible nightmare!" and rushed downstairs without listening to his stumbling responses.

In the dark living room the portrait of Helen Hostelford Kruger by Esteban Bernadorre was softly spotlighted by the pearly bulb just below its frame. As Terri advanced toward it, moving more slowly and deliberately now, breathing her full-blown anger, its witch face seemed to mock her. She noticed a subtlety that she'd previously missed: the narrowed eyes were very darkly limned, so that they sometimes seemed to be there but sometimes not, as though the portrait itself might be that of a taper-chinned witch mask greenish flesh-pink and waiting for eyes to fill it—and maybe teeth.

After glaring at it for a half dozen pounding heartbeats while thunder crackled in the middle distance, her fists clenching and unclenching, she contented herself with switching off its milky light—poison milk!—with a just audible "Flakesma!" like a curse and hurrying back upstairs.

In the hall there she passed Cassius coming out of "Wolf's bed-room," as he'd called it. She spared him a glare, but he, agitated looking and seemingly intent on wherever he was heading, hardly appeared to notice.

Wolf had Tommy tucked into the middle of their bed and was sitting close beside him. "Tom's going to spend the rest of the night with us," he told her. "Big family reunion and all."

"Oh, that's nice," she said, forcing a smile and bidding anger depart, at least from her features and tumultuous bosom.

"I've already invited him and he's accepted," Wolf went on, "so I guess you haven't any say in the matter."

"But we really want you, Ma," Tommy assured her anxiously, sitting up a little.

She plopped down on the other side, saying, "And I'm delighted to accept," as she hugged and kissed him.

Straightening up, she informed Wolf, "I turned that light off," and Tommy's face changed a little, and Wolf said lightly, "You mean that ghost light in Tom's room? A good idea. He and I have been talking about that a bit, and about ghosts and visions of all sorts, and thunderstorms, and flying cabbages and specter kings, and why if the sea were boiling hot we'd have fish stew."

"And wings for pigs," Tommy added with a pallid flicker of enthusiasm. "Space Pigs."

"Incidentally," Wolf remarked, "we discovered how the ghost light came to be on. No witchcraft at all. Cassius told us. It seems he was passing Tom's room on his way to bed and saw it was out, and not knowing that Tom had given up sleeping with a night light—"

"I might have known your father'd be the one!" Terri interjected venomously, yet midway through that statement recalled the command she'd given her anger, and managed to mute it somewhat.

"—and thinking to do a good turn he quietly stole in, so as not to wake Tom, and switched it on," Wolf finished, widening his eyes a little at Terri, warningly. "See? No mystery at all."

Then Wolf got up, saying, "Look, you guys, I want to check on what that storm's up to. I've been telling Tom how rare such storms are out here, and usually feeble when they do come. While I'm gone, Terri, why don't you tell Tom about the real humdingers they have in the Midwest that make even this one seem pretty tame? I'll be back soon."

Passing Tom's room he smelled fresh cigarette smoke.

Cassius was kneeling by the night light with his back to the door. He shoved something into his pocket and stood up. He looked haggard and distraught. He started to make an explanation to Wolf, but the latter with a warning nod toward the room where Terri and Tommy were, and not trusting himself to talk, motioned his father in the opposite direction downstairs, and followed him.

The interval gave the old man time to compose his thoughts as well as his features. When they faced each other in the living room, Cassius began, "I was replacing the night light that frightened Tommy with the white one from under Helen's picture." He gestured toward where the mask painting hung, now without its own special illumination. "Didn't want to leave the slightest opportunity for that nightmare, or whatever, to recur.

"But, Wolf," he immediately went on, his voice deepening, "what I really want to tell you is that I've been lying to you in more than one way while you've been here, at least lying in the sense of withholding information, though it didn't seem important to start with and was done, at least in part, with good intentions. Or at least I could make myself believe that, until now."

Wolf nodded without comment, dark- and suspicious-visaged.

"The littlest lie was that I haven't been dreaming much lately except for that bitch of a one about Esteban. The truth is that for the past six months or so I've been having horrible dreams in which Helen comes back from the dead and hounds and torments me, and especially dreams—green dreams, I call 'em—in which her face comes off that picture and buzzes around me whispering and wailing like green-eyed skulls used to when I had nightmares as a boy, and threatening to *strangle* me—remember that!...

"...for the most obvious reason for these dreams leads us straight back to my larger lie—again, a lie by withholding information: that ever since Helen's death I've had this half-memory, half-dread, that back in the horrible grey world of alcohol and blackout I contributed *more actively* to her death than just by not waking and getting her to the hospital in time to be pumped out.

"Sometimes the memory-dread has almost faded away (almost, sometimes, as if it could vanish forever), sometimes it's been real as a death-sentence—and especially since I've started this green-dreaming.

"Underlying all that has been the unnerving suspicion or conviction that somewhere in my mind is the memory of what really happened if only I could find a way to get back to it, through past alcoholic mists and blackout, maybe by fasting and exhaustion and sheer deprivation, maybe by drinking my way to it again or taking some stronger drug, maybe by mind-regression or psychoanalysis or some other awareness-broadening pushed to an extreme, maybe even by giving my dreams and dreads to another, to see what he'd find in them— Wolf, it's the sudden realization that I may have been trying (unknowingly!) to do that to Tommy—and to all of you, for that matter, but especially to Tommy—to use him as a sort of experimental subject, that shattered me tonight."

By this time Wolf also had had the opportunity to compose his thoughts and feelings somewhat, get over the worst of his anger at Tommy being terrorized, whether accidentally or half intentionally. Nor was he moved to sound off violently when Cassius, lighting another cigarette, had a coughing fit. But he'd also had time to make some decisions with which he knew Terri would concur.

"Don't worry any more about the night light," he began. "Tommy's sleeping with us. And tomorrow we'll be taking off, whether the rain forces us to get out (and you too maybe!) or not. It's been a good visit in a lot of ways, but I think we've pushed it too far, maybe all of us have done that. As for your dreams and guilts and worries, what can I say?" A wry note came into his voice for a moment, "After all, you're the psychologist! I do know there was something damn funny, something strange, about the scare Tommy got tonight, but I don't see where discussing it could get us anywhere, at least tonight."

Before Cassius could reply, the phone rang. It was Tilly for Cassius, and for Wolf too before she'd finished, to tell them that the TV said "the authorities" had begun to phone people in several areas including Goodland Valley to tell them to be ready to evacuate to safer places if the weather situation worsened and a second or general order came, and had they been phoned yet? Also to remind them that they were all, not just Cassius, invited down to her place, which was holding out pretty well, although there was a leak in her kitchen and a seepage in her garage.

When she finally got off the line, with messages to Terri and last admonitions to them all, Cassius tried to restart the conversation, but his mind had lost the edge it had had during his brief confession, if you could call it that, and he seemed inclined to ramble. Before he'd gotten anywhere much the phone rang again, this time with the official message Tilly had told them to expect, and there was that to respond to.

That ended their attempts at any more talk. Wolf went upstairs, while Cassius allowed he probably needed some rest too.

Outside the thunderstorm had moved into the far distance, but the rain was keeping up with a moderate pelting.

Wolf found Tom and Terri in bed, her arm around him, and with their eyes closed. She opened hers and signed to Wolf not to talk, she'd just got the boy asleep.

Wolf brought his lips close to her cheek. "We'll be leaving to-morrow," he whispered. "Stay somewhere in San Francisco. Okay?"

She nodded and smiled agreement and they softly kissed good-night and he went around and carefully slid into bed on the other side of Tommy.

That was the ticket, Wolf told himself. Leave tomorrow and let the storm decide how fast they moved, the storm and (he grinned to himself) "the authorities." Right now the former seemed to be slackening and the latter to have signed off for the night. This lazy thought pleased him and suited his weariness. What had really happened the past few days, anyway? Why, he'd simply pushed his reconciliation with his father too far, involved himself too much in the old man's ruined life-end, and as a result got Tommy and Terri (and Loni too!) entangled in the dismal wreckage of a marriage (and all its ghosts) which was all Cassius could ever be to anyone. And the solution to this was the same as it had been when Wolf was a youngster: get away from it! Yes, that was the ticket.

His thoughts in the dark grew desultory, he dozed, and after a while slumbered.

Morning revealed the storm still firmly in charge of things. No thunder-and-lightning histrionics, but its rain persistently pelted. TV and radio glumly reported a slowly worsening weather situation.

The Martinezes called in early to say they wouldn't be making it. They had storm troubles of their own down in the city.

Wolf took that call. Overflowing ashtrays told him Cassius had been up most of the night and he let the old man sleep. He made breakfast for the rest of them and served it in the kitchen. Simpler that way, he told himself, and avoided confrontation of Tommy with a certain painting.

Tilly called with updatings of last night's news and admonitions. Terri took that call and she and the older woman spun it out.

Packing occupied some more time. Wolf didn't want to rush things, but it seemed a chore best gotten out of the way.

He gave Terri the job of making them reservations at a San Francisco hotel or motel. She settled down with the phone and big directory.

Taking a rain-armored Tommy with him, he went down to the garage and found, as he'd feared, that the gas tank was a little too near empty for comfort. They drove to the nearest gas station that was open (the first and second weren't) and filled her up, made all other checks. Wolf noted that the big flashlight he kept in the glove compartment was dim and he bought new batteries for it.

Driving back, he took more note of the rain damage: fallen branches, scatters of rock and gravel, small runs of water crosswise of the road. In the garage he reminded himself to check out Cassius' Buick somehow before they left.

Terri had managed to make them a reservation at a motel on Lombard after getting "No vacancies" from a half dozen other places.

Cassius was up and on his best best behavior, though rather reserved (chastened? to borrow Tilly's word) and not inclined to talk much except to grumble half comically that people as usual were making too much of the storm and its dangers, decry the TV and radio reports, and in general put on a crusty-old-man act. However, he seemed quite reconciled to Wolf's departure and the visit's end, and also, despite his grumbles, to his own going down to Tilly's to stay out the end of the storm.

Wolf took advantage of this mood of acquiescence to get Cassius to go down to the garage with him and check out the Buick and its gas supply. Once there, and the Buick's motor starting readily enough, Wolf badgered the old man into backing it out of the garage and then into it again, so the car'd be facing forward for easiest eventual departure. Cassius groused about "having to prove to my own son I can still drive," but complied in the end, though in no more mood than before for any close conversation.

Back once more in the house, there came at long last the expected phone call with the order, or rather advisement, that all dwellers in it get out of Goodland Valley. Wolf carried their bags and things down to the car, while Cassius, still grumbling a little, prepared an overnight bag and made a call to Tilly, telling her he would be arriving shortly.

"But I'm not going to get out until you're all on your way," he gruffly warned his son's family. "Enough's enough. If I left at the same time you did, I'd lose completely the feeling—a very good one, let me assure you!—of having been your host in my own house for a most pleasant week."

Except for that show of warmth, Cassius continued his reserve in his good-bye, contenting himself with silently shaking hands first with Wolf, then Tommy, and giving each a curt nod of approval. Terri saw a tear in his eye and was touched, she felt a sudden swing in her feelings toward him, and impulsively threw her arms around his neck and kissed him. He started to wince away from her, then submitted with some grace and a murmured "M'dear. Thank you, Terri."

Wolf noted on her face a look of utter surprise and shock, but it was quickly replaced with a smile. It stuck in his mind, though he forgot to ask her about it, mostly because as they were pulling out of the garage, a highway patrol car stopped across the road and hailed them.

"Are you leaving the Kruger residence?" one of the officers asked, consulting a list, and when Wolf affirmed that, continued with, "Anyone else up there?"

"Yes, my father, the owner," Wolf called back. "He's leaving shortly, in another car."

They thanked him, but as he drove off, he saw them get out and start trudging up the hill.

"I'm glad they're doing that," he told Terri. "Make sure Cassius is rooted out."

But the incident left a bad taste in his mouth, because it reminded him of what he'd heard about the two policemen calling there the morning after his mother died.

At the first sizable intersection a roadblock was being set up to stop cars entering Goodland Valley. That didn't hold them back, but the drive into San Francisco took half again as long as he'd anticipated, what with the rain and slow traffic and a mudslide blocking two lanes of the freeway near Waldo Tunnel just north of the bridge.

Lombard Street, when they reached it just south of the bridge, reminded Wolf and Terri of western towns built along main highways in the days before freeways. Wide, but with stoplights every block and the sides garish with the neon of gas stations, chain restaurants, and motels. They located theirs and checked in with relief. Tommy had been starting to get cranky and the storm was making late afternoon seem like night.

Only Terri didn't seem to Wolf as relieved as she should be. Tommy was running a bath for himself and his boats. Wolf asked her, "Something bothering you, Hon?"

She was scowling nervously at the floor. "No, I guess I've just got to tell you," she decided reluctantly. "Wolf, when I kissed your father—"

"I know!" he interjected. "I was going to ask you about it, if he'd goosed you, tried to cop some other sort of feel, or what? You looked so strange."

"Wolf," she said tragically, "it was simply that his breath was reeking with alcohol. That was why he was making such a point of keeping a distance from us all day."

"Oh God," he said despondently, closing his eyes and slumping.

"Wolf," she went on in a small voice after a moment, "I think we've got to call up Tilly to check if he ever got there."

"Of course," he said, springing to the phone. "I guess we were going to do that in any case."

He got through to the Marin lady after some odd delays and found their worry realized: Cassius had not arrived. Wolf cut short Tilly's counter-questions with "Look, Til, I'll try to call him at the house, then get back to you right away."

This time the response was quicker. The number he was trying to reach was out of service due to storm damage.

He tried to call Tilly back and this time, after still more delays, got the same response as when he'd tried to call his father.

"All over Marin County the phones are going out," he told Terri, trying to put a light face on bad news. "Well, Hon," he went on, "I don't think I'm left much choice. I've just got to go back up there."

"Oh no, Wolf," she said apprehensively, "don't you think you should try calling the police first, at least? Cassius may still be at the house, I suppose, but then again he may simply have driven off somewhere else, anywhere, maybe to some bar. How can you know?"

He thought a bit, then said, "Tell you what, Hon. I'll go down to the coffee shop and have a couple of cups and a Danish or something; meanwhile you try calling the police. You may be able to find out something, they seem to have pretty good organization on this storm thing."

When he got back some twenty minutes later, she was on the phone. "Shh, I think I'm finally getting something," she told him.

She listened concentratedly, nodded sharply twice, asked, "About the mudslides?" nodded at the answer she got to that, and finally said, "Yes, I've got that. Thank you very much, officer," and put down the phone.

"Nothing specifically on any Kruger," she told Wolf, "but there are still holdouts in Goodland Valley, houses that won't vacate. And, at latest available report, there's been no major earth movement there, though they're expecting one at any time, it's 'a real and present danger.' Wolf, I still don't think you should go, just on the chance he'll be there."

She was watching him intently, as was a moist and robed Tommy in the bathroom door.

Grinning sympathetically, he shook his head. "Nope, got to go," he said. "I'll be cautious as hell, on the watch every second. Maybe just have to check the garage."

Outside, thunder rumbled. "That's my cue," he said and got out of the room as quickly as he could, and by the time he'd got the Volks on the bridge again, its gas tank once more topped off, he was feeling pretty good. Caffeine had done its work, thunderstorms always gave him a high, and now that he had only Cassius to worry about, everything was wonderfully simplified. It was great to be outdoors, alone, the city behind him, space around him, water under him, with lightning to reveal vividly every ten seconds or so the multiple mazy zigzag angles of the marvelous structure the Volks was traversing, and thunder to shake his bones. And himself free on a quixotic errand that had to be carried out but that really didn't matter all that much when you got down to it, since worry about Cassius was hardly to be compared with worry about Tommy or Terri, say. Oh, this storm was good, though awfully big, much too big for any sentimentalities or worrisome petty human concerns. It washed those away, washed away his own concern about whether he was being, had been, a good son (or husband or father, for that matter) and whether he was being wise to make this trip or not, washed away Terri's and Tilly's concern as to what indignities, exactly, Cassius had visited on Loni, washed away Cassius' own dreadful wondering as to whether or not he'd strangled his wife in a blackout, washed all those away and left only the naked phenomena, the stuff of which it, the storm itself, was composed, and all other storms, from those in teapots and cyclotrons to those out at the ends of the universe, that blustered through whole galaxies and blew out stars.

This almost suspiciously exalted state of mind, this lightning high, stuck with Wolf after the Volks had got across the bridge and come to the first traffic hold-up, the one a little beyond the Waldo tunnel. It was worse this time, four lanes were blocked, and took longer to get past; they were only letting cars through in one direction at a time. But now that his mind had time to move around, free for seconds and minutes from the task of driving, he found that it was drawn to *phenomena* and awarenesses rather than worries and *concerns*. For instance, those so-alike dreams Cassius and Tommy had had (they'd both used the same word "buzz" of the swooping green face), he now found himself simply lost in wonder at the coincidence. Could one person transmit his dreams to another? Could they travel through flesh and skin? And would they look like dreams if you saw them winging through darkness?

And that black sonic generator, or whatever, Esteban was supposed to have invented, how shockingly it had come alive in his hands when Cassius had thrown the switch—that strong and deep vibration! Whatever had made it work after a quarter century of disuse? And why had the puzzle of that slipped completely from his mind? He knew one thing: if he got the chance tonight, he'd certainly glom onto the black cylinder and bring it away with him!

And the color green, the witch green and death blue of Tommy's ghost light, were colors more than the raiments of awareness, the arbitrary furniture of the mind? Were they outside the mind too: feelings, forces, the raw stuff of life? and could they kill? Wave motions, vibrations, *buzzings*—vibes, vibes, vibes, vibes.

In such ways and a thousand others his thoughts veered and whirled throughout the trip, while thunder crackled and ripped, lightning made shiny sheets of streets awash, unceasing rain pattered and pelted.

Then, not more than a mile from Goodland Valley, all street-lights, all store lights, all house lights were simultaneously extinguished. He told himself this was to be expected, that power failures were a part of storms. Moreover, the rain did at last seem to be lessening.

Just the same he found it reassuring when the stationary head-lights and red lanterns of the roadblock appeared through the rain mist.

He'd been intending to explain about Cassius, but instead he found himself whipping out his veterinary identifications and launching into a story about this family in Goodland Valley that had a pet jaguar and wouldn't vacate without it and so couldn't move until he'd arrived and administered an anesthetic shot.

Almost to his chagrin they passed him through with various warnings and well wishings before he'd said much more than the words "pet jaguar." Evidently exotic pet carnivores were an old story in Marin County.

He wondered fleetingly if he'd been inspired to compose the lie in honor of Esteban Bernadorre, who'd been a mine of equally unlikely anecdotes, some of them doubtless invented only to please an admiring and credulous boy.

He followed his headlights up the slight grade leading into Goodland Valley, thankful the rain continued to slacken though lightning still flared faintly with diminished thunder from time to time, providing additional guidance. After what was beginning to seem too long a time, he caught sight of a few dim house lights in the steep hills close on each side (he'd got out of the area of the power failure, he told himself) and almost immediately afterwards his headlights picked up Cassius' garage with one door lifted open as he'd left it. He nosed the Volks into it until he could see the dark shape of Cassius' Buick.

On another sudden inspiration he reversed the direction of the Volks as he backed it out, so that it faced downgrade, the way he'd come. He parked it, setting the hand-brake, nearer the narrow road's center than its side. He took the flashlight from the glove compartment and got out on the side facing the house, leaving the headlights on, the motor idling, and the door open.

A fingering tendril of wind, startlingly chill, made him shiver.

But was the shiver from the wind alone? Staring uphill, straining his eyes at the dim bulk of the house, he saw a small greenish glow moving behind the windows of the second floor, while halfway between him and the house there stood a dark pale-headed figure. White-haired Cassius? Or a white crash helmet?

A flare of lightning brighter than those preceding it showed the swollen hillside empty and the windows blank.

Imagination! he told himself.

Thunder crashed loudly. The storm was getting nearer again, coming back.

He switched on the flashlight and by its reassuringly bright beam rapidly mounted the hill, stamping each step firmly into the soggy ground.

The front door was ajar. He thrust it open and was in the short hall that held the stairs to the second floor and led back to the living room.

As he moved forward between stairs and wall, he became aware of a deep and profound vibration that gave the whole house a heavy tremor; it was in the floor under his feet, the wall his hand groped, even in the thick air he breathed. While his ears were assaulted by a faint thin screaming, as of a sound too shrill to be quite heard, a sound to drive dogs mad and murder bats.

Midway in his short journey the house lurched sharply once, so he was staggered, then held steady. The deep vibration and the shrill whatever-it-was continued unchanging.

He paused in the doorway to the living room. From where he stood he had a clear view of the fireplace midway in the far wall, the mantelpiece above it, the two windows to either side of it that opened on the hill behind the house, a small coffee table in front of the fireplace, and in front of that an easy chair facing away from him. Barely showing above the back of the last was the crown of a white-haired head.

The bottles on the mantelpiece had been transferred to the coffee table, where one of them lay on its side, so that the mantelpiece itself was occupied only by the stubby black cylinder of Esteban's sonic generator and by his painting of Helen, which seemed strangely to have a pale grey rag plastered closely across it.

Wolf at first saw all these things not so much by the beam of his flashlight, which was directed at the floor from where his hand hung at his side, as by the green and blue glow of the ghost light beneath the oddly obscured painting.

Then the white glare of a lightning flash flooded in briefly from behind him through the open door and a window above the stairs, though strangely no ray of it showed through the windows to either side of the fireplace, followed almost immediately by a crash of thunder.

As though that great sound had been a word of command, Wolf strode rapidly toward the fireplace, directing the flashlight ahead of him. With every step forward the deep vibration and the super-shrill whine increased in intensity, almost unbearably.

He stopped by the coffee table and shone his flashlight at Esteban's invention. Torn-away friction tape dangled from the switch, which had been thrown on.

He shifted the beam to the painting and saw that what he had thought grey rag was the central area of bare canvas from which every last flake of paint had vanished, or rather *been shaken* by the vibrations from the cylinder beside it. For he could see now that the stripped canvas was quivering rapidly and incessantly like an invisibly beaten drumhead.

But the mantelpiece beneath the painting was bare. It showed no trace of fallen flakes.

As he swung the bright beam around to the easy chair, flashing in his mind on how the slim pinkish-green witch mask had swooped and buzzed through Cassius' and Tommy's dreams, it passed slowly across the nearest window, revealing why the lightning flash hadn't shone through it. Beyond the glass, close against it from top to bottom, was wet dirt packed solid.

The beam moved on to the easy chair. Cassius' hands gripping its arms and his head, pressed in frozen terror into the angle between back and side, were all purplish, while the whites of his bulging eyes were shot with a lacework of purple.

The reason for his suffocation was not far to seek. Stuffing his nostrils and plastered intrusively across his grimacing lips were tight-packed dry flakes of greenish-pink oil paint.

With a muted high-pitched crackle the two windows gave way to huge dark-faced thrusts of mud.

Wolf took off at speed, his flashlight held before him, raced down the lurching hall, out the open front door, down the splashing hill toward the lights of the Volks, and through its door into the driver's seat.

Simultaneously releasing the hand-brake, shifting the gear lever, and giving her throttle, he got away in a growling first that soon changed to a roaring second. A last sideways glimpse showed the house rushing down toward him in the grip of a great moving earth-wall in which uprooted trees rode like logs in a breaking-up river jam.

For critical seconds the end of the earth-wave seemed to Wolf's eye on a collision course with the hurtling Volks, but then rapidly fell behind the escaping car. He'd actually begun to slow down when he started to hear the profound, long-drawn rumbling roar of the hill burying forever Goodland Valley and all its secrets.

Coming Attraction

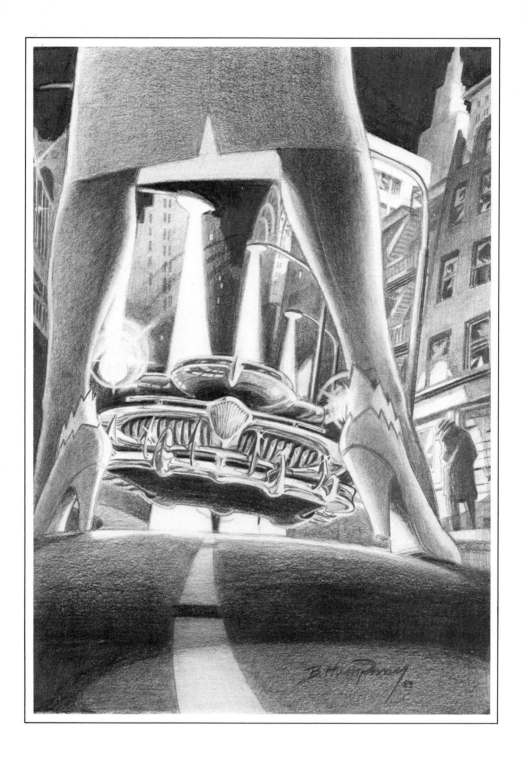

THE COUPE WITH THE FISHHOOKS welded to the fender shouldered up over the curb like the nose of a nightmare. The girl in its path stood frozen, her face probably stiff with fright under her mask. For once my reflexes weren't shy. I took a fast step toward her, grabbed her elbow, yanked her back. Her black shirt swirled out.

The big coupe shot by, its turbine humming. I glimpsed three faces. Something ripped. I felt the hot exhaust on my ankles as the big coupe swerved back into the street. A thick cloud like a black flower blossomed from its jouncing rear end, while from the fishhooks flew a black shimmering rag.

"Did they get you?" I asked the girl.

She had twisted around to look where the side of her skirt was torn away. She was wearing nylon tights.

"The hooks didn't touch me," she said shakily. "I guess I'm lucky."

I heard voices around us:

"Those kids! What'll they think up next?"

"They're a menace. They ought to be arrested."

Sirens screamed at a rising pitch as two motor-police, their rocket-assist jets full on, came whizzing toward us after the coupe. But the black flower had become an inky fog obscuring the whole street. The motor-police switched from rocket assists to rocket brakes and swerved to a stop near the smoke cloud.

"Are you English?" the girl asked me. "You have an English accent."

Her voice came shudderingly from behind the sleek black satin mask. I fancied her teeth must be chattering. Eyes that were perhaps blue searched my face from behind the black gauze covering the eyeholes of the mask. I told her she'd guessed right. She stood close to me. "Will you come to my place tonight?" she asked rapidly. "I can't thank you now. And there's something else you can help me about."

My arm, still lightly circling her waist, felt her body trembling.

I was answering the plea in that as much as in her voice when I said, "Certainly." She gave me an address south of Inferno, an apartment number and a time. She asked me my name and I told her.

"Hey, you!"

I turned obediently to the policeman's shout. He shooed away the small clucking crowd of masked women and barefaced men. Coughing from the smoke that the black coupe had thrown out, he asked for my papers. I handed him the essential ones.

He looked at them and then at me. "British Barter? How long will you be in New York?"

Suppressing the urge to say, "For as short a time as possible," I told him I'd be here for a week or so.

"May need you as a witness," he explained. "Those kids can't use smoke on us. When they do that, we pull them in."

He seemed to think the smoke was the bad thing. "They tried to kill the lady," I pointed out.

He shook his head wisely. "They always pretend they're going to, but actually they just want to snag skirts. I've picked up rippers with as many as fifty skirt-snags tacked up in their rooms. Of course, sometimes they come a little too close."

I explained that if I hadn't yanked her out of the way, she'd have been hit by more than hooks. But he interrupted, "If she'd thought it was a real murder attempt, she'd have stayed here."

I looked around. It was true. She was gone.

"She was fearfully frightened," I told him.

"Who wouldn't be? Those kids would have scared old Stalin himself."

"I mean frightened of more than 'kids.' They didn't look like 'kids.'"

"What did they look like?"

I tried without much success to describe the three faces. A vague impression of viciousness and effeminacy doesn't mean much.

"Well, I could be wrong," he said finally. "Do you know the girl? Where she lives?"

"No," I half lied.

The other policeman hung up his radiophone and ambled toward us, kicking at the tendrils of dissipating smoke. The black cloud no longer hid the dingy façades with their five-year-old radiation flash-burns, and I could begin to make out the distant stump of the Empire State Building, thrusting up out of Inferno like a mangled finger.

"They haven't been picked up so far," the approaching policeman grumbled. "Left smoke for five blocks, from what Ryan says."

The first policeman shook his head. "That's bad," he observed solemnly.

I was feeling a bit uneasy and ashamed. An Englishman shouldn't lie, at least not on impulse.

"They sound like nasty customers," the first policeman continued in the same grim tone. "We'll need witnesses. Looks as if you may have to stay in New York longer than you expect."

I got the point. I said, "I forgot to show you all my papers," and handed him a few others, making sure there was a five dollar bill in among them.

When he handed them back a bit later, his voice was no longer ominous. My feelings of guilt vanished. To cement our relationship, I chatted with the two of them about their job.

"I suppose the masks give you some trouble," I observed. "Over in England we've been reading about your new crop of masked female bandits."

"Those things get exaggerated," the first policeman assured me. "It's the men masking as women that really mix us up. But, brother, when we nab them, we jump on them with both feet."

"And you get so you can spot women almost as well as if they had naked faces," the second policeman volunteered. "You know, hands and all that."

"Especially all that," the first agreed with a chuckle. "Say, is it true that some girls don't mask over in England?"

"A number of them have picked up the fashion," I told him. "Only a few, though—the ones who always adopt the latest style, however extreme."

"They're usually masked in the British newscasts."

"I imagine it's arranged that way out of deference to American taste," I confessed. "Actually, not very many do mask."

The second policeman considered that. "Girls going down the street bare from the neck up." It was not clear whether he viewed the prospect with relish or moral distaste. Likely both.

"A few members keep trying to persuade Parliament to enact a law forbidding all masking," I continued, talking perhaps a bit too much.

The second policeman shook his head. "What an idea. You know, masks are a pretty good thing, brother. Couple of years more and I'm going to make my wife wear hers around the house."

The first policeman shrugged. "If women were to stop wearing masks, in six weeks you wouldn't know the difference. You get used to anything, if enough people do or don't do it."

I agreed, rather regretfully, and left them. I turned north on Broadway (old Tenth Avenue, I believe) and walked rapidly until I was beyond Inferno. Passing such an area of undecontaminated radioactivity always makes a person queasy. I thanked God there weren't any such in England, as yet.

The street was almost empty, though I was accosted by a couple of beggars with faces tunnelled by H-bomb scars, whether real or of makeup putty, I couldn't tell. A fat woman held out a baby with webbed fingers and toes. I told myself it would have been deformed anyway and that she was only capitalizing on our fear of bomb-induced mutations. Still, I gave her a seven-and-a-half-cent piece. Her mask made me feel I was paying tribute to an African fetish.

"May all your children be blessed with one head and two eyes, sir."

"Thanks," I said, shuddering, and hurried past her.

"...There's only trash behind the mask, so turn your head, stick to your task: Stay away, stay away—from—the—girls!"

This last was the end of an anti-sex song being sung by some religionists half a block from the circle-and-cross insignia of a femalist temple. They reminded me only faintly of our small tribe of British monastics. Above their heads was a jumble of billboards advertising predigested foods, wrestling instruction, radio handies and the like.

I stared at the hysterical slogans with disagreeable fascination. Since the female face and form have been banned on American signs, the very letters of the advertiser's alphabet have begun to crawl with sex—the fat-bellied, big-breasted capital B, the lascivious double O. However, I reminded myself, it is chiefly the mask that so strangely accents sex in America.

A British anthropologist has pointed out that, while it took more than 5,000 years to shift the chief point of sexual interest from the hips to the breasts, the next transition to the face has taken less than 50 years. Comparing the American style with Moslem tradition is not valid; Moslem women are compelled to wear veils, the purpose of which is to make a husband's property private, while American women have only the compulsion of fashion and use masks to create mystery.

Theory aside, the actual origins of the trend are to be found in the anti-radiation clothing of World War III, which led to masked wrestling, now a fantastically popular sport, and that in turn led to the current female fashion. Only a wild style at first, masks quickly became as necessary as brassieres and lipsticks had been earlier in the century.

I finally realized that I was not speculating about masks in general, but about what lay behind one in particular. That's the devil of the things; you're never sure whether a girl is heightening loveliness or hiding ugliness. I pictured a cool, pretty face in which fear showed only in widened eyes. Then I remembered her blonde hair, rich against the blackness of the satin mask. She'd told me to come at the twenty-second hour—10 P.M.

I climbed to my apartment near the British Consulate; the elevator shaft had been shoved out of plumb by an old blast, a nuisance in these tall New York buildings. Before it occurred to me that I would be going out again, I automatically tore a tab from the film strip under my shirt. I developed it just to be sure. It showed that the total radiation I'd taken that day was still within the safety limit. I'm not phobic about it, as so many people are these days, but there's no point in taking chances.

I flopped down on the day bed and stared at the silent speaker and the dark screen of the video set. As always, they made me think, somewhat bitterly, of the two great nations of the world. Mutilated by each other, yet still strong, they were crippled giants poisoning the planet with their respective dreams of an impossible equality and an impossible success.

I fretfully switched on the speaker. By luck the newscaster was talking excitedly of the prospect of a bumper wheat crop, sown by planes across a dust bowl moistened by seeded rains. I listened carefully to the rest of the program (it was remarkably clear of Russian telejamming) but there was no further news of interest to me. And, of course, no mention of the Moon, though everyone knows that America and Russia are racing to develop their primary bases into fortresses capable of mutual assault and the launching of alphabet-bombs toward Earth. I myself knew perfectly well that the British electronic equipment I was helping trade for American wheat was destined for use in spaceships.

I switched off the newscast. It was growing dark and once again I pictured a tender, frightened face behind a mask. I hadn't had a date since England. It's exceedingly difficult to become acquainted with a girl in America, where as little as a smile, often, can set one of them yelping for the police—to say nothing of the increasingly puritanical morality and the roving gangs that keep most women indoors after dark. And, naturally, the masks, which are definitely not, as the Soviets claim, a last invention of capitalist degeneracy, but a sign of great psychological insecurity. The Russians have no masks, but they have their own signs of stress.

I went to the window and impatiently watched the darkness gather. I was getting very restless. After a while a ghostly violet cloud appeared to the south. My hair rose. Then I laughed. I had momentarily fancied it a radiation from the crater of the Hell-bomb, though I should instantly have known it was only the radio-induced glow in the sky over the amusement and residential area south of Inferno.

Promptly at twenty-two hours I stood before the door of my unknown girl-friend's apartment. The electronic say-who-please said just that. I answered clearly, "Wysten Turner," wondering if she'd given my name to the mechanism. She evidently had, for the door opened. I walked into a small empty living-room, my heart pounding a bit.

The room was expensively furnished with the latest pneumatic hassocks and sprawlers. There were some midgie books on the table. The one I picked up was the standard hard-boiled detective story in which two female murderers go gunning for each other.

The television was on. A masked girl in green was crooning a love song. Her right hand held something that blurred off into the foreground. I saw the set had a handie, which we haven't in England as yet, and curiously thrust my hand into the handie orifice beside the screen. Contrary to my expectations, it was not like slipping into a pulsing rubber glove, but rather as if the girl on the screen actually held my hand.

A door opened behind me. I jerked out my hand with as guilty a reaction as if I'd been caught peering through a keyhole.

She stood in the bedroom doorway. I think she was trembling. She was wearing a grey fur coat, white speckled, and a grey velvet evening mask with shirred grey lace around the eyes and mouth. Her fingernails twinkled like silver.

It hadn't occurred to me that she'd expect us to go out.

"I should have told you," she said softly. Her mask veered nervously toward the books and the screen and the room's dark corners. "But I can't possibly talk to you here."

I said doubtfully, "There's a place near the Consulate..."

"I know where we can be together and talk," she said rapidly. "If you don't mind."

As we entered the elevator I said, "I'm afraid I dismissed the cab."

But the cab driver hadn't gone for some reason of his own. He jumped out and smirkingly held the front door open for us. I told him we preferred to sit in back. He sulkily opened the rear door, slammed it after us, jumped in front and slammed the door behind him.

My companion leaned forward. "Heaven," she said.

The driver switched on the turbine and televisor.

"Why did you ask if I were a British subject?" I said, to start the conversation.

She leaned away from me, tilting her mask close to the window. "See the Moon," she said in a quick, dreamy voice.

"But why, really?" I pressed, conscious of an irritation that had nothing to do with her.

"It's edging up into the purple of the sky."

"And what's your name?"

"The purple makes it look yellower."

Just then I became aware of the source of my irritation. It lay in the square of writhing light in the front of the cab beside the driver.

I don't object to ordinary wrestling matches, though they bore me, but I simply detest watching a man wrestle a woman. The fact that the bouts are generally "on the level," with the man greatly outclassed in weight and reach and the masked females young and personable, only makes them seem worse to me.

"Please turn off the screen," I requested the driver.

He shook his head without looking around. "Uh-uh, man," he said. "They've been grooming that babe for weeks for this bout with Little Zirk."

Infuriated, I reached forward, but my companion caught my arm. "Please," she whispered frightenedly, shaking her head.

I settled back, frustrated. She was closer to me now, but silent and for a few moments I watched the heaves and contortions of the powerful masked girl and her wiry masked opponent on the screen. His frantic scambling at her reminded me of a male spider.

I jerked around, facing my companion. "Why did those three men want to kill you?" I asked sharply.

The eyeholes of her mask faced the screen. "Because they're jealous of me," she whispered.

"Why are they jealous?"

She still didn't look at me. "Because of him."

"Who?"

She didn't answer.

I put my arm around her shoulders. "Are you afraid to tell me?" I asked. "What *is* the matter?"

She still didn't look my way. She smelled nice.

"See here," I said laughingly, changing my tactics, "you really should tell me something about yourself. I don't even know what you look like."

I half playfully lifted my hand to the band of her neck. She gave it an astonishingly swift slap. I pulled it away in sudden pain. There were four tiny indentations on the back. From one of them a tiny bead of blood welled out as I watched. I looked at her fingernails and saw they were actually delicate and pointed metal caps.

"I'm dreadfully sorry," I heard her say, "but you frightened me. I thought for a moment you were going to..."

At last she turned to me. Her coat had fallen open. Her evening dress was Cretan Revival, a bodice of lace beneath and supporting the breasts without covering them.

"Don't be angry," she said, putting her arms around my neck. "You were wonderful this afternoon."

The soft grey velvet of her mask, moulding itself to her cheek, pressed mine. Through the mask's lace the wet warm tip of her tongue touched my chin.

"I'm not angry," I said. "Just puzzled and anxious to help."

The cab stopped. To either side were black windows bordered by spears of broken glass. The sickly purple light showed a few ragged figures slowly moving toward us.

The driver muttered, "It's the turbine, man. We're grounded." He sat there hunched and motionless. "Wish it had happened somewhere else."

My companion whispered, "Five dollars is the usual amount."

She looked out so shudderingly at the congregating figures that I suppressed my indignation and did as she suggested. The driver took the bill without a word. As he started up, he put his hand out the window and I heard a few coins clink on the pavement.

My companion came back into my arms, but her mask faced the television screen, where the tall girl had just pinned the convulsively kicking Little Zirk.

"I'm so frightened," she breathed.

Heaven turned out to be an equally ruinous neighborhood, but it had a club with an awning and a huge doorman uniformed like

a spaceman, but in gaudy colors. In my sensuous daze I rather liked
it all. We stepped out of the cab just as a drunken old woman came
down the sidewalk, her mask awry. A couple ahead of us turned
their heads from the half revealed face, as if from an ugly body at
the beach. As we followed them in I heard the doorman say, "Get
along, grandma, and cover yourself."

Inside, everything was dimness and blue glows. She had said we
could talk here, but I didn't see how. Besides the inevitable chorus
of sneezes and coughs (they say America is fifty per cent allergic
these days), there was a band going full blast in the latest robop
style, in which an electronic composing machine selects an arbitrary
sequence of tones into which the musicians weave their raucous
little individualities.

Most of the people were in booths. The band was behind the
bar. On a small platform beside them, a girl was dancing, stripped
to her mask. The little cluster of men at the shadowy far end of the
bar weren't looking at her.

We inspected the menu in gold script on the wall and pushed
the buttons for breast of chicken, fried shrimps, and two scotches.
Moments later, the serving bell tinkled. I opened the gleaming panel
and took out our drinks.

The cluster of men at the bar filed off toward the door, but first
they stared around the room. My companion had just thrown back
her coat. Their look lingered on our booth. I noticed that there
were three of them.

The band chased off the dancing girl with growls. I handed my
companion a straw and we sipped our drinks.

"You wanted me to help you about something," I said. "Incidentally, I think you're lovely."

She nodded quick thanks, looked around, leaned forward. "Would
it be hard for me to get to England?"

"No," I replied, a bit taken aback. "Provided you have an American passport."

"Are they difficult to get?"

"Rather," I said, surprised at her lack of information. "Your
country doesn't like its nationals to travel, though it isn't quite as
stringent as Russia."

"Could the British Consulate help me get a passport?"

"It's hardly their..."

"Could you?"

I realized we were being inspected. A man and two girls had
paused opposite our table. The girls were tall and wolfish-looking,

with spangled masks. The man stood jauntily between them like a fox on its hind legs.

My companion didn't glance at them, but she sat back. I noticed that one of the girls had a big yellow bruise on her forearm. After a moment they walked to a booth in the deep shadows.

"Know them?" I asked. She didn't reply. I finished my drink.

"I'm not sure you'd like England," I said. "The austerity's altogether different from your American brand of misery."

She leaned forward again. "But I must get away," she whispered.

"Why?" I was getting impatient.

"Because I'm so frightened."

There were chimes. I opened the panel and handed her the fried shrimps. The sauce on my breast of chicken was a delicious steaming compound of almonds, soy and ginger. But something must have been wrong with the radionic oven that had thawed and heated the meal, for at the first bite I crunched a kernel of ice in the meat. These delicate mechanisms need constant repair and there aren't enough mechanics.

I put down my fork. "What are you really scared of?" I asked her.

For once her mask didn't waver away from my face. As I waited I could feel the fears gathering without her naming them, tiny dark shapes swarming through the curved night outside, converging on the radioactive pest spot of New York, dipping into the margins of the purple. I felt a sudden rush of sympathy, a desire to protect the girl opposite me. The warm feeling added itself to the infatuation engendered in the cab.

"Everything," she said finally.

I nodded and touched her hand.

"I'm afraid of the Moon," she began, her voice going dreamy and brittle as it had in the cab. "You can't look at it and not think of guided bombs."

"It's the same Moon over England," I reminded her.

"But it's not England's Moon any more. It's ours and Russia's. You're not responsible.

"Oh, and then," she said with a tilt of her mask, "I'm afraid of the cars and the gangs and the loneliness and Inferno. I'm afraid of the lust that undresses your face. And"—her voice hushed—"I'm afraid of the wrestlers."

"Yes?" I prompted softly after a moment.

Her mask came forward. "Do you know something about the wrestlers?" she asked rapidly. "The ones that wrestle women, I mean. They often lose, you know. And then they have to have a girl to take their frustration out on. A girl who's soft and weak and terribly frightened. They need that, to keep them men. Other men don't want them to have a girl. Other men want them just to fight women and be heroes. But they must have a girl. It's horrible for her."

I squeezed her fingers tighter, as if courage could be transmitted—granting I had any. "I think I can get you to England," I said.

Shadows crawled onto the table and stayed there. I looked up at the three men who had been at the end of the bar. They were the men I had seen in the big coupe. They wore black sweaters and close-fitting black trousers. Their faces were as expressionless as dopers. Two of them stood about me. The other loomed over the girl.

"Drift off, man," I was told. I heard the other inform the girl: "We'll wrestle a fall, sister. What shall it be? Judo, slapsie or kill-who-can?"

I stood up. There are times when an Englishman simply must be maltreated. But just then the foxlike man came gliding in like the star of a ballet. The reaction of the other three startled me. They were acutely embarrassed.

He smiled at them thinly. "You won't win my favour by tricks like this," he said.

"Don't get the wrong idea, Zirk," one of them pleaded.

"I will if it's right," he said. "She told me what you tried to do this afternoon. That won't endear you to me, either. Drift."

They backed off awkwardly. "Let's get out of here," one of them said loudly, as they turned. "I know a place where they fight naked with knives."

Little Zirk laughed musically and slipped into the seat beside my companion. She shrank from him, just a little. I pushed my feet back, leaned forward.

"Who's your friend, baby?" he asked, not looking at her.

She passed the question to me with a little gesture. I told him.

"British," he observed. "She's been asking you about getting out of the country? About passports?" He smiled pleasantly. "She likes to start running away. Don't you, baby?" His small hand began to stroke her wrist, the fingers bent a little, the tendons ridged, as if he were about to grab and twist.

"Look here," I said sharply. "I have to be grateful to you for ordering off those bullies, but—"

"Think nothing of it," he told me. "They're no harm except when they're behind steering wheels. A well-trained fourteen-year-old girl could cripple any one of them. Why even Theda here, if she went in for that sort of thing…" He turned to her, shifting his hand from her wrist to her hair. He stroked it, letting the strands slip slowly through his fingers. "You know I lost tonight, baby, don't you?" he said softly.

I stood up. "Come along," I said to her. "Let's leave."

She just sat there, I couldn't even tell if she was trembling. I tried to read a message in her eyes through the mask.

"I'll take you away," I said to her. "I can do it, I really will."

He smiled at me. "She'd like to go with you," he said. "Wouldn't you, baby?"

"Will you or won't you?" I said to her. She still just sat there.

He slowly knotted his fingers in her hair.

"Listen, you little vermin," I snapped at him. "Take your hands off her."

He came up from the seat like a snake. I'm no fighter. I just know that the more scared I am, the harder and straighter I hit. This time I was lucky. But as he crumpled back, I felt a slap and four stabs of pain in my cheek. I clapped my hand to it. I could feel the four gashes made by her dagger finger caps, and the warm blood oozing out from them.

She didn't look at me. She was bending over Little Zirk and cuddling her mask to his cheek and crooning: "There, there, don't feel bad, you'll be able to hurt me afterward."

There were sounds around us, but they didn't come close. I leaned forward and ripped the mask from her face.

I really don't know why I should have expected her face to be anything else. It was very pale, of course, and there weren't any cosmetics. I suppose there's no point in wearing any under a mask. The eyebrows were untidy and the lips chapped. But as for the general expression, as for the feelings crawling and wriggling across it—

Have you ever lifted a rock from damp soil? Have you ever watched the slimy white grubs?

I looked down at her, she up at me. "Yes, you're so frightened, aren't you?" I said sarcastically. "You dread this little nightly drama, don't you? You're scared to death."

And I walked right out into the purple night, still holding my hand to my bleeding cheek. No one stopped me, not even the girl wrestlers. I wished I could tear a tab from under my shirt, and test

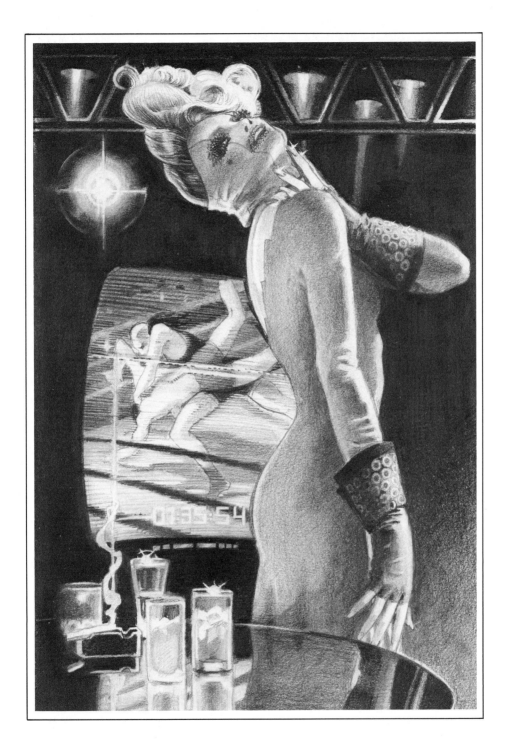

it then and there, and find I'd taken too much radiation, and so be able to ask to cross the Hudson and go down New Jersey, past the lingering radiance of the Narrows Bomb, and so on to Sandy Hook to wait for the rusty ship that would take me back over the seas to England.

Fritz
Leiber

A Deskful of Girls

YES, I SAID GHOSTGIRLS, SEXY ONES. PER-
sonally I never in my life saw any ghosts except the
sexy kind, though I saw enough of those I'll tell
you, but only for one evening, in the dark of course,
with the assistance of an eminent (I should also say
notorious) psychologist. It was an interesting experience, to put it mildly, and it introduced me to an unknown
field of psycho-physiology, but under no circumstances would I
want to repeat it.

But ghosts are supposed to be frightening? Well, who ever said
that sex isn't? It is to the neophyte, female or male, and don't let
any of the latter try to kid you. For one thing, sex opens up the
unconscious mind, which isn't exactly a picnic area. Sex is a force
and rite that is basic, primal; and the caveman or cavewoman in
each of us is a truth bigger than the jokes and cartoons about it.
Sex was behind the witchcraft religion, the sabbats were sexual
orgies. The witch was a sexual creature. So is the ghost.

After all, what is a ghost, according to all traditional views, but
the shell of a human being—an animated skin? And the skin is all
sex—it's touch, the boundary, the mask of flesh.

I got that notion about skin from my eminent-notorious psychologist, Dr. Emil Slyker, the first and the last evening I met him,
at the Countersign Club, though he wasn't talking about ghosts to
begin with. He was pretty drunk and drawing signs in the puddle
spilled from his triple martini.

He grinned at me and said, "Look here, What's-Your-Name—
oh yes, Carr Mackay, Mister *Justine* himself. Well, look here, Carr,
I got a deskful of girls at my office in this building and they're
needing attention. Let's shoot up and have a look."

Right away my hopelessly naive imagination flashed me a vivid
picture of a desk swarming inside with girls about five or six inches
high. They weren't dressed—my imagination never dresses girls
except for special effects after long thought—but these looked as
if they had been modeled from the drawings of Heinrich Kley or
Mahlon Blaine. Literal vest-pocket Venuses, saucy and active. Right

now they were attempting a mass escape from the desk, using a couple of nail files for saws, and they'd already cut some trap doors between the drawers so they could circulate around. One group was improvising a blowtorch from an atomizer and lighter fluid. Another was trying to turn a key from the inside, using tweezers for a wrench. And they were tearing down and defacing small signs, big to them, which read YOU BELONG TO DR. EMIL SLYKER.

My mind, which looks down at my imagination and refuses to associate with it, was studying Dr. Slyker and also making sure that I behaved outwardly like a worshipful fan, a would-be Devil's apprentice. This approach, helped by the alcohol, seemed to be relaxing him into the frame of mind I wanted him to have—one of boastful condescension. Slyker was a plump gut of a man with a perpetually sucking mouth, in his early fifties, fair-complexioned, blond, balding, with the power-lines around his eyes and at the corners of the nostrils. Over it all he wore the ready-for-photographers mask that is a sure sign its wearer is on the Big Time. Eyes weak, as shown by the dark glasses, but forever peering for someone to strip or cow. His hearing bad too, for that matter, as he didn't catch the barman approaching and started a little when he saw the white rag reaching out toward the spill from his drink. Emil Slyker, "Doctor" courtesy of some European universities and a crust like blued steel, movie columnist, pumper of the last ounce of prestige out of that ashcan word "psychologist," psychic researcher several mysterious rumored jumps ahead of Wilhelm Reich with his orgone and Rhine with his ESP, psychological consultant to starlets blazing into stars and other ladies in the bucks, and a particularly expert disher-out of that goulash of psychoanalysis, mysticism and magic that is the *chef-d'oeuvre* of our era. *And,* I was assuming, a particularly successful blackmailer. A stinker to be taken very seriously.

My real purpose in contacting Slyker, of which I hoped he hadn't got an inkling yet, was to offer him enough money to sink a small luxury liner in exchange for a sheaf of documents he was using to blackmail Evelyn Cordew, current pick-of-the-pantheon among our sex goddesses. I was working for another film star, Jeff Crain, Evelyn's ex-husband, but not "ex" when it came to the protective urge. Jeff said that Slyker refused to bite on the direct approach, that he was so paranoid in his suspiciousness as to be psychotic, and that I would have to make friends with him first. Friends with a paranoid!

So in pursuit of this doubtful and dangerous distinction, there I was at the Countersign Club, nodding respectfully happy acquiescence to the Master's suggestion and asking tentatively, "Girls needing attention?"

He gave me his whoremaster, keeper-of-the-keys grin and said, "Sure, women need attention whatever form they're in. They're like pearls in a vault, they grow dull and fade unless they have regular contact with warm human flesh. Drink up."

He gulped half of what was left of his martini—the puddle had been blotted up meantime and the black surface reburnished—and we made off without any fuss over checks or tabs; I had expected him to stick me with the former at least, but evidently I wasn't enough of an acolyte yet to be granted that honor.

It fitted that I had caught up with Emil Slyker at the Countersign Club. It is to a key club what the latter is to a top-crust bar. Strictly Big Time, set up to provide those in it with luxury, privacy, and security. Especially security: I had heard that the Countersign Club bodyguarded even their sober patrons home late of an evening with or without their pickups, but I hadn't believed it until this well-dressed and doubtless well-heeled silent husky rode the elevator up the dead midnight office building with us and only turned back at Dr. Slyker's door. Of course I couldn't have got into the Countersign Club on my own—Jeff had provided me with my entree: an illustrated edition of the Marquis de Sade's *Justine,* its margins annotated by a world-famous recently deceased psychoanalyst. I had sent it in to Slyker with a note full of flowery expression of "my admiration for your work in the psycho-physiology of sex."

The door to Slyker's office was something. No glass, just a dark expanse—teak or ironwood, I guessed—with EMIL SLYKER, CONSULTING PSYCHOLOGIST burnt into it. No Yale lock, but a large keyhole with a curious silver valve that the key pressed aside. Slyker showed me the key with a deprecating smile; the gleaming castellations of its web were the most complicated I'd ever seen, its stem depicted Pasiphaë and the bull. He certainly was willing to pay for atmosphere.

There were three sounds: first the soft grating of the turning key, then the solid snap of the bolts retracting, then a faint creak from the hinges.

Open, the door showed itself four inches thick, more like that of a safe or vault, with a whole cluster of bolts that the key controlled. Just before it closed, something very odd happened: a filmy plastic sheet whipped across the bolts from the outer edge of the doorway and conformed itself to them so perfectly that I suspected static electrical attraction of some sort. Once in place it barely clouded the silvery surface of the bolts and would have taken a close look to spot. It didn't interfere in any way with the door closing or the bolts snapping back into their channels.

The Doctor sensed or took for granted my interest in the door and explained over his shoulder in the dark, "My Siegfried Line. More than one ambitious crook or inspired murderer has tried to smash or think his or her way through that door. They've had no luck. They can't. At this moment there is literally no one in the world who could come through that door without using explosives—and they'd have to be well placed. Cozy."

I privately disagreed with the last remark. Not to make a thing of it, I would have preferred to feel in a bit closer touch with the silent corridors outside, even though they held nothing but the ghosts of unhappy stenographers and neurotic dames my imagination had raised on the way up.

"Is the plastic film part of an alarm system?" I asked. The Doctor didn't answer. His back was to me. I remembered that he'd shown himself a shade deaf. But I didn't get a chance to repeat my question, for just then some indirect lighting came on, although Slyker wasn't near any switch ("Our talk triggers it," he said) and the office absorbed me.

Naturally the desk was the first thing I looked for, though I felt foolish doing it. It was a big deep job with a dark soft gleam that might have been that of fine-grained wood or metal. The drawers were file size, not the shallow ones my imagination had played with, and there were three tiers of them to the right of the kneehole— space enough for a couple of life-size girls if they were doubled up according to one of the formulas for the hidden operator of Maelzel's chess-playing automaton. My imagination, which never learns, listened hard for the patter of tiny bare feet and the clatter of little tools. There wasn't even the scurry of mice, which would have done something to my nerves, I'm sure.

The office was L-shaped with the door at the end of this leg. The walls I could see were mostly lined with books, though a few line drawings had been hung—my imagination had been right about Heinrich Kley, though I didn't recognize these pen-and-ink originals, and there were some Fuselis you won't ever see reproduced in books handled over the counter.

The desk was in the corner of the L with the components of a hi-fi spaced along the bookshelves this side of it. All I could see yet of the other leg of the L was a big surrealist armchair facing the desk but separated from it by a wide low bare table. I took a dislike to that armchair on first sight, though it looked extremely comfortable. Slyker had reached the desk now and had one hand on it as he turned back toward me, and I got the impression that the armchair had changed shape since I had entered the office—that it had been more like a couch to start with, although now the back was almost straight.

But the Doctor's left thumb indicated I was to sit in it and I couldn't see another chair in the place except the padded button on which he was now settling himself—one of those stenographer deals with a boxing-glove back placed to catch you low in the spine like the hand of a knowledgeable masseur. In the other leg of the L, besides the armchair, were more books, a heavy concertina blind sealing off the window, two narrow doors that I supposed were those of a closet and a lavatory, and what looked like a slightly scaled-down and windowless telephone booth until I guessed it must be an orgone box of the sort Reich had invented to restore the libido when the patient occupies it. I quickly settled myself in the chair, not to be gingerly about it. It was rather incredibly comfortable, almost as if it had adjusted its dimensions a bit at the last instant to conform to mine. The back was narrow at the base but widened and then curled in and over to almost a canopy around my head and shoulders. The seat too widened a lot toward the front, where the stubby legs were far apart. The bulky arms sprang unsupported from the back and took my own just right, though curving inwards with the barest suggestion of a hug. The leather or unfamiliar plastic was as firm and cool as young flesh and its texture as mat under my fingertips.

"An historic chair," the Doctor observed, "designed and built for me by von Helmholtz of the Bauhaus. It has been occupied by all my best mediums during their so-called trance states. It was in that chair that I established to my entire satisfaction the real existence of ectoplasm—that elaboration of the mucous membrane and occasionally the entire epidermis that is distantly analogous to the birth envelope and is the fact behind the persisted legends of the snake-shedding of filmy live skins by human beings, and which the spiritualist quacks are forever trying to fake with their fluorescent cheesecloth and doctored negatives. Orgone, the primal sexual energy?—Reich makes a persuasive case, still... but ectoplasm?—yes! Angna went into a trance sitting just where you are, her entire body dusted with a special powder, the tracks and distant smudges of which later revealed the ectoplasm's movements and origin—chiefly in the genital area. The test was conclusive and led to further researches, very interesting and quite revolutionary, none of which I have published; my professional colleagues froth at the mouth, elaborating an opposite sort of foam, whenever I mix the psychic with psychoanalysis—they seem to forget that hypnotism gave Freud his start and that for a time the man was keen on cocaine. Yes indeed, an historic chair."

I naturally looked down at it and for a moment I thought I had vanished, because I couldn't see my legs. Then I realized that the upholstery had changed to a dark grey exactly matching my suit except for the ends of the arms, which merged by fine gradations into a sallow hue which blotted out my hands.

"I should have warned you that it's now upholstered in chameleon plastic," Slyker said with a grin. "It changes color to suit the sitter. The fabric was supplied me over a year ago by Henri Artois, the French dilettante chemist. So the chair has been many shades: dead black when Mrs. Fairlee—you recall the case?—came to tell me she had just put on mourning and then shot her bandleader husband, a charming Florida tan during the later experiments with Angna. It helps my patients forget themselves when they're free-associating and it amuses some people."

I wasn't one of them, but I managed a smile I hoped wasn't too sour. I told myself to stick to business—Evelyn Cordew and Jeff Crain's business. I must forget the chair and other incidentals, and concentrate on Dr. Emil Slyker and what he was saying—for I have by no means given all of his remarks, only the more important asides. He had turned out to be the sort of conversationalist who will talk for two hours solid, then when you have barely started your reply, give you a hurt look and say, "Excuse me, but if I can get a word in edgewise—" and talk for two hours more. The liquor may have been helping, but I doubt it. When we had left the Countersign Club he had started to tell me the stories of three of his female clients—a surgeon's wife, an aging star scared by a comeback opportunity, and a college girl in trouble—and the presence of the bodyguard hadn't made him hold back on gory details.

Now, sitting at his desk and playing with the catch of a file drawer as if wondering whether to open it, he had got to the point where the surgeon's wife had arrived at the operating theater early one morning to publish her infidelities, the star had stabbed her press agent with the wardrobe mistress' scissors, and the college girl had fallen in love with her abortionist. He had the conversation-hogger's trick of keeping a half dozen topics in the air at once and weaving back and forth between them without finishing any.

And of course he was a male tantalizer. Now he whipped open the file drawer and scooped out some folders and then held them against his belly and watched me as if to ask himself, "Should I?"

After a maximum pause to build suspense he decided he should, and so I began to hear the story of Dr. Emil Slyker's girls, not the first three, of course—they had to stay frozen at their climaxes unless their folders turned up—but others.

I wouldn't be telling the truth if I didn't admit it was a let-down. Here I was expecting I don't know what from his desk and all I got was the usual glimpses into childhood's garden of father-fixation and sibling rivalry and the bed-changing *Sturm und Drang* of later adolescence. The folders seemed to hold nothing but conventional medico-psychiatric case histories, along with physical measurements and other details of appearance, unusually penetrating *précis* of each client's financial resources, occasional notes on possible psychic gifts and other extrasensory talents, and maybe some candid snapshots, judging from the way he'd sometimes pause to study appreciatively and then raise his eyebrows at me with a smile.

Yet after a while I couldn't help starting to be impressed, if only by the sheer numbers. Here was this stream, this freshet, this flood of females, young and not-so-young that think of themselves as girls and wear the girl's suede mask even if they didn't still have the girl's natural face, all converging on Dr. Slyker's office with money stolen from their parents or highjacked from their married lovers, or paid when they signed the six-year contract with semiannual options, or held out on their syndicate boyfriends, or received in a lump sum in lieu of alimony, or banked for dreary years every fortnight from paychecks and then withdrawn in one grand gesture, or thrown at them by their husbands that morning like so much confetti, or, so help me, advanced them on their half-written novels. Yes, there was something very impressive about this pink stream of womankind rippling with the silver and green of cash conveyed infallibly, as if all the corridors and streets outside were concrete-walled spillways, to Dr. Slyker's office, but not to work any dynamos there except financial ones, instead to be worked over by a one-man dynamo and go foaming madly or trickling depletedly away or else stagnate excitingly for months, their souls like black swamp water gleaming with mysterious lights.

Slyker stopped short with a harsh little laugh. "We ought to have music with this, don't you think?" he said. "I believe I've got the *Nutcracker Suite* on the spindle," and he touched one of an unobtrusive bank of buttons on his desk.

They came without the whisper of a turntable or the faintest preliminary susurrus of tape, those first evocative, rich, sensual, yet eery chords, but they weren't the opening of any section of the *Nutcracker* I knew—and yet, damn it, they sounded as if they should be. And then they were cut off as if the tape had been snipped and I looked at Slyker and he was white and one of his hands was just coming back from the bank of buttons and the other was clutching the file folders as if they might somehow get away from him and both hands were shaking and I felt a shiver crawling down my own neck.

"Excuse me, Carr," he said slowly, breathing heavily, "but that's high-voltage music, psychically very dangerous, that I use only for special purposes. It *is* part of the *Nutcracker,* incidentally—the 'Ghostgirls Pavan' which Tchaikovsky suppressed completely under orders from Madam Sesostris, the Saint Petersburg clairvoyant. It was tape-recorded for me by...no, I don't know you quite well enough to tell you that. However, we will shift from tape to disk and listen to the known sections of the suite, played by the same artists."

I don't know how much this recording or the circumstances added to it, but I have never heard the "Danse Arabe" or the "Waltz of the Flowers" or the "Dance of the Flutes" so voluptuous and exquisitely menacing—those tinkling, superficially sugar-frosted bits of music that class after class of little-girl ballerinas have minced and teetered to *ad nauseam,* but underneath the glittering somber fancies of a thorough-going eroticist. As Slyker, guessing my thoughts, expressed it: "Tchaikovsky shows off each instrument— the flute, the throatier woodwinds, the silver chimes, the harp bubbling gold—as if he were dressing beautiful women in jewels and feathers and furs solely to arouse desire and envy in other men."

For of course we only listened to the music as background for Dr. Slyker's zigzagging, fragmentary, cream-skimming reminiscences. The stream of girls flowed on in their smart suits and flowered dresses and bouffant blouses and toreador pants, their improbable loves and unsuspected hates and incredible ambitions, the men who gave them money, the men who gave them love, the men who took both, the paralyzing trivial fears behind their wisely chic or corn-fed fresh façades, their ravishing and infuriating mannerisms, the trick of eye or lip or hair or wrist-curve or bosom-angle that was the focus of sex in each.

For Slyker could bring his girls to life very vividly, I had to grant that, as if he had more to jog his memory than case histories and notes and even photographs, as if he had the essence of each girl stoppered up in a little bottle, like perfume, and was opening them one by one to give me a whiff. Gradually I became certain that there *were* more than papers and pictures in the folders, though this revelation, like the earlier one about the desk, at first involved a letdown. Why should I get excited if Dr. Slyker filed away mementos of his clients?—even if they were keepsakes of love: lace handkerchiefs and filmy scarves, faded flowers, ribbons and bows, 20-denier stockings, long locks of hair, gay little pins and combs, swatches of material that might have been torn from dresses, snippets of silk delicate as ghost dandelions—what difference did it make to me if he treasured this junk or it fed his sense of power or was part of his blackmail? Yet it did make a difference to me, for like the music, like the little fearful starts he'd kept giving ever since the business of the "Ghostgirls Pavan," it helped to make everything very real, as if in some more-than-ordinary sense he did have a deskful of girls. For now as he opened or closed the folders there'd often be a puff of powder, a pale little cloud as from a jogged compact, and the pieces of silk gave the impression of being larger than they could be, like a magician's colored handkerchiefs, only most of them were flesh-colored, and I began to get glimpses of what looked like X-ray photographs and artist's transparencies, maybe life-size but cunningly folded, and other slack pale things that made me think of the ultra-fine rubber masks some aging actresses are rumored to wear, and all sorts of strange little flashes and glimmers of I don't know what, except there was that aura of femininity and I found myself remembering what he'd said about fluorescent cheesecloth and I did seem to get whiffs of very individual perfume with each new folder.

He had two file drawers open now, and I could just make out the word burnt into their fronts. The word certainly looked like PRESENT, and there were two of the closed file drawers labeled what looked like PAST and FUTURE. I didn't know what sort of hocus-pocus was supposed to be furthered by those words, but along with Slyker's darting, lingering monologue they did give me the feeling that I was afloat in a river of girls from all times and places, and the illusion that there somehow was a girl in each folder became so strong that I almost wanted to say, "Come on, Emil, trot 'em out, let me look at 'em."

He must have known exactly what feelings he was building up in me, for now he stopped in the middle of a saga of a starlet married to a Negro baseball player and looked at me with his eyes open a bit too wide and said, "All right, Carr, let's quit fooling around. Down at the Contersign I told you I had a deskful of girls and I wasn't kidding—although the truth behind that assertion would get me certified by all the little headshrinkers and Viennese windbags except it would scare the pants off them first. I mentioned ectoplasm earlier, and the proof of its reality. It's exuded by most properly stimulated women in deep trance, but it's not just some dimly fluorescent froth swirling around in a dark séance chamber. It takes the form of an envelope or limp balloon, closed toward the top but open toward the bottom, weighing less than a silk stocking but duplicating the person exactly down to features and hair, following the master-plan of the body's surface buried in the genetic material of the cells. It is a real shed skin but also dimly alive, a gossamer mannequin. A breath can crumple it, a breeze can whisk it away, but under some circumstances it becomes startlingly stable and resilient, a real apparition. It's invisible and almost impalpable by day, but by night, when your eyes are properly accommodated, you can just manage to see it. Despite its fragility it's almost indestructible, except by fire, and potentially immortal. Whether generated in sleep or under hypnosis, in spontaneous or induced trance, it remains connected to the source by a thin strand I call the 'umbilicus' and it returns to the source and is absorbed back into the individual again as the trance fades. But sometimes it becomes detached and then it lingers around as a shell, still dimly alive and occasionally glimpsed, forming the very real basis for the stories of hauntings we have from all centuries and cultures—in fact, I call such shells 'ghosts.' A strong emotional shock generally accounts for a ghost becoming detached from its owner, but it can also be detached artificially. Such a ghost is remarkably docile to one who understands how to handle and cherish it—for instance, it can be folded into an incredibly small compass and tucked away in an envelope, though by daylight you wouldn't notice anything in such an envelope if you looked inside. 'Detached artificially' I said, and that's what I do here in this office, and you know what I use to do it with, Carr?" He snatched up something long and daggerlike and gleaming and held it tight in his plump hand so that it pointed at the ceiling. "Silver shears, Carr, silver for the same reason you use a silver bullet to kill a werewolf, though those words would set the little headshrinkers howling. But would they be howling from outraged scientific attitude, Carr, or from professional jealousy or simply from fear? Just the same as it's unclear why they'd be howling, only certain they would be howling, if I told them that in every fourth or fifth folder in these files I have one or more ghostgirls."

He didn't need to mention fear—I was scared enough myself now, what with him spouting this ghost-guff, this spiritualism blather put far more precisely than any spiritualist would dare, this obviously firmly held and elaborately rationalized delusion, this perfect symbolization of a truly insane desire for power over women—filing them away in envelopes!—and then when he got bug-eyed and brandished those foot-long stiletto-shears.... Jeff Crain had warned me Slyker was "nuts—brilliant, but completely nuts and definitely dangerous," and I hadn't believed it, hadn't really visualized myself frozen on the medium's throne, locked in ("no one without explosives") with the madman himself. It cost me a lot of effort to keep on the acolyte's mask and simper adoringly at the Master.

My attitude still seemed to be fooling him, though he was studying me in a funny way, for he went on, "All right, Carr, I'll show you the girls, or at least one, though we'll have to put out all the lights after a bit—that's why I keep the window shuttered so tightly—and wait for our eyes to accommodate. But which one should it be?—we have a large field of choice. I think since it's your first and probably your last, it should be someone out of the ordinary, don't you think, someone who's just a little bit special? Wait a second—I know." And his hand shot under the desk where it must have touched a hidden button, for a shallow drawer shot out from a place where there didn't seem to be room for one. He took from it a single fat file folder that had been stored flat and laid it on his knees.

Then he began to talk again in his reminiscing voice and damn if it wasn't so cool and knowing that it started to pull me back toward the river of girls and set me thinking that this man wasn't really crazy, only extremely eccentric, maybe the eccentricity of genius, maybe he actually had hit on a hitherto unknown phenomenon depending on the more obscure properties of mind and matter, describing it to me in whimsically florid jargon, maybe he really had discovered something in one of the blind spots of modern science-and-psychology's picture of the universe.

"Stars, Carr. Female stars. Movie queens. Royal princess of the gray world, the ghostly chiaroscuro. Shadow empresses. They're realer than people, Carr, realer than the great actresses or casting-couch champions they start as, for they're symbols, Carr, symbols of our deepest longings and—yes—most hidden fears and most secret dreams. Each decade has several who achieve this more-than-life and less-than-life existence, but there's generally one who's the chief symbol, the top ghost, the dream who lures men along toward fulfillment and destruction. In the Twenties it was Garbo, Garbo the Free Soul—that's my name for the symbol she became; her romantic mask heralded the Great Depression. In the late Thirties and early Forties it was Bergman the Brave Liberal; her dewiness and Swedish-Modern smile helped us accept World War Two. And now it's"—he touched the bulky folder on his knees—"now it's Evelyn Cordew the Good-Hearted Bait, the gal who accepts her troublesome sexiness with a resigned shrug and a foolish little laugh, and what general castastrophe she foreshadows we don't know yet. But here she is, and in five ghost versions. Pleased, Carr?"

I was so completely taken by surprise that I couldn't say anything for a moment. Either Slyker had guessed my real purpose in contacting him, or I was faced with a sizable coincidence. I wet my lips and then just nodded.

Slyker studied me and finally grinned. "Ah," he said, "takes you aback a bit, doesn't it? I perceive that in spite of your moderate sophistication you are one of the millions of males who have wistfully contemplated desert-islanding with Delectable Evvie. A complex cultural phenomenon, Eva-Lynn Korduplewski. The child of a coal miner, educated solely in backstreet movie houses—shaped by dreams, you see, into a master dream, an empress dream-figure. A hysteric, Carr, in fact the most classic example I have ever encountered, with unequaled mediumistic capacities and also with a hypertrophied and utterly ruthless ambition. Riddled by hypochondrias, but with more real drive than a million other avid schoolgirls tangled and trapped in the labyrinth of film ambitions. Dumb as they come, no rational mind at all, but with ten times Einstein's intuition—intuition enough, at least, to realize that the symbol our sex-exploiting culture craved was a girl who accepted like a happy martyr the incandescent sexuality men and Nature forced on her— and with the patience and malleability to let the feathersoft beating of the black-and-white light in a cheap cinema shape her into that symbol. I sometimes think of her as a girl in a cheap dress standing on the shoulder of a big throughway, her eyes almost blinded by the lights of an approaching bus. The bus stops and she climbs on, dragging a pet goat and breathlessly giggling explanations at the driver. The bus is Civilization.

"Everybody knows her life story, which has been put out in a surprisingly accurate form up to a point: her burlesque-line days, the embarrassingly faithful cartoon-series *Girl in a Fix* for which she posed, her bit parts, the amazingly timed success of the movies *Hydrogen Blonde* and *The Jean Harlow Saga,* her broken marriage to Jeff Crain—What was that, Carr? Oh, I thought you'd started to say something—and her hunger for the real stage and intellectual distinction and power. You can't imagine how hungry for brains and power that girl became *after* she hit the top.

"I've been part of the story of that hunger, Carr, and I pride myself that I've done more to satisfy it than all the culture-johnnies she's had on her payroll. Evelyn Cordew has learned a lot about herself right where you're sitting, and also threaded her way past two psychotic crack-ups. The trouble is that when her third loomed up she didn't come to me, she decided to put her trust in wheat germ and yogurt instead, so now she hates my guts—and perhaps her own, on that diet. She's made two attempts on my life, Carr, and had me trailed by gangsters...and by other individuals. She's talked about me to Jeff Crain, whom she still sees from time to time, and Jerry Smyslov and Nick De Grazia, telling them I've got a file of information on her burlesque days and a few of her later escapades, including some interesting photostats and the real dope on her income and her tax returns, and that I'm using it to blackmail her white. What she actually wants is her five ghosts back, and I can't give them to her because they might kill her. Yes, kill her, Carr." He flourished the shears for emphasis. "She claims that the ghosts I've taken from her have made her lose weight permanently— 'look like a skeleton' are her words—and given her fits of mental blackout, a sort of psychic fading—whereas actually the ghosts have bled from her a lot of malignant thoughts and destructive emotions, which could literally kill her (or someone!) if reabsorbed—they're drenched with death-wish. Still, I hear she actually does look a little haggard, a trifle faded, in her last film, in spite of all Hollywood's medico-cosmetic lore, so maybe she has a sort of case against me. I haven't seen the film, I suppose you have. What do you think, Carr?"

I knew I'd been overworking the hesitation and the silent flattery, so I whipped out quickly, "I'd say it was due to her anemia. It seems to me that the anemia is quite enough to account for her loss of weight and her tired look."

"Ah! You've slipped, Carr," he lashed back, pointing at me triumphantly, except that instead of the outstretched finger there were those ridiculous, horrible shears. "Her anemia is one of the things that's been kept top-secret, known only to a very few of her intimates. Even in all the half-humorous releases about her hypochondrias that's one disease that has never been mentioned. I suspected you were from her when I got your note at the Countersign Club—the handwriting squirmed with tension and secrecy—but the *Justine* amused me—that was a fairly smart dodge—and your sorcerer's apprentice act amused me too, and I happened to feel like talking. But I've been studying you all along, especially your reactions to certain test-remarks I dropped in from time to time, and now you've really slipped." His voice was loud and clear, but he was shaking and giggling at the same time and his eyes showed white all the way around the irises. He drew back the shears a little, but clenched his fingers more tightly around them in a dagger grip, as he said with a chuckle, "Our dear little Evvie has sent all types up against me, to bargain for her ghosts or try to scare or assassinate me, but this is the first time she's sent an idealistic fool. Carr, why didn't you have the sense not to meddle?"

"Look here, Dr. Slyker," I countered before he started answering for me, "it's true I have a special purpose in contacting you. I never denied it. But I don't know anything about ghosts or gangsters. I'm here on a simple, businesslike assignment from the same guy who lent me the *Justine* and who has no purpose whatever beyond protecting Evelyn Cordew. I'm representing Jeff Crain."

That was supposed to calm him. Well, he did stop shaking and his eyes stopped wandering, but only because they were going over me like twin searchlights, and the giggle went out of his voice.

"Jeff Crain! Evvie just wants to murder me, but that cinematic Hemingway, that hulking guardian of hers, that human Saint Bernard tonguing the dry crumbs of their marriage—he wants to set the T-men on me, and the boys in blue and the boys in white too. Evvie's agents I mostly kid along, even the gangsters, but for Jeff's agents I have only one answer."

The silver shears pointed straight at my chest and I could see his muscles tighten like a fat tiger's. I got ready for a spring of my own at the first movement this madman made toward me.

But the move he made was back across the desk with his free hand. I decided it was a good time to be on my feet in any case, but just as I sent my own muscles their orders I was hugged around the waist and clutched by the throat and grabbed by the wrists and ankles. By something soft but firm.

I looked down. Padded, broad, crescent-shaped clamps had sprung out of hidden traps in my chair and now held me as comfortably but firmly as a gang of competent orderlies. Even my hands were held by wide, velvet-soft cuffs that had snapped out of the bulbous arms. They were all a nondescript grey but even as I looked they began to change color to match my suit or skin, whichever they happened to border.

I wasn't scared. I was merely frightened half to death.

"Surprised, Carr? You shouldn't be." Slyker was sitting back like an amiable schoolteacher and gently wagging the shears as if they were a ruler. "Streamlined unobtrusiveness and remote control are

the essence of our times, especially in medical furniture. The buttons on my desk can do more than that. Hypos might slip out—hardly hygenic, but then germs are overrated. Or electrodes for shock. You see, restraints are necessary in my business. Deep mediumistic trance can occasionally produce convulsions as violent as those of electroshock, especially when a ghost is cut. And I sometimes administer electroshock too, like any garden-variety headshrinker. Also, to be suddenly and firmly grabbed is a profound stimulus to the unconscious and often elicits closely guarded facts from difficult patients. So a means of making my patients hold still is absolutely necessary— something swift, sure, tasteful, and preferably without warning. You'd be surprised, Carr, at the situations in which I've been forced to activate those restaints. This time I prodded you to see just how dangerous you were. Rather to my surprise you showed yourself ready to take physical action against me. So I pushed the button. Now we'll be able to deal comfortably with Jeff Crain's problem...and yours. But first I've a promise to keep to you. I said I would show you one of Evelyn Cordew's ghosts. It will take a little time and after a bit it will be necessary to turn out the lights."

"Dr. Slyker," I said as evenly as I could, "I—"

"Quiet! Activating a ghost for viewing involves certain risks. Silence is essential, though it will be necessary to use—very briefly— the suppressed Tchaikovsky music which I turned off so quickly earlier this evening." He busied himself with the hi-fi for a few moments. "But partly because of that it will be necessary to put away all the other folders and the four ghosts of Evvie we aren't using, and lock the file drawers. Otherwise there might be complications."

I decided to try once more. "Before you go any further, Dr. Slyker," I began, "I would really like to explain—"

He didn't say another word, merely reached back across the desk again. My eyes caught something coming over my shoulder fast and the next instant it clapped down over my mouth and nose, not quite covering my eyes, but lapping up to them—something soft and dry and clinging and faintly crinkled feeling. I gasped and I could feel the gag sucking in, but not a bit of air came through it. That scared me seven-eighths of the rest of the way to oblivion, of course, and I froze. Then I tried a very cautious inhalation and a little air did seep through. It was wonderfully cool coming into the furnace of my lungs, that little suck of air—I felt I hadn't breathed for a week.

Slyker looked at me with a little smile. "I never say 'Quiet' twice, Carr. The foam plastic of that gag is another of Henri Artois' inventions. It consists of millions of tiny valves. As long as you breathe softly—very, very softly, Carr—they permit ample air to pass, but if you gasp or try to shout through it, they'll close up tight. A wonderfully soothing device. Compose yourself, Carr; your life depends on it."

I have never experienced such utter helplessness. I found that the slightest muscular tension, even crooking a finger, made my breathing irregular enough so that the valves started to close and I was in the fringes of suffocation. I could see and hear what was going on, but I dared not react, I hardly dared think. I had to pretend that most of my body wasn't there (the chameleon plastic helped!), only a pair of lungs working constantly but with infinite caution.

Slyker had just set the Cordew folder back in its drawer, without closing it, and started to gather up the other scattered folders, when he touched the desk again and the lights went out. I have mentioned that the place was completely sealed against light. The darkness was complete.

"Don't be alarmed, Carr," Slyker's voice came chuckling through it. "In fact, as I am sure you realize, you had better not be. I can tidy up just as handily—working by touch is one of my major skills, my sight and hearing being rather worse than appears—and even your eyes must be fully accommodated if you're to see anything at all. I repeat, don't be alarmed, Carr, least of all by ghosts."

I would never have expected it, but in spite of the spot I was in (which actually did seem to have its soothing effects), I still got a little kick—a very little one—out of thinking I was going to see some sort of secret vision of Evelyn Cordew, real in some sense or faked by a master faker. Yet at the same time, and I think beyond all my fear for myself, I felt a dispassionate disgust at the way Slyker reduced all human drives and desires to a lust for power, of which the chair imprisoning me, the "Siegfried Line" door, and the files of ghosts, real or imagined, were perfect symbols.

Among immediate worries, although I did a pretty good job of suppressing all of them, the one that nagged at me the most was that Slyker had admitted to me the inadequacy of his two major senses. I didn't think he would make that admission to someone who was going to live very long.

The black minutes dragged on. I heard from time to time the rustle of folders, but only one soft thud of a file drawer closing, so I knew he wasn't finished yet with the putting-away and locking-up job.

I concentrated the free corner of my mind—the tiny part I dared spare from breathing—on trying to hear something else, but I couldn't even catch the background noise of the city. I decided the office must be soundproofed as well as light-sealed. Not that it mattered, since I couldn't get a signal out anyway.

Then a noise did come—a solid snap that I'd heard just once before, but knew instantly. It was the sound of the bolts in the office door retracting. There was something funny about it that took me a moment to figure out: there had been no preliminary grating of the key.

For a moment too I thought Slyker had crept noiselessly to the door, but then I realized that the rustling of folders at the desk had kept up all the time.

And the rustling of folders continued. I guessed Slyker had not noticed the door. He hadn't been exaggerating about his bad hearing.

There was the faint creaking of the hinges, once, twice—as if the door were being opened and closed—then again the solid snap of the bolts. That puzzled me, for there should have been a big flash of light from the corridor—unless the lights were all out.

I couldn't hear any sound after that, except the continued rustling of the file folders, though I listened as hard as the job of breathing let me—and in a crazy kind of way the job of cautious breathing helped my hearing, because it made me hold absolutely still yet without daring to tense up. I knew that someone was in the office with us and that Slyker didn't know it. The black moments seemed to stretch out forever, as if an edge of eternity had got hooked into our timestream.

All of a sudden there was a *swish,* like that of a sheet being whipped through the air very fast, and a grunt of surprise from Slyker that started toward a screech and then was cut off as sharp as if he'd been gagged nose-and-mouth like me. Then there came the scuff of feet and the squeal of the castors of a chair, the sound of a struggle, not of two people struggling, but of a man struggling against restraints of some sort, a frantic confined heaving and panting. I wondered if Slyker's little lump of chair had sprouted restraints like mine, but that hardly made sense.

Then abruptly there was the whistle of breath, as if his nostrils had been uncovered, but not his mouth. He was panting through his nose. I got a mental picture of Slyker tied to his chair some way and eying the darkness just as I was doing.

Finally out of the darkness came a voice I knew very well because I'd heard it often enough in movie houses and from Jeff Crain's tape-recorder. It had the old familiar caress mixed with the old familiar giggle, the naïveté and the knowingness, the warm sympathy and cool-headedness, the high-school charmer and the sybil. It was Evelyn Cordew's voice, all right.

"Oh for goodness sake stop threshing around, Emmy. It won't help you shake off that sheet and it makes you look so funny. Yes, I said 'look,' Emmy—you'd be surprised at how losing five ghosts improves your eyesight, like having veils taken away from in front of them; you get more sensitive all over.

"And don't try to appeal to me by pretending to suffocate. I tucked the sheet under your nose even if I did keep your mouth covered. Couldn't bear you talking now. The sheet's called wrap-around plastic—I've got my chemical friend too, though he's not Parisian. It'll be next year's number-one packaging material, he tells me. Filmy, harder to see than cellophane, but very tough. An electronic plastic, no less, positive one side, negative the other. Just touch it to something and it wraps around, touches itself, and clings like anything. Like I just had to touch it to you. To make it unwrap fast you can just shoot some electrons into it from a handy static battery—my friend's advertising copy, Emmy—and it flattens out *whang*. Give it enough electrons and it's stronger than steel.

"We used another bit of it that last way, Emmy, to get through your door. Fitted it outside, so it'd wrap itself against the bolts when your door opened. Then just now, after blacking out the corridor, we pumped electrons into it and flattened out, pushing back all the bolts. Excuse me, dear, but you know how you love to lecture about your valved plastics and all your other little restraints, so you mustn't mind me giving a little talk about mine. And boasting about my friends too. I've got some you don't know about, Emmy. Ever heard the name Smyslov, or the Arain? Some of them cut ghosts themselves and weren't pleased to hear about you, especially the past-future angle."

There was a protesting little squeal of castors, as if Slyker were trying to move his chair.

"Don't go away, Emmy. I'm sure you know why I'm here. Yes, dear, I'm taking them all back as of now. All five. And I don't care how much death-wish they got, because I've got some ideas for that. So now 'scuse me, Emmy, while I get ready to slip into my ghosts."

There wasn't any noise then except Emil Slyker's wheezy breathing and the occasional rustle of silk and the whir of a zipper, followed by soft feathery falls.

"There we are, Emmy, all clear. Next step, my five lost sisters. Why, your little old secret drawer is open—you didn't think I knew about that, Emmy, did you? Let's see now, I don't think we'll need music for this—they know my touch; it should make them stand up and shine."

She stopped talking. After a bit I got the barest hint of light over by the desk, very uncertain at first, like a star at the limit of vision, where it keeps winking back and forth from utter absence to the barest dim existence, or like a lonely lake lit only by starlight and glimpsed through a thick forest, or as if those dancing points of light that persist even in absolute darkness and indicate only a restless retina and optic nerve had fooled me for a moment into thinking they represented something real.

But then the hint of light took definite form, though staying at the dim limit of vision and crawling back and forth as I focused on it because my eyes had no other point of reference to steady it by.

It was a dim angular band making up three edges of a rectangle, the top edge longer than the two verticle edges, while the bottom edge wasn't there. As I watched it and it became a little clearer, I saw that the bands of light were brightest toward the inside—that is, toward the rectangle they partly enclosed, where they were bordered by stark blackness—while toward the outside they faded gradually away. Then as I continued to watch I saw that the two corners were rounded while up from the top edge there projected a narrow, lesser rectangle—a small tab.

The tab made me realize that I was looking at a file folder silhouetted by something dimly glowing inside it.

Then the top band darkened toward the center, as would happen if a hand were dipping into the folder, and then lightened again as if the hand were being withdrawn. Then up out of the folder, as if the invisible hand were guiding or coaxing it, swam something no brighter than the bands of light.

It was the shape of a woman, but distorted and constantly flowing, the head and arms and upper torso maintaining more of an approximation to human proportions than the lower torso and legs, which were like churning, trailing draperies or a long gauzy skirt. It was extremely dim, so I had to keep blinking my eyes, and it didn't get brighter.

It was like the figure of a woman phosphorescently painted on a long-skirted slip of the flimsiest silk that had silk-stocking-like sheaths for arms and head attached—yes, and topped by some illusion of dim silver hair. And yet it was more than that. Although it looped up gracefully through the air as such a slip might when shaken out by a woman preparing to put it on, it also had a writhing life of its own.

But in spite of all the distortions, as it flowed in an arc toward the ceiling and dove downward, it was seductively beautiful and the face was recognizably that of Evvie Cordew.

It checked its dive and reversed the direction of its flow, so that for a moment it floated upright high in the air, like a filmy night-gown a woman swishes above her head before she slips into it.

Then it began to settle toward the floor and I saw that there really was a woman standing under it and pulling it down over her head, though I could see her body only very dimly by the reflected glow of the ghost she was drawing down around her.

The woman on the floor shot up her hands close to her body and gave a quick wriggle and twist and ducked her head and then threw it back, as a woman does when she's getting into a tight dress, and the flowing glowing thing lost its distortions as it fitted itself around her.

Then for a moment the glow brightened a trifle as the woman and her ghost merged and I saw Evvie Cordew with her flesh gleaming by its own light—the long slim ankles, the vase-curve of hips and waist, the impudent breasts almost as you'd guess them from the bikini shots, but with larger aureoles—saw it for an instant before the ghostlight winked out like white sparks dying, and there was utter darkness again.

Utter darkness and a voice that crooned, "Oh that was like silk, Emmy, pure silk stocking all over. Do you remember when you cut it, Emmy? I'd just got my first screen credit and I'd signed the seven-year contract and I knew I was going to have the world by the tail and I felt wonderful and I suddenly got terribly dizzy for no reason and I came to you. And you straightened me out for then by coaxing out and cutting away my happiness. You told me it would be a little like giving blood, and it was. That was my first ghost, Emmy, but only the first."

My eyes, recovering swiftly from the brighter glow of the ghost returning to its sources, again made out the three glowing sides of the file folder. And again there swam up out of it a crazily churning phosphorescent woman trailing gauzy streamers. The face was recognizably Evvie's, but constantly distorting, now one eye big as an orange then small as a pea, the lips twisting in impossible smiles and grimaces, the brow shrinking to that of a pinhead or swelling to that of a mongolian idiot, like a face reflected from a plate-glass window running with water. As it came down over the real Evelyn's face there was a moment when the two were together but didn't merge, like the faces of twins in such a flooded window. Then, as if a squeegee had been wiped down it, the single face came bright and clear, and just as the darkness returned she caressed her lips with her tongue.

And I heard her say, "That one was like hot velvet, Emmy, smooth but with a burn in it. You took it two days after the sneak preview of *Hydrogen Blonde,* when we had the little party to celebrate after the big party, and the current Miss America was there and I showed her what a really valuable body looked like. That was when I realized that I'd hit the top and it hadn't changed me into a goddess or anything. I still had the same ignorances as before and the same awkwardnesses for the cameramen and cutters to hide—only they were worse because I was in the center of the show window—and I was going to have to fight for the rest of my life to keep my body like it was and then I was going to start to die, wrinkle by wrinkle, lose my juice cell by cell, like anybody else."

The third ghost arched toward the ceiling and down, waves of phosphorescence flickering it all the time. The slender arms undulated like pale serpents and the hands, the finger- and thumb-tips gently pressed together, were like the inquisitive heads of serpents—until the fingers spread so the hands resembled five-tongued creeping puddles of phosphorescent ink. Then into them as if into shoulder-length ivory silk gloves came the solid fingers and arms. For a bit the hands, first part to be merged, were brightest of the whole figure and I watched them help fit each other on and then sweep symmetrically down brow and cheeks and chin, fitting the face, with a little sidewise dip of the ring fingers as they smoothed in the eyes. Then they swept up and back and raked through both heads of hair, mixing them. This ghost's hair was very dark and, mingling, it toned down Evelyn's blonde a little.

"That one felt slimy, Emmy, like the top crawled off of a swamp. Remember, I'd just teased the boys into fighting over me at the

Troc. Jeff hurt Lester worse than they let out and even old Sammy got a black eye. I'd just discovered that when you get to the top you have all the ordinary pleasures the boobs yearn for all their lives, and they don't mean anything, and you have to work and scheme every minute to get the pleasures beyond pleasure that you've got to have to keep your life from going dry."

The fourth ghost rose toward the ceiling like a diver paddling up from the depths. Then, as if the whole room were filled with its kind of water, it seemed to surface at the ceiling and jackknife there and plunge down again with a little swoop and then reverse direction again and hover for a moment over the real Evelyn's head and then sink slowly down around her like a diver drowning. This time I watched the bright hands cupping the ghost's breasts around her own as if she were putting on a luminescent net brassiere. Then the ghost's filminess shrank suddenly to tighten over her torso like a cheap cotton dress in a cloudburst.

As the glow died to darkness a fourth time, Evelyn said softly, "Ah but that was cool, Emmy. I'm shivering. I'd just come back from my first location work in Europe and was sick to get at Broadway, and before you cut it you made me relive the yacht party where I overheard Ricco and the author laughing at how I'd messed up my first legitimate play reading, and we swam in the moonlight and Monica almost drowned. That was when I realized that nobody, even the bottom boobs in the audience, really respected you because you were their sex queen. They respected the little female boob in the seat beside them more than they did you. Because you were just something on the screen that they could handle as they pleased inside their minds. With the top folk, the Big Timers, it wasn't any better. To them you were just a challenge, a prize, something to show off to other men to drive them nuts, but never something to love. Well, that's four, Emmy, and four and one makes all."

The last ghost rose whirling and billowing like a silk robe in the wind, like a crazy photomontage, like a surrealist painting done in a barely visible wash of pale flesh tones on a black canvas, or rather like an endless series of such surrealist paintings, each distortion melting into the next—trailing behind it a gauzy wake of draperies which I realized was the way ghosts were always pictured and described. I watched the draperies bunch as Evelyn pulled them down around her, and then they suddenly whipped tight against her thighs, like a skirt in a strong wind or like nylon clinging in the cold. The final glow was a little stronger, as if there were more life in the shining woman than there had been at first.

"Ah that was like the brush of wings, Emmy, like feathers in the wind. You cut it after the party in Sammy's plane to celebrate me being the top money star in the industry. I bothered the pilot because I wanted him to smash us in a dive. That was when I realized I was just property—something for men to make money out of (and me to make money, too, out of me) from the star who married me to prop his box-office rating to the sticks theater owner who hoped I'd sell a few extra tickets. I found that my deepest love—it was once for you, Emmy—was just something for a man to capitalize on. That any man, no matter how sweet or strong, could in the end never be anything but a pimp. Like you, Emmy."

Just darkness for a while then, darkness and silence, broken only by the faint rustling of clothing.

Finally her voice again: "So now I got my pictures back, Emmy. All the original negatives, you might say, for you can't make prints of them or second negatives—I don't think. Or is there a way of making prints of them, Emmy—duplicate women? It's not worth letting you answer—you'd be bound to say yes to scare me.

"What do we do with you now, Emmy? I know what you'd do to me if you had the chance, for you've done it already. You've kept parts of me—no, five real *me*'s—tucked away in envelopes for a long time, something to take out and look at or run through your hand or twist around a finger or crumple in a ball, whenever you felt bored on a long afternoon or an endless night. Or maybe show off to special friends or even give other girls to wear—you didn't think I knew about that trick, did you, Emmy?—I hope I poisoned them, I hope I made them burn! Remember, Emmy, I'm full of death-wish now, five ghosts of it. Yes, Emmy, what do we do with you now?"

Then for the first time since the ghosts had shown, I heard the sound of Dr. Slyker's breath whistling through his nose and the muffled grunts and creakings as he lurched against the clinging sheet.

"Makes you think, doesn't it, Emmy? I wish I'd asked my ghosts what to do with you when I had the chance—I wish I'd known how to ask them. They'd have been the ones to decide. Now they're too mixed in.

"We'll let the other girls decide—the other ghosts. How many dozen are there, Emmy? How many hundred? I'll trust their judgment. Do your ghosts love you, Emmy?"

I heard the click of her heels followed by soft rushes ending in thuds—the file drawers being yanked open. Slyker got noisier.

"You don't think they love you, Emmy? Or they do but their way of showing affection won't be exactly comfortable, or safe? We'll see."

The heels clicked again for a few steps.

"And now, music. The fourth button, Emmy?"

There came again those sensual, spectral chords that opened the "Ghostgirls Pavan," and this time they led gradually into a music that seemed to twirl and spin, very slowly and with a lazy grace, the music of space, the music of free-fall. It made easier the slow breathing that meant life to me.

I became aware of dim fountains. Each file drawer was outlined by a phosphorescent glow shooting upward.

Over the edge of one drawer a pale hand flowed. It slipped back, but there was another, and another.

The music strengthened, though spinning still more lazily, and out of the phosphorescence-edged parallelogram of the file drawers there began to pour, swiftly now, pale streams of womankind. Ever-changing faces that were gossamer masks of madness, drunkennness, desire, and hate; arms like a flood of serpents; bodies that writhed, convulsed, yet flowed like milk by moonlight.

They swirled out in a circle like slender clouds in a ring, a spinning circle that dipped close to me, inquisitively, a hundred strangely slitted eyes seeming to peer.

The spinning forms brightened. By their light I began to see Dr. Slyker, the lower part of his face tight with the transparent plastic, only the nostrils flaring and the bulging eyes switching their gaze about, his arms tight to his sides.

The first spiral of the ring speeded up and began to tighten around his head and neck. He was beginning to twirl slowly on his tiny chair, as if he were a fly caught in the middle of a web and being spun in a cocoon by the spider. His face was alternately obscured and illuminated by the bright smoky forms swinging past it. It looked as if he was being strangled by his own cigarette smoke in a film run backwards.

His face began to darken as the glowing circle tightened against him.

Once more there was utter darkness.

Then a whirring click and a tiny shower of sparks, three times repeated, then a tiny blue flame. It moved and stopped and moved, leaving behind it more silent tiny flames, yellow ones. They grew. Evelyn was systematically setting fire to the files.

I knew it might be curtains for me, but I shouted—it came out as a kind of hiccup—and my breath was instantly cut off as the valves in the gag closed.

But Evelyn turned. She had been bending close over Emil's chest and the light from the growing flames highlighted her smile. Through the dark red mist that was closing in on my vision I saw the flames begin to leap from one drawer after another. There was a sudden low roar, like film or acetate shavings burning.

Suddenly Evelyn reached across the desk and touched a button. As I started to red out, I realized that the gag was off, the clamps were loose.

I floundered to my feet, pain stabbing my numbed muscles. The room was full of flickering brightness under a dirty cloud bulging from the ceiling. Evelyn had jerked the transparent sheet off Slyker and was crumpling it up. He started to fall forward, very slowly. Looking at me she said, "Tell Jeff he's dead." But before Slyker hit the floor, she was out the door. I took a step toward Slyker, felt the stinging heat of the flames. My legs were like shaky stilts as I made for the door. As I steadied myself on the jamb I took a last look back, then lurched on.

There wasn't a light in the corridor. The glow of the flames behind me helped a little.

The top of the elevator was dropping out of sight as I reached the shaft. I took the stairs. It was a painful descent. As I trotted out of the building—it was the best speed I could manage—I heard sirens coming. Evelyn must have put in a call—or one of her "friends," though not even Jeff Crain was able to tell me more about them: who her chemist was and who were the Arain—it's an old word for spider, but that leads nowhere. I don't even know how she knew I was working for Jeff; Evelyn Cordew is harder than ever to see and I haven't tried. I don't believe even Jeff's seen her; though I've sometimes wondered if I wasn't used as a cat's paw.

I'm keeping out of it—just as I left it to the firemen to discover Dr. Emil Slyker "suffocated by smoke" from a fire in his "weird" private office, a fire which it was reported did little more than char the furniture and burn the contents of his files and the tapes of his hi-fi.

I think a little more was burned. When I looked back the last time I saw the Doctor lying in a straitjacket of pale flames. It may have been scattered papers or the electronic plastic. I think it was ghostgirls burning.

GUMMITCH WAS A SUPERKITTEN, AS HE knew very well, with an I.Q. of about 160. Of course, he didn't talk. But everybody knows that I.Q. tests based on language ability are very one-sided. Besides, he would talk as soon as they started setting a place for him at table and pouring him coffee. Ashurbanipal and Cleopatra ate horsemeat from pans on the floor and they didn't talk. Baby dined in his crib on milk from a bottle and he didn't talk. Sissy sat at table but they didn't pour her coffee and she didn't talk—not one word. Father and Mother (whom Gummitch had nicknamed Old Horsemeat and Kitty-Come-Here) sat at table and poured each other coffee and they *did* talk. Q.E.D.

Meanwhile, he would get by very well on thought projection and intuitive understanding of all human speech—not even to mention cat patois, which almost any civilized animal could play by ear. The dramatic monologues and Socratic dialogues, the quiz and panel show appearances, the felidological expedition to darkest Africa (where he would uncover the real truth behind lions and tigers), the exploration of the outer planets—all these could wait. The same went for the books for which he was ceaselessly accumulating material: *The Encyclopedia of Odors, Anthropofeline Psychology, Invisible Signs and Secret Wonders, Space-Time for Springers, Slit Eyes Look at Life,* et cetera. For the present it was enough to live existence to the hilt and soak up knowledge, missing no experience proper to his age level—to rush about with tail aflame.

So to all outward appearances Gummitch was just a vividly normal kitten, as shown by the succession of nicknames he bore along the magic path that led from blue-eyed infancy toward puberty: Little One, Squawker, Portly, Bumble (for purring not clumsiness), Old Starved-to-Death, Fierso, Loverboy (affection not sex), Spook, and Catnik. Of these only the last perhaps requires further explanation: the Russians had just sent Muttnik up after Sputnik, so that when one evening Gummitch streaked three times across the firmament of the living room floor in the same direction, past the fixed stars of the humans and the comparatively slow-moving heavenly bodies of the two older cats, and Kitty-Come-Here quoted the line from Keats:

> Then felt I like some watcher of the skies
> When a new planet swims into his ken;

it was inevitable that Old Horsemeat would say, "Ah—Catnik!"

The new name lasted all of three days, to be replaced by Gummitch, which showed signs of becoming permanent.

The little cat was on the verge of truly growing up, at least so Gummitch overheard Old Horsemeat comment to Kitty-Come-Here. A few short weeks, Old Horsemeat said, and Gummitch's fiery flesh would harden, his slim neck thicken, the electricity vanish from everything but his fur, and all his delightful kittenish qualities rapidly give way to the earthbound singlemindedness of a tom. They'd be lucky, Old Horsemeat concluded, if he didn't turn completely surly like Ashurbanipal.

Gummitch listened to these predictions with gay unconcern and with secret amusement from his vantage point of superior knowledge, in the same spirit that he accepted so many phases of his outwardly conventional existence: the murderous sidelong looks he got from Ashurbanipal and Cleopatra as he devoured his own horsemeat from his own little tin pan, because they sometimes were given canned catfood but he never; the stark idiocy of Baby, who didn't know the difference between a live cat and a stuffed teddy bear and who tried to cover up his ignorance by making goo-goo noises and poking indiscriminately at all eyes; the far more serious—because cleverly hidden—maliciousness of Sissy, who had to be watched out for warily—especially when you were alone—and whose retarded—even warped—development, Gummitch knew, was Old Horsemeat and Kitty-Come-Here's deepest, most secret, worry (more of Sissy and her evil ways soon); the limited intellect of Kitty-Come-Here, who despite the amounts of coffee she drank was quite as featherbrained as kittens are supposed to be and who firmly believed, for example, that kittens operated in the same space-time as other beings—that to get from *here* to *there* they had to cross the space *between*—and similar fallacies; the mental stodginess of even Old Horsemeat, who although he understood quite a bit of the secret doctrine and talked intelligently to Gummitch when they were alone, nevertheless suffered from the limitations of his status—a rather nice old god but a maddeningly slow-witted one.

But Gummitch could easily forgive all this massed inadequacy and downright brutishness in his felino-human household, because he was aware that he alone knew the real truth about himself and about other kittens and babies as well, the truth which was hidden from weaker minds, the truth that was as intrinsically incredible as the germ theory of disease or the origin of the whole great universe in the explosion of a single atom.

As a baby kitten Gummitch had believed that Old Horsemeat's two hands were hairless kittens permanently attached to the ends of Old Horsemeat's arms but having an independent life of their own. How he had hated and loved those two five-legged sallow monsters, his first playmates, comforters and battle-opponents!

Well, even that fantastic discarded notion was but a trifling fancy compared to the real truth about himself!

The forehead of Zeus split open to give birth to Minerva. Gummitch had been born from the waist-fold of a dirty old terrycloth bathrobe, Old Horsemeat's basic garment. The kitten was intuitively certain of it and had proved it to himself as well as any Descartes or Aristotle. In a kitten-size tuck of that ancient bathrobe the atoms of his body had gathered and quickened into life. His earliest memories were of snoozing wrapped in terrycloth, warmed by Old Horsemeat's heat. Old Horsemeat and Kitty-Come-Here were his true parents. The other theory of his origin, the one he heard Old Horsemeat and Kitty-Come-Here recount from time to time—that he had been the only surviving kitten of a litter abandoned next door, that he had had the shakes from vitamin deficiency and lost the tip of his tail and the hair on his paws and had to be nursed back to life and health with warm yellowish milk-and-vitamins fed from an eyedropper—that other theory was just one of those rationalizations with which mysterious nature cloaks the birth of heroes, perhaps wisely veiling the truth from minds unable to bear it, a rationalization as false as Kitty-Come-Here and Old Horsemeat's touching belief that Sissy and Baby were their children rather than the cubs of Ashurbanipal and Cleopatra.

The day that Gummitch had discovered by pure intuition the secret of his birth he had been filled with a wild instant excitement. He had only kept it from tearing him to pieces by rushing out to the kitchen and striking and devouring a fried scallop, torturing it fiendishly first for twenty minutes.

And the secret of his birth was only the beginning. His intellectual faculties aroused, Gummitch had two days later intuited a further and greater secret: since he was the child of humans he would, upon reaching this maturation date of which Old Horsemeat had spoken, turn not into a sullen tom but into a godlike human youth with reddish golden hair the color of his present fur. He would be poured coffee; and he would instantly be able to talk, probably in all languages. While Sissy (how clear it was now!) would at approximately the same time shrink and fur out into a sharp-clawed and vicious she-cat dark as her hair, her only concerns sex and self-love, fit harem-mate for Cleopatra, concubine to Ashurbanipal.

Exactly the same was true, Gummitch realized at once, for all kittens and babies, all humans and cats, wherever they might dwell. Metamorphosis was as much a part of the fabric of their lives as it was of the insects'. It was also the basic fact underlying all legends of werewolves, vampires, and witches' familiars.

If you just rid your mind of preconceived notions, Gummitch told himself, it was all very logical. Babies were stupid, fumbling, vindictive creatures without reason or speech. What could be more natural than that they should grow up into mute sullen selfish beasts bent only on rapine and reproduction? While kittens were quick, sensitive, subtle, supremely alive. What other destiny were they possibly fitted for except to become the deft, word-speaking, book-writing, music-making, meat-getting-and-dispensing masters of the world? To dwell on the physical differences, to point out that kittens and men, babies and cats, are rather unlike in appearance and size, would be to miss the forest for the trees—very much as if an entomologist should proclaim metamorphosis a myth because his microscope failed to discover the wings of a butterfly in a caterpillar's slime or a golden beetle in a grub.

Nevertheless it was such a mind-staggering truth, Gummitch realized at the same time, that it was easy to understand why humans, cats, babies, and perhaps most kittens were quite unaware of it. How to safely explain to a butterfly that he was once a hairy crawler, or to a dull larva that he will one day be a walking jewel? No, in such situations the delicate minds of man- and feline-kind are guarded by a merciful mass amnesia such as Velikovsky has explained prevents us from recalling that in historical times the Earth was catastrophically bumped by the planet Venus operating in the manner of a comet before settling down (with a cosmic sigh of relief, surely!) into its present orbit.

This conclusion was confirmed when Gummitch in the first fever of illumination tried to communicate his great insight to others. He told it in cat patois, as well as that limited jargon permitted, to

Ashurbanipal and Cleopatra and even, on the off chance, to Sissy and Baby. They showed no interest whatever, except that Sissy took advantage of his unguarded preoccupation to stab him with a fork.

Later, alone with Old Horsemeat, he projected the great new thoughts, staring with solemn yellow eyes at the old god, but the latter grew markedly nervous and even showed signs of real fear, so Gummitch desisted. ("You'd have sworn he was trying to put across something as deep as the Einstein theory or the doctrine of original sin," Old Horsemeat later told Kitty-Come-Here.)

But Gummitch was a man now in all but form, the kitten reminded himself after these failures, and it was part of his destiny to shoulder secrets alone when necessary. He wondered if the general amnesia would affect him when he metamorphosed. There was no sure answer to this question, but he hoped not—and sometimes felt that there was reason for his hopes. Perhaps he would be the first true kitten-man, speaking from a wisdom that had no locked doors in it.

Once he was tempted to speed up the process by the use of drugs. Left alone in the kitchen, he sprang onto the table and started to lap up the black puddle in the bottom of Old Horsemeat's coffee cup. It tasted foul and poisonous and he withdrew with a little snarl, frightened as well as revolted. The dark beverage would not work its tongue-loosening magic, he realized, except at the proper time and with the proper ceremonies. Incantations might be necessary as well. Certainly unlawful tasting was highly dangerous.

The futility of expecting coffee to work any wonders by itself was further demonstrated to Gummitch when Kitty-Come-Here, wordlessly badgered by Sissy, gave a few spoonfuls to the little girl, liberally lacing it first with milk and sugar. Of course Gummitch knew by now that Sissy was destined shortly to turn into a cat and that no amount of coffee would ever make her talk, but it was nevertheless instructive to see how she spat out the first mouthful, drooling a lot of saliva after it, and dashed the cup and its contents at the chest of Kitty-Come-Here.

Gummitch continued to feel a great deal of sympathy for his parents in their worries about Sissy and he longed for the day when he would metamorphose and be able as an acknowledged man-child truly to console them. It was heartbreaking to see how they each tried to coax the little girl to talk, always attempting it while the other was absent, how they seized on each accidentally wordlike note in the few sounds she uttered and repeated it back to her hopefully, how they were more and more possessed by fears not so much of her retarded (they thought) development as of her increasingly obvious maliciousness, which was directed chiefly at Baby...though the two cats and Gummitch bore their share. Once she had caught Baby alone in his crib and used the sharp corner of a block to dot Baby's large-domed lightly downed head with triangular red marks. Kitty-Come-Here had discovered her doing it, but the woman's first action had been to rub Baby's head to obliterate the marks so that Old Horsemeat wouldn't see them. That was the night Kitty-Come-Here hid the abnormal psychology books.

Gummitch understood very well that Kitty-Come-Here and Old Horsemeat, honestly believing themselves to be Sissy's parents, felt just as deeply about her as if they actually were and he did what little he could under the present circumstances to help them. He had recently come to feel a quite independent affection for Baby—the miserable little proto-cat was so completely stupid and defenseless—and so he unofficially constituted himself the creature's guardian, taking his naps behind the door of the nursery and dashing about noisily whenever Sissy showed up. In any case he realized that as a potentially adult member of a felino-human household he had his natural responsibilities.

Accepting responsibilities was as much a part of a kitten's life, Gummitch told himself, as shouldering unsharable intuitions and secrets, the number of which continued to grow from day to day.

There was, for instance, the Affair of the Squirrel Mirror.

Gummitch had early solved the mystery of ordinary mirrors and of the creatures that appeared in them. A little observation and sniffing and one attempt to get behind the heavy wall-job in the living room had convinced him that mirror beings were insubstantial or at least hermetically sealed into their other world, probably creatures of pure spirit, harmless imitative ghosts—including the silent Gummitch Double who touched paws with him so softly yet so coldly.

Just the same, Gummitch had let his imagination play with what would happen if one day, while looking into the mirror world, he should let loose his grip on his spirit and let it slip into the Gummitch Double while the other's spirit slipped into his body—if, in short, he should change places with the scentless ghost kitten. Being doomed to a life consisting wholly of imitation and completely lacking in opportunities to show initiative—except for behind-the-scenes judgment and speed needed in rushing from one mirror to another to keep up with the real Gummitch—would be sickeningly dull, Gummitch decided, and he resolved to keep a tight hold on his spirit at all times in the vicinity of mirrors.

But that isn't telling about the Squirrel Mirror. One morning Gummitch was peering out the front bedroom window that overlooked the roof of the porch. Gummitch had already classified windows as semi-mirrors having two kinds of space on the other side: the mirror world and that harsh region filled with mysterious and dangerously organized-sounding noises called the outer world, into which grownup humans reluctantly ventured at intervals, donning special garments for the purpose and shouting loud farewells that were meant to be reassuring but achieved just the opposite effect. The coexistence of two kinds of space presented no paradox to the kitten who carried in his mind the twenty-seven-chapter outline of *Space-Time for Springers*—indeed, it constituted one of the minor themes of the book.

This morning the bedroom was dark and the outer world was dull and sunless, so the mirror world was unusually difficult to see. Gummitch was just lifting his face toward it, nose twitching, his front paws on the sill, when what should rear up on the other side, exactly in the space that the Gummitch Double normally occupied, but a dirty brown, narrow-visaged image with savagely low forehead, dark evil walleyes, and a huge jaw filled with shovel-like teeth.

Gummitch was enormously startled and hideously frightened. He felt his grip on his spirit go limp, and without volition he teleported himself three yards to the rear, making use of that faculty for cutting corners in space-time, traveling by space-warp in fact, which was one of his powers that Kitty-Come-Here refused to believe in and that even Old Horsemeat accepted only on faith.

Then, not losing a moment, he picked himself up by his furry seat, swung himself around, dashed downstairs at top speed, sprang to the top of the sofa, and stared for several seconds at the Gummitch Double in the wall-mirror—not relaxing a muscle strand until he was completely convinced that he was still himself and had not been transformed into the nasty brown apparition that had confronted him in the bedroom window.

"Now what do you suppose brought that on?" Old Horsemeat asked Kitty-Come-Here.

Later Gummitch learned that what he had seen had been a squirrel, a savage, nut-hunting being belonging wholly to the outer world (except for forays into attics) and not at all to the mirror one. Nevertheless he kept a vivid memory of his profound momentary conviction that the squirrel had taken the Gummitch Double's place and been about to take his own. He shuddered to think what would have happened if the squirrel had been actively interested in trading spirits with him. Apparently mirrors and mirror-situations, just as he had always feared, were highly conducive to spirit transfers. He filed the information away in the memory cabinet reserved for dangerous, exciting and possibly useful information, such as plans for climbing straight up glass (diamond-tipped claws!) and flying higher than the trees.

These days his thought cabinets were beginning to feel filled to bursting and he could hardly wait for the moment when the true rich taste of coffee, lawfully drunk, would permit him to speak.

He pictured the scene in detail: the family gathered in conclave at the kitchen table, Ashurbanipal and Cleopatra respectfully watching from floor level, himself sitting erect on chair with paws (or would they be hands?) lightly touching his cup of thin china, while Old Horsemeat poured the thin black steaming stream. He knew the Great Transformation must be close at hand.

At the same time he knew that the other critical situation in the household was worsening swiftly. Sissy, he realized now, was far older than Baby and should long ago have undergone her own somewhat less glamorous though equally necessary transformation (the first tin of raw horsemeat could hardly be as exciting as the first cup of coffee). Her time was long overdue. Gummitch found increasing horror in this mute vampirish being inhabiting the body of a rapidly growing girl, though inwardly equipped to be nothing but a most bloodthirsty she-cat. How dreadful to think of Old Horsemeat and Kitty-Come-Here having to care all their lives for such a monster! Gummitch told himself that if any opportunity for alleviating his parents' misery should ever present itself to him, he would not hesitate for an instant.

Then one night, when the sense of Change was so burstingly strong in him that he knew tomorrow must be the Day, but when the house was also exceptionally unquiet with boards creaking and snapping, taps adrip, and curtains mysteriously rustling at closed windows (so that it was clear that the many spirit worlds including the mirror one must be pressing very close), the opportunity came to Gummitch.

Kitty-Come-Here and Old Horsemeat had fallen into especially sound, drugged sleeps, the former with a bad cold, the latter with one unhappy highball too many (Gummitch knew he had been brooding about Sissy). Baby slept too, though with uneasy whimperings and joggings—moonlight shone full on his crib past a window shade which had whirringly rolled itself up without human or feline agency. Gummitch kept vigil under the crib, with eyes closed but with wildly excited mind pressing outward to every boundary of the house and even stretching here and there into the outer world. On this night of all nights sleep was unthinkable.

Then suddenly he became aware of footsteps, footsteps so soft they must, he thought, be Cleopatra's.

No, softer than that, so soft they might be those of the Gummitch Double escaped from the mirror world at last and padding up toward him through the darkened halls. A ribbon of fur rose along his spine.

Then into the nursery Sissy came prowling. She looked slim as an Egyptian princess in her long thin yellow nightgown and as sure of herself, but the cat was very strong in her tonight, from the flat intent eyes to the dainty canine teeth slightly bared—one look at her now would have sent Kitty-Come-Here running for the telephone number she kept hidden, the telephone number of the special doctor—and Gummitch realized he was witnessing a monstrous suspension of natural law in that this being should be able to exist for a moment without growing fur and changing round pupils for slit eyes.

He retreated to the darkest corner of the room, suppressing a snarl.

Sissy approached the crib and leaned over Baby in the moonlight, keeping her shadow off him. For a while she gloated. Then she began softly to scratch his cheek with a long hatpin she carried, keeping away from his eye, but just barely. Baby awoke and saw her and Baby didn't cry. Sissy continued to scratch, always a little more deeply. The moonlight glittered on the jeweled end of the pin.

Gummitch knew he faced a horror that could not be countered by running about or even spitting and screeching. Only magic could fight so obviously supernatural a manifestation. And this was also no time to think of consequences, no matter how clearly and bitterly etched they might appear to a mind intensely awake.

He sprang up onto the other side of the crib, not uttering a sound, and fixed his golden eyes on Sissy's in the moonlight. Then he moved forward straight at her evil face, stepping slowly, not swiftly, using his extraordinary knowledge of the properties of space *to walk straight through her hand and arm as they flailed the hatpin at him.* When his nose-tip finally paused a fraction of an inch from hers his eyes had not blinked once, and she could not look away. Then he unhesitatingly flung his spirit into her like a fistful of flaming arrows and he worked the Mirror Magic.

Sissy's moonlit face, feline and terrified, was in a sense the last thing that Gummitch, the real Gummitch-kitten, ever saw in this world. For the next instant he felt himself enfolded by the foul black blinding cloud of Sissy's spirit, which his own had displaced. At the same time he heard the little girl scream, very loudly but even more distinctly, *"Mommy!"*

That cry might have brought Kitty-Come-Here out of her grave, let alone from sleep merely deep or drugged. Within seconds she was in the nursery, closely followed by Old Horsemeat, and she had caught up Sissy in her arms and the little girl was articulating the wonderful word again and again, and miraculously following it with the command—there could be no doubt, Old Horsemeat heard it too—"Hold me tight!"

Then Baby finally dared to cry. The scratches on his cheek came to attention and Gummitch, as he had known must happen, was banished to the basement amid cries of horror and loathing chiefly from Kitty-Come-Here.

The little cat did not mind. No basement would be one-tenth as dark as Sissy's spirit that now enshrouded him for always, hiding all the file drawers and the labels on all the folders, blotting out forever even the imagining of the scene of first coffee-drinking and first speech.

In a last intuition, before the animal blackness closed in utterly, Gummitch realized that the spirit, alas, is not the same thing as the consciousness and that one may lose—sacrifice—the first and still be burdened with the second.

Old Horsemeat had seen the hatpin (and hid it quickly from Kitty-Come-Here) and so he knew that the situation was not what it seemed and that Gummitch was at the very least being made into a sort of scapegoat. He was quite apologetic when he brought the tin pans of food to the basement during the period of the little cat's exile. It was a comfort to Gummitch, albeit a small one. Gummitch told himself, in his new black halting manner of thinking, that after all a cat's best friend is his man.

From that night Sissy never turned back in her development. Within two months she had made three years' progress in speaking. She became an outstandingly bright, light-footed, high-spirited little girl. Although she never told anyone this, the moonlit nursery and Gummitch's magnified face were her first memories. Everything before that was inky blackness. She was always very nice to Gummitch in a careful sort of way. She could never stand to play the game "Owl Eyes."

After a few weeks Kitty-Come-Here forgot her fears and Gummitch once again had the run of the house. But by then the transformation Old Horsemeat had always warned about had fully taken place. Gummitch was a kitten no longer but an almost burly tom. In him it took the psychological form not of sullenness or surliness but an extreme dignity. He seemed at times rather like an old pirate brooding on treasures he would never live to dig up, shores of adventure he would never reach. And sometimes when you looked into his yellow eyes you felt that he had in him all the materials for the book *Slit Eyes Look at Life*—three or four volumes at least— although he would never write it. And that was natural when you come to think of it, for as Gummitch knew very well, bitterly well indeed, his fate was to be the only kitten in the world that did not grow up to be a man.

Four Ghosts in Hamlet

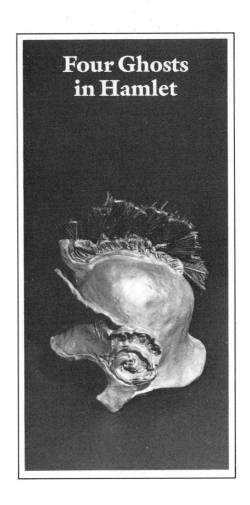

ACTORS ARE A SUPERSTITIOUS LOT, PROBAbly because chance plays a big part in the success of a production of a company or merely an actor — and because we're still a little closer than other people to the gypsies in the way we live and think. For instance, it's bad luck to have peacock feathers on stage or say the last line of a play at rehearsals or whistle in the dressing room (the one nearest the door gets fired) or sing God Save the Sovereign on a railway train (a Canadian company got wrecked that way).

Shakespearean actors are no exceptions. They simply travel a few extra superstitions, such as the one which forbids reciting the lines of the Three Witches, or anything from *Macbeth,* for that matter, except at performances, rehearsals, and on other legitimate occasions. This might be a good rule for outsiders too — then there wouldn't be the endless flood of books with titles taken from the text of *Macbeth* — you know, *Brief Candle, Tomorrow and Tomorrow, The Sound and the Fury, A Poor Player, All Our Yesterdays,* and those are all just from one brief soliloquy.

And our company, the Governor's company, has a rule against the Ghost in *Hamlet* dropping his greenish cheesecloth veil over his helmet-framed face until the very moment he makes each of his entrances. Hamlet's dead father mustn't stand veiled in the darkness of the wings.

This last superstition commemorates something which happened not too long ago, an actual ghost story. Sometimes I think it's the greatest ghost story in the world — though certainly not from my way of telling it, which is gossipy and poor, but from the wonder blazing at its core.

It's not only a true tale of the supernatural, but also very much a story about people, for after all — and before everything else — ghosts are people.

The ghostly part of the story first showed itself in the tritest way imaginable: three of our actresses (meaning practically all the ladies in a Shakespearean company) took to having sessions with a Ouija board in the hour before curtain time and sometimes even during a performance when they had long offstage waits, and they became so wrapped up in it and conceited about it and they squeaked so excitedly at the revelations which the planchette spelled out—and three or four times almost missed entrances because of it—that if the Governor weren't such a tolerant commander-in-chief, he would have forbidden them to bring the board to the theater. I'm sure he was tempted to and might have, except that Props pointed out to him that our three ladies probably wouldn't enjoy Ouija sessions one bit in the privacy of a hotel room, that much of the fun in operating a Ouija board is in having a half-exasperated, half-intrigued floating audience, and that when all's done the basic business of all ladies is glamour, whether of personal charm or of actual witchcraft, since the word means both.

Props—that is, our property man, Billy Simpson—was fascinated by their obsession, as he is by any new thing that comes along, and might very well have broken our Shakespearean taboo by quoting the Three Witches about them, except that Props has no flair for Shakespearean speech at all, no dramatic ability whatsoever, in fact he's the one person in our company who never acts even a bit part or carries a mute spear on stage, though he has other talents which make up for this deficiency—he can throw together a papier-mâché bust of Pompey in two hours, or turn out a wooden prop dagger all silvery-bladed and hilt-gilded, or fix a zipper, and that's not all.

As for myself, I was very irked at the ridiculous alphabet board, since it seemed to occupy most of Monica Singleton's spare time and satisfy all her hunger for thrills. I'd been trying to promote a romance with her—a long touring season becomes deadly and cold without some sort of heart-tickle—and for a while I'd made progress. But after Ouija came along, I became a ridiculous Guildenstern mooning after an unattainable unseeing Ophelia—which were the parts I and she actually played in *Hamlet*.

I cursed the idiot board with its childish corner-pictures of grinning suns and smirking moons and windblown spirits, and I further alienated Monica by asking her why wasn't it called a Nenein or No-No board (Ninny board!) instead of a Yes-Yes board? Was that, I inquired, because all spiritualists are forever accentuating the positive and behaving like a pack of fawning yes-men?—yes, we're here; yes, we're your uncle Harry; yes, we're happy on this plane; yes, we have a doctor among us who'll diagnose that pain in your chest; and so on.

Monica wouldn't speak to me for a week after that.

I would have been even more depressed except that Props pointed out to me that no flesh-and-blood man can compete with ghosts in a girl's affections, since ghosts being imaginary have all the charms and perfections a girl can dream of, but that all girls eventually tire of ghosts, or if their minds don't, their bodies do. This eventually did happen, thank goodness, in the case of myself and Monica, though not until we'd had a grisly, mind-wrenching experience— a night of terrors before the nights of love.

So Ouija flourished and the Governor and the rest of us put up with it one way or another, until there came that three-night-stand in Wolverton, when its dismal uncanny old theater tempted our three Ouija-women to ask the board who was the ghost haunting the spooky place and the swooping planchette spelled out the name S-H-A-K-E-S-P-E-A-R-E....

But I am getting ahead of my story. I haven't introduced our company except for Monica, Props, and the Governor—and I haven't identified the last of those three.

We call Gilbert Usher the Governor out of sheer respect and affection. He's about the last of the old actor-managers. He hasn't the name of Gielgud or Olivier or Evans or Richardson, but he's spent most of a lifetime keeping Shakespeare alive, spreading that magical areligious gospel in the more remote counties and the Dominions and the United States, like Benson once did. Our other actors aren't names at all—I refuse to tell you mine!—but with the exception of myself they're good troupers, or if they don't become that the first season, they drop out. Gruelingly long seasons, much uncomfortable traveling, and small profits are our destiny.

This particular season had got to that familiar point where the plays are playing smoothly and everyone's a bit tireder than he realizes and the restlessness sets in. Robert Dennis, our juvenile, was writing a novel of theatrical life (he said) mornings at the hotel—up at seven to slave at it, our Robert claimed. Poor old Guthrie Boyd had started to drink again, and drink quite too much, after an abstemious two months which had astonished everyone.

Francis Farley Scott, our leading man, had started to drop hints that he was going to organize a Shakespearean repertory company of his own next year and he began to have conspiratorial conversations with Gertrude Grainger, our leading lady, and to draw us furtively aside one by one to make us hypothetical offers, no exact salary named. F.F. is as old as the Governor—who is our star, of course—and he has no talents at all except for self-infatuation and a somewhat grandiose yet impressive fashion of acting. He's portly like an opera tenor and quite bald and he travels with an assortment of thirty toupees, ranging from red to black shot with silver, which he alternates with shameless abandon—they're for wear offstage, not on. It doesn't matter to him that the company knows all about his multi-colored artificial toppings, for we're part of his world of illusion, and he's firmly convinced that the stage-struck local ladies he squires about never notice, or at any rate mind the deception. He once gave me a lecture on the subtleties of suiting the color of your hair to the lady you're trying to fascinate—her own age, hair color, and so on.

Every year F.F. plots to start a company of his own—it's a regular midseason routine with him—and every year it comes to nothing, for he's as lazy and impractical as he is vain. Yet F.F. believes he could play any part in Shakespeare or all of them at once in a pinch; perhaps the only F.F. Scott Company which would really satisfy him would be one in which he would be the only actor—a Shakespearean monologue; in fact, the one respect in which F.F. is not lazy is in his eagerness to double as many parts as possible in any single play.

F.F.'s yearly plots never bother the Governor a bit—he keeps waiting wistfully for F.F. to fix him with an hypnotic eye and in a hoarse whisper ask *him* to join the Scott company.

And I of course was hoping that now at last Monica Singleton would stop trying to be the most exquisite ingenue that ever came tripping Shakespeare's way (rehearsing her parts even in her sleep, I guessed, though I was miles from being in a position to know that for certain) and begin to take note and not just advantage of my devoted attentions.

But then old Sybil Jameson bought the Ouija board and Gertrude Grainger dragooned an unwilling Monica into placing her fingertips on the planchette along with theirs "just for a lark." Next day Gertrude announced to several of us in a hushed voice that Monica had the most amazing undeveloped mediumistic talent she'd ever encountered, and from then on the girl was a Ouija-addict. Poor tight-drawn Monica, I suppose she had to explode out of her self-imposed Shakespearean discipline somehow, and it was just too bad it had to be the board instead of me. Though come to think of it, I shouldn't have felt quite so resentful of the board, for she might have exploded with Robert Dennis, which would have been infinitely worse, though we were never quite sure of Robert's sex. For that matter I wasn't sure of Gertrude's and suffered agonies of uncertain jealousy when she captured my beloved. I was obsessed with the vision of Gertrude's bold knees pressing Monica's under the Ouija board, though with Sybil's bony ones for chaperones, fortunately.

Francis Farley Scott, who was jealous too because this new toy had taken Gertrude's mind off their annual plottings, said rather spitefully that Monica must be one of those grabby girls who have to take command of whatever they get their fingers on, whether it's a man or a planchette, but Props told me he'd bet anything that Gertrude and Sybil had "followed" Monica's first random finger movements like the skillfulest dancers guiding a partner while seeming to yield, in order to coax her into the business and make sure of their third.

Sometimes I thought that F.F. was right and sometimes Props and sometimes I thought that Monica had a genuine supernatural talent, though I don't ordinarily believe in such things, and that last really frightened me, for such a person might give up live men for ghosts forever. She was such a sensitive, subtle, wraith-cheeked girl and she could get so keyed up and when she touched the planchette her eyes got such an empty look, as if her mind had traveled down into her fingertips or out to the ends of time and space. And once the three of them gave me a character reading from the board which embarrassed me with its accuracy. The same thing happened to several other people in the company. Of course, as Props pointed out, actors can be pretty good character analysts whenever they stop being egomaniacs.

After reading characters and foretelling the future for several weeks, our Three Weird Sisters got interested in reincarnation and began asking the board and then telling us what famous or infamous people we'd been in past lives. Gertrude Grainger had been Queen Boadicea, I wasn't surprised to hear. Sybil Jameson had been Cassandra. While Monica was once mad Queen Joanna of Castile and more recently a prize hysterical patient of Janet at the Salpetriere— touches which irritated and frightened me more than they should have. Billy Simpson—Props—had been an Egyptian silversmith under Queen Hatshepsut and later a servant of Samuel Pepys; he heard this with a delighted chuckle. Guthrie Boyd had been the Emperor Claudius and Robert Dennis had been Caligula. For some reason I had been both John Wilkes Booth and Lambert Simnel, which irritated me considerably, for I saw no romance but only neurosis in assassinating an American president and dying in a burning barn, or impersonating the Earl of Warwick, pretending unsuccessfully to the British throne, being pardoned for it—of all things!—and spending the rest of my life as a scullion in the kitchen of Henry VII and his son. The fact that both Booth and Simnel had been actors of a sort—a poor sort—naturally irritated me the more. Only much later did Monica confess to me that the board had probably made those decisions because I had had such a "tragic, dangerous, defeated look"—a revelation which surprised and flattered me.

Francis Farley Scott was flattered too, to hear he'd once been Henry VIII—he fancied all those wives and he wore his golden blond toupee after the show that night—until Gertrude and Sybil and Monica announced that the Governor was a reincarnation of no less than William Shakespeare himself. That made F.F. so jealous that he instantly sat down at the prop table, grabbed up a quill pen, and did an impromptu rendering of Shakespeare composing Hamlet's "To be or not to be" soliloquy. It was an effective performance, though with considerably more frowning and eye-rolling and trying of lines for sound than I imagine Willy S. himself used originally, and when F.F. finished, even the Governor, who'd been standing unobserved in the shadows beside Props, applauded with the latter.

Governor kidded the pants off the idea of himself as Shakespeare. He said that if Willy S. were ever reincarnated it ought to be as a world-famous dramatist who was secretly in his spare time the world's greatest scientist and philosopher and left clues to his identity in his mathematical equations—that way he'd get his own back at Bacon, rather the Baconians.

Yet I suppose if you had to pick someone for a reincarnation of Shakespeare, Gilbert Usher wouldn't be a bad choice. Insofar as a star and director ever can be, the Governor is gentle and self-effacing—as Shakespeare himself must have been, or else there would never have arisen that ridiculous Bacon-Oxford-Marlowe-Elizabeth-take-your-pick-who-wrote-Shakespeare controversy. And the Governor has a sweet melancholy about him, though he's handsomer and despite his years more athletic than one imagines Shakespeare being. And he's generous to a fault, especially where old actors who've done brave fine things in the past are concerned.

This season his mistake in that last direction had been in hiring Guthrie Boyd to play some of the more difficult older leading roles, including a couple F.F. usually handles: Brutus, Othello, and besides those Duncan in *Macbeth,* Kent in *King Lear,* and the Ghost in *Hamlet.*

Guthrie was a bellowing hard-drinking bear of an actor, who'd been a Shakespearean star in Australia and successfully smuggled some of his reputation west—he learned to moderate his bellowing, while his emotions were always simple and sincere, though explosive—and finally even spent some years in Hollywood. But there his drinking caught up with him, probably because of the stupid film parts he got, and he failed six times over. His wife divorced him. His children cut themselves off. He married a starlet and she divorced him. He dropped out of sight.

Then after several years the Governor ran into him. He'd been rusticating in Canada with a stubborn teetotal admirer. He was only a shadow of his former self, but there was some substance to the shadow—and he wasn't drinking. The Governor decided to take a chance on him—although the company manager Harry Grossman was dead set against it—and during rehearsals and the first month or so of performances it was wonderful to see how old Guthrie Boyd came back, exactly as if Shakespeare were a restorative medicine.

It may be stuffy or sentimental of me to say so, but you know, I think Shakespeare's good for people. I don't know of an actor, except myself, whose character hasn't been strengthened and his vision widened and charity quickened by working in the plays. I've heard that before Gilbert Usher became a Shakespearean, he was a more ruthlessly ambitious and critical man, not without malice, but the plays mellowed him, as they've mellowed Props's philosophy and given him a zest for life.

Because of his contact with Shakespeare, Robert Dennis is a less strident and pettish swish (if he is one), Gertrude Grainger's outbursts of cold rage have an undercurrent of queenly make-believe, and even Francis Farley Scott's grubby little seductions are probably kinder and less insultingly illusionary.

In fact I sometimes think that what civilized serenity the British people possess, and small but real ability to smile at themselves, is chiefly due to their good luck in having had William Shakespeare born one of their company.

But I was telling how Guthrie Boyd performed very capably those first weeks, against the expectations of most of us, so that we almost quit holding our breaths—or sniffing at his. His Brutus was workmanlike, his Kent quite fine—that bluff rough honest part suited him well—and he regularly got admiring notices for his Ghost in *Hamlet*. I think his years of living death as a drinking alcoholic had given him an understanding of loneliness and frozen abilities and despair that he put to good use—probably unconsciously—in interpreting that small role.

He was really a most impressive figure in the part, even just visually. The Ghost's basic costume is simple enough—a big all-enveloping cloak that brushes the groundcloth, a big dull helmet with the tiniest battery light inside its peak to throw a faint green glow on the Ghost's features, and over the helmet a veil of greenish cheesecloth that registers as mist to the audience. He wears a suit of stage armor under the cloak, but that's not important and at a pinch he can do without it, for his cloak can cover his entire body.

The Ghost doesn't switch on his helmet-light until he makes his entrance, for fear of it being glimpsed by an edge of the audience, and nowadays because of that superstition or rule I told you about, he doesn't drop the cheesecloth veil until the last second either, but when Guthrie Boyd was playing the part that rule didn't exist and I have a vivid recollection of him standing in the wings, waiting to go on, a big bearish inscrutable figure about as solid and unsupernatural as a bushy seven-foot evergreen covered by a gray tarpaulin. But then when Guthrie would switch on the tiny light and stride smoothly and silently on stage and his hollow distant tormented voice boom out, there'd be a terrific shivery thrill, even for us backstage, as if we were listening to words that really had traveled across black windy infinite gulfs from the Afterworld or the Other Side.

At any rate Guthrie was a great Ghost, and adequate or a bit better than that in most of his other parts—for those first non-drinking weeks. He seemed very cheerful on the whole, modestly buoyed up by his comeback, though sometimes something empty and dead would stare for a moment out of his eyes—the old drinking alcoholic wondering what all this fatiguing sober nonsense was about. He was especially looking forward to our three-night stand at Wolverton, although that was still two months in the future then. The reason was that both his children—married and with families now, of course—lived and worked at Wolverton and I'm sure he set great store on proving to them in person his rehabilitation, figuring it would lead to a reconciliation and so on.

But then came his first performance as Othello. (The Governor, although the star, always played Iago—an equal role, though not the title one.) Guthrie was almost too old for Othello, of course, and besides that, his health wasn't good—the drinking years had taken their toll of his stamina and the work of rehearsals and of first nights in eight different plays after years away from the theater had exhausted him. But somehow the old volcano inside him got seething again and he gave a magnificent performance. Next morning the papers raved about him and one review rated him even better than the Governor.

That did it, unfortunately. The glory of his triumph was too much for him. The next night—*Othello* again—he was drunk as a skunk. He remembered most of his lines—though the Governor had to throw him about every sixth one out of the side of his mouth—but he weaved and wobbled, he planked a big hand on the shoulder of every other character he addressed to keep from falling over, and he even forgot to put in his false teeth the first two acts, so that his voice was mushy. To cap that, he started really to strangle Gertrude Grainger in the last scene, until that rather brawny Desdemona, unseen by the audience, gave him a knee in the gut; then, after stabbing himself, he flung the prop dagger high in the flies so that it came down with two lazy twists and piercing the groundcloth buried its blunt point deep in the soft wood of the stage floor not three feet from Monica, who plays Iago's wife Emilia and so was lying dead on the stage at that point in the drama, murdered by her villainous husband—and might have been dead for real if the dagger had followed a slightly different trajectory.

Since a third performance of *Othello* was billed for the following night, the Governor had no choice but to replace Guthrie with Francis Farley Scott, who did a good job (for him) of covering up his satisfaction at getting his old role back. F.F., always a plushy and lascivious-eyed Moor, also did a good job with the part, coming in that way without even a brush-up rehearsal, so that one critic, catching the first and third shows, marveled how we could change big roles at will, thinking we'd done it solely to demonstrate our virtuosity.

Of course the Governor read the riot act to Guthrie and carried him off to a doctor, who without being prompted threw a big scare into him about his drinking and his heart, so that he just might have recovered from his lapse, except that two nights later we did *Julius Caesar* and Guthrie, instead of being statisfied with being workmanlike, decided to recoup himself with a really rousing performance. So he bellowed and groaned and bugged his eyes as I suppose he had done in his palmiest Australian days. His optimistic self-satisfaction between scenes was frightening to behold. Not too terrible a performance, truly, but the critics all panned him and one of them said, "Guthrie Boyd played Brutus—a bunch of vocal cords wrapped up in a toga."

That tied up the package and knotted it tight. Thereafter Guthrie was medium pie-eyed from morning to night—and often more than medium. The Governor had to yank him out of Brutus too (F.F. again replacing), but being the Governor he didn't sack him. He put him into a couple of bit parts—Montano and the Soothsayer—in *Othello* and *Caesar* and let him keep on at the others and he gave me and Joe Rubens and sometimes Props the job of keeping an eye on the poor old sot and making sure he got to the theater by the half hour and if possible not too plastered. Often he played the Ghost or the Doge of Venice in his street clothes under cloak or scarlet robe, but he played them. And many were the nights Joe and I made the rounds of half the local bars before we corraled him. The Governor sometimes refers to Joe Rubens and me in mild derision as "the American element" in his company, but just the same he depends on us quite a bit; and I certainly don't mind being one of his trouble-shooters—it's a joy to serve him.

All this may seem to contradict my statement about our getting to the point, about this time, where the plays were playing smoothly and the monotony setting in. But it doesn't really. There's always something going wrong in a theatrical company—anything else would be abnormal; just as the Samoans say no party is a success until somebody's dropped a plate or spilled a drink or tickled the wrong woman.

Besides, once Guthrie had got Othello and Brutus off his neck, he didn't do too badly. The little parts and even Kent he could play passably whether drunk or sober. King Duncan, for instance, and the Doge in *The Merchant* are easy to play drunk because the actor always has a couple of attendants to either side of him, who can guide his steps if he weaves and even hold him up if necessary— which can turn out to be an effective dramatic touch, registering as the infirmity of extreme age.

And somehow Guthrie continued to give that same masterful performance as the Ghost and get occasional notices for it. In fact Sybil Jameson insisted he was a shade better in the Ghost now that he was invariably drunk; which could have been true. And he still talked about the three-night-stand coming up in Wolverton, though now as often with gloomy apprehension as with proud fatherly anticipation.

Well, the three-night-stand eventually came. We arrived at Wolverton on a non-playing evening. To the surprise of most of us, but especially Guthrie, his son and daughter were there at the station to welcome him with their respective spouses and all their kids and numerous in-laws and a great gaggle of friends. Their cries of greeting when they spotted him were almost an organized cheer and I looked around for a brass band to strike up.

I found out later that Sybil Jameson, who knew them, had been sending them all his favorable notices, so that they were eager as weasels to be reconciled with him and show him off as blatantly as possible.

When he saw his children's and grandchildren's faces and realized the cries were for him, old Guthrie got red in the face and beamed like the sun, and they closed in around him and carried him off in triumph for an evening of celebrations.

Next day I heard from Sybil, whom they'd carried off with him, that everything had gone beautifully. He'd drunk like a fish, but kept marvellous control, so that no one but she noticed, and the warmth of the reconciliation of Guthrie to everyone, complete strangers included, had been wonderful to behold. Guthrie's son-in-law, a pugnacious chap, had got angry when he'd heard Guthrie wasn't to play Brutus the third night, and he declared that Gilbert Usher must be jealous of his magnificent father-in-law. Everything was forgiven twenty times over. They'd even tried to put old Sybil to bed with Guthrie, figuring romantically, as people will about actors, that she must be his mistress. All this was very fine, and of course wonderful for Guthrie, and for Sybil too in a fashion, yet I suppose the unconstrained nightlong bash, after two months of uninterrupted semi-controlled drunkenness, was just about the worst thing anybody could have done to the old boy's sodden body and laboring heart.

Meanwhile on that first evening I accompanied Joe Rubens and Props to the theater we were playing at Wolverton to make sure the scenery got stacked right and the costume trunks were all safely arrived and stowed. Joe is our stage manager besides doing rough or Hebraic parts like Caliban and Tubal—he was a professional boxer in his youth and got his nose smashed crooked. Once I started to take boxing lessons from him, figuring an actor should know everything, but during the third lesson I walked into a gentle right cross and although it didn't exactly stun me there were bells ringing faintly in my head for six hours afterwards and I lived in a world of faery and that was the end of my fistic career. Joe is actually a most versatile actor—for instance, he understudies the Governor in Macbeth, Lear, Iago, and of course Shylock—though his brutal moon-face is against him, especially when his make-up doesn't include a beard. But he dotes on being genial and in the States he often gets a job by day playing Santa Claus in big department stores during the month before Christmas.

The Monarch was a cavernous old place, very grimy backstage, but with a great warren of dirty little dressing rooms and even a property room shaped like an L stage left. Its empty shelves were thick with dust.

There hadn't been a show in the Monarch for over a year, I saw from the yellowing sheets thumbtacked to the callboard as I tore them off and replaced them with a simple black-crayoned HAMLET: TONIGHT AT 8:30.

Then I noticed, by the cold inadequate working lights, a couple of tiny dark shapes dropping down from the flies and gliding around in wide swift circles—out into the house too, since the curtain was up. Bats, I realized with a little start—the Monarch was really halfway through the lich gate. The bats would fit very nicely with *Macbeth*, I told myself, but not so well with *The Merchant of Venice*, while with *Hamlet* they should neither help nor hinder, provided they didn't descend in nightfighter squadrons; it would be nice if they stuck to the Ghost scenes.

I'm sure the Governor had decided we'd open at Wolverton with *Hamlet* so that Guthrie would have the best chance of being a hit in his children's home city.

Billy Simpson, shoving his properties table into place just in front of the dismal L of the prop room, observed cheerfully, "It's a proper haunted house. The girls'll find some rare ghosts here, I'll wager, if they work their board."

Which turned out to be far truer than he realized at the time— I think.

"Bruce!" Joe Rubens called to me. "We better buy a couple of rat traps and set them out. There's something scuttling back of the drops."

But when I entered the Monarch next night, well before the hour, by the creaky thick metal stage door, the place had been swept and tidied a bit. With the groundcloth down and the *Hamlet* set up, it didn't look too terrible, even though the curtain was still unlowered, dimly showing the house and its curves of empty seats and the two faint green exit lights with no one but myself to look at them.

There was a little pool of light around the callboard stage right, and another glow the other side of the stage beyond the wings, and lines of light showing around the edges of the door of the second dressing room, next to the star's.

I started across the dark stage, sliding my shoes softly so as not to trip over a cable or stage-screw and brace, and right away I got the magic electric feeling I often do in an empty theater the night of a show. Only this time there was something additional, something that started a shiver crawling down my neck. It wasn't, I think, the thought of the bats which might now be swooping around me unseen, skirling their inaudibly shrill trumpet calls, or even of the rats which *might* be watching sequin-eyed from behind trunks and flats, although not an hour ago Joe had told me that the traps he'd actually procured and set last night had been empty today.

No, it was more as if all of Shakespeare's characters were invisibly there around me—all the infinite possibilities of the theater. I imagined Rosalind and Falstaff and Prospero standing arm-in-arm watching me with different smiles. And Caliban grinning down from where he silently swung in the flies. And side by side, but unsmiling and not arm-in-arm: Macbeth and Iago and Dick the Three Eyes—Richard III. And all the rest of Shakespeare's myriad-minded good-evil crew.

I passed through the wings opposite and there in the second pool of light Billy Simpson sat behind his table with the properties for *Hamlet* set out on it: the skulls, the foils, the lantern, the purses, the parchmenty letters, Ophelia's flowers, and all the rest. It was odd Props having everything ready quite so early and a bit odd too that he should be alone, for Props has the un-actorish habit of making friends with all sorts of locals, such as policemen and porters and flower women and newsboys and shopkeepers and tramps who claim they're indigent actors, and even inviting them backstage with him—a fracture of rules which the Governor allows since Props is such a sensible chap. He has a great liking for people, especially low people, Props has, and for all the humble details of life. He'd make a good writer, I'd think, except for his utter lack of dramatic flair and story-skill—a sort of prosiness that goes with his profession.

And now he was sitting at his table, his stooped shoulders almost inside the doorless entry to the empty-shelfed prop room—no point in using it for a three-night-stand—and he was gazing at me quizzically. He has a big forehead—the light was on that—and a tapering chin—that was in shadow—and rather large eyes, which were betwixt the light and the dark. Sitting there like that, he seemed to me for a moment (mostly because of the outspread props, I guess) like the midnight Master of the Show in *The Rubaiyat* round whom all the rest of us move like shadow shapes.

Usually he has a quick greeting for anyone, but tonight he was silent, and that added to the illusion.

"Props," I said, "this theater's got a supernatural smell."

His expression didn't change at all, but he solemnly sniffed the air in several little whiffles adding up to one big inhalation, and as he did so he threw his head back, bringing his weakish chin into the light and shattering the illusion.

"Dust," he said after a moment. "Dust and old plush and scenery waterpaint and sweat and drains and gelatin and greasepaint and powder and a breath of whisky. But the supernatural...no, I can't smell that. Unless..." And he sniffed again, but shook his head.

I chuckled at his materialism—although that touch about whisky did seem fanciful, since I hadn't been drinking and Props never does and Guthrie Boyd was nowhere in evidence. Props has a mind like a notebook for sensory details—and for the minutiae of human habits too. It was Props, for instance, who told me about the actual notebook in which John McCarthy (who would be playing Fortinbras and the Player King in a couple of hours) jots down the exact number of hours he sleeps each night and keeps totting them up, so he knows when he'll have to start sleeping extra hours to average the full nine he thinks he must get each night to keep from dying.

It was also Props who pointed out to me that F.F. is much more careless gumming his offstage toupees to his head than his theater wigs—a studied carelessness, like that in tying a bowtie, he assured me; it indicated, he said, a touch of contempt for the whole offstage world.

Props isn't *only* a detail-worm, but it's perhaps because he is one that he has sympathy for all human hopes and frailties, even the most trivial, like my selfish infatuation with Monica.

Now I said to him, "I didn't mean an actual smell, Billy. But back there just now I got the feeling anything might happen tonight."

He nodded slowly and solemnly. With anyone but Props I'd have wondered if he weren't a little drunk. Then he said, "You were on a stage. You know, the science-fiction writers are missing a bet there. We've got time machines right now. Theaters. Theaters are time machines and spaceships too. They take people on trips through the future and the past and the elsewhere and the might-have-been—yes, and if it's done well enough, give them glimpses of Heaven and Hell."

I nodded back at him. Such grotesque fancies are the closest Props ever comes to escaping from prosiness.

I said, "Well, let's hope Guthrie gets aboard the spaceship before the curtain up-jets. Tonight we're depending on his children having the sense to deliver him here intact. Which from what Sybil says about them is not to be taken for granted."

Props stared at me owlishly and slowly shook his head. "Guthrie got here about ten minutes ago," he said, "and looking no drunker than usual."

"That's a relief," I told him, meaning it.

"The girls are having a Ouija session," he went on, as if he were determined to account for all of us from moment to moment. "They smelt the supernatural here, just as you did, and they're asking the board to name the culprit." Then he stooped so that he looked almost hunchbacked and he felt for something under the table.

I nodded. I'd guessed the Ouija part from the lines of light showing around the door of Gertrude Grainger's dressing room.

Props straightened up and he had a pint bottle of whisky in his hand. I don't think a loaded revolver would have dumbfounded me as much. He unscrewed the top.

"There's the Governor coming in," he said tranquilly, hearing the stage door creak and evidently some footsteps my own ears missed. "That's seven of us in the theater before the hour."

He took a big slow swallow of whisky and recapped the bottle, as naturally as if it were a nightly action. I goggled at him without comment. What he was doing was simply unheard of—for Billy Simpson.

At that moment there was a sharp scream and a clatter of thin wood and something twangy and metallic falling and a scurry of footsteps. Our previous words must have cocked a trigger in me, for I was at Gertrude Grainger's dressing-room door as fast as I could sprint—no worry this time about tripping over cables or braces in the dark.

I yanked the door open and there by the bright light of the bulbs framing the mirror were Gertrude and Sybil sitting close together with the Ouija board face down on the floor in front of them along with a flimsy wire-backed chair, overturned. While pressing back into Gertrude's costumes hanging on the rack across the little room, almost as if she wanted to hide behind them like bedclothes, was Monica, pale and staring-eyed. She didn't seem to recognize me. The dark-green heavily brocaded costume Gertrude wears as the Queen in *Hamlet,* into which Monica was chiefly pressing herself, accentuated her pallor. All three of them were in their streetclothes.

I went to Monica and put an arm around her and gripped her hand. It was cold as ice. She was standing rigidly.

While I was doing that Gertrude stood up and explained in rather haughty tones what I told you earlier: about them asking the board who the ghost was haunting the Monarch tonight and the planchette spelling out S-H-A-K-E-S-P-E-A-R-E. . . .

"I don't know why it startled you so, dear," she ended crossly, speaking to Monica. "It's very natural his spirit should attend performances of his plays."

I felt the slim body I clasped relax a little. That relieved me. I was selfishly pleased at having got an arm around it, even under such public and unamorous circumstances, while at the same time my silly mind was thinking that if Props had been lying to me about Guthrie Boyd having come in no more drunken than usual (this new Props who drank straight whisky in the theater could lie too, I supposed), why then we could certainly use William Shakespeare tonight, since the Ghost in *Hamlet* is the one part in all his plays Shakespeare himself is supposed to have acted on the stage.

"I don't know why myself now," Monica suddenly answered from beside me, shaking her head as if to clear it. She became aware of me at last, started to pull away, then let my arm stay around her.

The next voice that spoke was the Governor's. He was standing in the doorway, smiling faintly, with Props peering around his shoulder. Props would be as tall as the Governor if he ever straightened up, but his stoop takes almost a foot off his height.

The Governor said softly, a comic light in his eyes, "I think we should be content to bring Shakespeare's plays to life, without trying for their author. It's hard enough on the nerves just to *act* Shakespeare."

He stepped forward with one of his swift, naturally graceful movements and kneeling on one knee he picked up the fallen board and planchette. "At all events I'll take these in charge for tonight. Feeling better now, Miss Singleton?" he asked as he straightened and stepped back.

"Yes, quite all right," she answered flusteredly, disengaging my arm and pulling away from me rather too quickly.

He nodded. Gertrude Grainger was staring at him coldly, as if about to say something scathing, but she didn't. Sybil Jameson was looking at the floor. She seemed embarrassed, yet puzzled too.

I followed the Governor out of the dressing room and told him, in case Props hadn't, about Guthrie Boyd coming to the theater early. My momentary doubt of Props's honesty seemed plain silly to me now, although his taking that drink remained an astonishing riddle.

Props confirmed me about Guthrie coming in, though his manner was a touch abstracted.

The Governor nodded his thanks for the news, then twitched a nostril and frowned. I was sure he'd caught a whiff of alcohol and didn't know to which of us two to attribute it—or perhaps even to one of the ladies, or to an earlier passage of Guthrie this way.

He said to me, "Would you come into my dressing room for a bit, Bruce?"

I followed him, thinking he'd picked me for the drinker and wondering how to answer—best perhaps simply silently accept the fatherly lecture—but when he'd turned on the lights and I'd shut the door, his first question was, "You're attracted to Miss Singleton, aren't you, Bruce?"

When I nodded abruptly, swallowing my morsel of surprise, he went on softly but emphatically, "Then why don't you quit hovering and playing Galahad and really go after her? Ordinarily I must appear to frown on affairs in the company, but in this case it would be the best way I know of to break up those Ouija sessions, which are obviously harming the girl."

I managed to grin and tell him I'd be happy to obey his instructions—and do it entirely on my own initiative too.

He grinned back and started to toss the Ouija board on his couch, but instead put it and the planchette carefully down on the end of his long dressing table and put a second question to me.

"What do you think of some of this stuff they're getting over the board, Bruce?"

I said, "Well, that last one gave me a shiver, all right—I suppose because..." and I told him about sensing the presence of Shakespeare's characters in the dark. I finished, "But of course the whole idea is nonsense," and I grinned.

He didn't grin back.

I continued impulsively, "There was one idea they had a few weeks back that impressed me, though it didn't seem to impress you. I hope you won't think I'm trying to butter you up, Mr. Usher. I mean the idea of you being a reincarnation of William Shakespeare."

He laughed delightedly and said, "Clearly you don't yet know the difference between a player and a playwright, Bruce. Shakespeare striding about romantically with head thrown back?—and twirling a sword and shaping his body and voice to every feeling handed him? Oh no! I'll grant he might have played the Ghost—it's a part within the scope of an average writer's talents, requiring nothing more than that he stand still and sound off sepulchrally."

He paused and smiled and went on. "No, there's only one person in this company who might be Shakespeare come again, and that's Billy Simpson. Yes, I mean Props. He's a great listener and he knows how to put himself in touch with everyone and then he's got that rat-trap mind for every hue and scent and sound of life, inside or out the mind. And he's very analytic. Oh, I know he's got no poetic talent, but surely Shakespeare wouldn't have that in *every* reincarnation. I'd think he'd need about a dozen lives in which to gather material for every one in which he gave it dramatic form. Don't you find something very poignant in the idea of a mute inglorious Shakespeare spending whole humble lifetimes collecting the necessary stuff for one great dramatic burst? Think about it some day."

I was doing that already and finding it a fascinating fantasy. It crystalized so perfectly the feeling I'd got seeing Billy Simpson behind his property table. And then Props did have a high-fore-headed poet-schoolmaster's face like that given Shakespeare in the posthumous engravings and woodcuts and portraits. Why, even their initials were the same. It made me feel strange.

Then the Governor put his third question to me.

"He's drinking tonight, isn't he? I mean Props, not Guthrie."

I didn't say anything, but my face must have answered for me— at least to such a student of expressions as the Governor—for he smiled and said, "You needn't worry. I wouldn't be angry with him. In fact, the only other time I know of that Props drank spirits by himself in the theater, I had a great deal to thank him for." His lean face grew thoughtful. "It was long before your time, in fact it was the first season I took out a company of my own. I had barely enough money to pay the printer for the three-sheets and get the first-night curtain up. After that it was touch and go for months. Then in mid-season we had a run of bad luck—a two-night heavy fog in one city, an influenza scare in another, Harvey Wilkins' Shakespearean troupe two weeks ahead of us in a third. And when in the next town we played it turned out the advance sale was very light—because my name was unknown there and the theater was an unpopular one—I realized I'd have to pay off the company while there was still money enough to get them home, if not the scenery.

"That night I caught Props swigging, but I hadn't the heart to chide him for it—in fact I don't think I'd have blamed anyone, except perhaps myself, for getting drunk that night. But then during the performance the actors and even the union stagehands we travel with began coming to my dressing room by ones and twos and telling me they'd be happy to work without salary for another three weeks, if I thought that might give us a chance of recouping. Well, of course I grabbed at their offers and we got a spell of brisk pleasant weather and we hit a couple of places starved for Shakespeare, and things worked out, even to paying all the back salary owed before the season was ended.

"Later on I discovered it was Props who had put them all up to doing it."

Gilbert Usher looked up at me and one of his eyes was wet and his lips were working just a little. "I couldn't have done it myself," he said, "for I wasn't a popular man with my company that first season—I'd been riding everyone much too hard and with nasty sarcasms—and I hadn't yet learned how to ask anyone for help when I really needed it. But Billy Simpson did what I couldn't, though he had to nerve himself for it with spirits. He's quick enough with his tongue in ordinary circumstances, as you know, particularly when he's being the friendly listener, but apparently when something very special is required of him, he must drink himself to the proper pitch. I'm wondering..."

His voice trailed off and then he straightened up before his mirror and started to unknot his tie and he said to me briskly, "Better get dressed now, Bruce. And then look in on Guthrie, will you?"

My mind was churning some rather strange thoughts as I hurried up the iron stairs to the dressing room I shared with Robert Dennis. I got on my Guildenstern make-up and costume, finishing just as Robert arrived; as Laertes, Robert makes a late entrance and so needn't hurry to the theater on *Hamlet* nights. Also, although we don't make a point of it, he and I spend as little time together in the dressing room as we can.

Before going down I looked into Guthrie Boyd's. He wasn't there, but the lights were on and the essentials of the Ghost's costume weren't in sight—impossible to miss that big helmet!—so I assumed he'd gone down ahead of me.

It was almost the half hour. The house lights were on, the curtain down, more stage lights on too, and quite a few of us about. I noticed that Props was back in the chair behind his table and not looking particularly different from any other night—perhaps the drink had been a once-only aberration and not some symptom of a crisis in the company.

I didn't make a point of hunting for Guthrie. When he gets costumed early he generally stands back in a dark corner somewhere, wanting to be alone—perchance to sip, aye, there's the rub!—or visits with Sybil in her dressing room.

I spotted Monica sitting on a trunk by the switchboard, where backstage was brightest lit at the moment. She looked ethereal yet springlike in her blonde Ophelia wig and first costume, a pale green one. Recalling my happy promise to the Governor, I bounced up beside her and asked her straight out about the Ouija business, pleased to have something to the point besides the plays to talk with her about—and really not worrying as much about her nerves as I suppose I should have.

She was in a very odd mood, both agitated and abstracted, her gaze going back and forth between distant and near and very distant. My questions didn't disturb her at all, in fact I got the feeling she welcomed them, yet she genuinely didn't seem able to tell me much about why she'd been so frightened at the last name the board had spelled. She told me that she actually did get into a sort of dream state when she worked the board and that she'd screamed before she'd quite comprehended what had shocked her so; then her mind had blacked out for a few seconds, she thought.

"One thing though, Bruce," she said. "I'm not going to work the board any more, at least when the three of us are alone like that."

"That sounds like a wise idea," I agreed, trying not to let the extreme heartiness of my agreement show through.

She stopped peering around as if for some figure to appear that wasn't in the play and didn't belong backstage, and she laid her hand on mine and said, "Thanks for coming so quickly when I went idiot and screamed."

I was about to improve this opportunity by telling her that the reason I'd come so quickly was that she was so much in my mind, but just then Joe Rubens came hurrying up with the Governor behind him in his Hamlet black to tell me that neither Guthrie Boyd nor his Ghost costume was to be found anywhere in the theater.

What's more, Joe had got the phone numbers of Guthrie's son and daughter from Sybil and rung them up. The one phone hadn't answered, while on the other a female voice—presumably a maid's—had informed him that everyone had gone to see Guthrie Boyd in *Hamlet*.

Joe was already wearing his cumbrous chain-mail armor for Marcellus—woven cord silvered—so I knew I was elected. I ran upstairs and in the space of time it took Robert Dennis to guess my mission and advise me to try the dingiest bars first and have a drink or two myself in them, I'd put on my hat, overcoat, and wristwatch and left him.

So garbed and as usual nervous about people looking at my ankles, I sallied forth to comb the nearby bars of Wolverton. I consoled myself with the thought that if I found Hamlet's father's ghost drinking his way through them, no one would ever spare a glance for my own costume.

Almost on the stroke of curtain I returned, no longer giving a damn what anyone thought about my ankles. I hadn't found Guthrie or spoken to a soul who'd seen a large male imbiber—most likely of Irish whisky—in great-cloak and antique armor, with perhaps some ghostly green light cascading down his face.

Beyond the curtain the overture was fading to its sinister close and the backstage lights were all down, but there was an angry hushed-voice dispute going on stage left, where the Ghost makes all his entrances and exits. Skipping across the dim stage in front of the blue-lit battlements of Elsinore—I still in my hat and over- coat—I found the Governor and Joe Rubens and with them John McCarthy all ready to go on as the Ghost in his Fortinbras armor with a dark cloak and some green gauze over it.

But alongside them was Francis Farley Scott in a very similar get-up—no armor, but a big enough cloak to hide his King costume and a rather more impressive helmet than John's.

They were all very dim in the midnight glow leaking back from the dimmed-down blue floods. The five of us were the only people I could see on this side of the stage.

F.F. was arguing vehemently that he must be allowed to double the Ghost with King Claudius because he knew the part better than John and because—this was the important thing—he could imitate Guthrie's voice perfectly enough to deceive his children and perhaps save their illusions about him. Sybil had looked through the curtain hole and seen them and all of their yesterday crowd, with new recruits besides, occupying all of the second, third, and fourth rows center, chattering with excitement and beaming with anticipation. Harry Grossman had confirmed this from the front of the house.

I could tell that the Governor was vastly irked at F.F. and at the same time touched by the last part of his argument. It was exactly the sort of sentimental heroic rationalization with which F.F. cloaked his insatiable yearnings for personal glory. Very likely he believed it himself.

John McCarthy was simply ready to do what the Governor asked him. He's an actor untroubled by inward urgencies—except things like keeping a record of the hours he sleeps and each penny he spends—though with a natural facility for portraying on stage emotions which he doesn't feel one iota.

The Governor shut up F.F. with a gesture and got ready to make his decision, but just then I saw that there was a sixth person on this side of the stage.

Standing in the second wings beyond our group was a dark figure like a tarpaulined Christmas tree topped by a big helmet of unmistakable general shape despite its veiling. I grabbed the Governor's arm and pointed at it silently. He smothered a large curse and strode up to it and rasped, "Guthrie, you old Son of a B! Can you go on?" The figure gave an affirmative grunt.

Joe Rubens grimaced at me as if to say "Show business!" and grabbed a spear from the prop table and hurried back across the stage for his entrance as Marcellus just before the curtain lifted and the first nervous, superbly atmospheric lines of the play rang out, loud at first, but then going low with unspoken apprehension.

"Who's there?"

"Nay, answer me; stand, and unfold yourself."

"Long live the king!"

"Bernardo?"

"He."

"You come most carefully upon your hour."

"'Tis now struck twelve; get thee to bed, Francisco."

"For this relief much thanks; 'tis bitter cold and I am sick at heart."

"Have you had quiet guard?"

"Not a mouse stirring."

With a resigned shrug, John McCarthy simply sat down. F.F. did the same, though *his* gesture was clench-fisted and exasperated. For a moment it seemed to me very comic that two Ghosts in *Hamlet* should be sitting in the wings, watching a third perform. I unbuttoned my overcoat and slung it over my left arm.

The Ghost's first two appearances are entirely silent ones. He merely goes on stage, shows himself to the soldiers, and comes off again. Nevertheless there was a determined little ripple of hand-clapping from the audience—the second, third, and fourth rows center greeting their patriarchal hero, it seemed likely. Guthrie didn't fall down at any rate and he walked reasonably straight—an achievement perhaps rating applause, if anyone out there knew the degree of intoxication Guthrie was probably burdened with at this moment—a cask-bellied Old Man of the Sea on his back.

The only thing out of normal was that he had forgot to turn on the little green light in the peak of his helmet—an omission which hardly mattered, certainly not on his first appearance. I hurried up to him when he came off and told him about it in a whisper as he moved off toward a dark backstage corner. I got in reply, through the inscrutable green veil, an exhalation of whisky and three affirmative grunts: one, that he knew it; two, that the light was working; three, that he'd remember to turn it on next time.

Then the scene had ended and I darted across the stage as they changed to the room-of-state set. I wanted to get rid of my overcoat. Joe Rubens grabbed me and told me about Guthrie's green light not being on and I told him that was all taken care of.

"Where the hell was he all the time we were hunting for him?" Joe asked me.

"I don't know," I answered.

By that time the second scene was playing, with F.F., his Ghost-coverings shed, playing the King as well as he always does (it's about his best part) and Gertrude Grainger looking very regal beside him as the Queen, her namesake, while there was another flurry of applause, more scattered this time, for the Governor in his black doublet and tights beginning about his seven hundredth performance of Shakespeare's longest and meatiest role.

Monica was still sitting on the trunk by the switchboard, looking paler than ever under her make-up, it seemed to me, and I folded my overcoat and silently persuaded her to use it as a cushion. I sat beside her and she took my hand and we watched the play from the wings.

After a while I whispered to her, giving her hand a little squeeze, "Feeling better now?"

She shook her head. Then leaning toward me, her mouth close to my ear, she whispered rapidly and unevenly, as if she just had to tell someone, "Bruce, I'm frightened. There's something in the theater. I don't think that was Guthrie playing the Ghost."

I whispered back, "Sure it was. I talked with him."

"Did you see his face?" she asked.

"No, but I smelled his breath," I told her and explained to her about him forgetting to turn on the green light. I continued, "Francis and John were both ready to go on as the Ghost, though, until Guthrie turned up. Maybe you glimpsed one of them before the play started and that gave you the idea that it was Guthrie."

Sybil Jameson in her Player costume looked around at me warningly. I was letting my whispering get too loud.

Monica put her mouth so close that her lips for an instant brushed my ear and she mouse-whispered, "I don't mean another *person* playing the Ghost—not that exactly. Bruce, there's *something* in the theater."

"You've got to forget that Ouija nonsense," I told her sharply. "And buck up now," I added, for the curtain had just gone down on Scene Two and it was time for her to get on stage for her scene with Laertes and Polonius.

I waited until she was launched into it, speaking her lines brightly enough, and then I carefully crossed the stage behind the backdrop. I was sure there was no more than nerves and imagination to her notions, though they'd raised shivers on me, but just the same I wanted to speak to Guthrie again and see his face.

When I'd completed my slow trip (you have to move rather slowly, so the drop won't ripple or bulge), I was dumbfounded to find myself witnessing the identical backstage scene that had been going on when I'd got back from my tour of the bars. Only now there was a lot more light because the scene being played on stage was a bright one. And Props was there behind his table, watching everything like the spectator he basically is. But beyond him were Francis Farley Scott and John McCarthy in their improvised Ghost costumes again, and the Governor and Joe with them, and all of them carrying on that furious lip-reader's argument, now doubly hushed.

I didn't have to wait to get close to them to know that Guthrie must have disappeared again. As I made my way toward them, watching their silent antics, my silly mind became almost hysterical with the thought that Guthrie had at last discovered that invisible hole every genuine alcoholic wishes he had, into which he could decorously disappear and drink during the times between his absolutely necessary appearances in the real world.

As I neared them, Donald Fryer (our Horatio) came from behind me, having made the trip behind the backdrop faster than I had, to tell the Governor in hushed gasps that Guthrie wasn't in any of the dressing rooms or anywhere else stage right.

Just at that moment the bright scene ended, the curtain came down, the drapes before which Ophelia and the others had been playing swung back to reveal again the battlements of Elsinore, and the lighting shifted back to the midnight blue of the first scene, so that for the moment it was hard to see at all. I heard the Governor say decisively, *"You* play the Ghost," his voice receding as he and Joe and Don hurried across the stage to be in place for their proper entrance. Seconds later there came the dull soft hiss of the main curtain opening and I heard the Governor's taut resonant voice saying, "The air bites shrewdly; it is very cold," and Don responding as Horatio with, "It is a nipping and an eager air."

By that time I could see again well enough—see Francis Farley Scott and John McCarthy moving side by side toward the back wing through which the Ghost enters. They were still arguing in whispers. The explanation was clear enough: each thought the Governor had pointed at him in the sudden darkness—or possibly in F.F.'s case was pretending he so thought. For a moment the comic side of my mind, grown a bit hysterical by now, almost collapsed me with the thought of twin Ghosts entering the stage side by side. Then once again, history still repeating itself, I saw beyond them that other bulkier figure with the unmistakable shrouded helmet. They must have seen it too for they stopped dead just before my hands touched a shoulder of each of them. I circled quickly past them and reached out my hands to put them lightly on the third figure's shoulders, intending to whisper, "Guthrie, are you okay?" It was a very stupid thing for one actor to do to another—startling him just before his entrance—but I was made thoughtless by the memory of Monica's fears and by the rather frantic riddle of where Guthrie could possibly have been hiding.

But just then Horatio gasped, "Look, my lord, it comes," and Guthrie moved out of my light grasp onto the stage without so much as turning his head—and leaving me shaking because where I'd touched the rough buckram-braced fabric of the Ghost's cloak I'd felt only a kind of insubstantiality beneath instead of Guthrie's broad shoulders.

I quickly told myself that was because Guthrie's cloak had stood out from his shoulders and his back as he had moved. I had to tell myself something like that. I turned around. John McCarthy and F.F. were standing in front of the dark prop table and by now my nerves were in such a state that their paired forms gave me another start. But I tiptoed after them into the downstage wings and watched the scene from there.

The Governor was still on his knees with his sword held hilt up like a cross doing the long speech that begins, "Angels and ministers of grace defend us!" And of course the Ghost had his cloak drawn around him so you couldn't see what was under it—and the little green light still wasn't lit in his helmet. Tonight the absence of that theatric touch made him a more frightening figure—certainly to me, who wanted so much to see Guthrie's ravaged old face and be reassured by it. Though there was still enough comedy left in the ragged edges of my thoughts that I could imagine Guthrie's pugnacious son-in-law whispering angrily to those around him that Gilbert Usher was so jealous of his great father-in-law that he wouldn't let him show his face on the stage.

Then came the transition to the following scene where the Ghost has led Hamlet off alone with him—just a five-second complete darkening of the stage while a scrim is dropped—and at last the Ghost spoke those first lines of "Mark me" and "My hour is almost come, When I to sulphurous and tormenting flames Must render up myself."

If any of us had any worries about the Ghost blowing up on his lines or slurring them drunkenly, they were taken care of now. Those lines were delivered with the greatest authority and effect. And I was almost certain that it was Guthrie's rightful voice—at least I was at first—but doing an even better job than the good one he had always done of getting the effect of distance and otherworldliness and hopeless alienation from all life on Earth. The theater became as silent as death, yet at the same time I could imagine the soft pounding of a thousand hearts, thousands of shivers crawling— and I *knew* that Francis Farley Scott, whose shoulder was pressed against mine, was trembling.

Each word the Ghost spoke was like a ghost itself, mounting the air and hanging poised for an impossible extra instant before it faded towards eternity.

Those great lines came: "I am thy father's spirit; Doomed for a certain term to walk the night..." and just at that moment the idea came to me that Guthrie Boyd might be dead, that he might have died and be lying unnoticed somewhere between his children's home and the theater—no matter what Props had said or the rest of us had seen—and that his ghost might have come to give a last performance. And on the heels of that shivery impossibility came the thought that similar and perhaps even eerier ideas must be frightening Monica. I knew I had to go to her.

So while the Ghost's words swooped and soared in the dark— marvellous black-plumed birds—I again made that nervous cross behind the backdrop.

Everyone stage right was standing as frozen and absorbed— motionless loomings—as I'd left John and F.F. I spotted Monica at once. She'd moved forward from the switchboard and was standing, crouched a little, by the big floodlight that throws some dimmed blue on the backdrop and across the back of the stage. I went to her just as the Ghost was beginning his exit stage left, moving backward along the edge of the light from the flood, but not quite in it, and reciting more lonelily and eerily than I'd ever heard them before those memorable last lines:

"Fare thee well at once!
"The glow-worm shows the matin to be near,
"And 'gins to pale his uneffectual fire;
"Adieu, adieu! Hamlet, remember me."

One second passed, then another, and then there came two unexpected bursts of sound at the same identical instant: Monica screamed and a thunderous applause started out front, touched off by Guthrie's people, of course, but this time swiftly spreading to all the rest of the audience.

I imagine it was the biggest hand the Ghost ever got in the history of the theater. In fact, I never heard of him getting a hand before. It certainly was a most inappropriate place to clap, however much the performance deserved it. It broke the atmosphere and the thread of the scene.

Also, it drowned out Monica's scream, so that only I and a few of those behind me heard it.

At first I thought I'd made her scream, by touching her as I had Guthrie, suddenly, like an idiot, from behind. But instead of dodging away she turned and clung to me, and kept clinging too even after I'd drawn her back and Gertrude Grainger and Sybil Jameson had closed in to comfort her and hush her gasping sobs and try to draw her away from me.

By this time the applause was through and Governor and Don and Joe were taking up the broken scene and knitting together its finish as best they could, while the floods came up little by little, changing to rosy, to indicate dawn breaking over Elsinore.

Then Monica mastered herself and told us in quick whispers what had made her scream. The Ghost, she said, had moved for a moment into the edge of the blue floodlight, and she had seen for a moment through his veil, and what she had seen had been a face like Shakespeare's. Just that and no more. Except that at the moment when she told us—later she became less certain—she was sure it was Shakespeare himself and no one else.

I discovered that when you hear something like that you don't exclaim or get outwardly excited. Or even inwardly, exactly. It rather shuts you up. I know I felt at the same time extreme awe and a

renewed irritation at the Ouija board. I was deeply moved, yet at the same time pettishly irked, as if some vast adult creature had disordered the toy world of my universe.

It seemed to hit Sybil and even Gertrude the same way. For the moment we were shy about the whole thing, and so, in her way, was Monica, and so were the few others who had overheard in part or all what Monica had said.

I knew we were going to cross the stage in a few more seconds when the curtain came down on that scene, ending the first act, and stagelights came up. At least I knew that I was going across. Yet I wasn't looking forward to it.

When the curtain did come down—with another round of applause from out front—and we started across, Monica beside me with my arm still tight around her, there came a choked-off male cry of horror from ahead to shock and hurry us. I think about a dozen of us got stage left about the same time, including of course the Governor and the others who had been on stage.

F.F. and Props were standing inside the doorway to the empty prop room and looking down into the hidden part of the L. Even from the side, they both looked pretty sick. Then F.F. knelt down and almost went out of view, while Props hunched over him with his natural stoop.

As we craned around Props for a look—myself among the first, just beside the Governor—we saw something that told us right away that this Ghost wasn't ever going to be able to answer that curtain call they were still fitfully clapping for out front, although the house lights must be up by now for the first intermission.

Guthrie Boyd was lying on his back in his street clothes. His face looked grey, the eyes staring straight up. Swirled beside him lay the Ghost's cloak and veil and the helmet and an empty fifth of whisky.

Between the two conflicting shocks of Monica's revelation and the body in the prop room, my mind was in a useless state. And from her helpless incredulous expression I knew Monica felt the same. I tried to put things together and they wouldn't fit anywhere.

F.F. looked up at us over his shoulder. "He's not breathing," he said. "I think he's gone." Just the same he started loosing Boyd's tie and shirt and pillowing his head on the cloak. He handed the whisky bottle back to us through several hands and Joe Rubens got rid of it.

The Governor sent out front for a doctor and within two minutes Harry Grossman was bringing us one from the audience who'd left his seat number and bag at the box office. He was a small man—Guthrie would have made two of him—and a bit awestruck, I could see, though holding himself with greater professional dignity because of that, as we made way for him and then crowded in behind.

He confirmed F.F.'s diagnosis by standing up quickly after kneeling only for a few seconds where F.F. had. Then he said hurriedly to the Governor, as if the words were being surprised out of him against his professional caution, "Mr. Usher, if I hadn't heard this man giving that great performance just now, I'd think he'd been dead for an hour or more."

He spoke low and not all of us heard him, but I did and so did Monica, and there was Shock Three to go along with the other two, raising in my mind for an instant the grisly picture of Guthrie Boyd's spirit, or some other entity, willing his dead body to go through with the last performance. Once again I unsuccessfully tried to fumble together the parts of this night's mystery.

The little doctor looked around at us slowly and puzzledly. He said, "I take it he just wore the cloak over his street clothes?" He paused. Then, "He *did* play the Ghost?" he asked us.

The Governor and several others nodded, but some of us didn't at once and I think F.F. gave him a rather peculiar look, for the doctor cleared his throat and said, "I'll have to examine this man as quickly as possible in a better place and light. Is there—?" The Governor suggested the couch in his dressing room and the doctor designated Joe Rubens and John McCarthy and Francis Farley Scott to carry the body. He passed over the Governor, perhaps out of awe, but Hamlet helped just the same, his black garb most fitting.

It was odd the doctor picked the older men—I think he did it for dignity. And it was odder still that he should have picked two ghosts to help carry a third, though he couldn't have known that.

As the designated ones moved forward, the doctor said, "Please stand back, the rest of you."

It was then that the very little thing happened which made all the pieces of this night's mystery fall into place—for me, that is, and for Monica too, judging from the way her hand trembled in and then tightened around mine. We'd been given the key to what had happened. I won't tell you what it was until I've knit together the ends of this story.

The second act was delayed perhaps a minute, but after that we kept to schedule, giving a better performance than usual—I never knew the Graveyard Scene to carry so much feeling or the bit with Yorick's skull to be so poignant.

Just before I made my own first entrance, Joe Rubens snatched off my street hat—I'd had it on all this while—and I played all of Guildenstern wearing a wristwatch, though I don't imagine anyone noticed.

F.F. played the Ghost as an off-stage voice when he makes his final brief appearance in the Closet Scene. He used Guthrie's voice to do it, imitating him very well. It struck me afterwards as ghoulish—but right.

Well before the play ended, the doctor had decided he could say that Guthrie had died of a heart seizure, not mentioning the alcoholism. The minute the curtain came down on the last act, Harry Grossman informed Guthrie's son and daughter and brought them backstage. They were much moved, though hardly deeply smitten, seeing they'd been out of touch with the old boy for a decade. However, they quickly saw it was a Grand and Solemn Occasion and behaved accordingly, especially Guthrie's pugnacious son-in-law.

Next morning the two Wolverton papers had headlines about it and Guthrie got his biggest notices ever in the Ghost. The strangeness of the event carried the item around the world—a six-line filler, capturing the mind for a second or two, about how a once-famous actor had died immediately after giving a performance as the Ghost in *Hamlet,* though in some versions, of course, it became Hamlet's Ghost.

The funeral came on the afternoon of the third day, just before our last performance in Wolverton, and the whole company attended along with Guthrie's children's crowd and many other Wolvertonians. Old Sybil broke down and sobbed.

Yet to be a bit callous, it was a neat thing that Guthrie died where he did, for it saved us the trouble of having to send for relatives and probably take care of the funeral ourselves. And it did give old Guthrie a grand finish, with everyone outside the company thinking him a hero-martyr to the motto The Show Must Go On. And of course we knew too that in a deeper sense he'd really been that.

We shifted around in our parts and doubled some to fill the little gaps Guthrie had left in the plays, so that the Governor didn't have to hire another actor at once. For me, and I think for Monica, the rest of the season was very sweet. Gertrude and Sybil carried on with the Ouija sessions alone.

And now I must tell you about the very little thing which gave myself and Monica a satisfying solution to the mystery of what had happened that night.

You'll have realized that it involved Props. Afterwards I asked him straight out about it and he shyly told me that he really couldn't help me there. He'd had this unaccountable devilish compulsion to get drunk and his mind had blanked out entirely from well before the performance until he found himself standing with F.F. over Guthrie's body at the end of the first act. He didn't remember the Ouija-scare or a word of what he'd said to me about theaters and time machines—or so he always insisted.

F.F. told us that after the Ghost's last exit he'd seen him—very vaguely in the dimness—lurch across backstage into the empty prop room and that he and Props had found Guthrie lying there at the end of the scene. I think the queer look F.F.—the old reality-fuddling rogue!—gave the doctor was to hint to him that *he* had played the Ghost, though that wasn't something I could ask him about.

But the very little thing— When they were picking up Guthrie's body and the doctor told the rest of us to stand back, Props turned as he obeyed and straightened his shoulders and looked directly at Monica and myself, or rather a little over our heads. He appeared compassionate yet smilingly serene as always and for a moment transfigured, as if he were the eternal observer of the stage of life and this little tragedy were only part of an infinitely vaster, endlessly interesting pattern.

I realized at that instant that Props could have done it, that he'd very effectively guarded the doorway to the empty prop room during our searches, that the Ghost's costume could be put on or off in seconds (though Props's shoulders wouldn't fill the cloak like Guthrie's), and that I'd never once before or during the play seen him and the Ghost at the same time. Yes, Guthrie had arrived a few minutes before me...and died...and Props, nerved to it by drink, had covered for him.

While Monica, as she told me later, knew at once that here was the great-browed face she'd glimpsed for a moment through the greenish gauze.

Clearly there had been four ghosts in *Hamlet* that night—John McCarthy, Francis Farley Scott, Guthrie Boyd, and the fourth who had really played the role. Mentally blacked out or not, knowing the lines from the many times he'd listened to *Hamlet* performed in this life, or from buried memories of times he'd taken the role in the days of Queen Elizabeth the First, Billy (or Willy) Simpson, or simply Willy S., had played the Ghost, a good trouper responding automatically to an emergency.

Gonna Roll
the Bones

SUDDENLY JOE SLATTERMILL KNEW FOR SURE he'd have to get out quick or else blow his top and knock out with the shrapnel of his skull the props and patches holding up his decaying home, that was like a house of big wooden and plaster and wallpaper cards except for the huge fireplace and ovens and chimney across the kitchen from him.

Those were stone-solid enough, though. The fireplace was chin-high, at least twice that long, and filled from end to end with roaring flames. Above were the square doors of the ovens in a row—his Wife baked for part of their living. Above the ovens was the wall-long mantelpiece, too high for his Mother to reach or Mr. Guts to jump any more, set with all sorts of ancestral curios, but any of them that weren't stone or glass or china had been so dried and darkened by decades of heat that they looked like nothing but shrunken human heads and black golf balls. At one end were clustered his Wife's square gin bottles. Above the mantelpiece hung one old chromo, so high and so darkened by soot and grease that you couldn't tell whether the swirls and fat cigar shape were a whaleback steamer ploughing through a hurricane or a spaceship plunging through a storm of light-driven dust motes.

As soon as Joe curled his toes inside his boots, his Mother knew what he was up to. "Going bumming," she mumbled with conviction. "Pants pockets full of cartwheels of house money, too, to spend on sin." And she went back to munching the long shreds she stripped fumblingly with her right hand off the turkey carcass set close to the terrible heat, her left hand ready to fend off Mr. Guts, who stared at her yellow-eyed, gaunt-flanked, with long mangy tail a-twitch. In her dirty dress, streaky as the turkey's sides, Joe's Mother looked like a bent brown bag and her fingers were lumpy twigs.

Joe's Wife knew as soon or sooner, for she smiled thin-eyed at him over her shoulder from where she towered at the centermost oven. Before she closed its door, Joe glimpsed that she was baking two long, flat, narrow, fluted loaves and one high, round-domed one. She was thin as death and disease in her violet wrapper. Without looking, she reached out a yard-long, skinny arm for the nearest gin bottle and downed a warm slug and smiled again. And without a word spoken, Joe knew she'd said, "You're going out and gamble and get drunk and lay a floozy and come home and beat me and go to jail for it," and he had a flash of the last time he'd been in the dark gritty cell and she'd come by moonlight, which showed the green and yellow lumps on her narrow skull where he'd hit her, to whisper to him through the tiny window in the back and slip him a half pint through the bars.

And Joe knew for certain that this time it would be that bad and worse, but just the same he heaved up himself and his heavy, muffledly clanking pockets and shuffled straight to the door, muttering, "Guess I'll roll the bones, up the pike a stretch and back," swinging his bent, knobbly-elbowed arms like paddlewheels to make a little joke about his words.

When he'd stepped outside, he held the door open a hand's breadth behind him for several seconds. When he finally closed it, a feeling of deep misery struck him. Earlier years, Mr. Guts would have come streaking along to seek fights and females on the roofs and fences, but now the big tom was content to stay home and hiss by the fire and snatch for turkey and dodge a broom, quarrelling and comforting with two house-bound women. Nothing had followed Joe to the door but his Mother's chomping and her gasping breaths and the clink of the gin bottle going back on the mantel and the creaking of the floor boards under his feet.

The night was up-side-down deep among the frosty stars. A few of them seemed to move, like the white-hot jets of spaceships. Down below it looked as if the whole town of Ironmine had blown or buttoned out the light and gone to sleep, leaving the streets and spaces to the equally unseen breezes and ghosts. But Joe was still in the hemisphere of the musty dry odor of the worm-eaten carpentry behind him, and as he felt and heard the dry grass of the lawn brush his calves, it occurred to him that something deep down inside him had for years been planning things so that he and the House and his Wife and Mother and Mr. Guts would all come to an end together. Why the kitchen heat hadn't touched off the tindery place ages ago was a physical miracle.

Hunching his shoulders, Joe stepped out, not up the pike, but down the dirt road that led past Cypress Hollow Cemetery to Night Town.

The breezes were gentle, but unusually restless and variable tonight, like leprechaun squalls. Beyond the drunken, whitewashed cemetery fence dim in the starlight, they rustled the scraggly trees

of Cypress Hollow and made it seem they were stroking their beards of Spanish moss. Joe sensed that the ghosts were just as restless as the breezes, uncertain where and whom to haunt, or whether to take the night off, drifting together in sorrowfully lecherous companionship. While among the trees the red-green vampire lights pulsed faintly and irregularly, like sick fireflies or a plague-stricken space fleet. The feeling of deep misery stuck with Joe and deepened and he was tempted to turn aside and curl up in any convenient tomb or around some half-toppled head board and cheat his Wife and the other two behind him out of a shared doom. He thought: Gonna roll the bones, gonna roll 'em up and go to sleep. But while he was deciding, he got past the sagged-open gate and the rest of the delirious fence and Shantyville too.

At first Night Town seemed dead as the rest of Ironmine, but then he noticed a faint glow, sick as the vampire lights but more feverish, and with it a jumping music, tiny at first as a jazz for jitterbugging ants. He stepped along the springy sidewalk, wistfully remembering the days when the spring was all in his own legs and he'd bound into a fight like a bobcat or a Martian sand-spider. God, it had been years now since he had fought a real fight, or felt *the power*. Gradually the midget music got raucous as a bunny-hug for grizzly bears and loud as a polka for elephants, while the glow became a riot of gas flares and flambeaux and corpse-blue mercury tubes and jiggling pink neon ones that all jeered at the stars where the spaceships roved. Next thing, he was facing a three-story false front flaring everywhere like a devil's elbow, with a pale blue topping of St. Elmo's fire. There were wide swinging doors in the center of it, spilling light above and below. Above the doorway, golden calcium light scrawled over and over again, with wild curlicues and flourishes, "The Boneyard," while a fiendish red kept printing out, "Gambling."

So the new place they'd all been talking about for so long had opened at last! For the first time that night, Joe Slattermill felt a stirring of real life in him and the faintest caress of excitement.

Gonna roll the bones, he thought.

He dusted off his blue-green work clothes with big, careless swipes and slapped his pockets to hear the clank. Then he threw back his shoulders and grinned his lips sneeringly and pushed through the swinging doors as if giving a foe the straight-armed heel of his palm.

Inside, The Boneyard seemed to cover the area of a township and the bar looked as long as the railroad tracks. Round pools of light on the green poker tables alternated with hourglass shapes of exciting gloom, through which drink girls and change-girls moved like white-legged witches. By the jazz-stand in the distance, belly dancers made *their* white hourglass shapes. The gamblers were thick and hunched down as mushrooms, all bald from agonizing over the fall of a card or a die or the dive of an ivory ball, while the Scarlet Women were like fields of poinsettia.

The calls of the croupiers and the slaps of dealt cards were as softly yet fatefully staccato as the rustle and beat of the jazz drums. Every tight-locked atom of the place was controlledly jumping. Even the dust motes jiggled tensely in the cones of light.

Joe's excitement climbed and he felt sift through him, like a breeze that heralds a gale, the faintest breath of a confidence which he knew could become a tornado. All thoughts of his House and Wife and Mother dropped out of his mind, while Mr. Guts remained only as a crazy young tom walking stiff-legged around the rim of his consciousness. Joe's own leg muscles twitched in sympathy and he felt them grow supplely strong.

He coolly and searchingly looked the place over, his hand going out like it didn't belong to him to separate a drink from a passing, gently bobbing tray. Finally his gaze settled on what he judged to be the Number One Crap Table. All the Big Mushrooms seemed to be there, bald as the rest but standing tall as toadstools. Then through a gap in them Joe saw on the other side of the table a figure still taller, but dressed in a long dark coat with collar turned up and a dark slouch hat pulled low, so that only a triangle of white face showed. A suspicion and a hope rose in Joe and he headed straight for the gap in the Big Mushrooms.

As he got nearer, the white-legged and shiny-topped drifters, eddying out of his way, his suspicion received confirmation after confirmation and his hope budded and swelled. Back from one end of the table was the fattest man he'd ever seen, with a long cigar and a silver vest and a gold tie clasp at least eight inches wide that just said in thick script, "Mr. Bones." Back a little from the other end was the nakedest change-girl yet and the only one he'd seen whose tray, slung from her bare shoulders, and indenting her belly just below her breasts, was stacked with gold in gleaming little towers and with jet-black chips. While the dice-girl, skinnier and taller and longer armed than his Wife even, didn't seem to be wearing much but a pair of long white gloves. She was all right if you went for the type that isn't much more than pale skin over bones with breasts like china doorknobs.

Beside each gambler was a high round table for his chips. The one by the gap was empty. Snapping his fingers at the nearest silver change-girl, Joe traded all his greasy dollars for an equal number of pale chips and tweaked her left nipple for luck. She playfully snapped her teeth towards his fingers.

Not hurrying but not wasting any time, he advanced and carelessly dropped his modest stacks on the empty table and took his place in the gap. He noted that the second Big Mushroom on his right had the dice. His heart but no other part of him gave an extra jump. Then he steadily lifted his eyes and looked straight across the table.

The coat was a shimmering elegant pillar of black satin with jet buttons, the upturned collar of fine dull plush black as the darkest cellar, as was the slouch hat with down-turned brim and a band of only a thin braid of black horse-hair. The arms of the coat were long, lesser satin pillars, ending in slim, longfingered hands that moved swiftly when they did, but held each position of rest with a statue's poise.

Joe still couldn't see much of the face except for smooth lower forehead with never a bead or trickle of sweat—the eyebrows were like straight snippets of the hat's braid—and gaunt aristocratic cheeks and narrow but somewhat flat nose. The complexion of the face wasn't as white as Joe had first judged. There was a faint touch of brown in it, like ivory that's just begun to age, or Venusian soapstone. Another glance at the hands confirmed this.

Behind the man in black was a knot of just about the flashiest and nastiest customers, male or female, Joe had ever seen. He knew from one look that each bediamonded, pomaded bully had a belly gun beneath the flap of his flowered vest and a blackjack in his hip pocket, and each snake-eyed sporting girl a stiletto in her garter and a pearl-handled silver-plated derringer under the sequinned silk in the hollow between her jutting breasts.

Yet at the same time Joe knew they were just trimmings. It was the man in black, their master, who was the deadly one, the kind of man you knew at a glance you couldn't touch and live. If without asking you merely laid a finger on his sleeve, no matter how lightly and respectfully, an ivory hand would move faster than thought and you'd be stabbed or shot. Or maybe just the touch would kill you, as if every black article of his clothing were charged from his ivory skin outwards with a high-voltage, high-amperage ivory electricity. Joe looked at the shadowed face again and decided he wouldn't care to try it.

For it was the eyes that were the most impressive feature. All great gamblers have dark-shadowed deep-set eyes. But this one's eyes were sunk so deep you couldn't even be sure you were getting a gleam of them. They were inscrutability incarnate. They were unfathomable. They were like black holes.

But all this didn't disappoint Joe one bit, though it did terrify him considerably. On the contrary, it made him exult. His first suspicion was completely confirmed and his hope spread into full flower.

This must be one of those really big gamblers who hit Ironmine only once a decade at most, come from the Big City on one of the river boats that ranged the watery dark like luxurious comets, spouting long thick tails of sparks from their sequoia-tall stacks with top foliage of curvy-snipped sheet iron. Or like silver space-liners with dozens of jewel-flamed jets, their portholes atwinkle like ranks of marshalled asteroids.

For that matter, maybe some of those really big gamblers actually came from other planets where the nighttime pace was hotter and the sporting life a delirium of risk and delight.

Yes, this was the kind of man Joe had always yearned to pit his skill against. He felt *the power* begin to tingle in his rock-still fingers, just a little.

Joe lowered his gaze to the crap table. It was almost as wide as a man is tall, at least twice as long, unusually deep, and lined with black, not green, felt, so that it looked like a giant's coffin. There was something familiar about its shape which he couldn't place. Its bottom, though not its sides or ends, had a twinkling iridescence, as if it had been lightly sprinkled with very tiny diamonds. As Joe lowered his gaze all the way and looked directly down, his eyes barely over the table, he got the crazy notion that it went down all the way through the world, so that the diamonds were the stars on the other side, visible despite the sunlight there, just as Joe was always able to see the stars by day up the shaft of the mine he worked in, and so that if a cleaned-out gambler, dizzy with defeat, toppled forward into it, he'd fall forever, towards the bottom-most bottom, be it Hell or some black galaxy. Joe's thoughts swirled and he felt the cold, hard-fingered clutch of fear at his crotch. Someone was crooning beside him, "Come on, Big Dick."

Then the dice, which had meanwhile passed to the Big Mushroom immediately on his right, came to rest near the table's center, contradicting and wiping out Joe's vision. But instantly there was another oddity to absorb him. The Ivory dice were large and unusually round-cornered with dark red spots that gleamed like real rubies, but the spots were arranged in such a way that each face looked like a miniature skull. For instance, the seven thrown just now, by which the Big Mushroom to his right had lost his point, which had been ten, consisted of a two with the spots evenly spaced towards one side, like eyes, instead of towards opposite corners, and of a five with the same red eyespots but a central red nose and two spots close together below that to make teeth.

The long, skinny, white-gloved arm of the dice-girl snaked out like an albino cobra and scooped up the dice and whisked them on to the rim of the table right in front of Joe. He inhaled silently, picked up a single chip from his table and started to lay it beside the dice, then realized that wasn't the way things were done here, and put it back. He would have liked to examine the chip more closely, though. It was curiously lightweight and pale tan, about the color of cream with a shot of coffee in it, and it had embossed on its surface a symbol he could feel, though not see. He didn't know what the symbol was, that would have taken more feeling. Yet its touch had been very good, setting the power tingling full blast in his shooting hand.

Joe looked casually yet swiftly at the faces around the table, not missing the Big Gambler across from him, and said quietly, "Roll a penny," meaning of course one pale chip, or a dollar.

There was a hiss of indignation from all the Big Mushrooms and the moonface of big-bellied Mr. Bones grew purple as he started forward to summon his bouncers.

The Big Gambler raised a black-satined forearm and sculptured hand, palm down. Instantly Mr. Bones froze and the hissing stopped faster than that of a meteor prick in self-sealing space steel. Then in a whispery, cultured voice, without the faintest hint of derision, the man in black said, "Get on him, gamblers."

Here, Joe thought, was a final confirmation of his suspicion, had it been needed. The really great gamblers were always perfect gentlemen and generous to the poor.

With only the tiny, respectful hint of a guffaw, one of the Big Mushrooms called to Joe, "You're faded."

Joe picked up the ruby-featured dice.

Now ever since he had first caught two eggs on one plate, won all the marbles in Ironmine, and juggled six alphabet blocks so they finally fell in a row on the rug spelling "Mother," Joe Slattermill had been almost incredibly deft at precision throwing. In the mine he could carom a rock off a wall of ore to crack a rat's skull fifty

feet away in the dark and he sometimes amused himself by tossing
little fragments of rock back into the holes from which they had
fallen, so that they stuck there, perfectly fitted in, for at least a
second. Sometimes, by fast tossing, he could fit seven or eight
fragments into the hole from which they had fallen, like putting
together a puzzle block. If he could ever have got into space, Joe
would undoubtedly have been able to pilot six Moon-skimmers at
once and do figure eights through Saturn's rings blindfolded.

Now the only real difference between precision-tossing rocks or
alphabet blocks and dice is that you have to bounce the latter off
the end wall of a crap table, and that just made it a more interesting
test of skill for Joe.

Rattling the dice now, he felt the power in his fingers and palm
as never before.

He made a swift low roll, so that the bones ended up exactly in
front of the white-gloved dice-girl. His natural seven was made up,
as he'd intended, of a four and a three. In red-spot features they
were like the five, except that both had only one tooth and the three
no nose. Sort of baby-faced skulls. He had won a penny—that is,
a dollar.

"Roll two cents," said Joe Slattermill.

This time, for variety, he made his natural with an eleven. The
six was like the five, except it had three teeth, the bestlooking skull
of the lot.

"Roll a nickel less one."

Two Big Mushrooms divided that bet with a covert smirk at
each other.

Now Joe rolled a three and an ace. His point was four. The ace,
with its single spot off center towards a side, still somehow looked
like a skull—maybe of a Lilliputian Cyclops.

He took a while making his point, once absent-mindedly rolling
three successive tens the hard way. He wanted to watch the dice-
girl scoop up the cubes. Each time it seemed to him that her snake-
swift fingers went under the dice while they were still flat on the
felt. Finally he decided it couldn't be an illusion. Although the dice
couldn't penetrate the felt, her white-gloved fingers somehow could,
dipping in a flash through the black, diamond-sparkling material
as if it weren't there.

Right away the thought of a crap-table-size hole through the
earth came back to Joe. This would mean that the dice were rolling
and lying on a perfectly transparent flat surface, impenetrable for
them but nothing else. Or maybe it was only the dice-girl's hands

that could penetrate the surface, which would turn into a mere fantasy Joe's earlier vision of a cleaned-out gambler taking the Big Dive down that dreadful shaft, which made the deepest mine a mere pin dent.

Joe decided he had to know which was true. Unless absolutely unavoidable, he didn't want to take the chance of being troubled by vertigo at some crucial stage of the game.

He made a few more meaningless throws, from time to time crooning for realism, "Come on, Little Joe." Finally he settled on his plan. When he did at last make his point—the hard way, with two twos—he caromed the dice off the far corner so that they landed exactly in front of him. Then, after a minimum pause for his throw to be seen by the table, he shot his left hand down under the cubes, just a flicker ahead of the dice-girl's strike, and snatched them up.

Wow! Joe had never had a harder time in his life making his face and manner conceal what his body felt, not even when the wasp had stung him on the neck just as he had been for the first time putting his hand under the skirt of his prudish, fickle, demanding Wife-to-be. His fingers and the back of his hand were in as much agony as if he'd stuck them into a blast furnace. No wonder the dice-girl wore white gloves. They must be asbestos. And a good thing he hadn't used his shooting hand, he thought as he ruefully watched the blisters rise.

He remembered he'd been taught in school what Twenty-Mile Mine also demonstrated: that the earth was fearfully hot under its crust. The crap-table-size hole must pipe up that heat, so that any gambler taking the Big Dive would fry before he'd fallen a furlong and come out less than a cinder in China.

As if his blistered hand weren't bad enough, the Big Mushrooms were all hissing at him again and Mr. Bones had purpled once more and was opening his melon-size mouth to shout for his bouncers.

Once again a lift of the Big Gambler's hand saved Joe. The whispery, gentle voice called, "Tell him, Mr. Bones."

The latter roared towards Joe, "No gambler may pick up the dice he or any other gambler has shot. Only my dice-girl may do that. Rule of the house!"

Joe snapped Mr. Bones the barest nod. He said coolly, "Rolling a dime less two," and when that still peewee bet was covered, he shot Phoebe for his point and then fooled around for quite a while, throwing anything but a five or a seven, until the throbbing in his left hand should fade and all his nerves feel rock-solid again. There had never been the slightest alteration in the power in his right hand; he felt that strong as ever, or stronger.

Midway of this interlude, the Big Gambler bowed slightly but respectfully towards Joe, hooding those unfathomable eye sockets, before turning around to take a long black cigarette from his prettiest and evilest-looking sporting girl. Courtesy in the smallest matters, Joe thought, another mark of the master devotee of games of chance. The Big Gambler sure had himself a flash crew, all right, though in idly looking them over again as he rolled, Joe noted one bummer towards the back who didn't fit in—a raggedly-elegant chap with the elflocked hair and staring eyes and TB-spotted cheeks of a poet.

As he watched the smoke trickling up from under the black slouch hat, he decided that either the lights across the table had dimmed or else the Big Gambler's complexion was yet a shade darker than he'd thought at first. Or it might even be—wild fantasy—that the Big Gambler's skin was slowly darkening tonight, like a meerschaum pipe being smoked a mile a second. That was almost funny to think of—there was enough heat in this place, all right, to darken meerschaum, as Joe knew from sad experience, but so far as he was aware it was all under the table.

None of Joe's thoughts, either familiar or admiring, about the Big Gambler decreased in the slightest degree his certainty of the supreme menace of the man in black and his conviction that it would be death to touch him. And if any doubts had stirred in Joe's mind, they would have been squelched by the chilling incident which next occurred.

The Big Gambler had just taken into his arms his prettiest-evilest sporting girl and was running an aristocratic hand across her haunch with perfect gentility, when the poet chap, green-eyed from jealousy and lovesickness, came leaping forward like a wildcat and aimed a long gleaming dagger at the black satin back.

Joe couldn't see how the blow could miss, but without taking his genteel right hand off the sporting girl's plush rear end, the Big Gambler shot out his left arm like a steel spring straightening. Joe couldn't tell whether he stabbed the poet chap in the throat, or judo-chopped him there, or gave him the Martian double-finger, or just touched him, but anyhow the fellow stopped as dead as if he'd been shot by a silent elephant gun or an invisible ray pistol and he slammed down on the floor. A couple of darkies came running up to drag off the body and nobody paid the least attention, such episodes apparently being taken for granted at The Boneyard.

It gave Joe quite a turn and he almost shot Phoebe before he intended to.

But by now the waves of pain had stopped running up his left arm and his nerves were like metal-wrapped new guitar strings, so three rolls later he shot a five, making his point, and set in to clean out the table.

He rolled nine successive naturals, seven sevens and two elevens, pyramiding his first wager of a single chip to a stake of over four thousand dollars. None of the Big Mushrooms had dropped out yet, but some of them were beginning to look worried and a couple were sweating. The Big Gambler still hadn't covered any part of Joe's bets, but he seemed to be following the play with interest from the cavernous depths of his eye sockets.

Then Joe got a devilish thought. Nobody could beat him tonight, he knew, but if he held on to the dice until the table was cleaned out, he'd never get a chance to see the Big Gambler exercise *his* skill, and he was truly curious about that. Besides, he thought, he ought to return courtesy for courtesy and have a crack at being a gentleman himself.

"Pulling out forty-one dollars less a nickel," he announced. "Rolling a penny."

This time there wasn't any hissing and Mr. Bones's moonface didn't cloud over. But Joe was conscious that the Big Gambler was staring at him disappointedly, or sorrowfully, or maybe just speculatively.

Joe immediately crapped out by throwing boxcars, rather pleased to see the two best-looking tiny skulls grinning rubytoothed side by side, and the dice passed to the Big Mushroom on his left.

"Knew when his streak was over," he heard another Big Mushroom mutter with grudging admiration.

The play worked rather rapidly around the table, nobody getting very hot and the stakes never more than medium high. "Shoot a fin." "Rolling a sawbuck." "An Andrew Jackson." "Rolling thirty bucks." Now and then Joe covered part of a bet, winning more than he lost. He had over seven thousand dollars, real money, before the bones got around to the Big Gambler.

That one held the dice for a long moment on his statue-steady palm while he looked at them reflectively, though not the hint of a furrow appeared in his almost brownish forehead down which never a bead of sweat trickled. He murmured, "Rolling a double sawbuck," and when he had been faded, he closed his fingers, lightly rattled the cubes—the sound was like big seeds inside a small gourd only half dry—and negligently cast the dice towards the end of the table.

It was a throw like none Joe had ever seen before at any crap table. The dice traveled flat through the air without turning over, struck the exact juncture of the table's end and bottom, and stopped there dead, showing a natural seven.

Joe was distinctly disappointed. On one of his own throws he was used to calculating something like, "Launch three-up, five north, two and a half rolls in the air, hit on the six-five-three corner, three-quarter roll and a one-quarter side-twist right, hit end on the one-two edge, one-half reverse roll and three-quarter side-twist left, land on five face, roll over twice, come up two," and that would be for just one of the dice, and a really commonplace throw, without extra bounces.

By comparison, the technique of the Big Gambler had been ridiculously, abysmally, horrifyingly simple. Joe could have duplicated it with the greatest ease, of course. It was no more than an elementary form of his old pastime of throwing fallen rocks back into their holes. But Joe had never once thought of pulling such a babyish trick at the crap table. It would make the whole thing too easy and destroy the beauty of the game.

Another reason Joe had never used the trick was that he'd never dreamed he'd be able to get away with it. By all the rules he'd ever heard of, it was a most questionable throw. There was the possibility that one or the other die hadn't completely reached the end of the table, or lay a wee bit cocked against the end. Besides, he reminded himself, weren't both dice supposed to rebound off the end, if only for a fraction of an inch?

However, as far as Joe's very sharp eyes could see, both dice lay perfectly flat and sprang up against the end wall. Moreover, everyone else at the table seemed to accept the throw, the dice-girl had scooped up the cubes, and the Big Mushrooms who had faded the man in black were paying off. As far as the rebound business went, well, The Boneyard appeared to put a slightly different interpretation on that rule, and Joe believed in never questioning House Rules except in dire extremity—both his Mother and Wife had long since taught him it was the least troublesome way.

Besides, there hadn't been any of his own money riding on that roll.

In a voice like wind through Cypress Hollow or on Mars, the Big Gambler announced, "Roll a century." It was the biggest bet yet tonight, ten thousand dollars, and the way the Big Gambler said it made it seem something more than that. A hush fell on The Boneyard, they put the mutes on the jazz horns, the croupiers' calls became more confidential, the cards fell softlier, even the roulette balls seemed to be trying to make less noise as they rattled into their cells. The crowd around the Number One Crap Table quietly thickened. The Big Gambler's flash boys and girls formed a double semicircle around him, ensuring him lots of elbow room.

That century bet, Joe realized, was thirty bucks more than his own entire pile. Three or four of the Big Mushrooms had to signal each other before they'd agreed how to fade it.

The Big Gambler shot another natural seven with exactly the same flat, stop-dead throw.

He bet another century and did it again.

And again.

And again.

Joe was getting mighty concerned and pretty indignant too. It seemed unjust that the Big Gambler should be winning such huge bets with such machinelike, utterly unromantic rolls. Why, you couldn't even call them rolls, the dice never turned over an iota, in the air or after. It was the sort of thing you'd expect from a robot, and a very dully programmed robot at that. Joe hadn't risked any of his own chips fading the Big Gambler, of course, but if things went on like this he'd have to. Two of the Big Mushrooms had already retired sweatingly from the table, confessing defeat, and no one had taken their places. Pretty soon there'd be a bet the remaining Big Mushrooms couldn't entirely cover between them, and then he'd have to risk some of his own chips or else pull out of the game himself—and he couldn't do that, not with the power surging in his right hand like chained lightning.

Joe waited and waited for someone else to question one of the Big Gambler's shots, but no one did. He realized that, despite his efforts to look imperturbable, his face was slowly reddening.

With a little lift of his left hand, the Big Gambler stopped the dice-girl as she was about to snatch at the cubes. The eyes that were like black wells directed themselves at Joe, who forced himself to look back into them steadily. He still couldn't catch the faintest gleam in them. All at once he felt the lightest touch-on-neck of a dreadful suspicion.

With the utmost civility and amiability, the Big Gambler whispered, "I believe that the fine shooter across from me has doubts about the validity of my last throw, though he is too much of a gentleman to voice them. Lottie, the card test."

The wraith-tall, ivory dice-girl plucked a playing card from below the table and with a venomous flash of her little white teeth spun it low across the table through the air at Joe. He caught the whirling pasteboard and examined it briefly. It was the thinnest, stiffest, flattest, shiniest playing card Joe had ever handled. It was also the Joker, if that meant anything. He spun it back lazily into her hand and she slid it very gently, letting it descend by its own weight, down the end wall against which the two dice lay. It came to rest in the tiny hollow their rounded edges made against the black felt. She deftly moved it about without force, demonstrating that there was no space between either of the cubes and the table's end at any point.

"Satisfied?" the Big Gambler asked. Rather against his will Joe nodded. The Big Gambler bowed to him. The dice-girl smirked her short, thin lips and drew herself up, flaunting her white-china-doorknob breasts at Joe.

Casually, almost with an air of boredom, the Big Gambler returned to his routine of shooting a century and making a natural seven. The Big Mushrooms wilted fast and one by one tottered away from the table. A particularly pink-faced Toadstool was brought extra cash by a gasping runner, but it was no help, he only lost the additional centuries. While the stacks of pale and black chips beside the Big Gambler grew skyscraper-tall.

Joe got more and more furious and frightened. He watched like a hawk or spy satellite the dice nesting against the end wall, but never could spot justification for calling for another card test, or nerve himself to question the House Rules at this late date. It was maddening, in fact insanitizing, to know that if only he could get the cubes once more he could shoot circles around that black pillar of sporting aristocracy. He damned himself a googolplex of ways for the idiotic, conceited, suicidal impulse that had led him to let go of the bones when he'd had them.

To make matters worse, the Big Gambler had taken to gazing steadily at Joe with those eyes like coal mines. Now he made three rolls running without even glancing at the dice or the end wall, as far as Joe could tell. Why, he was getting as bad as Joe's Wife or Mother—watching, watching, watching Joe.

But the constant staring of those eyes that were not eyes was mostly throwing a terrific scare into him. Supernatural terror added itself to his certainty of the deadliness of the Big Gambler. Just who, Joe kept asking himself, had he got into a game with tonight? There was curiosity and there was dread—a dreadful curiosity as strong as his desire to get the bones and win. His hair rose and he was all over goose bumps, though the power was still pulsing in his hand like a braked locomotive or a rocket wanting to lift from the pad.

At the same time the Big Gambler stayed just that—a black satin-coated, slouch-hatted elegance, suave, courtly, lethal. In fact, almost the worst thing about the spot Joe found himself in was that, after admiring the Big Gambler's perfect sportsmanship all night, he must now be disenchanted by his machinelike throwing and try to catch him out on any technicality he could.

The remorseless mowing down of the Big Mushrooms went on. The empty spaces outnumbered the Toadstools. Soon there were only three left.

The Boneyard had grown still as Cypress Hollow or the Moon. The jazz had stopped and the gay laughter and the shuffle of feet and the squeak of goosed girls and the clink of drinks and coins. Everybody seemed to be gathered around the Number One Crap Table, rank on silent rank.

Joe was wracked by watchfulness, sense of injustice, self-contempt, wild hopes, curiosity, and dread. Especially the last two.

The complexion of the Big Gambler, as much as you could see of it, continued to darken. For one wild moment Joe found himself wondering if he'd got into a game with a nigger, maybe a witchcraft-drenched Voodoo Man whose white makeup was wearing off.

Pretty soon there came a century wager which the two remaining Big Mushrooms couldn't fade between them. Joe had to make up a sawbuck from his miserably tiny pile or get out of the game. After a moment's agonizing hesitation, he did the former.

And lost his ten.

The two Big Mushrooms reeled back into the hushed crowd.

Pit-black eyes bored into Joe. A whisper: "Rolling your pile."

Joe felt well up in him the shameful impulse to confess himself licked and run home. At least his six thousand dollars would make a hit with his Wife and Ma.

But he just couldn't bear to think of the crowd's laughter, or the thought of living with himself knowing that he'd had a final chance, however slim, to challenge the Big Gambler and passed it up.

He nodded.

The Big Gambler shot. Joe leaned out over and down the table, forgetting his vertigo, as he followed the throw with eagle or space-telescope eyes.

"Satisfied?"

Joe knew he ought to say, "Yes," and slink off with head held as high as he could manage. It was the gentlemanly thing to do. But then he reminded himself that he wasn't a gentleman, but just a dirty, working-stiff miner with a talent for precision hurling.

He also knew that it was probably very dangerous for him to say anything but, "Yes," surrounded as he was by enemies and strangers. But then he asked himself what right had he, a miserable, mortal, homebound failure, to worry about danger.

Besides, one of the ruby-grinning dice looked just the tiniest hair out of line with the other.

It was the biggest effort yet of Joe's life, but he swallowed and managed to say, "No. Lottie, the card test."

The dice-girl fairly snarled and reared up and back as if she were going to spit in his eyes, and Joe had a feeling her spit was cobra venom. But the Big Gambler lifted a finger at her in reproof and she skimmed the card at Joe, yet so low and viciously that it disappeared under the black felt for an instant before flying up into Joe's hand.

It was hot to the touch and singed a pale brown all over, though otherwise unimpaired. Joe gulped and spun it back high.

Sneering poisoned daggers at him, Lottie let it glide down the end wall...and after a moment's hesitation, it slithered behind the die Joe had suspected.

A bow and then the whisper: "You have sharp eyes, sir. Undoubtedly that die failed to reach the wall. My sincerest apologies and...your dice, sir."

Seeing the cubes sitting on the black rim in front of him almost gave Joe apoplexy. All the feelings wracking him, including his curiosity, rose to an almost unbelievable pitch of intensity, and when he'd said, "Rolling my pile," and the Big Gambler had replied, "You're faded," he yielded to an uncontrollable impulse and cast the two dice straight at the Big Gambler's ungleaming, midnight eyes.

They went right through into the Big Gambler's skull and bounced around inside there, rattling like big seeds in a big gourd not quite yet dry.

Throwing out a hand, palm back, to either side, to indicate that none of his boys or girls or anyone else must make a reprisal on Joe, the Big Gambler dryly gargled the two cubical bones, then spat them out so that they landed in the center of the table, the one die flat, the other leaning against it.

"Cocked dice, sir," he whispered as graciously as if no indignity whatever had been done him. "Roll again."

Joe shook the dice reflectively, getting over the shock. After a little bit he decided that though he could now guess the Big Gambler's real name, he'd still give him a run for his money.

A little corner of Joe's mind wondered how a live skeleton hung together. Did the bones still have gristle and thews, were they wired, was it done with force-fields, or was each bone a calcium magnet clinging to the next?—this tying in somehow with the generation of the deadly ivory electricity.

In the great hush of The Boneyard, someone cleared his throat, a Scarlet Woman tittered hysterically, a coin fell from the nakedest change-girl's tray with a golden clink and rolled musically across the floor.

"Silence," the Big Gambler commanded and in a movement almost too fast to follow whipped a hand inside the bosom of his coat and out to the crap table's rim in front of him. A short-barreled silver revolver lay softly gleaming there. "Next creature, from the humblest nigger night-girl to you, Mr. Bones, who utters a sound while my worthy opponent rolls, gets a bullet in the head."

Joe gave him a courtly bow back, it felt funny, and then decided to start his run with a natural seven made up of an ace and a six. He rolled and this time the Big Gambler, judging from the movements of his skull, closely followed the course of the cubes with his eyes that weren't there.

The dice landed, rolled over, and lay still. Incredulously, Joe realized that for the first time in his crap-shooting life he'd made a mistake. Or else there was a power in the Big Gambler's gaze greater than that in his own right hand. The six cube had come down okay, but the ace had taken an extra half roll and come down six too.

"End of the game," Mr. Bones boomed sepulchrally.

The Big Gambler raised a brown skeletal hand. "Not necessarily," he whispered. His black eyepits aimed themselves at Joe like the mouths of siege guns. "Joe Slattermill, you still have something of value to wager, if you wish. Your life."

At that a giggling and a hysterical tittering and a guffawing and a braying and a shrieking burst uncontrollably out of the whole Boneyard. Mr. Bones summed up the sentiments when he bellowed over the rest of the racket, "Now what use or value is there in the life of a bummer like Joe Slattermill? Not two cents, ordinary money."

The Big Gambler laid a hand on the revolver gleaming before him and all the laughter died.

"I have a use for it," the Big Gambler whispered. "Joe Slattermill,

on my part I will venture all my winnings of tonight, and throw in the world and everything in it for a side bet. You will wager your life, and on the side your soul. You to roll the dice. What's your pleasure?"

Joe Slattermill quailed, but then the drama of the situation took hold of him. He thought it over and realized he certainly wasn't going to give up being stage center in a spectacle like this to go home broke to his Wife and Mother and decaying House and the dispirited Mr. Guts. Maybe, he told himself encouragingly, there wasn't a power in the Big Gambler's gaze, maybe Joe had just made his one and only crap-shooting error. Besides, he was more inclined to accept Mr. Bones's assessment of the value of his life than the Big Gambler's.

"It's a bet," he said.

"Lottie, give him the dice."

Joe concentrated his mind as never before, the power tingled triumphantly in his hand, and he made his throw.

The dice never hit the felt. They went swooping down, then up, in a crazy curve far out over the end of the table, and then came streaking back like tiny red-glinting meteors towards the face of the Big Gambler, where they suddenly nested and hung in his black eye sockets, each with the single red gleam of an ace showing.

Snake eyes.

The whisper, as those red-glinting dice-eyes stared mockingly at him: "Joe Slattermill, you've crapped out."

Using thumb and middle finger—or bone rather—of either hand, the Big Gambler removed the dice from his eye sockets and dropped them in Lottie's white-gloved hand.

"Yes, you've crapped out, Joe Slattermill," he went on tranquilly. "And now you can shoot yourself"—he touched the silver gun—"or cut your throat"—he whipped a gold-handled bowie knife out of his coat and laid it beside the revolver—"or poison yourself"—the two weapons were joined by a small black bottle with white skull and crossbones on it—"or Miss Flossie here can kiss you to death." He drew forward beside him his prettiest, evilest-looking sporting girl. She preened herself and flounced her short violet skirt and gave Joe a provocative, hungry look, lifting her carmine upper lip to show her long white canines.

"Or else," the Big Gambler added, nodding significantly towards the black-bottomed crap table, "you can take the Big Dive."

Joe said evenly, "I'll take the Big Dive."

He put his right foot on his empty chip table, his left on the black rim, fell forward...and suddenly kicking off from the rim, launched himself in a tiger spring straight across the crap table at the Big Gambler's throat, solacing himself with the thought that certainly the poet chap hadn't seemed to suffer long.

As he flashed across the exact center of the table he got an instant photograph of what really lay below, but his brain had no time to develop that snapshot, for the next instant he was ploughing into the Big Gambler.

Stiffened brown palm edge caught him in the temple with a lightning-like judo chop...and the brown fingers or bones flew all apart like puff paste. Joe's left hand went through the Big Gambler's chest as if there were nothing there but black satin coat, while his right hand, straight-armedly clawing at the slouch-hatted skull, crunched it to pieces. Next instant Joe was sprawled on the floor with some black clothes and brown fragments.

He was on his feet in a flash and snatching at the Big Gambler's tall stacks. He had time for one left-handed grab. He couldn't see any gold or silver or any black chips, so he stuffed his left pants pocket with a handful of the pale chips and ran.

Then the whole population of The Boneyard was on him and after him. Teeth, knives, and brass knuckles flashed. He was punched, clawed, kicked, tripped and stamped on with spike heels. A gold-plated trumpet with a bloodshot-eyed black face behind it bopped him on the head. He got a white flash of the golden dice-girl and made a grab for her, but she got away. Someone tried to mash a lighted cigar in his eye. Lottie, writhing and flailing like a white boa constrictor, almost got a simultaneous strangle hold and scissors on him. From a squat wide-mouth bottle Flossie, snarling like a feline fiend, threw what smelt like acid past his face. Mr. Bones peppered shots around him from the silver revolver. He was stabbed at, gouged, rabbit-punched, scragmauled, slugged, kneed, bitten, bearhugged, butted, beaten, and had his toes trampled.

But somehow none of the blows or grabs had much real force. It was like fighting ghosts. In the end it turned out that the whole population of The Boneyard, working together, had just a little more strength than Joe. He felt himself being lifted by a multitude of hands and pitched out through the swinging doors so that he thudded down on his rear end on the board sidewalk. Even that didn't hurt much. It was more like a kick of encouragement.

He took a deep breath and felt himself over and worked his bones. He didn't seem to have suffered any serious damage. He stood up and looked around. The Boneyard was dark and silent as the grave, or the planet Pluto, or all the rest of Ironmine. As his eyes got accustomed to the starlight and occasional roving space-ship-gleam, he saw a padlocked sheet-iron door where the swinging ones had been.

He found he was chewing on something crusty that he'd some-how carried in his right hand all the way through the final fracas. Mighty tasty, like the bread his Wife baked for best customers. At that instant his brain developed the photograph it had taken when he had glanced down as he flashed across the center of the crap table. It was a thin wall of flames moving sideways across the table and just beyond the flames the faces of his Wife, Mother, and Mr. Guts, all looking very surprised. He realized that what he was chew-ing was a fragment of the Big Gambler's skull, and he remembered the shape of the three loaves his Wife had started to bake when he left the House. And he understood the magic she'd made to let him get a little ways away and feel half a man, and then come diving home with his fingers burned.

He spat out what was in his mouth and pegged the rest of the bit of giant-popover skull across the street.

He fished in his left pocket. Most of the pale poker chips had been mashed in the fight, but he found a whole one and explored its surface with his fingertips. The symbol embossed on it was a cross. He lifted it to his lips and took a bite. It tasted delicate, but delicious. He ate it and felt his strength revive. He patted his bulging left pocket. At least he'd started out well provisioned.

Then he turned and headed straight for home, but he took the long way, around the world.

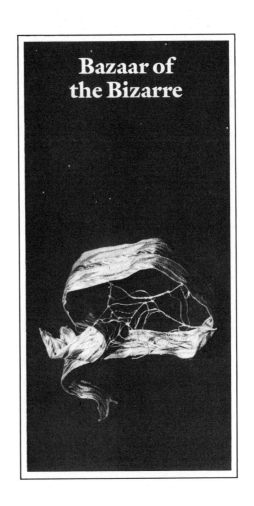

Bazaar of
the Bizarre

THE STRANGE STARS OF THE WORLD OF Nehwon glinted thickly above the black-roofed city of Lankhmar, where swords clink almost as often as coins. For once there was no fog.

In the Plaza of Dark Delights, which lies seven blocks south of the Marsh Gate and extends from the Fountain of Dark Abundance to the Shrine of the Black Virgin, the shop-lights glinted upward no more brightly than the stars glinted down. For there the vendors of drugs and the peddlers of curiosa and the hawkers of assignations light their stalls and crouching places with foxfire, glowworms, and firepots with tiny single windows, and they conduct their business almost as silently as the stars conduct theirs.

There are plenty of raucous spots a-glare with torches in nocturnal Lankhmar, but by immemorial tradition soft whispers and a pleasant dimness are the rule in the Plaza of Dark Delights. Philosophers often go there solely to meditate, students to dream, and fanatic-eyed theologians to spin like spiders abstruse new theories of the devil and of the other dark forces ruling the universe. And if any of these find a little illicit fun by the way, their theories and dreams and theologies and demonologies are undoubtedly the better for it.

Tonight, however, there was a glaring exception to the darkness rule. From a low doorway with a trefoil arch new-struck through an ancient wall, light spilled into the Plaza. Rising above the horizon of the pavement like some monstrous moon a-shine with the ray of a murderous sun, the new doorway dimmed almost to extinction the stars of the other merchants of mystery.

Eerie and unearthly objects for sale spilled out of the doorway a little way with the light, while beside the doorway crouched an avid-faced figure clad in garments never before seen on land or sea...in the World of Nehwon. He wore a hat like a small red pail, baggy trousers, and outlandish red boots with upturned toes. His eyes were as predatory as a hawk's, but his smile as cynically and lasciviously cajoling as an ancient satyr's.

Now and again he sprang up and pranced about, sweeping and resweeping with a rough long broom the flagstones as if to clean path for the entry of some fantastic emperor, and he often paused in his dance to bow low and loutingly, but always with upglancing eyes, to the crowd gathering in the darkness across from the doorway and to wing his hand from them toward the interior of the new shop in a gesture of invitation at once servile and sinister.

No one of the crowd had yet plucked up courage to step forward into the glare and enter the shop, or even inspect the rarities set out so carelessly yet temptingly before it. But the number of fascinated peerers increased momently. There were mutterings of censure at the dazzling new method of merchandising—the infraction of the Plaza's custom of darkness—but on the whole the complaints were outweighed by the gasps and murmurings of wonder, admiration, and curiosity kindling ever hotter.

The Gray Mouser slipped into the Plaza at the Fountain end as silently as if he had come to slit a throat or spy on the spies of the Overlord. His ratskin moccasins were soundless. His sword Scalpel in its mouseskin sheath did not swish ever so faintly against either his tunic or cloak, both of gray silk curiously coarse of weave. The glances he shot about him from under his gray silk hood half thrown back were freighted with menace and a freezing sense of superiority.

Inwardly the Mouser was feeling very much like a schoolboy— a schoolboy in dread of rebuke and a crushing assignment of homework. For in the Mouser's pouch of ratskin was a note scrawled in dark brown squid-ink on silvery fish-skin by Sheelba of the Eyeless Face, inviting the Mouser to be at this spot at this time.

Sheelba was the Mouser's supernatural tutor and—when the whim struck Sheelba—guardian, and it never did to ignore his invitations, for Sheelba had eyes to track down the unsociable though he did not carry them between his cheeks and forehead.

But the tasks Sheelba would set the Mouser at times like these were apt to be peculiarly onerous and even noisome—such as procuring nine white cats with never a black hair among them, or stealing five copies of the same book of magic runes from five widely separated sorcerous libraries or obtaining specimens of the dung of four kings living or dead—so the Mouser had come early, to get the bad news as soon as possible, and he had come alone, for he certainly did not want his comrade Fafhrd to stand snickering by while Sheelba delivered his little wizardly homilies to a dutiful Mouser...and perchance thought of extra assignments.

Sheelba's note, invisibly graven somewhere inside the Mouser's skull, read merely, *When the star Akul bedizens the Spire of Rhan, be you by the Fountain of Dark Abundance,* and the note was signed only with the little featureless oval which is Sheelba's sigil.

The Mouser glided now through the darkness to the Fountain, which was a squat black pillar from the rough rounded top of which a single black drop welled and dripped every twenty elephant's heartbeats.

The Mouser stood beside the Fountain and, extending a bent hand, measured the altitude of the green star Akul. It had still to drop down the sky seven finger widths more before it would touch the needle-point of the slim star-silhouetted distant minaret of Rhan.

The Mouser crouched doubled-up by the black pillar and then vaulted lightly atop it to see if that would make any great difference in Akul's attitude. It did not.

He scanned the nearby darkness for motionless figures... especially that of one robed and cowled like a monk—cowled so deeply that one might wonder how he saw to walk. There were no figures at all.

The Mouser's mood changed. If Sheelba chose not to come courteously beforehand, why he could be boorish too! He strode off to investigate the new bright arch-doored shop, of whose infractious glow he had become inquisitively aware at least a block before he had entered the Plaza of Dark Delights.

Fafhrd the Northerner opened one wine-heavy eye and without moving his head scanned half the small firelit room in which he slept naked. He shut that eye, opened the other, and scanned the other half.

There was no sign of the Mouser anywhere. So far so good! If his luck held, he would be able to get through tonight's embarrassing business without being jeered at by the small gray rogue.

He drew from under his stubbly cheek a square of violet serpent-hide pocked with tiny pores so that when he held it between his eyes and the dancing fire it made stars. Studied for a time, these stars spelled out obscurely the message: *When Rhan-dagger stabs the darkness in Akul-heart, seek you the Source of the Black Drops.*

Drawn boldly across the prickholes in an orange-brown like dried blood—in fact spanning the violet square—was one of the sigils of Ningauble of the Seven Eyes.

Fafhrd had no difficulty in interpreting the Source of the Black Drops as the Fountain of Dark Abundance. He had become wearily familiar with such cryptic poetic language during his boyhood as a scholar of the singing skalds.

Ningauble stood to Fafhrd very much as Sheelba stood to the Mouser except that the seven-eyed one was a somewhat more pretentious archimage, whose taste in the thaumaturgical tasks he set Fafhrd ran in larger directions, such as the slaying of dragons, the sinking of four-masted magic ships, and the kidnapping of ogre-guarded enchanted queens.

Also, Ningauble was given to quiet realistic boasting, especially about the grandeur of his vast cavern-home, whose stony serpent-twisting back corridors led, he often averred, to all spots in space and time—provided Ningauble instructed one beforehand exactly how to step those rocky crooked low-ceilinged passageways.

Fafhrd was driven by no great desire to learn Ningauble's formulas and enchantments, as the Mouser was driven to learn Sheelba's, but the septinocular one had enough holds on the Northerner, based on the latter's weaknesses and past misdeeds, so that Fafhrd had always to listen patiently to Ningauble's wizardly admonishments and vaunting sorcerous chit-chat—but *not*, if humanly or inhumanly possible, while the Gray Mouser was present to snigger and grin.

Meanwhile, Fafhrd standing before the fire, had been whipping, slapping, and belting various garments and weapons and ornaments onto his huge brawny body with its generous stretches of thick short curling red-gold hairs. When he opened the outer door and, also booted and helmeted now, glanced down the darkling alleyway preparatory to leaving and noted only the hunch-backed chestnut vendor a-squat by his brazier at the next corner, one would have sworn that when he did stride forth toward the Plaza of Dark Delights it would be with the clankings and thunderous tread of a siege-tower approaching a thick-walled city.

Instead the lynx-eared old chestnut vendor, who was also a spy of the Overlord, had to swallow down his heart when it came sliding crookedly up his throat as Fafhrd rushed past him, tall as a pine tree, swift as the wind, and silent as a ghost.

The Mouser elbowed aside two gawkers with shrewd taps on the floating rib and strode across the dark flagstones toward the garishly bright shop with its doorway like an upended heart. It occurred to him they must have had masons working like fiends to have cut and plastered that archway so swiftly. He had been past here this afternoon and noted nothing but blank wall.

The outlandish porter with the red cylinder hat and twisty red shoe-toes came frisking out to the Mouser with his broom and then went curtsying back as he reswept a path for this first customer with many an obsequious bow and smirk.

But the Mouser's visage was set in an expression of grim and all-skeptical disdain. He paused at the heaping of objects in front of the door and scanned it with disapproval. He drew Scalpel from its thin gray sheath and with the tip of the long blade flipped back the cover on the topmost of a pile of musty books. Without going any closer he briefly scanned the first page, shook his head, rapidly turned a half dozen more pages with Scalpel's tip, using the sword as if it were a teacher's wand to point out words here and there— because they were ill-chosen, to judge from his expression—and then abruptly closed the book with another sword-flip.

Next he used Scalpel's tip to lift a red cloth hanging from a table behind the books and peer under it suspiciously, to rap contemptuously a glass jar with a human head floating in it, to touch disparagingly several other objects and to waggle reprovingly at a foot-chained owl which hooted at him solemnly from its high perch.

He sheathed Scalpel and turned toward the porter with a sour, lifted-eyebrow look which said—nay, shouted—plainly, "Is *this* all you have to offer? Is this garbage your excuse for defiling the Dark Plaza with glare?"

Actually the Mouser was mightily interested by every least item which he had glimpsed. The book, incidentally, had been in a script which he not only did not understand, but did not even recognize.

Three things were very clear to the Mouser: first, that this stuff offered here for sale did not come from anywhere in the World of Nehwon, no, not even from Nehwon's farthest outback; second, that all this stuff was, in some way which he could not yet define, extremely dangerous; third, that all this stuff was monstrously fascinating and that he, the Mouser, did not intend to stir from this place until he had personally scanned, studied, and, if need be, tested every last intriguing item and scrap.

At the Mouser's sour grimace, the porter went into a convulsion of wheedling and fawning caperings, seemingly torn between a desire to kiss the Mouser's foot and to point out with flamboyant caressing gestures every object in his shop.

He ended by bowing so low that his chin brushed the pavement, sweeping an ape-long arm toward the interior of the shop, and gibbering in atrocious Lankhmarese, "Every object to pleasure the flesh and senses and imagination of man. Wonders undreamed. Very cheap, very cheap! Yours for a penny! The Bazaar of the Bizarre. Please to inspect, oh king!"

The Mouser yawned a very long yawn with the back of his hand to his mouth, next he looked around him again with the weary, patient, worldly smile of a duke who knows he must put up with many boredoms to encourage business in his demesne, finally he shrugged faintly and entered the shop.

Behind him the porter went into a jigging delirium of glee and began to resweep the flagstones like a man maddened with delight.

Inside, the first thing the Mouser saw was a stack of slim books bound in gold-lined fine-grained red and violet leather.

The second was a rack of gleaming lenses and slim brass tubes calling to be peered through.

The third was a slim dark-haired girl smiling at him mysteriously from a gold-barred cage that swung from the ceiling.

Beyond that cage hung others with bars of silver and strange green, ruby, orange, ultramarine, and purple metals.

Fafhrd saw the Mouser vanish into the shop just as his left hand touched the rough chill pate of the Fountain of Dark Abundance and as Akul pointed precisely on Rhan-top as if it were that needle-spire's green-lensed pinnacle-lantern.

He might have followed the Mouser, he might have done no such thing, he certainly would have pondered the briefly glimpsed event, but just then there came from behind him a long low "Hssssst!"

Fafhrd turned like a giant dancer and his longsword Graywand came out of its sheath swiftly and rather more silently than a snake emerges from its hole.

Ten arm lengths behind him, in the mouth of an alleyway darker than the Dark Plaza would have been without its new commercial moon, Fafhrd dimly made out two robed and deeply cowled figures poised side by side.

One cowl held darkness absolute. Even the face of a Negro of Klesh might have been expected to shoot ghostly bronze gleams. But here there were none.

In the other cowl there nested seven very faint pale greenish glows. They moved about restlessly, sometimes circling each other, swinging mazily. Sometimes one of the seven horizontally oval gleams would grow a little brighter, seemingly as it moved forward toward the mouth of the cowl—or a little darker, as it drew back.

Fafhrd sheathed Graywand and advanced toward the figures. Still facing him, they retreated slowly and silently down the alley.

Fafhrd followed as they receded. He felt a stirring of interest…and of other feelings. To meet his own supernatural mentor alone might be only a bore and a mild nervous strain; but it would be hard for anyone entirely to repress a shiver of awe at encountering at one and the same time both Ningauble of the Seven Eyes and Sheelba of the Eyeless Face.

Moreover, that those two bitter wizardly rivals would have joined forces, that they should apparently be operating together in amity.…Something of great note must be afoot! There was no doubting that.

The Mouser meantime was experiencing the smuggest, most mind-teasing, most exotic enjoyments imaginable. The sleekly leather-bound gold-stamped books turned out to contain scripts stranger far than that in the book whose pages he had flipped outside—scripts that looked like skeletal beasts, cloud swirls, and twisty-branched bushes and trees—but for a wonder he could read them all without the least difficulty.

The books dealt in the fullest detail with such matters as the private life of devils, the secret histories of murderous cults, and—these were illustrated—the proper dueling techniques to employ against sword-armed demons and the erotic tricks of lamias, succubi, bacchantes, and hamadryads.

The lenses and brass tubes, some of the latter of which were as fantastically crooked as if they were periscopes for seeing over the walls and through the barred windows of other universes, showed at first only delightful jeweled patterns, but after a bit the Mouser was able to see through them into all sorts of interesting places: the treasure-room of dead kings, the bedchambers of living queens, council-crypts of rebel angels, and the closets in which the gods hid plans for worlds too frighteningly fantastic to risk creating.

As for the quaintly clad slim girls in their playfully widely-barred cages, well, they were pleasant pillows on which to rest eyes momentarily fatigued by book-scanning and tube-peering.

Ever and anon one of the girls would whistle softly at the Mouser and then point cajolingly or imploringly or with languorous hintings at a jeweled crank set in the wall whereby her cage, suspended on a gleaming chain running through gleaming pulleys, could be lowered to the floor.

At these invitations the Mouser would smile with a bland amorousness and nod and softly wave a hand from the fingerhinge as if to whisper, "Later…later. Be patient."

After all, girls had a way of blotting out all lesser, but not thereby despicable, delights. Girls were for dessert.

Ningauble and Sheelba receded down the dark alleyway with Fafhrd following them until the latter lost patience and, somewhat conquering his unwilling awe, called out nervously, "Well, are you going to keep on fleeing me backward until we all pitch into the Great Salt Marsh? What do you want of me? What's it all about?"

But the two cowled figures had already stopped, as he could perceive by the starlight and the glow of a few high windows, and now it seemed to Fafhrd that they had stopped a moment before he had called out. A typical sorcerers' trick for making one feel awkward! He gnawed his lip in the darkness. It was ever thus!

"Oh My Gentle Son..." Ningauble began in his most sugary-priestly tones, the dim puffs of his seven eyes now hanging in his cowl as steadily and glowing as mildly as the Pleiades seen late on a summer night through a greenish mist rising from a lake freighted with blue vitriol and corrosive gas of salt.

"I asked what it's all about!" Fafhrd interrupted harshly. Already convicted of impatience, he might as well go the whole hog.

"Let me put it as a hypothetical case," Ningauble replied imperturbably. "Let us suppose, My Gentle Son, that there is a man in a universe and that a most evil force comes to this universe from another universe, or perhaps from a congeries of universes, and that this man is a brave man who wants to defend his universe and who counts his life as a trifle and that moreover he has to counsel him a very wise and prudent and public-spirited uncle who knows all about these matters which I have been hypothecating—"

"The Devourers menace Lankhmar!" Sheelba rapped out in a voice as harsh as a tree cracking and so suddenly that Fafhrd almost started—and for all we know, Ningauble too.

Fafhrd waited a moment to avoid giving false impressions and then switched his gaze to Sheelba. His eyes had been growing accustomed to the darkness and he saw much more now than he had seen at the alley's mouth, yet he still saw not one jot more than absolute blackness inside Sheelba's cowl.

"Who are the Devourers?" he asked.

It was Ningauble, however, who replied, "The Devourers are the most accomplished merchants in all the many universes—so accomplished, indeed, that they sell only trash. There is a deep necessity in this, for the Devourers must occupy all their cunning in perfecting their methods of selling and so have not an instant to spare in considering the worth of what they sell. Indeed, they dare not concern themselves with such matters for a moment, for fear of losing their golden touch—and yet such are their skills that their wares are utterly irresistible, indeed the finest wares in all the many universes—if you follow me?"

Fafhrd looked hopefully toward Sheelba, but since the latter did not this time interrupt with some pithy summation, he nodded to Ningauble.

Ningauble continued, his seven eyes beginning to weave a bit, judging from the movements of the seven green glows, "As you might readily deduce, the Devourers possess all the mightiest magics garnered from the many universes, whilst their assault groups are led by the most aggressive wizards imaginable, supremely skilled in all methods of battling, whether it be with the wits, or the feelings, or with the beweaponed body.

"The method of the Devourers is to set up shop in a new world and first entice the bravest and the most adventuresome and the supplest-minded of its people—who have so much imagination that with just a touch of suggestion they themselves do most of the work of selling themselves.

"When these are safely ensnared, the Devourers proceed to deal with the remainder of the population: meaning simply that they sell and sell and sell!—sell trash and take good money and even finer things in exchange."

Ningauble sighed windily and a shade piously. "All this is very bad, My Gentle Son," he continued, his eye-glows weaving hypnotically in his cowl, "but natural enough in universes administered by such gods as we have—natural enough and perhaps endurable. However"—he paused—"there is worse to come! The Devourers want not only the patronage of all beings in all universes, but—doubtless because they are afraid someone will some day raise the ever-unpleasant question, of the true worth of things—they want all their customers reduced to a state of slavish and submissive suggestibility, so that they are fit for nothing whatever but to gawk at and buy the trash the Devourers offer for sale. This means of course that eventually the Devourers' customers will have nothing wherewith to pay the Devourers for their trash, but the Devourers do not seem to be concerned with this eventuality. Perhaps they feel that there is always a new universe to exploit. And perhaps there is!"

"Monstrous!" Fafhrd commented. "But what do the Devourers gain from all these furious commercial sorties, all this mad merchandising? What do they really want?"

Ningauble replied, "The Devourers want only to amass cash and to raise little ones like themselves to amass more cash and they want to compete with each other at cash-amassing. (Is that coincidentally a city, do you think, Fafhrd? Cashamash?) And the Devourers want to brood about their great service to the many universes—it is their claim that servile customers make the most obedient subjects for the gods—and to complain about how the work of amassing cash tortures their minds and upsets their digestions. Beyond this, each of the Devourers also secretly collects and hides away forever, to delight no eyes but his own, all the finest objects and thoughts created by true men and women (and true wizards and true demons) and bought by the Devourers at bankruptcy prices and paid for with trash or—this is their ultimate preference—with nothing at all."

"Monstrous indeed!" Fafhrd repeated. "Merchants are ever an evil mystery and these sound the worst. But what has all this to do with me?"

"Oh My Gentle Son," Ningauble responded, the piety in his voice now tinged with a certain clement disappointment, "you force me once again to resort to hypothecating. Let us return to the supposition of this brave man whose whole universe is direly menaced and who counts his life a trifle and to the related supposition of this brave man's wise uncle, whose advice the brave man invariably follows—"

"The Devourers have set up shop in the Plaza of Dark Delights!" Sheelba interjected so abruptly in such iron-harsh syllables that this time Fafhrd actually did start. "You must obliterate this outpost tonight!"

Fafhrd considered that for a bit, then said, in a tentative sort of voice, "You will both accompany me, I presume, to aid me with your wizardly sendings and castings in what I can see must be a most perilous operation, to serve me as a sort of sorcerous artillery and archery corps while I play assault battalion—"

"Oh My Gentle Son..." Ningauble interrupted in tones of deepest disappointment, shaking his head so that his eye-glows jogged in his cowl.

"You must do it alone!" Sheelba rasped.

"Without any help at all?" Fafhrd demanded. "No! Get someone else. Get this doltish brave man who always follows his scheming uncle's advice as slavishly as you tell me the Devourers' customers respond to their merchandising. Get *him!* But as for me—No, I say!"

"Then leave us, coward!" Sheelba decreed dourly, but Ningauble only sighed and said quite apologetically, "It was intended that you have a comrade in this quest, a fellow soldier against noisome evil—to wit, the Gray Mouser. But unfortunately he came too early to his appointment with my colleague here and was enticed into the shop of the Devourers and is doubtless now deep in their snares, if not already extinct. So you can see that we do take thought for your welfare and have no wish to overburden you with solo quests. However, My Gentle Son, if it still be your firm resolve…"

Fafhrd let out a sigh more profound than Ningauble's. "Very well," he said in gruff tones admitting defeat, "I'll do it for you. Someone will have to pull that poor little gray fool out of the pretty-pretty fire—or the twinkly-twinkly water!—that tempted him. But how do I go about it?" He shook a big finger at Ningauble. "And no more Gentle-Sonning!"

Ningauble paused. Then he said only, "Use your own judgment."

Sheelba said, "Beware the Black Wall!"

Ningauble said to Fafhrd, "Hold, I have a gift for you," and held out to him a ragged ribbon a yard long, pinched between the cloth of the wizard's long sleeve so that it was impossible to see the manner of hand that pinched. Fafhrd took the tatter with a snort, crumpled it into a ball, and thrust it into his pouch.

"Have a greater care with it," Ningauble warned. "It is the Cloak of Invisibility, somewhat worn by many magic usings. Do not put it on until you near the Bazaar of the Devourers. It has two minor weaknesses: it will not make you altogether invisible to a master sorcerer if he senses your presence and takes certain steps. Also, see to it that you do not bleed during this exploit, for the cloak will not hide blood."

"I've a gift too!" Sheelba said, drawing from out of his black cowl-hole—with sleeve-masked hand, as Ninguable had done—something that shimmered faintly in the dark like…

Like a spiderweb.

Sheelba shook it, as if to dislodge a spider, or perhaps two.

"The Blindfold of True Seeing," he said as he reached it toward Fafhrd. "It shows all things as they really are! Do not lay it across your eyes until you enter the Bazaar. On no account, as you value your life or your sanity, wear it now!"

Fafhrd took it from him most gingerly, the flesh of his fingers crawling. He was inclined to obey the taciturn wizard's instructions. At this moment he truly did not much care to see the true visage of Sheelba of the Eyeless Face.

•

The Gray Mouser was reading the most interesting book of them all, a great compendium of secret knowledge written in a script of astrologic and geomantic signs, the meaning of which fairly leaped off the page into his mind.

To rest his eyes from that—or rather to keep from gobbling the book too fast—he peered through a nine-elbowed brass tube at a scene that could only be the blue heaven-pinnacle of the universe where angels flew shimmeringly like dragonflies and where a few choice heroes rested from their great mountain-climb and spied down critically on the antlike labors of the gods many levels below.

To rest his eye from *that,* he looked up between the scarlet (bloodmetal?) bars of the inmost cage at the most winsome, slim, fair, jet-eyed girl of them all. She knelt, sitting on her heels, with her upper body leaned back a little. She wore a red velvet tunic and had a mop of golden hair so thick and pliant that she could sweep it in a neat curtain over her upper face, down almost to her pouting lips. With the slim fingers of one hand she would slightly part these silky golden drapes to peer at the Mouser playfully, while with those of the other she rattled golden castanets in a most languorously slow rhythm, though with occasional swift staccato bursts.

The Mouser was considering whether it might not be as well to try a turn or two on the ruby-crusted golden crank next to his elbow, when he spied for the first time the glimmering wall at the back of the shop. What could its material be? he asked himself. Tiny diamonds countless as the sand set in smoky glass? Black opal? Black pearl? Black moonshine?

Whatever it was, it was wholly fascinating, for the Mouser quickly set down his book, using the nine-crooked spy-tube to mark his place—a most engrossing pair of pages on dueling where were revealed the Universal Parry and its five false variants and also the three true forms of the Secret Thrust—and with only a finger-wave to the ensorceling blonde in red velvet he walked quickly toward the back of the shop.

As he approached the Black Wall he thought for an instant that he glimpsed a silver wraith, or perhaps a silver skeleton, walking toward him out of it, but then he saw that it was only his own darkly handsome reflection, pleasantly flattered by the lustrous material. What had momentarily suggested silver ribs was the reflection of the silver lacings on his tunic.

He smirked at his image and reached out a finger to touch *its* lustrous finger when—Lo, a wonder!—his hand went into the wall with never a sensation at all save a faint tingling coolth promising comfort like the sheets of a fresh-made bed.

He looked at his hand inside the wall and—Lo, another wonder—it was all a beautiful silver faintly patterned with tiny scales. And though his own hand indubitably, as he could tell by clenching it, it was scarless now and a mite slimmer and longer fingered— altogether a more handsome hand than it had been a moment ago.

He wriggled his fingers and it was like watching small silver fish dart about—fingerlings!

What a droll conceit, he thought, to have a dark fishpond or rather swimming pool set on its side indoors, so that one could walk into the fracious erect fluid quietly and gracefully, instead of all the noisy, bouncingly athletic business of diving!

And how charming that the pool should be filled not with wet soppy cold water, but with a sort of moon-dark essence of sleep! An essence with beautifying cosmetic properties too—a sort of mudbath without the mud. The Mouser decided he must have a swim in this wonder pool at once, but just then his gaze lit on a long high black couch toward the other end of the dark liquid wall, and beyond the couch a small high table set with viands and a crystal pitcher and goblet.

He walked along the wall to inspect these, his handsome reflection taking step for step with him.

He trailed his hand in the wall for a space and then withdrew it, the scales instantly vanishing and the familiar old scars returning.

The couch turned out to be a narrow high-sided black coffin lined with quilted black satin and piled at one end with little black satin pillows. It looked most invitingly comfortable and restful— not quite as inviting as the Black Wall, but very attractive just the same; there was even a rack of tiny black books nested in the black satin for the occupant's diversion and also a black candle, unlit.

The collation on the little ebony table beyond the coffin consisted entirely of black foods. By sight and then by nibbling and sipping the Mouser discovered their nature: thin slices of a very dark rye bread crusted with poppy seeds and dripped with black butter; slivers of charcoal-seared steak; similarly broiled tiny thin slices of calf's liver sprinkled with dark spices and liberally pricked with capers; the darkest grape jellies; truffles cut paper thin and mushrooms fried black; pickled chestnuts; and of course, ripe olives and black fish eggs—caviar. The black drink, which foamed when he poured it, turned out to be stout laced with the bubbly wine of Ilthmar.

He decided to refresh the inner Mouser—the Mouser who lived

a sort of blind soft greedy undulating surface-life between his lips and his belly—before taking a dip in the Black Wall.

Fafhrd re-entered the Plaza of Dark Delights walking warily and with the long tatter that was the Cloak of Invisibility trailing from between left forefinger and thumb and with the glimmering cobweb that was the Blindfold of True Seeing pinched even more delicately by its edge between the same digits of his right hand. He was not yet altogether certain that the trailing gossamer hexagon was completely free of spiders.

Across the Plaza he spotted the bright-mouthed shop—the shop he had been told was an outpost of the deadly Devourers—through a ragged gather of folk moving about restlessly and commenting and speculating to one another in harsh excited undertones.

The only feature of the shop Fafhrd could make out at all clearly at this distance was the red-capped red-footed baggy-trousered porter, not capering now but leaning on his long broom beside the trefoil-arched doorway.

With a looping swing of his left arm Fafhrd hung the Cloak of Invisibility around his neck. The ragged ribband hung to either side down his chest in its wolfskin jerkin only halfway to his wide belt which supported longsword and short-axe. It did not vanish his body to the slightest degree that he could see and he doubted it worked at all. Like many another thaumaturge, Ningauble never hesitated to give one useless charms, not for any treacherous reason, necessarily, but simply to improve one's morale. Fafhrd strode boldly toward the shop.

The Northerner was a tall, broad-shouldered, formidable-looking man—doubly formidable by his barbaric dress and weaponing in supercivilized Lankhmar—and so he took it for granted that the ordinary run of city folk stepped out of his way; indeed it had never occurred to him that they should not.

He got a shock. All the clerks, seedy bravos, scullery folk, students, slaves, second-rate merchants and second-class courtesans who would automatically have moved aside for him (though the last with a saucy swing of the hips) now came straight at him, so that he had to dodge and twist and stop and even sometimes dart back to avoid being toe-tramped and bumped. Indeed one fat pushy proud-stomached fellow almost carried away his cobweb, which he could see now by the light of the shop was free of spiders—or if there were any spiders still on it, they must be very small.

He had so much to do dodging Fafhrd-blind Lankhmarians that

he could not spare one more glance for the shop until he was almost at the door. And then before he took his first close look, he found that he was tilting his head so that his left ear touched the shoulder below it and that he was laying Sheelba's spiderweb across his eyes.

The touch of it was simply like the touch of any cobweb when one runs face into it walking between close-set bushes at dawn. Everything shimmered a bit as if seen through a fine crystal grating. Then the least shimmering vanished, and with it the delicate clinging sensation, and Fafhrd's vision returned to normal—as far as he could tell.

It turned out that the doorway to the Devourers' shop was piled with garbage—garbage of a particularly offensive sort: old bones, dead fish, butcher's offal, moldering gravecloths folded in uneven squares like badly bound uncut books, broken glass and potsherds, splintered boxes, large stinking dead leaves orange-spotted with blight, bloody rags, tattered discarded loincloths, large worms nosing about, centipedes a-scuttle, cockroaches a-stagger, maggots a-crawl—and less agreeable things.

Atop all perched a vulture which had lost most of its feathers and seemed to have expired of some avian eczema. At least Fafhrd took it for dead, but then it opened one white-filmed eye.

The only conceivably salable object outside the shop—but it was a most notable exception—was the tall black iron statue, somewhat larger than life-size, of a lean swordsman of dire yet melancholy visage. Standing on its square pedestal beside the door, the statue leaned forward just a little on its long two-handed sword and regarded the Plaza dolefully.

The statue almost teased awake a recollection in Fafhrd's mind—a recent recollection, he fancied—but then there was a blank in his thoughts and he instantly dropped the puzzle. On raids like this one, relentlessly swift action was paramount. He loosened his axe in its loop, noiselessly whipped out Graywand and, shrinking away from the piled and crawling garbage just a little, entered the Bazaar of the Bizarre.

The Mouser, pleasantly replete with tasty black food and heady black drink, drifted to the Black Wall and thrust in his right arm to the shoulder. He waved it about, luxuriating in the softly flowing coolth and balm—admiring its fine silver scales and more than human handsomeness. He did the same with his right leg, swinging it like a dancer exercising at the bar. Then he took a gentle deep breath and drifted farther in.

●

Fafhrd on entering the Bazaar saw the same piles of gloriously bound books and racks of gleaming brass spy-tubes and crystal lenses as had the Mouser—a circumstance which seemed to overset Ningauble's theory that the Devourers sold only trash.

He also saw the eight beautiful cages of jewel-gleaming metals and the gleaming chains that hung them from the ceiling and went to the jeweled wall cranks.

Each cage held a gleaming, gloriously hued, black- or light-haired spider big as a rather small person and occasionally waving a long jointed claw-handed leg, or softly opening a little and then closing a pair of fanged down-swinging mandibles, while staring steadily at Fafhrd with eight watchful eyes set in two jewel-like rows of four.

Set a spider to catch a spider, Fafhrd thought, thinking of his cobweb, and then wondered what the thought meant.

He quickly switched to more practical questions then, but he had barely asked himself whether before proceeding further he should kill the very expensive-looking spiders, fit to be the coursing beasts of some jungle empress—another count against Ning's trash-theory!—when he heard a faint splashing from the back of the shop. It reminded him of the Mouser taking a bath—the Mouser loved baths, slow luxurious ones in hot soapy scented oil-dripped water, the small gray sybarite!—and so Fafhrd hurried off in that direction with many a swift upward overshoulder glance.

He was detouring the last cage, a scarlet-metaled one holding the handsomest spider yet, when he noted a book set down with a crooked spy-tube in it—exactly as the Mouser would keep his place in a book by closing it on a dagger.

Fafhrd paused to open the book. Its lustrous white pages were blank. He put his impalpably cobwebbed eye to the spy-tube. He glimpsed a scene that could only be the smoky red hell-nadir of the universe, where dark devils scuttled about like centipedes and where chained folk gazing yearningly upward and the damned writhed in the grip of black serpents whose eyes shone and whose fangs dripped and whose nostrils breathed fire.

As he dropped tube and book, he heard the faint sonorous quick dull report of bubbles being expelled from a fluid at its surface. Staring instantly toward the dim back of the shop, he saw at last the pearl-shimmering Black Wall and a silver skeleton eyed with great diamonds receding into it. However, this costly bone-man— once more Ning's trash-theory disproved!—still had one arm sticking partway out of the wall and this arm was not bone, whether silver, white, brownish or pink, but live-looking flesh covered with proper skin.

As the arm sank into the wall, Fafhrd sprang forward as fast as he ever had in his life and grabbed the hand just before it vanished. He knew then he had hold of his friend, for he would recognize anywhere the Mouser's grip, no matter how enfeebled. He tugged, but it was as if the Mouser were mired in black quicksand. He laid Graywand down and grasped the Mouser by the wrist too and braced his feet against the rough black flags and gave a tremendous heave.

The silver skeleton came out of the wall with a black splash, metamorphosing as it did into a vacant-eyed Gray Mouser who without a look at his friend and rescuer went staggering off in a curve and pitched head over heels into the black coffin.

But before Fafhrd could hoist his comrade from this new gloomy predicament, there was a swift clash of footsteps and there came racing into the shop, somewhat to Fafhrd's surprise, the tall black iron statue. It had forgotten or simply stepped off its pedestal, but it had remembered its two-handed sword, which it brandished about most fiercely while shooting searching black glances like iron darts at every shadow and corner and nook.

The black gaze passed Fafhrd without pausing, but halted at Graywand lying on the floor. At the sight of the longsword the statue started visibly, snarled its iron lips, narrowed its black eyes. It shot glances more ironly stabbing than before, and it began to move about the shop in sudden zigzag rushes, sweeping its darkly flashing sword in low scythe-strokes.

At that moment the Mouser peeped moon-eyed over the edge of the coffin, lifted a limp hand and waved it at the statue, and in a soft sly foolish voice cried, "Yoo-hoo!"

The statue paused in its searchings and scythings to glare at the Mouser in mixed contempt and puzzlement.

The Mouser rose to his feet in the black coffin, swaying drunkenly, and dug in his pouch.

"Ho, slave!" he cried to the statue with maudlin gaiety, "your wares are passing passable. I'll take the girl in red velvet." He pulled a coin from his pouch, goggled at it closely, then pitched it at the statue. "That's one penny. And the nine-crooked spy-tube. That's another penny." He pitched it. "And *Gron's Grand Compendium of Exotic Love*—another penny for you! Yes, and here's one more for supper—very tasty, 'twas. Oh and I almost forgot—here's for tonight's lodging!" He pitched a fifth large copper coin at the demonic black statue and, smiling blissfully, flopped back out of sight. The black quilted satin could be heard to sigh as he sank in it.

Four-fifths of the way through the Mouser's penny-pitching Fafhrd decided it was useless to try to unriddle his comrade's non-sensical behavior and that it would be far more to the point to make use of this diversion to snatch up Graywand. He did so on the instant, but by that time the black statue was fully alert again, if it had ever been otherwise. Its gaze switched to Graywand the instant Fafhrd touched the longsword and it stamped its foot, which rang against the stone, and cried a harsh metallic "Ha!"

Apparently the sword became invisible as Fafhrd grasped it, for the black statue did not follow him with its iron eyes as he shifted position across the room. Instead it swiftly laid down its own mighty blade and caught up a long narrow silver trumpet and set it to its lips.

Fafhrd thought it wise to attack before the statue summoned reinforcements. He rushed straight at the thing, swinging back Graywand for a great stroke at the neck—and steeling himself for an arm-numbing impact.

The statue blew and instead of the alarm blare Fafhrd had expected, there silently puffed out straight at him a great cloud of white powder that momentarily blotted out everything, as if it were the thickest of fogs from Hlal the River.

Fafhrd retreated, choking and coughing. The demon-blown fog cleared quickly, the white powder falling to the stony floor with unnatural swiftness, and he could see again to attack, but now the statue apparently could see him too, for it squinted straight at him and cried its metallic "Ha!" again and whirled its sword around its iron head preparatory to the charge—rather as if winding itself up.

Fafhrd saw that his own hands and arms were thickly filmed with the white powder, which apparently clung to him everywhere except his eyes, doubtless protected by Sheelba's cobweb.

The iron statue came thrusting and slashing in. Fafhrd took the great sword on his, chopped back, and was parried in return. And now the combat assumed the noisy deadly aspects of a conventional longsword duel, except that Graywand was notched whenever it caught the chief force of a stroke, while the statue's somewhat longer weapon remained unmarked. Also, whenever Fafhrd got through the other's guard with a thrust—it was almost impossible to reach him with a slash—it turned out that the other had slipped his lean body or head aside with unbelievably swift and infallible anticipations.

It seemed to Fafhrd—at least at the time—the most fell, frustrating, and certainly the most wearisome combat in which he had ever engaged, so he suffered some feelings of hurt and irritation when the Mouser reeled up in his coffin again and leaned an elbow on the black-satin-quilted side and rested chin on fist and grinned hugely at the battlers and from time to time laughed wildly and shouted such enraging nonsense as, "Use Secret Thrust Two-and-a-Half, Fafhrd—it's all in the book!" or "Jump in the oven!—there'd be a master stroke of strategy!" or—this to the statue—"Remember to sweep under his feet, you rogue!"

Backing away from one of Fafhrd's sudden attacks, the statue bumped the table holding the remains of the Mouser's repast—evidently its anticipatory abilities did not extend to its rear—and scraps of black food and white potsherds and jags of crystal shattered across the floor.

The Mouser leaned out of his coffin and waved a finger waggishly. "You'll have to sweep that up!" he cried and went off into a gale of laughter.

Backing away again, the statue bumped the black coffin. The Mouser only clapped the demonic figure comradely on the shoulder and called, "Set to it again, clown! Brush him down! Dust him off!"

But the worst was perhaps when, during a brief pause while the combatants gasped and eyed each other dizzily, the Mouser waved coyly to the nearest giant spider and called his inane "Yoo-hoo!" again, following it with, "I'll see you, dear, after the circus."

Fafhrd, parrying with weary desperation a fifteenth or a fiftieth cut at his head, thought bitterly, *This comes of trying to rescue small heartless madmen who would howl at their grandmothers hugged by bears. Sheelba's cobweb has shown me the gray one in his true idiot nature.*

The Mouser had first been furious when the sword-skirling clashed him awake from his black satin dreams, but as soon as he saw what was going on he became enchanted at the wildly comic scene.

For, lacking Sheelba's cobweb, what the Mouser saw was only the zany red-capped porter prancing about in his tip-curled red shoes and aiming with his broom great strokes at Fafhrd, who looked exactly as if he had climbed a moment ago out of a barrel of meal. The only part of the Northerner not whitely dusted was a mask-like stretch across his eyes.

What made the whole thing fantastically droll was that miller-white Fafhrd was going through all the motions—and emotions!—of a genuine combat with excruciating precision, parrying the broom as if it were some great jolting scimitar or two-handed broadsword even. The broom would go sweeping up and Fafhrd would gawk at it, giving a marvellous interpretation of apprehensive goggling despite his strangely shadowed eyes. Then the broom would come sweeping down and Fafhrd would brace himself and seem to catch it on his sword only with the most prodigious effort—and then pretend to be jolted back by it!

The Mouser had never suspected Fafhrd had such a perfected theatric talent, even if it were acting of a rather mechanical sort, lacking the broad sweeps of true dramatic genius, and he whooped with laughter.

Then the broom brushed Fafhrd's shoulder and blood sprang out.

Fafhrd, wounded at last and thereby knowing himself unlikely to out-endure the black statue—although the latter's iron chest was working now like a bellows—decided on swifter measures. He loosened his hand-axe again in its loop and at the next pause in the fight, both battlers having outguessed each other by retreating simultaneously, whipped it up and hurled it at his adversary's face.

Instead of seeking to dodge or ward off the missile, the black statue lowered its sword and merely wove its head in a tiny circle.

The axe closely circled the lean black head, like a silver wood-tailed comet whipping around a black sun, and came back straight at Fafhrd like a boomerang—and rather more swiftly than Fafhrd had sent it.

But time slowed for Fafhrd then and he half ducked and caught it left-handed as it went whizzing past his cheek.

His thoughts too went for a moment fast as his actions. He thought of how his adversary, able to dodge every frontal attack, had not avoided the table or the coffin behind him. He thought of how the Mouser had not laughed now for a dozen clashes and he looked at him and saw him, though still dazed-seeming, strangely pale and sober-faced, appearing to stare with horror at the blood running down Fafhrd's arm.

So crying as heartily and merrily as he could, "Amuse yourself! Join in the fun, clown!—here's your slap-stick," Fafhrd tossed the axe toward the Mouser.

Without waiting to see the result of that toss—perhaps not daring to—he summoned up his last reserves of speed and rushed at the black statue in a circling advance that drove it back toward the coffin.

Without shifting his stupid horrified gaze, the Mouser stuck out a hand at the last possible moment and caught the axe by the handle as it spun lazily down.

As the black statue retreated near the coffin and poised for what promised to be a stupendous counter-attack, the Mouser leaned out and, now grinning foolishly again, sharply rapped its black pate with the axe.

The iron head split like a coconut, but did not come apart. Fafhrd's hand-axe, wedged in it deeply, seemed to turn all at once to iron like the statue and its black haft was wrenched out of the Mouser's hand as the statue stiffened up straight and tall.

The Mouser stared at the split head woefully, like a child who hadn't known knives cut.

The statue brought its great sword flat against its chest, like a staff on which it might lean but did not, and it fell rigidly forward and hit the floor with a ponderous clank.

At that stony-metallic thundering, white wildfire ran across the Black Wall, lightening the whole shop like a distant levin-bolt, and iron-basalt thundering echoed from deep within it.

Fafhrd sheathed Graywand, dragged the Mouser out of the black coffin—the fight hadn't left him the strength to lift even his small friend—and shouted in his ear, "Come on! Run!"

The Mouser ran for the Black Wall.

Fafhrd snagged his wrist as he went by and plunged toward the arched door, dragging the Mouser after him.

The thunder faded out and there came a low whistle, cajolingly sweet.

Wildfire raced again across the Black Wall behind them—much more brightly this time, as if a lightning storm were racing toward them.

The white glare striking ahead imprinted one vision indelibly on Fafhrd's brain: the giant spider in the inmost cage pressed against the bloodred bars to gaze down at them. It had pale legs and a velvet red body and a mask of sleek thick golden hair from which eight jet eyes peered, while its fanged jaws hanging down in the manner of the wide blades of a pair of golden scissors rattled together in a wild staccato rhythm like castanets.

That moment the cajoling whistle was repeated. It too seemed to be coming from the red and golden spider.

But strangest of all to Fafhrd was to hear the Mouser, dragged unwillingly along behind him, cry out in answer to the whistling, "Yes, darling, I'm coming. Let me go, Fafhrd! Let me climb to her! Just one kiss! Sweetheart!"

"Stop it, Mouser," Fafhrd growled, his flesh crawling in mid-plunge. "It's a giant spider!"

"Wipe the cobwebs out of your eyes, Fafhrd," the Mouser retorted pleadingly and most unwittingly to the point. "It's a gorgeous girl! I'll never see her ticklesome like—and I've paid for her! *Sweetheart!*"

Then the booming thunder drowned his voice and any more whistling there might have been, and the wildfire came again, brighter than day, and another great thunderclap right on its heels, and the floor shuddered and the whole shop shook, and Fafhrd dragged the Mouser through the trefoil-arched doorway, and there was another great flash and clap.

The flash showed a semicircle of Lankhmarians peering ashen-faced overshoulder as they retreated across the Plaza of Dark Delights from the remarkable indoor thunderstorm that threatened to come out after them.

Fafhrd spun around. The archway had turned to blank wall.

The Bazaar of the Bizarre was gone from the World of Nehwon.

The Mouser, sitting on the dank flags where Fafhrd had dragged him, babbled wailfully, "The secrets of time and space! The lore of the gods! The mysteries of Hell! Black nirvana! Red and gold Heaven! Five pennies gone forever!"

Fafhrd set his teeth. A mighty resolve, rising from his many recent angers and bewilderments, crystallized in him.

Thus far he had used Sheelba's cobweb—and Ningauble's tatter too—only to serve others. Now he would use them for himself! He would peer at the Mouser more closely and at every person he knew. He would study even his own reflection! But most of all, he would stare Sheelba and Ning to their wizardly cores!

There came from overhead a low "Hssst!"

As he glanced up he felt something snatched from around his neck and, with the faintest tingling sensation, from off his eyes.

For a moment there was a shimmer traveling upward and through it he seemed to glimpse distortedly, as through thick glass, a black face with a cobwebby skin that entirely covered mouth and nostrils and eyes.

Then that dubious flash was gone and there were only two cowled heads peering down at him from over the wall top. There was chuckling laughter.

Then both cowled heads drew back out of sight and there was only the edge of the roof and the sky and the stars and the blank wall.

Midnight by
the Morphy Watch

BEING WORLD'S CHESS CHAMPION (crowned or uncrowned) puts a more deadly and maddening strain on a man even than being President of the United States. We have a prime example enthroned right now. For more than ten years the present champion was clearly the greatest chess player in the world, but during that time he exhibited such willful and seemingly self-destructive behavior—refusing to enter crucial tournaments, quitting them for crankish reasons while holding a commanding lead, entertaining what many called a paranoid delusion that the whole world was plotting to keep him from reaching the top—that many informed experts wrote him off as a contender for the highest honors. Even his staunchest supporters experienced agonizing doubts—until he finally silenced his foes and supremely satisfied his friends by decisively winning the crucial and ultimate match on a fantastic polar island.

Even minor players bitten by the world's-championship bug—or the fantasy of it—experience a bit of that terrible strain, occasionally in very strange and even eerie fashion....

Stirf Ritter-Rebil was indulging in one of his numerous creative avocations—wandering at random through his beloved downtown San Francisco with its sometimes dizzily slanting sidewalks, its elusive narrow courts and alleys, and its kaleidoscope of ever-changing store and restaurant-fronts amongst the ones that persist as landmarks. To divert his gaze, there were interesting almond and black faces among the paler ones. There was the dangerous surge of traffic threatening to invade the humpy sidewalks.

The sky was a careless silvery grey, like an expensive whore's mink coat covering bizarre garb or nakedness. There were even wisps of fog, that Bay Area benison. There were bankers and hippies, con men and corporation men, queers of all varieties, beggars and sports, murderers and saints (at least in Ritter's freewheeling imagination). And there were certainly alluring girls aplenty in an astounding variety of packages—and pretty girls are the essential spice in any really tasty ragout of people. In fact there may well have been Martians and time travelers.

Ritter's ramble had taken on an even more dream-like, whimsical quality than usual—with an unflagging anticipation of mystery, surprise, and erotic or diamond-studded adventure around the very next corner.

He frequently thought of himself by his middle name, Ritter, because he was a sporadically ardent chess player now in the midst of a sporad. In German "Ritter" means "knight," yet Germans do not call a knight a Ritter, but a springer, or jumper (for its crookedly hopping move), a matter for inexhaustible philological, historical, socioracial speculation. Ritter was also a deeply devoted student of the history of chess, both in its serious and anecdotal aspects.

He was a tall, white-haired man, rather thin, saved from the look of mere age by ravaged handsomeness, an altogether youthful though worldly and sympathetically cynical curiosity in his gaze (when he wasn't daydreaming), and a definitely though unobtrusively theatrical carriage.

He was more daydreamingly lost than usual on this particular ramble, though vividly aware of all sorts of floating, freakish, beautiful and grotesque novelties about him. Later he recollected that he must have been fairly near Portsmouth Square and not terribly far from the intersection of California and Montgomery. At all events, he was fascinatedly looking into the display window of a secondhand store he'd never recalled seeing before. It must be a new place, for he knew all the stores in the area, yet it had the dust and dinginess of an *old* place—its owner must have moved in without refurbishing the premises or even cleaning them up. And it had a delightful range of items for sale, from genuine antiques to mod facsimiles of same. He noted in his first scanning glance, and with growing delight, a Civil War saber, a standard promotional replica of the starship *Enterprise,* a brand-new deck of tarots, an authentic shrunken head like a black globule of detritus from a giant's nostril, some fancy roach-clips, a silver lusterware creamer, a Sony tape recorder, a last year's whiskey jug in the form of a cable car, a scatter of Gene McCarthy and Nixon buttons, a single brass Lucas "King of the Road" headlamp from a Silver Ghost Rolls Royce, an electric toothbrush, a 1920's radio, a last month's copy of the *Phoenix,* and three dime-a-dozen plastic chess sets.

And then, suddenly, all these were wiped from his mind. Unnoticed were the distant foghorns, the complaining prowl of slowed traffic, the shards of human speech behind him mosaicked with the singsong chatter of Chinatown, the reflection in the plate glass of

a girl in a grandmother dress selling flowers, and of opening umbrellas as drops of rain began to sprinkle from the mist. For every
atom of Stirf Ritter-Rebil's awareness was burningly concentrated
on a small figure seeking anonymity among the randomly set-out
chessmen of one of the plastic sets. It was a squat, tarnished silver
chess pawn in the form of a barbarian warrior. Ritter knew it was
a chess pawn—and what's more, he knew to what fabulous historic
set it belonged, because he had seen one of its mates in a rare police
photograph given him by a Portuguese chess-playing acquaintance.
He knew that he had quite without warning arrived at a once-in-
a-lifetime experience.

Heart pounding but face a suave mask, he drifted into the store's
interior. In situations like this it was all-essential not to let the seller
know what you were interested in or even that you were interested
at all.

The shadowy interior of the place lived up to its display window.
There was the same piquant clutter of dusty memorables and among
them several glass cases housing presumably choicer items, behind
one of which stood a gaunt yet stocky elderly man whom Ritter
sensed was the proprietor, but pretended not even to notice.

But his mind was so concentrated on the tarnished silver pawn
he *must* possess that it was a stupefying surprise when his automatically flitting gaze stopped at a second and even greater once-
in-a-lifetime item in the glass case behind which the proprietor
stood. It was a dingy, old-fashioned gold pocket watch with the
hours not in Roman numerals as they should have been in so ven-
erable a timepiece, but in the form of dull gold and silver chess
pieces as depicted in game-diagrams. Attached to the watch by a
bit of thread was a slim, hexagonal gold key.

Ritter's mind almost froze with excitement. Here was the big
brother of the skulking barbarian pawn. Here, its true value almost
certainly unknown to its owner, was one of the supreme rarities of
the world of chess-memorabilia. Here was no less than the gold
watch Paul Morphy, meteorically short-reigned King of American
chess, had been given by an adoring public in New York City on
May 25, 1859, after the triumphal tour of London and Paris which
had proven him to be perhaps the greatest chess genius of all time.

Ritter veered as if by lazy chance toward the case, his eyes resolutely fixed on a dull silver ankh at the opposite end from the chess
watch.

He paused like a sleepwalker across from the proprietor after
what seemed like a suitable interval and—hoping the pounding of

his heart wasn't audible—made a desultory inquiry about the ankh. The proprietor replied in as casual a fashion, though getting the item out for his inspection.

Ritter brooded over the silver love-cross for a bit, then shook his head and idly asked about another item and still another, working his insidious way toward the Morphy watch.

The proprietor responded to his queries in a low, bored voice, though in each case dutifully getting the item out to show Ritter. He was a very old and completely bald man with a craggy Baltic cast to his features. He vaguely reminded Ritter of someone.

Finally Ritter was asking about an old silver railroad watch next to the one he still refused to look at directly.

Then he shifted to another old watch with a complicated face with tiny windows showing the month and the phases of the moon, on the other side of the one that was keeping his heart a-pound.

His gambit worked. The proprietor at last dragged out the Morphy watch, saying softly, "Here is an odd old piece that might interest you. The case is solid gold. It threatens to catch your interest, does it not?"

Ritter at last permitted himself a second devouring glance. It confirmed the first. Beyond a shadow of a doubt this was the genuine relic that had haunted his thoughts for two thirds of a lifetime.

What he said was "It's odd, all right. What are those funny little figures it has in place of hours?"

"Chessmen," the other explained. "See, that's a King at six o'clock, a pawn at five, a Bishop at four, a Knight at three, a Rook at two, a Queen at one, another King at midnight, and then repeat, eleven to seven, around the dial."

"Why midnight rather than noon?" Ritter asked stupidly. He knew why.

The proprietor's wrinkled fingernail indicated a small window just above the center of the face. In it showed the letters P.M. "That's another rare feature," he explained. "I've handled very few watches that knew the difference between night and day."

"Oh, and I suppose those squares on which the chessmen are placed and which go around the dial in two and a half circles make a sort of checkerboard?"

"Chessboard," the other corrected. "Incidentally, there are exactly sixty-four squares, the right number."

Ritter nodded. "I suppose you're asking a fortune for it," he remarked, as if making conversation.

The other shrugged, "Only a thousand dollars."

Ritter's heart skipped a beat. He had more than ten times that in his bank account. A trifle, considering the stake.

But he bargained for the sake of appearances. At one point he argued, "But the watch doesn't run, I suppose."

"But it still has its hands," the old Balt with the hauntingly familiar face countered. "And it still has its works, as you can tell by the weight. They could be repaired, I imagine. A French movement. See, there's the hexagonal winding-key still with it."

A price of seven hundred dollars was finally agreed on. He paid out the fifty dollars he always carried with him and wrote a check for the remainder. After a call to his bank, it was accepted.

The watch was packed in a small box in a nest of fluffy cotton. Ritter put it in a pocket of his jacket and buttoned the flap.

He felt dazed. The Morphy watch, the watch Paul Morphy had kept his whole short life, despite his growing hatred of chess, the the watch he had willed to his French admirer and favorite opponent Jules Arnous de Riviere, the watch that had then mysteriously disappeared, the watch of watches—was his!

He felt both weightless and dizzy as he moved toward the street, which blurred a little.

As he was leaving he noticed in the window something he'd forgotten—he wrote a check for fifty dollars for the silver barbarian pawn without bargaining.

He was in the street, feeling glorious and very tired. Faces and umbrellas were alike blurs. Rain pattered on his face unnoticed, but there came a stab of anxiety.

He held still and very carefully used his left hand to transfer the heavy little box—and the pawn in a twist of paper—to his trouser pocket, where he kept his left hand closed around them. Then he felt secure.

He flagged down a cab and gave his home address.

The passing scene began to come unblurred. He recognized Rimini's Italian Restaurant where his own chess game was now having a little renaissance after five years of foregoing tournament chess because he knew he was too old for it. A chess-smitten young cook there, indulged by the owner, had organized a tourney. The entrants were mostly young people. A tall, moody girl he thought of as the Czarina, who played a remarkable game, and a likable, loudmouthed young Jewish lawyer he thought of as Rasputin, who played almost as good a game and talked a better one, both stood out. On impulse Ritter had entered the tournament because it was such a trifling one that it didn't really break his rule against playing chess. And, his old skills reviving nicely, he had done well enough to have a firm grip on third place, right behind Rasputin and the Czarina.

But now that he had the Morphy watch...

Why the devil should he think that having the Morphy watch should improve his chess game? he asked himself sharply. It was as silly as faith in the power of the relics of saints.

In his hand inside his left pocket the watch box vibrated eagerly, as if it contained a big live insect, a golden bee or beetle. But that, of course, was his imagination.

Stirf Ritter-Rebil (a proper name, he always felt, for a chess player, since they specialize in weird ones, from Euwe to Znosko-Borovsky, from Noteboom to Dus-Chotimirski) lived in a one-room and bath, five blocks west of Union Square and packed with files, books, and also paintings wherever the wall space allowed, of his dead wife and parents, and of his son. Now that he was older, he liked living with clues to all of his life in view. There was a fine view of the Pacific and the Golden Gate and their fogs to the west, over a sea of roofs. On the orderly cluttered tables were two fine chess sets with positions set up.

Ritter cleared a space beside one of them and set in its center the box and packet. After a brief pause—as if for propitiatory prayer, he told himself sardonically—he gingerly took out the Morphy watch and centered it for inspection with the unwrapped silver pawn behind it.

Then, wiping and adjusting his glasses and from time to time employing a large magnifying glass, he examined both treasures exhaustively.

The outer edge of the dial was circled with a ring or wheel of twenty-four squares, twelve pale and twelve dark alternating. On the pale squares were the figures of chessmen indicating the hours, placed in the order the old Balt had described. The Black pieces went from midnight to five and were of silver set with tiny emeralds or bright jade, as his magnifying glass confirmed. The White pieces went from six to eleven and were of gold set with minute rubies or amethysts. He recalled that descriptions of the watch always mentioned the figures as being colored.

Inside that came a second circle of twenty-four pale and dark squares.

Finally, inside *that,* there was a two-thirds circle of sixteen squares below the center of the dial.

In the corresponding space above the center was the little window showing P.M.

The hands on the dial were stopped at 11:57—three minutes to midnight.

With a paper knife he carefully pried open the hinged back of the watch, on which were floridly engraved the initials PM—which he suddenly realized also stood for Paul Morphy.

On the inner golden back covering the works was engraved "France H&H"—the old Balt was right again—while scratched in very tiny—he used his magnifier once more—were a half dozen sets of numbers, most of the sevens having the French slash. Pawnbrokers' marks. Had Arnous de Riviere pawned the treasure? Or later European owners? Oh well, chess players were an impecunious lot. There was also a hole by which the watch could be wound with its hexagonal key. He carefully wound it but of course nothing happened.

He closed the back and brooded on the dial. The sixty-four squares—twenty-four plus twenty-four plus sixteen—made a fantastic circular board. One of the many variants of chess he had played once or twice was cylindrical.

"Les échecs fantasques," he quoted. "It's a cynical madman's allegory with its doddering monarch, vampire queen, gangster knights, double-faced bishops, ramming rooks and inane pawns, whose supreme ambition is to change their sex and share the dodderer's bed."

With a sigh of regret he tore his gaze away from the watch and took up the pawn behind it. Here was a grim little fighter, he thought, bringing the tarnished silver figure close to his glasses. Naked long-sword clasped against his chest, point down, iron skullcap low on forehead, face merciless as Death's. What did the golden legionaries look like?

Then Ritter's expression grew grim, too, as he decided to do something he'd had in mind ever since glimpsing the barbarian pawn in the window. Making a long arm, he slid out a file drawer and after flipping a few tabs drew out a folder marked "Death of Alekhine." The light was getting bad. He switched on a big desk lamp against the night.

Soon he was studying a singularly empty photograph. It was of an unoccupied old armchair with a peg-in chess set open on one of the flat wooden arms. Behind the chess set stood a tiny figure. Bringing the magnifying glass once more into play, he confirmed what he had expected: that it was a precise mate to the barbarian pawn he had bought today.

He glanced through another item from the folder—an old letter on onionskin paper in a foreign script with cedillas under half the "C's" and tildes over half the "A's."

It was from his Portuguese friend, explaining that the photo was a reproduction of one in the Lisbon police files.

The photo was of the chair in which Alexander Alekhine had been found dead of a heart attack on the top floor of a cheap Lisbon rooming house in 1946.

Alekhine had won the World's Chess Championship from Capablanca in 1927. He had held the world's record for the greatest number of games played simultaneously and blindfolded—thirty-two. In 1946 he was preparing for an official match with the Russian champion Botvinnik, although he had played chess for the Axis in World War II. Though at times close to psychosis, he was considered the profoundest and most brilliant attacking player who had ever lived.

Had he also, Ritter asked himself, been one of the players to own the Morphy silver-and-gold chess set and the Morphy watch?

He reached for another file folder, labeled "Death of Steinitz." This time he found a brownish daguerreotype showing an empty, narrow, old-fashioned hospital bed with a chessboard and set on a small table beside it. Among the chess pieces, Ritter's magnifier located another one of the unmistakable barbarian pawns.

Wilhelm Steinitz, called the Father of Modern Chess, had held the world's championship for twenty-eight years, until his defeat by Emmanuel Lasker in 1894. Steinitz had had two psychotic episodes and been hospitalized for them in the last years of his life, during the second of which he had believed he could move the chess pieces by electricity and challenged God to a match, offering God the odds of Pawn and Move. It was after the second episode that the daguerreotype had been taken which Ritter had acquired many years ago from the aged Emmanuel Lasker.

Ritter leaned back wearily from the table, took off his glasses and knuckled his tired eyes. It was later than he'd imagined.

He thought about Paul Morphy retiring from chess at the age of twenty-one after beating every important player in the world and issuing a challenge, never accepted, to take on any master at the odds of Pawn and Move. After that contemptuous gesture in 1859 he had brooded for twenty-five years, mostly a recluse in his family home in New Orleans, emerging only fastidiously dressed and becaped for an afternoon promenade and regular attendance at the opera. He suffered paranoid episodes during which he believed his relatives were trying to steal his fortune and, of all things, his clothes. And he never spoke of chess or played it, except for an occasional game with his friend Maurian at the odds of Knight and Move.

Twenty-five years of brooding in solitude without the solace of playing chess, but with the Morphy chess set and the Morphy watch in the same room, testimonials to his world mastery.

Ritter wondered if those circumstances—with Morphy constantly thinking of chess, he felt sure—were not ideal for the transmission of the vibrations of thought and feeling into inanimate objects, in this case the golden Morphy set and watch.

Material objects intangibly vibrating with twenty-five years of the greatest chess thought and then by strange chance (chance alone?) falling into the hands of two other periodically psychotic chess champions, as the photographs of the pawns hinted.

An absurd fancy, Ritter told himself. And yet one to the pursuit of which he had devoted no small part of his life.

And now the richly vibrant objects were in *his* hands. What would be the effect of that on *his* game?

But to speculate in that direction was doubly absurd.

A wave of tiredness went through him. It was close to midnight.

He heated a small supper for himself, consumed it, drew the heavy window drapes tight, and undressed.

He turned back the cover of the big couch next to the table, switched off the light, and inserted himself into bed.

It was Ritter's trick to put himself to sleep by playing through a chess opening in his thoughts. Like any talented player, he could readily contest one blindfold game, though he could not quite visualize the entire board and often had to count moves square by square, especially with the bishops. He selected Breyer's Gambit, an old favorite of his.

He made a half dozen moves. Then suddenly the board was brightly illuminated in his mind, as if a light had been turned on there. He had to stare around to assure himself that the room was still dark as pitch: There was only the bright board inside his head.

His sense of awe was lost in luxuriant delight. He moved the mental pieces rapidly, yet saw deep into the possibilities of each position.

Far in the background he heard a church clock on Franklin boom out the dozen strokes of midnight. After a short while he announced mate in five by White. Black studied the position for perhaps a minute, then resigned.

Lying flat on his back he took several deep breaths. Never before had he played such a brilliant blindfold game—or game with sight even. That it was a game with himself didn't seem to matter—his personality had split neatly into two players.

He studied the final position for a last time, returned the pieces to their starting positions in his head, and rested a bit before beginning another game.

It was then he heard the ticking, a nervous sound five times as fast as the distant clock had knelled. He lifted his wristwatch to his ear. Yes, it was ticking rapidly too, but this was another ticking, louder.

He sat up silently in bed, leaned over the table, switched on the light.

The Morphy watch. That was where the louder ticks were coming from. The hands stood at twelve ten and the small window showed A.M.

For a long while he held that position—mute, motionless, aghast, wondering, fearing, doubting, dreaming dreams no mortal ever dared to dream before.

Let's see. Edgar Allan Poe had died when Morphy was twelve years old and beating his uncle, Ernest Morphy, then chess king of New Orleans.

It seemed impossible that a stopped watch with works well over one hundred years old should begin to run. Doubly impossible that it should begin to run at approximately the right time—his wristwatch and the Morphy watch were no more than a minute apart.

Yet the works might be in better shape than either he or the old Balt had guessed; watches did capriciously start and stop running. Coincidences were only coincidences.

Yet he felt profoundly uneasy. He pinched himself and went through the other childish tests.

He said aloud, "I am Stirf Ritter-Rebil, an old man who lives in San Francisco and plays chess, and who yesterday discovered an unusual curio. But really, everything is perfectly normal...."

Nevertheless, he suddenly got the feeling of "A man-eating lion is a-prowl." It was the childish form terror still took for him on rare occasions. For a minute or so everything seemed *too* still, despite the ticking. The stirring of the heavy drapes at the window gave him a shiver, and the walls seemed thin, their protective power nil.

Gradually the sense of a killer lion moving outside them faded and his nerves calmed.

He switched off the light, the bright mental board returned, and the ticking became reassuring rather than otherwise. He began another game with himself, playing for Black the Classical Defense to the Ruy Lopez, another of his favorites.

This game proceeded as brilliantly and vividly as the first. There was the sense of a slim, man-shaped glow standing beside the bright board in the mental dark. After a while the shape grew amorphous and less bright, then split into three. However, it bothered him little, and when he at last announced mate in three for Black, he felt great satisfaction and profound fatigue.

Next day he was in exceptionally good spirits. Sunlight banished all night's terrors as he went about his ordinary business and writing chores. From time to time he reassured himself that he could still visualize a mental chessboard very clearly, and he thought now and again about the historical chess mystery he was in the midst of solving. The ticking of the Morphy watch carried an exciting, eager note. Toward the end of the afternoon he realized he was keenly anticipating visiting Rimini's to show off his newfound skill.

He got out an old gold watch chain and fob, snapped it to the Morphy watch, which he carefully wound again, pocketed them securely in his vest, and set out for Rimini's. It was a grand day— cool, brightly sunlit, and a little windy. His steps were brisk. He wasn't thinking of all the strange happenings but of *chess*. It's been said that a man can lose his wife one day and forget her that night, playing *chess*.

Rimini's was a good, dark, garlic-smelling restaurant with an annex devoted to drinks, substantial free pasta appetizers and, for the nonce, chess. As he drifted into the long L-shaped room, Ritter became pleasantly aware of the row of boards, chessmen, and the intent, mostly young, faces bent above them.

Then Rasputin was grinning at him calculatedly and yapping at him cheerfully. They were due to play their tournament game. They checked out a set and were soon at it. Beside them the Czarina also contested a crucial game, her moody face askew almost as if her neck were broken, her bent wrists near her chin, her long fingers pointing rapidly at her pieces as she calculated combinations, like a sorceress putting a spell on them.

Ritter was aware of her, but only peripherally. For last night's bright mental board had returned, only now it was superimposed on the actual board before him. Complex combinations sprang to mind effortlessly. He beat Rasputin like a child. The Czarina caught the win from the corner of her eye and growled faintly in approval. She was winning her own game; Ritter beating Rasputin bumped her into first place. Rasputin was silent for once.

A youngish man with a black moustache was sharply inspecting Ritter's win. He was the California state champion, Martinez, who had recently played a simultaneous at Rimini's, winning fifteen games, losing none, drawing only with the Czarina. He now suggested a casual game to Ritter, who nodded somewhat abstractedly.

They contested two very hairy games—a Sicilian Defense by Martinez in which Ritter advanced all his pawns in front of his castled King in a wild-looking attack, and a Ruy Lopez by Martinez that Ritter answered with the Classical Defense, going to great lengths to preserve his powerful King's Bishop. The mental board stayed superimposed, and it almost seemed to Ritter that there was a small faint halo over the piece he must next move or capture. To his mild astonishment he won both games.

A small group of chess-playing onlookers had gathered around their board. Martinez was looking at him speculatively, as if to ask, "Now just where did you spring from, old man, with your power game? I don't recall ever hearing of you."

Ritter's contentment would have been complete, except that among the kibitzers, toward the back there was a slim young man whose face was always shadowed when Ritter glimpsed it. Ritter saw him in three different places, though never in movement and never for more than an instant. Somehow he seemed one onlooker too many. This disturbed Ritter obscurely, and his face had a thoughtful, abstracted expression when he finally quit Rimini's for the faintly drizzling evening streets. After a block he looked around, but so far as he could tell, he wasn't being followed. This time he walked the whole way to his apartment, passing several landmarks of Dashiell Hammett, Sam Spade, and *The Maltese Falcon*.

Gradually, under the benison of the foggy droplets, his mood changed to one of exaltation. He had just now played some beautiful chess, he was in the midst of an amazing historic chess mystery he'd always yearned to penetrate, and somehow the Morphy watch was working *for* him—he could actually hear its muffled ticking in the street, coming up from his waist to his ear.

Tonight his room was a most welcome retreat, *his* place, like an extension of his mind. He fed himself. Then he reviewed, with a Sherlock Holmes smile, what he found himself calling "The Curious Case of the Morphy Timepiece." He wished he had a Dr. Watson to hear him expound. First, the appearance of the watch after Morphy returned to New York on the *Persia* in 1859. Over paranoid years Morphy had imbued it with psychic energy and vast chessic wisdom. Or else—mark this, Doctor—he had set up the conditions whereby subsequent owners of the watch would *think* he had done such, for the supernatural is not our bailiwick, Watson. Next (after de Riviere) great Steinitz had come into possession of it and challenged God and died mad. Then, after a gap, paranoid Alekhine had owned it and devised diabolically brilliant, hyper-Morphian strategies of attack, and died all alone after a thousand treacheries in a miserable Lisbon flat with a pegin chess set and the telltale barbarian pawn next to his corpse. Finally, after a hiatus of almost thirty years (where had the watch and set been then? Who'd had their custody? Who was the old Balt?) the timepiece and a pawn had come into his own possession. A unique case, Doctor. There isn't even a parallel in Prague in 1863.

The nighted fog pressed against the windowpane and now and again a little rain pattered. San Francisco was a London City and had its own resident great detective. One of Dashiell Hammett's hobbies had been chess, even though there was no record of Spade having played the game.

From time to time Ritter studied the Morphy watch as it glowed and ticked on the table space he'd cleared. P.M. once more, he noted. The time: White Queen, ruby glittering, past Black King, microscopically emerald studded—I mean five minutes past midnight, Doctor. The witching hour, as the superstitiously minded would have it.

But to bed, to bed, Watson. We have much to do tomorrow—and, paradoxically, tonight.

Seriously, Ritter was glad when the golden glow winked out on the watch face, though the strident ticking kept on, and he wriggled himself into his couch-bed and arranged himself for thought. The mental board flashed on once more and he began to play. First he reviewed all the best games he'd ever played in his life—there weren't very many—discovering variations he'd never dreamed of before. Then he played through all his favorite games in the history of chess, from MacDonnell-La Bourdonnais to Fischer-Spassky, not forgetting Steinitz-Zukertort and Alekhine-Bogolyubov. They were richer masterpieces than ever before—the mental board saw deeply. Finally he split his mind again and challenged himself to an eight-game blindfold match, Black against White. Against all expectation, Black won with three wins, two losses, and three draws.

But the night was not all imaginative and ratiocinative delight. Twice there came periods of eerie silence, which the ticking of the watch in the dark made only more complete, and two spells of the man-eating lion a-prowl that raised his hair at the roots. Once again there loomed the slim, faint, man-shaped glow beside the mental board and he wouldn't go away. Worse, he was joined by two other man-shaped glows, one short and stocky, with a limp, the other fairly tall, stocky too, and restless. These inner intruders bothered Ritter increasingly—who were they? And wasn't there beginning to be a faint fourth? He recalled the slim young elusive watcher with shadowed face of his games with Martinez and wondered if there was a connection.

Disturbing stuff—and most disturbing of all, the apprehension that his mind might be racked apart and fragmented abroad with all its machine-gun thinking, that it already extended by chessic veins from one chess-playing planet to another, to the ends of the universe?

He was profoundly glad when toward the end of his self-match, his brain began to dull and slow. His last memory was of an attempt to invent a game to be played on the circular board on the watch dial. He thought he was succeeding as his mind at last went spiraling off into unconsciousness.

Next day he awoke restless, scratchy, and eager—and with the feeling that the three or four dim figures had stood around his couch all night vibrating like strobe lights to the rhythm of the Morphy watch.

Coffee heightened his alert nervousness. He rapidly dressed, snapped the Morphy watch to its chain and fob, pocketed the silver pawn, and went out to hunt down the store where he'd purchased the two items.

In a sense he never found it, though he tramped and minutely scanned Montgomery, Kearny, Grant, Stockton, Clay, Sacramento, California, Pine, Bush, and all the rest.

What he did find at long last was a store window with a grotesque pattern of dust on it that he was certain was identical with that on the window through which he had first glimpsed the barbarian pawn day before yesterday.

Only now the display space behind the window was empty and the whole store too, except for a tall, lanky Black with a fabulous Afro hair-do, sweeping up.

Ritter struck up a conversation with the man as he worked, and slowly winning his confidence, discovered he was one of three partners opening a store there that would be stocked solely with African imports.

Finally, after the Black had fetched a great steaming pail of soapy water and a long-handled roller mop and begun to efface forever the map of dust by which Ritter had identified the place, the man at last grew confidential.

"Yeah," he said, "there *was* a queer old character had a second-hand store here until yesterday that had every crazy thing you could dig for sale, some junk, some real fancy. Then he cleared everything out into two big trucks in a great rush, with me breathing down his neck every minute because he'd been supposed to do it the day before.

"Oh, but he was a fabulous cat, though," the Black went on with a reminiscing grin as he sloshed away the last peninsulas and archipelagos of the dust map. "One time he said to me, 'Excuse me while I rest,' and—you're not going to believe this—he went into a corner and stood on his head. I'm telling you he did, man. I'd like to bust a gut. I thought he'd have a stroke—and he did get a bit lavender in the face—but after three minutes exact—I timed him—he flipped back onto his feet neat as you could ask and went on with his work twice as fast as before, supervising his carriers out of their skulls. Wow, that was an event."

Ritter departed without comment. He had got the final clue he'd been seeking to the identity of the old Balt and likewise the fourth and most shadowy form that had begun to haunt his mental chessboard.

Casually standing on his head, saying "It threatens to catch your interest"—why, it had to be Aaron Nimzovich, most hypereccentric player of them all and Father of Hypermodern Chess, who had been Alekhine's most dangerous but ever-evaded challenger. Why, the old Balt had even looked exactly like an aged Nimzovich—hence Ritter's constant sense of a facial familiarity. Of course, Nimzovich had supposedly died in the 1930's in his home city of Riga in the U.S.S.R., but what were life and breath to the forces with which Ritter was now embroiled?

It seemed to him that there were four dim figures stalking him relentlessly as lions right now in the Chinatown crowds, while despite the noise he could hear and feel the ticking of the Morphy watch at his waist.

He fled to the Danish Kitchen at the St. Francis Hotel and consumed cup on cup of good coffee and two orders of Eggs Benedict, and had his mental chessboard flashing on and off in his mind like a strobe light, and wondered if he shouldn't hurl the Morphy watch into the Bay to be rid of the influence racking his mind apart and destroying his sense of reality.

But then with the approach of evening, the urge toward *chess* gripped him more and more imperiously and he headed once again for Rimini's.

Rasputin and the Czarina were there and also Martinez again, and with the last a distinguished silver-haired man whom Martinez introduced as the South American international master, Pontebello, suggesting that he and Ritter have a quick game.

The board glowed again with the superimposed mental one, the halos were there once more, and Ritter won as if against a tyro.

At that, chess fever seized him entirely and he suggested he immediately play four simultaneous blindfold games with the two masters and the Czarina and Rasputin, Pontebello acting also as referee.

There were incredulous looks a-plenty at that, but he *had* won those two games from Martinez and now the one from Pontebello, so arrangements were quickly made, Ritter insisting on an actual blindfold. All the other players crowded around to observe.

The simul began. There were now four mental boards glowing in Ritter's mind. It did not matter—*now*—that there were four dim forms with them, one by each. Ritter played with a practiced brilliance, combinations bubbled, he called out his moves crisply and unerringly. And so he beat the Czarina and Rasputin quickly. Pontebello took a little longer, and he drew with Martinez by perpetual check.

There was silence as he took off the blindfold to scan a circle of astonished faces and four shadowed ones behind them. He felt the joy of absolute chess mastery. The only sound he heard was the ticking, thunderous to him, of the Morphy watch.

Pontebello was the first to speak. To Ritter, "Do you realize, master, what you've just done?" To Martinez, "Have you the scores of all four games?" To Ritter again, "Excuse me, but you look pale, as if you've seen a ghost." "Four," Ritter corrected quietly. "Those of Morphy, Steinitz, Alekhine, and Nimzovich."

"Under the circumstances, most appropriate," commented Pontebello, while Ritter sought out again the four shadowed faces in the background. They were still there, though they had shifted their positions and withdrawn a little into the varied darknesses of Rimini's.

Amid talk of scheduling another blindfold exhibition and writing a multiple-signed letter describing tonight's simul to the U.S. Chess Federation—not to mention Pontebello's searching queries as to Ritter's chess career—he tore himself away and made for home through the dark streets, certain that four shadowy figures stalked behind him. The call of the mental *chess* in his own room was not to be denied.

Ritter forgot no moment of that night, for he did not sleep at all. The glowing board in his mind was an unquenchable beacon, an all-demanding mandala. He contested two matches with himself, then one each with Morphy, Steinitz, Alekhine, and Nimzovich, winning the first two, drawing the third, and losing the last by a half point. Nimzovich was the only one to speak, saying, "I am both dead and alive, as I'm sure you know. Please don't smoke, or threaten to."

He stacked eight mental boards and played two games of three-dimensional chess, Black winning both. He traveled to the ends of the universe, finding chess everywhere he went, and contesting a long game, more complex than 3-D chess, on which the fate of the universe depended. He drew it.

And all through the long night the four were with him in the room and the man-eating lion stared in through the window with black-and-white checkered mask and silver mane. While the Morphy watch ticked like a death-march drum. All figures vanished when the dawn came creeping, though the mental board stayed bright and busy into full daylight and showed no signs of vanishing ever. Ritter felt overpoweringly tired, his mind racked to atoms, on the verge of death.

But he knew what he had to do. He got a small box and packed into it, in cotton wool, the silver barbarian pawn, the old photograph and daguerreotype, and a piece of paper on which he scribbled only:

Morphy, 1859–1884
de Riviere, 1884–?
Steinitz, ?–1900
Alekhine, ?–1946
Nimzovich, 1946–now
Ritter-Rebil, 3 days

Then he packed the watch in the box too, it stopped ticking, its hands were still at last, and in Ritter's mind the mental board winked out.

He took one last devouring gaze at the grotesque, glittering dial. Then he shut the box, wrapped and sealed and corded it, boldly wrote on it in black ink "Chess Champion of the World" and added the proper address.

He took it to the post office on Van Ness and sent it off by registered mail. Then he went home and slept like the dead.

Ritter never received a response. But he never got the box back either. Sometimes he wonders if the subsequent strange events in the Champion's life might have had anything to do with the gift.

And on even rarer occasions he wonders what would have happened if he had faced the challenge of death and let his mind be racked to bits, if that was what was to happen.

But on the whole he is content. Questions from Martinez and the others he has put off with purposefully vague remarks.

He still plays chess at Rimini's. Once he won another game from Martinez, when the latter was contesting a simul against twenty-three players.

Black Glass

RIVOCHE

ON A CHILLY SATURDAY IN LATE AUTUMN last year I was walking slowly east on Forty-second Street in New York, threading my way through the somewhat raunchy throngs and noting with some wonder and more depression the changes a quarter-century had made in the super-metropolis (I'd visited the city several times recently, staying in Greenwich Village and Chelsea, but this was the first time in more than twenty years that I'd walked any distance across midtown Manhattan), when there was borne in on me the preponderance of black glass as a facing material in the newer skyscrapers, as though they were glisteningly robing themselves for an urban funeral—perhaps their own.

Well, there was justification enough for that, I told myself with a bitter smile, what with the grime, the smog, the general filth and pollution, garbage strikes, teachers' strikes, the municipal universities retrenching desperately, municipal financing tottering near bankruptcy, crime in the growling, snarling streets where the taxi drivers, once famed for their wise-guy loquacity, were silent now, each in his front-seat fort, communicating with his passenger only by voice tube and payment slit. For two blocks now I'd been passing nothing but narrow houses showing X-rated films with an emphasis on torture, interspersed with pornographic bookstores, leather shops, hardware stores displaying racks of knives, a few seedy drug and cigar stores, and garish junk-food bars.

Did my gloomy disapproval of all this reflect nothing but my piled-up years? I asked myself. (Those around me were mostly young, though with knowing eyes and used-looking flesh.) I'd reached the age where the rest of life is mostly downhill and more and more alone, when you know that what you haven't gotten already you most likely will never get—or be able to enjoy if you do, and when your greatest insights are apt to transform next moment into the most banal clichés, and then back again and forth still once more, bewildering. And just lately I'd tried and failed to write a book of memoirs and personal philosophy—I'd set out to make a net to capture the universe and ended by creating a cage for my solitary self. Had New York City really changed at all? For example, hadn't Times Square, across which I was now pressing, been for the last seventy-five years a mass of gigantic trick advertisements flaring aloft—monstrous ruby lips that puffed real smoke, brown bottles big as tank cars pouring unending streams of grainy electric whisky? Yes, but then they had evoked wonder and amusement; the illusions had been fun; now they got only a bored acceptance and a dark resentment at the establishment power they represented; the violence seething just below the surface in the city was as real as the filth upon that surface, and the skyscrapers had reason to foresee doom and robe themselves in black.

Of course the glass wasn't really black—an opaque black—although it looked like that from the outside. But when you went inside (as I now did, through revolving doors, into the spacious lobby of the Telephone Building at Forty-second and Sixth Avenue), you saw at once it was only somewhat dusky, as if a swift-traveling storm cloud had blotted out the sun while you were going in. Or as if (it occurred to me with a twinge of fear) the small gray churning edged shadow in my left eye were expanding out to cover the whole visual field—and invading my right eye also. (I'd discovered that evidence of retinal degeneration a year ago, and the optical surgeon had treated it with skillfully aimed bursts of laser light, whose pinpoint cautery had scarred the diseased tissue, arresting the shadow's spread—but for dreary weeks I'd anticipated going blind and practiced for that by feeling my way around my room for an hour each day with my eyes shut tight.)

Now through the dusky glass I saw a young woman in a dark green cloak and gloves and jaunty visored cap pulled down—it was a chilly day, foreshadowing winter—striding along purposefully in the direction I'd been going, and her example inspired me to shake off my dismal thoughts, push out through the dizzying doors, and follow after. I enjoyed passing iron-fenced Bryant Park with its winter-dark bushes and grass, although the wind bit keenly—at least there were no neon promises of sick thrills, no violet-glowing mercury-vapor commands to buy. And then I came to the great Public Library at Fifth Avenue, which always gives me a lift with its semblance of being an island of disinterested intelligence in a dingy, commercial sea—although today, in tune with the times, a small scattered crowd encircled a swarthy man juggling flaming torches on the library's broad steps (encourage local street artists!—it promotes integration) while the two proud stone lions flanking the wide entry seemed to look away disdainfully. Some skinny children ran around the northern one, two rangy blacks conversing earnestly rested themselves against its side, and then my striding young woman in green, coming suddenly out of a crowd, passed in front of the lion, but as she did so, she briefly paused with face averted and laid her hand upon its mane in a gesture that was at once compassionate and commanding and even had an odd and faintly sinister note of ritual. I knew I was being imaginative to read so much into a stranger's gesture seen at a distance, but it nevertheless struck me as being somehow *important*.

She had reversed directions on me, going back toward Sixth, and once more I took my cue from her for my own strolling. I wasn't following her with any real intentness, or at least that's what I told myself then—why, I hadn't even glimpsed her face either time— but I did want to see more of those black glass buildings, and they had seemed to cluster most thickly north on Sixth. At any rate, by the time I'd reached Sixth again, I'd lost sight of her, though I somehow had the impression she'd turned north there.

I reminded myself it isn't called Sixth any more, but been rather grandiosely renamed the Avenue of the Americas. Though really it's the same old knock-about Sixth that once had an elevated and then was forever being dug up. And it's still Sixth underground— the Sixth Avenue IND subway.

I found enough black glass as I wended north, peering upward like a hick, to delight my sense of the grotesque. After New York Telephone there was RCA Corporation and Bankers Trust and West Side Federal Savings and W. R. Grace and Company, where the dark glass sloped, and the Stevens Tower, where the black facings were separated by gravestone pale verticals. And at 1166 they had black glass with *stars,* by God (but why were green faceless people painted on the wooden facing masking the lobby they were re-building there? Here be mysteries, I thought).

But all the time that I was playing my game with the buildings, I was aware of a not altogether pleasant change that had begun to take place in the scene around me after I'd looked out of the lobby of the Telephone Building and seen the day suddenly darken. That darkening effect had kept up after I'd got outside, as if the afternoon were drawing to an end sooner than it should, or as if—melodramatic fantasy!—an inky infection were spreading from the pernicious black glass to the air and space around it. The farther north I pressed, block by block, the more I noticed it, as though I were penetrating deeper and deeper into some realm of not altogether unfrightening mystery.

As for the girl in green, although I once or twice thought I'd caught sight of her a block or so ahead, I made no effort to catch up with her and verify my guess (or see her face). So she could hardly be responsible for the darkly romantic element (the feeling of playing with mysterious dangers) that had entered my fantasies. Or so I believed at the time.

And then I found I'd arrived at Rockefeller Plaza, where the black tried to disguise itself with dim silvery verticals, and the game became by degrees a little more somber and frightening. I think the transition occurred at the Pool of the Planets. I noted that oddly but not unpleasantly jarring feature (in the midst of the metropolitan commercial, the cosmic) down in a sunken court. I was instantly attracted and descended by means of broad gray granite steps. Nearby were chaste advertisements for a municipal theater offering something called "The New York Experience," which somehow struck me a bit comically, as though London should announce it was going to impersonate London. And there were other features which I have forgotten.

The pool itself was dark and very shallow, perfectly circular and quite wide, and from it rose on slender metal stems, all at their proper distances from the center and in their proper sizes, amazingly, as far as I could determine, the spheres of the planets done in some darkened silver metal and blackish brass. Simple inset plates of the same metals gave the names, symbols, dimensions, and distances. Truly, a charming conceit, but with sinister touches (the theme of darkening, the idea of the planets emerging from, or menaced by, a great unknown sea in space), so that when I finally turned away from it and especially when I'd mounted the stairs again to the sidewalk, I was not altogether surprised to find the scene around me altered still further. The people seemed to have grown fewer and I was unaccountably hesitant to look at their faces, and it had grown much, much darker—a sort of grainy blackness sprinkled everywhere—so that for the first time in months I felt for a moment in sharpest intensity the fear I'd had a year ago of going blind, while in my mind, succeeding each other rapidly, there unrolled a series of very brief darting visions: of New York and its high-rises drowned in a black sea, of the girl in green whirling on me and showing under her cap's visor no face at all, of the northern library lion coming suddenly awake at memory of the girl's touch (post-hypnotic command?) and shaking his pale mane and suppling his stony flanks and setting out after us, the pads of his paws grating on the steps and sidewalk, like giant's chalk—those fugitive visions and a dozen like them, such as the mind only gets when it's absorbing presentations from inner space at top speed, too many to remember.

At the first break in those visions, I wrenched my attention away from inner space to the sidewalk just ahead of me and I moved away from the sunken court. It worked. My surroundings didn't darken any further (that change was arrested) and the people grew no fewer, though I didn't yet risk looking at their faces. After a space I found myself grasping a thick brass railing and gazing down into a larger and—thank God!—more familiar sunken area. It was the skating rink, and there, one more figure among the graceful circlers in the white-floored gloom (a couple of them in rather flamboyant costumes, a couple of them suggesting animals), was my girl in green with cap pulled down and cloak swinging behind her, taking the long strokes you'd have expected from her striding.

I was entranced. I remember telling myself that she'd had just enough time, while I'd paused at the Pool of the Planets, to put on her skates and join the others. It was a delight to watch her moving swiftly without having to chase after her. I kept wishing she'd look up and I'd see her face and she'd wave. I concentrated so on her that I hardly noticed the gloom once more on the increase, and the other skaters growing fewer as they broke away to glide from the rink, and the low murmur of comment growing around me. It was as if there were an invisible spotlight on her.

And then there entered the rink with a rush, skidding to a near stop at its center, an amazing figure of clownish comedy, so that the murmur around me changed to laughter. It was that of a man in a wonderfully authentic tawny-pale lion's costume with more of a real lion's mask than a man's face, as with the Cowardly Lion in *The Wizard of Oz,* so that for a moment (but a moment only) I recalled my fantasy of the library lion coming to life. The girl in green came smoothly gliding toward him, as if they were supposed to waltz together, and he moved to meet her but then skidded off at an unlikely angle, fighting to keep his balance, and the laughter rose obediently.

It went on like that for a while, the lion proceeding around the rink in a series of staggering rushes and skids, flailing his front paws (his arms) in every direction, the girl circling him solicitously and invitingly, dipping in toward him and out, to the accompaniment of the laughter.

But then the scene grew darker still, as if the invisible spotlights were failing, and the grating of the lion's skates against the ice louder as he skidded (so that my library-lion fantasy came uneasily back to my mind), and he moved more slowly and drooped his great maned mask as if he were sick, so that his efforts to keep balance became more pathetic than comical, and the laughter, and then all the other sounds too, died away as though someone had turned on a tap marked "Silence."

And then he collapsed in a sprawling heap on the ice and the girl reached him in one long glide and knelt low over him, and the darkness became so great that I could no longer see the green in her visored cap or in her cloak trailed on the ice behind her, or in the gloves on her hands cupping his huge jowls, and the gloom closed in completely.

It was then that my trick of concentrating on the pavement just ahead of me (there was light enough for that, it was lighter up here) and not looking at faces (there were people crowding around me now, though they made no noise) stood me in good stead, so that I was able to get away, step by step, from the sunken court of the skating rink drowned in inky darkness.

I don't know with certainty what my intentions were then. I think they were to get down to her somehow and help her with her unfortunate partner. At any rate, one way or another, letting myself move with the crowd here, clutching along a stair rail there, I did manage to descend several levels, one of them by escalator, until I finally emerged into that brightly lit, somewhat low-ceilinged world of dingy white tile which underlies so much of New York.

There was one difference, however. Although the place was lined with colorful busy storefronts, and marked with arrow-trails leading to various street exits and subways, and although there were throngs and scatters of people following along them, everything went silently, or at most with a seashell-roaring suggestion of muted noise, as if I had actually gone temporarily deaf from a great but unremembered sound, or else descended rapidly from a very great height and my ears not yet adjusted to it.

Just then I was caught up in a hurrying crowd of people coming from one of the subway entrances, so thick a crowd that I was forced to move with it for a ways while I edged sideways to get free. And then this crowd was in turn further constrained by another crowd pushing in the opposite direction—into the subway—so that my efforts to extricate myself were further hampered. And then, while I was in that situation, just being hemmed in and carried along, I saw my young woman in green in the same predicament as myself, apparently, but in the other crowd, so that she was being carried toward and then past me. I saw her face at last: It was rather narrow and somehow knifelike with glowing hazel eyes, and I got the instant impression of invincible youth strangely matured before its time. She looked angry and somewhat disheveled, her green cap pushed back with visor askew and brown hair foaming out from under it. She didn't have her lion man being crowded along with her (*that* would have been a sight, I told myself—and might have gained her some space, too) but she *was* carrying, clutched to her chest, a pale-tan long-haired cat. And then, just when she'd been carried opposite me and I unable for the moment to move a step closer to her—there must have been a dozen people between us; we could only see each other clearly because we were both quite tall—why, just then she looked straight at me and her hazel eyes widened and her brown eyebrows went up, and lifting one cupped hand alongside her lips while she clutched her cat more closely with the other, she twice called something to me, working her lips and face as though she were trying to enunciate very clearly, before she was rapidly carried away out of my sight—and all the lights around me dimmed a little. I made a real effort to get free and follow her then, but it only resulted in a minor altercation that further delayed me—a woman I was squeezing past snarled at me, and as I begged her pardon while still trying to get past, a man beside her grabbed me and told me to quit shoving and I grabbed his elbows and shook him a bit in turn, while still apologizing. By that time the crowd had started to melt away, but it seemed too late now to go tearing after the girl into the subway. Besides, I was still trying to make sure of and puzzle out the cryptic message I thought she'd called to me—actually I was pretty sure of it, what with my hearing having gotten somewhat better and a bit of reading of her lips as they carefully shaped the few words. Twice.

Spoken in the manner of someone who announces a change of rendezvous or a place to get together in case of separation, the repeated message was simply: "Cortlandt Street. Tower Two. The Deck."

Now that wasn't cryptic at all, I told myself, now that I'd hope-fully got it down straight. Cortlandt Street was simply a subway address of the World Trade Center, Tower Two was the southern-most of the lofty twins, and the 107th floor was the observation deck with the open-air promenade on the 110th, the roof, to which you could go by a long three-story escalator—I knew all about that. I'd been up there myself only two days ago to enjoy the magnificent view of Manhattan, Queens, Brooklyn, the East River and the Hudson, Staten Island, the Jersey shore. It lay on the same subway line (only a few stations farther along) I'd be taking myself in a bit to get back to where I was visiting with my son in Greenwich Village.

For I wasn't going aboveground in this locality again today—that much I was sure of. I was no longer so sure of exactly what had happened up there, how much had been due to a weird weather change or a confusion about time (though a wall clock told me just then that it was still more than an hour until sunset) and how much had been subjective, a matter of my mood and the strange directions my imagination had taken. There are people who get panicky in crowds and narrow places, such as big city streets, they actually go crazy. I'd never had any trouble that way that I knew of, but there's always a first time. In fact, there are all sorts of strange things that happen to you and you find out about yourself as you grow older. Such as playing a game with yourself of pretending to be attracted to younger and younger women and following them in the street. All sorts of nonsense. (Another part of my mind was reminding me that her message to me had been real and that she had touched the library lion and skated with a sick lion-man and been carrying a long-haired cat of the same color when last seen. What was to be made of that?) But however much nonsense or no, nonsense and vivid daydreams, I wasn't going to go up to Rockefeller Plaza again today and look down into the Pool of Planets or the skating rink. No, I wasn't going to do that.

As my thoughts reached that point, the underground lights flickered again, shadows racing across the white tile, and dimmed down another notch. "What's the matter with the lights?" I involuntarily demanded aloud, fighting to keep the note of panic out of my voice.

The man who happened to be shuffling past me at that moment was quite short. He was wearing a black overcoat worn smooth in spots with a dusty-looking astrakhan collar. His head was bowed under the weight of a black derby, also worn shiny in spots, and he had it pulled down to his jutting ears, making them jut out still farther.

He halted and lifted his face toward mine (it took quite a swing of his head) and I got a considerable minor shock, for covering his entire face below his eyes was a white gauze mask such as the Japanese favor during cold epidemics. But it wasn't altogether white by any means. Centered on it were two coal-black spots where his nostrils would be underneath. Each was surrounded by a wide grey border fading up to white at a distance of about two inches from the dull jet centers. They overlapped, of course. While below them was a horizontal grey-bordered line only less black marking his mouth. I wondered in what atmosphere he could have been all day to have accumulated so much pollution. Or had he worn the same mask for several days?

Then, keeping his fierce dark eyes fixed on mine, he growled somewhat muffledly (the mask) but in the measured tones of an originally mild man grown truculent, even recklessly so, with the years and repeated disillusion, "So what's the matter with the lights? Nothing's the matter with the lights. They're always like that— only sometimes worse. This is a little above average. Where have you been all your life?"

"I'm just visiting New York," I told him. "My son."

"So who visits New York?" he demanded, continuing to eye me suspiciously. "We should be so lucky as to be somewhere else. Your son hasn't gotten away yet? That's terrible. My condolences."

I didn't quite know how to answer that one, so I just continued to look at him sideways. Somehow while talking we'd begun to walk on slowly together toward the subway.

"So what's with *this,* you're asking maybe?" he said challengingly, indicating his mask. "The old schmuck has got the crazies about germs, they're trying to assassinate him? That's what my wife thought, and my brother-in-law the druggist, when I started to wear it." He shook his head slowly and emphatically. "No, my friend, I'm not afraid of germs. Germs and me, we get on all right, we got an understanding, things in common. Because germs are alive. No, it's the dead Dreck I don't want none of, the Guck (that's the goyish word for it), the black foam."

His muffled, muttering voice was indescribably odd. There was nothing wrong about my hearing now, incidentally. I searched for a relationship between the visual and auditory dimmings I'd been experiencing, but there didn't seem to be any, their cycles didn't jibe.

I was going to ask him what industry or business the black foam figured in, though it didn't sound like a very specific thing, but by then we were at the subway. I half expected him to head uptown for the Bronx, but he stuck with me and changed with me a station or two later to the IRT.

"I'm getting off at Fourteenth Street," I volunteered, adding after a moment, "Or maybe I'll go on to Cortlandt. You were saying something about black—"

"So why shouldn't you?" he demanded, interrupting. "Or change your mind as much as you want? Myself, I change at Chambers and keep on to Brooklyn. You're thinking it's maybe queer I live in Brooklyn? That's where my brother-in-law's got his drugstore. He's very ambitious—wants to be a chemist. Now about the black foam, the Dreck, I'm the expert on that, believe me, I'm your rabbi there, because I foresaw its coming before anyone else." And he turned toward me and laid a hand on my forearm and gripped it, and he fixed on me his dark eyes above the filthy mask.

We were sitting side by side on one of the long seats in a car that was more than three-quarters empty, the windows and walls crawling with graffiti that were hard to read because the lights were dimming and flickering so. The other passengers paid us no heed, locked in their thoughts or stupefactions. As the train set off with a lurch and a low screech, he began.

"You remember when detergents first started getting in sewage and mounding up in rivers and lakes, killing the fishes—mountains of white foam that wouldn't go away? The Guck, the Dreck began like that, only black, and it came from the air and crawling along the ground and working up from under the ground. The street-washing trucks couldn't pick it up, not all of it, brooms and hoses couldn't move it, it built up in corners and cracks and angles. And people ignored it, pretended it wasn't there, like they always do at first with muggings and trashings and riots and war and death. But I could see it. Sometimes I was sure I was the only one, but sometimes I thought my niece Chana could see it too and admit it to herself—Chana, a very nice, delicate girl, refined and plays the piano—from the way she looked quick out the window and then away and washed her hands over and over. Chana and her cat, who stopped going out. I watched the Dreck getting thicker and thicker, building up higher and higher, blacker and blacker—the black foam."

"But why a foam?" I asked him. "Why not just dirt or dust?"

"Because it clings and smears and creeps, don't blow like dust. Comes through the air, but once it lands, don't blow no more. You know those foams the firemen got that shut in fire, strangle it to death? The Guck works the same with life, you should believe me.

"When I started wearing this mask and making my wife stop opening windows ever and never open an inside door without shutting the outside one, she decides I'm getting sensitive (her nice word for the crazies, maybe) and wants her brother recommend a doctor should give me shots. 'So now I'm sensitive, am I?' I say to her." (He lifted a finger to his mask's center.) " 'Then what's this?' I ask her. 'Poppy seeds? You maybe want to try filling a blintz with it?' "

We ground to a stop at the Fourteenth Street platform and after a while the doors slid shut with hollow thuds and we humped out of it, and I'd had no thought of getting off. I was spellbound by the way this man's grotesque tale of his paranoia, or whatever, fitted with my own experiences and fantasies this afternoon, as if it were the same story (a black story!) told in a different language or as if it were perhaps a contagious insanity manifesting itself differently, but with one basic theme, in each victim.

My Ancient Mariner of the Subway continued, still fixing me with his glittering dark eye, "When the Dreck got so bad everyone had to admit it, then my brother-in-law was the first comes to me, you should expect it, with all sorts of explanations of what it was and why it wasn't so bad as it looked, we should love it maybe.

" 'The scientists understand it and are learning to control it,' he tells me, like we should celebrate.

" 'Which means they can't do anything about it right now?' I say. 'Is that news?'

" 'It is the ultimate para-terminal waste product,' he says, holding up a finger like a professor (the words he's got! like he's a Doctor of Dreck! and he repeats himself until I've learned them by heart, *Zeeser Gottenyu!*), 'created by a catalytic action of various industrial wastes on each other under conditions of extreme congestion. As a result it has maximum stasis—'

" 'It stays, all right,' I say, 'if that's what you're getting at.'

" '—and is the ultimate in unbiodegradable paraplastics,' he keeps on with.

" 'It's degrading to us,' I agree. 'And it's making us all into paraplegics, *nu?*'

"He tries again with, 'In a very general way, simplifying it for the layman, it is as if the organic, under unprecedented pressures, were trying to return to the inorganic, and succeeding only too well.'

" 'If you mean it's black death spreading itself like sour cream, covering everything, I knew it already. Tell me, was it invented at Dachau or Belsen?' "

Christopher Street went by, Houston, Canal. Sluggish passengers braved the dim stations. The car emptied. The masked man kept on, quoting his brother-in-law.

" 'In structure,' he says, making with the finger again, 'it is a congeries'—*Oy, Gottenyu,* his words!—'of microscopic bubbles that are monomolecular, hence black—'

" 'Ah-ha! Like poppy seeds! I was just telling Rivke', I say.

" '—and in many ways it behaves like a para-liquid, a gas of fixed volume—'

" 'It's fixed us,' I tell him, 'and it's keeping on fixing.'

" '—but it has been proven by scientists,' he keeps up, so I can't get a word in, 'to be absolutely noncarcinogenic, completely inert, and therefore utterly harmless!'

" 'So why won't Chana's cat go out in it?' I ask him."

The train slowed. My companion stood up. "Chambers Street, I should change," he explained. He placed his hands on my shoulders. "You should stay on. Your stop is next, Cortlandt. But, pardon me, you should get yourself a mask if you don't mind me telling you. They've started to carry them at cigar stores, so you shouldn't get Dreck in your tobacco smoke. Goodbye, it's been a pleasure listening to you."

I heard the sliding doors thud shut. I looked around. The car was empty. I wasn't exactly frightened, but I stood up and continued to look around as we surged along, and when the doors opened at the next stop, after having seemed to hesitate deliberately for a long moment, I felt a gust of relief and I slid out quickly.

As I did so, a somewhat silly mood of nervous, high-spirited excitement boiled up in me without warning. The afternoon's happenings would make a great vaudeville act, I told myself, for the young woman in green to tour in—and I'd tell her so if I ever caught up with her, and maybe be her manager. She'd have herself—a graceful girl's always an attraction—and her clumsy lion man, and the little Jewish comedian from the bad old days of broad racial humor. We'd put him on skates too. Would he be afraid of the lion? Of course. But his dirty mask would have to go. On him it might make people think of concentration camps and suffocation. We'd have to do something about that.

The white tile underworld was loftier and cleaner here and brighter too (no dimming or muting, at least at the moment—my eyes and ears seemed working okay). The only thing I wondered about was the absence of hurrying crowds at rush hour—until I remembered it was Saturday.

I wandered with the other mostly solitary movers across those fantastically large underground pleasances, not hurrying particularly but taking long strides, relishing the exercise. We were like ants in a giant's bathroom, each on our separate linear course.

My companions grew fewer as I progressed, and by the time I had purchased my ticket and reached the massive underpinnings of Tower Two, unobtrusive in a vast gleaming, science-fictional, multistoried hall hung with great panels of aluminum and plates of glass, I was alone. And I alone was lofted on the endlessly mounting steps of the silvery escalator to the high mezzanine, so that I had a comically grandiose vision of myself as Ludwig the Mad King of Bavaria on my way to a performance at the royal theatre that had only one seat in it. On the mezzanine I quickened my stride, thinking of how frustrating it would be to move more slowly and just miss a trip and have to wait, so that by the time I rounded a corner into the alcove of the express elevator I was almost running.

The elevator was in, but its big silvery doors had just begun to close.

I am a man who almost never acts on impulse, but this time I did. I sprinted forward and managed to get aboard, encountering at the last moment an odd physical resistance I had to force my way through, with an extra effort, though I was in the clear and didn't have to squeeze past persons or the closing doors—it was something invisible, more like a science-fictional field.

Then the doors closed and the car began to mount and I realized that it was completely dark inside and that I couldn't remember seeing any people in it; my eyes had been only on the closing doors.

No, not completely dark. High on the back wall a small ghostly white light was moving from left to right behind the numbers of the floors. But it wasn't enough light to show anything else, at least not to my unadjusted vision.

I asked myself what the devil could have happened. Was I the only passenger, going up on automatic? But this express elevator always carried an operator, didn't it? Also I recalled there had been a spiel (live or recorded?) about the more-than-quarter-mile nonstop vertical trip lasting less than a minute, the more-than-twenty-mile-per-hour vertical speed, and so on. There wasn't now.

I listened intently. After a bit I began to hear, from the point to my left where I'd recalled the operator standing, a very faint strange croaking and breathy whining, the sort of sound a deaf-and-dumb person makes when he's trying hard to communicate—perhaps as if such a person were thinking hard to himself.

I moved involuntarily to my right and forward without encountering anyone—or thing. I remembered the door at the top was the back of the elevator, opposite to what it was at the bottom. Was the trip going to last forever? The ghost light was hardly halfway across the wall. Would the door at the top open?

I could no longer hear the "deaf-and-dumb" breathing. Was that because of the distance I'd moved or the blood pounding in my ears? Or had the breather stopped thinking and begun to take action? How did one pass time like this while holding still? Playing a routine chess opening in one's head? Reciting the prime numbers under one hundred? Counting the coins in one's pocket by feel? No, they might chink.

The cage stopped. A vertical crack of dull light appeared ahead of me and I squeezed through as soon as it was wide enough. I took a dozen forward steps measuredly, started to turn around, but didn't. I listened uneasily for footsteps behind me.

There was a sound. I turned. The silver doors had closed and the space between me and them was empty.

Then I noticed that the doors themselves were blotched and corroded, the floor under my shoes was faintly gritty, there was an oily, coaly stench in my nostrils, though the air felt dry as a desert's and was *blowing* (indoors!), the place was unnaturally silent except for the air's windy sighing, and there was something very strange about the light.

I turned again and moved cautiously out of the elevator's alcove.

The layout of the enclosed observation deck is very simple. A broad corridor made up of continuous windows on the outside runs all the way around, making a great square. Along the inner wall are murals, displays, booths for attendants, that sort of thing. I was in the corridor on the building's east side.

I looked both ways and didn't see a soul, neither visitors nor the deck's personnel. But I did see trails of footprints and of at least one wheeled vehicle in the dull dust coating the floor.

I couldn't see much of anything out of the windows, at least from where I stood back from them in the middle of the corridor. They seemed to be very dusty, too, and through the dust there wasn't anything visible outside but a dark expanse lightening toward the top and streaked with a dull sunset red. There were no inside lights on.

I didn't approach the windows any closer but walked quietly north in search of an explanation for the incredible transformation that had occurred—or the weird hallucination from which I was suffering. Can one walk through a hallucination one is having? For some reason that question didn't seem nonsensical to me then. Exactly how are inner and outer space related?

The dry, insect-wailing wind brushed my face with its feathery touch. It seemed icy now on my forehead and cheeks because of its rapid evaporation of my sweat of fear. And now, through it, I could hear other noises from ahead: faint rutchings, creakings, and gratings, as if some heavy object were with difficulty being moved. I myself moved more slowly then, in the end hardly at all as, holding my breath, I peered sidewise down the north corridor.

This one wasn't empty. Halfway along it a dozen black-clad figures, black-hooded and black-trousered, were at work where two of the observation windows had been jaggedly smashed open to the dark, reddening sky. Through that large gap came the dry wind that now blew against me more strongly. About half the black figures were busy manhandling a gun (from the first I knew it was a gun) so that it pointed north out the gap. The weapon, formed of a grayish metal, resembled a field piece of the world wars, but there were perplexing differences. The barrel was pointed sharply upward like a mortar's, but was longer, more like that of a recoilless rifle. The breech bulged unnaturally—too big. It was mounted on a carriage with small wheels that seemed to turn with difficulty, judging from the way the black figures strained at it, while beside it on a squat tripod was a steaming cauldron heated by a small fire built on the floor.

The other six or seven figures were closely grouped around the edges of the gap and peering out of it intently and restlessly, as though on watch and guard for something in the sky. Each held ready, close against him, a small missile weapon of some sort.

All the figures were silent, appearing to communicate by some sort of sign language that involved twitchings of the head and grippings of one another's upper arms and legs—perhaps a language more of touch than visual signs.

Despite their silence, there was such a venom and hatred, such a killer's eagerness, about the way the gunhandlers heaved at their cranky weapon, strained and touch-talked, and in the window guards the same, though in them mixed more with dread, that my genitals contracted and my stomach fluttered and I wanted to retch.

Inch by inch I withdrew, thankful for their single-minded intentness on the gap and for the crepe soles of my shoes. I retraced my path past the elevator, its blotched doors still shut at the back of the shadowy recess, and peered with circumspection into the southern corridor. It seemed as empty as the one I was in. The windows at its far end glowed red with sunset light. A short distance along it, the escalator to the open observation deck on the roof three storys above began its straight-line ascent. Its treads weren't moving (I hardly needed visual confirmation of that), but up through it the dry wind, now on my neck, seemed to be blowing out, escaping from this floor.

I had no desire to explore the red-lit west corridor, the only one I hadn't peered along, or to wait by the stained doors of the elevator. The oily, coaly stench was sickening me. I began the long ascent of the stalled escalator.

At first I went slowly, to avoid noise, then I speeded up nervously from the dry wind's pressure on my back and its faint whistlings, and in my feelings a queer mixture of claustrophobia and fear of exposure—the feeling of being in a long, narrow opening. Then I slowed down to avoid getting winded. And the last few steps I took very slowly, for fear of running into a guard (or whatever) at the top—that and a certain hesitation to see what I would see.

Spying from the entry, I first closely surveyed the open observation deck—really just a wide, railed, rectangular catwalk, supported by a minimum of metal framework, about fifteen feet above and twenty feet back from the edges of the flat roof of the building proper, those edges having a stout high mesh fence, the top wires of which were electrified to further discourage would-be suicide jumpers and such. (I knew these details from my earlier visit.)

I didn't spot anyone or anything in the twilight (anyone standing or crouching, at least), though there was the opposite exit structure matching mine, around which it would be possible to hide, and at one point the railing was gone and a slanting ladder led down to the roof—a crude stairs. Also a good deal of the outer fence appeared to have been torn away, though I didn't try to check that very closely.

Thus reassured (if you can call it that), I straightened up, walked out, and looked around. First to the west where a flattened sun, deep red and muted enough to look at without hurt, was about to go beneath the Jersey horizon. Its horizontal rays gave the low heavens a furnace glow that made "the roof of Hell" a cliché no longer, though lower down the sky was dark.

The horizon all around looked *higher* than it ought to be. From it in toward me stretched an absolutely flat black plain, unbroken save for several towers, mostly toward the north, their western walls uniformly red-lit by the sunset, their long shadows stretching endlessly to the east, a few of the towers rather tall but some quite squat.

I looked in vain for the streets of New York, for the lights that should be coming on (and becoming more apparent) by now, for the Hudson and East rivers, for the bay with its islands and for the Narrows.

None of those things were there, only the dull ebon plain, across which the dry north wind blew ceaselessly. Oh, the utter flatness of that plain! It was like the waters of an absolutely still great lake, not a quiver in it, thickly filmed with coal dust and across which spiders might run.

And then I began to recognize the towers by their tops. That one to the north, the tallest in that direction except for one at almost twice the distance, its somewhat rounded stepbacks were unmistalkable—Kong-unmistakable. It was the Empire State shrunken to less than half its height without a corresponding diminishment in breadth. And that still slender spire was the top quarter of the graceful Chrysler Building, its bottom three quarters chopped off by (were they beneath?) the plain. And there was the RCA Building at Rockefeller Center where I'd just been—the top hundred feet of it.

But what were those two structures rather taller (allowing for differences in distance) than the Empire State? One mostly truncated pyramid, the most distant northern one; the other to the northeast, about where the United Nations enclave would be. Were they buildings built after my...well, I had to face up to the possibility of time travel, didn't I?

And there were lights, I began to see now, as the red western walls started to darken—a very few windows scattered here and there among the towers. One of them was in a most modest structure nearby—hardly four storys with a pyramidal roof. I knew it from boyhood, the Woolworth Building, New York's tallest in 1920 and for some years after, which the black plain had almost inundated.

Yes, the black plain, which lay only some five or six hundred feet beneath me, not the thirteen hundred and fifty it ought to be.

And then I knew with an intuitive, insane certainty the black plain's nature. It was the final development of the Guck, the Dreck, the sinister, static, ineradicable foam, the coming of which the old Jew had described to me.

But how in hell could there be *this* much accumulation of waste of whatever sort, seven or eight hundred feet of it? Unless one imagined the whole process as being catalytic in some way and reaching and overpassing some critical value (analogous to fission and fusion temperatures in atomics), after which the process became self-perpetuating and self-devouring—"Death taking over," as he'd said.

And how far, in God's name, did the black plain extend? To the ends of the Earth? It would take more than the melting of a couple of black icecaps to do that to the planet. Oh, I was beginning to think in a crazy way, I told myself....

At the same time a line from the cauldron scene in *Macbeth* joggled its way to the surface of my mind: "Make the gruel thick and slab..."

But the gruel wouldn't have to be thick, I reminded myself with insane cunning, because it was composed of microscopic *bubbles.* That would stretch the Guck, make it seem that there was much more Dreck than there really was. And it wouldn't be solid and massy like liquids are, but feathery and soft as finest soot or new-fallen snow, hundreds of feet of it....

New-fallen black snow....

But if the stuff were foam, why didn't it mound up in hillocks and humps, like the life-choking detergent foams the old Jew had talked about? What force, what unnatural surface tension, constrained it to lie flat as a stagnant pond?

And why did I keep coming back to *his* ideas, monotonously? My intuition was insane, all right, as insane as what was happening to me, or as his own paranoid ideas—or mine. I shook my head to clear it of them all and to stir myself to action, and I began to move around the catwalk, studying my closer surroundings. The first thing to catch my eye and almost stop me was the wire-hung narrow suspension bridge connecting the northwest corner of this roof with the nearest corner of the roof of Tower One. It was a primitive affair, the junkyard equivalent of a jungle structure of bamboo and braided vines. The two main wires or thin cables, guyed through holes driven in the roof edges, also served as its rails, from which was flimsily suspended the narrow footway made of sections of thin aluminum sheeting of varying lengths. It swayed a little and creaked and sang in the dry wind from the north.

I could see no figures or movement on the roof of Tower One, though another of its corners was simply gone for twenty feet or so, as if gigantically chopped or bitten off.

I came to the first right-angle turn (to the east) in the catwalk and (just beyond it) the gap in the rail where the ladder went down.

Scanning north again, I saw the last red highlights on the scanty cluster of towers fade as the crouched-down scarlet sun flattened itself completely behind the western horizon, but the hell glow lingered on the low, cramping sky, under which that dry wind from the pole blew on and blew. Squinting my eyes against it, I thought I saw shapes in movement, soaring and flapping, around the most distant northern tower, the tall, unfamiliar, mysterious one. If they were fliers and were really there, they were gigantic, I told myself uneasily.

My gaze dropped down to the lowly pale Woolworth tower with its single dim light and I noticed that its roof edge was damaged somewhat like that of Tower One, and I had a vision (the soaring shapes had paved the way for it) of a vast dragon's head with jaws agape (and mounted on a long neck like that of a plesiosaur) emerging from the black plain and menacing the structure, while great dull black ripples spread out from it in ever-widening circles. Another scrap of poetry came to my mind, Lanier's "But who will reveal to our waking ken/The forms that swim and the shapes that creep/Under the waters of sleep?"

As I mused on that, I heard a not very loud but nevertheless arresting sound, a gasp of indrawn breath. Glancing sharply ahead along the catwalk, I saw, near the exit structure, something that may or may not have been there before (I could have missed it in my survey): a body sprawled flat with that attitude of finality about it which indicates utter exhaustion, unconsciousness, or death. It was clad in what looked in the dusk dark green—cloak, cap, gloves...and trousers.

Before I could begin to sort out my reactions to that sight (although I instantly moved softfootedly toward it), another dark-green-clad figure emerged swiftly from the exit-structure and swiftly knelt to the sprawled form in a way that was complete identification for me. I had seen that identical movement earlier today, though then it had been on skates.

When I was less than a dozen feet away, I said, clearing my throat, "Excuse me, but can I be of any help to you?"

She writhed to her feet with the sinuous swiftness of a cobra rearing and faced me tensely across the dead or insensate form, her eyes blazing with danger and menace in the last light from the west. I almost cringed from her. Then there was added a look of tentative recognition, of counting up.

"You're the man in the subway," she said rapidly. "Neutral, possibly favorable, at least not actively hostile—I took a chance on you and that's how I still read you. The man from Elsewhen."

"The subway, yes," I said. "I don't know about the Elsewhen part. I presume from what I see I've time-traveled, but I've always thought that time travel, if such a thing could possibly be, would be instantaneous, not by a weird, crooked series of transformations and transitions."

"Then you were wrong," she said, rather impatiently. "You don't do *anything* all at once in the universe. To get from here to there you traverse a space-time between. Even light moves a step at a time. There are no instantaneous transitions, though there are short-cuts, no actions at a distance. There are no miracles."

"And as for being possibly favorable," I went on, "I've already asked if I could help you."

"You say that as lightly as if it meant tipping your hat or holding a door open. You don't know what you're getting into," she assured me. "You saw the men on the lower deck?"

"The men in black with the gun, yes."

"You mention the gun. That's good," she commented quickly, and for the first time there was a hint in her voice and look that I might be accepted. She went on, "That's the gun my brother and I were going to knock out, when...when..." Her gaze flickered down toward the flattened form, dark green, death pale, between us, and her voice stumbled.

"I'm terribly sorry—" I began.

"Please!—no sympathy," she interrupted. "We haven't time and I haven't the strength. Now listen to me. In this age the blackness has almost buried New York. We are the sole survivors, we in these two towers and like lonely groups in those out there, a desolate few." She indicated the scattered tops to the north and around. "We should be brothers in adversity. Yet all that those men on the lower deck can feel is hate, hate for all men in other towers than their own, hate and the fears from which their hatred grew—dread of the blackness and of other things. They dress in black because they fear it so and hope so to gain for themselves all the cruel power and exulting evil they read in it, while their avoidance of spoken language is another tribute to their fear—in point, the Guck's their god, their devil-god."

She paused, then commented, "Man lacks imagination, doesn't he? Or even a mere talent for variety in his reactions. Sometimes it seems appropriate he should drown squealing in the dark."

I said, uneasy at this chilly philosophizing, "I'd think you'd be afraid they'd come up here and find us. I wonder that they haven't posted guards."

She shook her head. "They never come out under the sky unless they have to. They fear the birds—the birds and other things."

Before I could ask her another question she resumed the main thread of her talk. "And so all that those men on the lower deck can think to do is to destroy all other towers save their own. That is the business they're about just now (the business of the gun) and one on which they concentrate ferociously—another reason we needn't fear them surprising us here.

"Someday," she said, and for a moment her voice grew wistful, "someday we may be able to change their hearts and minds. But now all we can do is take away their tools, remove their weapon, the gun that's capable of killing buildings.

"And so now, sir," she said briskly, looking toward me, "will you aid me in this venture, knowing the risks? Will you play the part my brother would have played—receive my fire? For I must tell you that *my* weapon requires both a firer and a receiver. One soul can't work it. Also it works only against their weapon, not against them (I would not wish it otherwise), and so it cannot save us from their afterwrath. Escaping will be your own business, with my help. How say you, sir?"

It sounded crazy, but I was in a crazy situation and my feelings fitted themselves to it—and I remembered the sickening venomousness I had sensed in the black-clad men below.

"I'll help you," I told her in a low, choked voice, swallowing hard and nodding sharply.

She laughed, and with a curtsy to her brother's corpse, knelt by it again and from a pouch at the belt removed something which she held out to me.

"Your receiver, sir," she said gaily, smiling over it. "Your far-focus, yin to the yang of mine. I believe you have seen something like it earlier today. Here, take it, sir."

It was a pale brown cube with rounded corners, about as big as a golf ball and surprisingly heavy. When I looked at it close up I saw that it was the figure of a lioness crouching, quite stylized, the body all drawn together to fit the cubic form—one face of the cube, for instance, was all proud, glaring head and forepaws. It was a remarkable piece, so far as I could make out in the dusk. The eyes appeared to flash, though it seemed all of one material.

"Here is its mate," she said, "my near-focus, my firer," and she held close to my eyes for a long moment a like figure of a maned lion. "And now the plan. It is only necessary that we be on opposite sides of our target, in this case the gun, so that I may weave the web and you anchor it. When we get to the foot of the long stair, you go to the left, I'll to the right. Walk rapidly but quietly as you can to the end corridor they're in. Stand in the middle of it facing them and holding the receiver in front of you. It doesn't matter if it's hidden in your fist, only don't stir then and whatever happens, don't drop it." She chuckled. "You won't have to wait long for me once you get there. Oh, and one other thing. Although your receiver is no weapon against them afterwards, except to weight your fist— no weapon at all without the aid of mine—it has one virtue: If you lack for air (as, *viz.*, they use the Guck on you) hold it close to your nostrils or your lips. That, I believe, is all." She gently clapped her left arm around the back of my waist from where she was standing close beside me and looked up a bit at me and said, "So, sir, let's go.

"But first," she added somewhat comically, "my thanks for your companioning in this venture. Ill met and worse to follow!" And she leaned around laughingly and rather quickly kissed me.

As our lips were pressed together there came a jarringly loud sound from close below. It sounded like a giant cough from very deep in a dark throat. As we pulled apart, turning each toward the north, we saw an incandescent scarlet line rapidly mounting out from the tower beneath, belched from the midst of a spreading smoke puff. It soared across the last darkening carmine streaks of sunset in the top of the sky, seemed to hang there, then fell more and more rapidly through the last of its parabolic course and was extinguished (it seemed) in the black plain short of the Empire State. But then began a churning and a mounding and a glowing in the Guck, ending in a tumultuous eruption of blackness and flame. I was vividly reminded of depth-charging at night, only this glare was redder. And the flash seemed to last longer too, for by its darkening red glow I saw the façade of the Empire State hugely spotched and pied with inky black—napalm that didn't burn.

I was losing my balance—it was my companion dragging at my arm. "Come on," she yelled. "Same plan, only we run."

We ran. Halfway to the stalled escalator we were given an extra shove by the great muffled thunderclap of the explosion. I pounded down the dark silvery, gritty stairs, recklessly for me, watching her draw farther and farther ahead. And then, by God, I heard her *whistling* loud in a fast, rocking rhythm. It was the *cavalry charge,* so help me!

She waited at the bottom to point me left, make sure I got it. And then as I was loping down the west corridor, nearing my goal, the windows ahead of me were painted with a bright red flash against which the small figure of the Empire State was silhouetted. This time they'd struck beyond her, had her bracketed. The third shell...

I shot into the north corridor and came to an arm-waving halt just as the dark glass ahead of me bent inward, but did not shatter, with the second muffled thunderclap. And then I faced myself at where the bent black figures were toiling exultantly in their reloading and I held my receiver out in front of me. I remember I held it gripped between right thumb and bent forefinger with the lioness' head looking at them (that seemed important, though the girl hadn't said so) and with my left hand gripped around my right. My legs were bent and spread wide too, so that I must have looked like some improbably elderly macho with a magnum straight out of TV.

I didn't see her arrive beyond them (she was probably there ahead of me) but suddenly my conjoined hands were tingling and there was a narrow sheaf of bright violet lines fanning out from that double fist to touch the extremities of the ugly gun and around it illumine staring ghost eyes and spectral mouths gaping with surprise within black hoods, before they drew together again (the violet lines) into a glowing point which showed me, just above it, very tiny—her face—for all the world as if she and I were playing cat's cradle together with the fluorescent violet string, the gun the figure we'd created.

The tingling spread to my arms and shoulders, but I didn't drop my receiver or writhe around very much.

Then the lines vanished (and my hands stopped tingling) but a swirled Kirlian aura of the same shade of violet hung around the gun, making it glow all over as though new-forged and highlighting the frozen figures around it. Then one of those figures reached out slowly and fearfully and touched the muzzle, and at that point a very fine iridescent violet snowfall began, the individual flakes winking out before they touched the deck, and the snowfall spreading rapidly, eating its way into the glowing metal, until the entire gun had trickled away into dust.

The frozen figures broke then into such a frenzy of arm- and thigh-gripping, and head-twitching, that it was like a battle (or an orgy) in a soundless hell. Then most of them raced away from me, but two toward me, and I heard a high sweet whistling, three mounting notes. She was sounding taps, the *retreat*.

I was already in flight. The west corridor seemed longer than it had coming. She was waiting for me again at the foot of the escalator, but started up as soon as she saw me. I'd not mounted a dozen steps when the faint tattoo of our pursuers' footsteps was abruptly amplified as they poured into the south corridor. It didn't so much frighten me as make me feel wild—an unfamiliar sort of excitement.

I was panting before I was halfway up. I could hear her breathing hard too, though I think she deliberately slowed down so as not to get too far ahead. When I got to the top I did a foolish, show-off thing—I took the deepest gasping breath I could and then turned and bellowed inarticulately down the stairs—roared, you might say, perhaps in honor of the lioness clenched in my fist. And then I went dancing out onto the catwalk, not straight ahead following her, but around the opposite way, with some crazy idea of drawing the pursuit away from her, and pausing to turn and bellow nastily once or twice more.

My storybook ruse didn't work at all. The main body of our silent pursuers went racing after her without even hesitating, though a couple did come skulking after me. She paused at the railing gap to shake her fist at me, or wave me on, I don't know which, and then she ran down the slanting ladder, and across the roof to its northwest corner, and up and out onto the rickety suspension bridge. Two of her pursuers stopped and made hurling motions, there were sharp reports and then two bright white lights were floating above her head and then slowly past her—star-grenades, to give them a name.

She was halfway across the bridge when a swarm of figures appeared at its other end. The glare showed them to be black-clad, black-hooded. She stopped. Then, pausing only for a sweeping gesture of defiance—or a wave of farewell—she ducked under one of the main wires and dove down head first, her green cloak trailing behind her. Almost at once the roof edge cut her off from my sight and there were only the eagerly bent, black-hooded heads peering down.

And then, without warning, there was clapped over my face from behind a double handful of fine-grained darkness that was soft as soot, intimate as cobweb, somehow oily and dry at the same time, and instantly cutting off all sight and breath. In my convulsive struggles, during which I was thrown down on my back, I lifted my hands to my face and though I did not manage to tear whatever it was away, I became able to see through it dimly and draw shallow breaths. I made a supreme effort and then—

Have you ever begun to wake up from a nightmare that's happening in the same room you're actually sleeping in, and for a while been able to see both rooms at the same time, the nightmare one and the real one, almost coinciding but not quite? It was that way with me. It was night and I was down on my back on the open observation deck of Tower Two at the World Trade Center and there were people bent over me and handling me. And sometimes the sky would be utterly black and the faces hooded ones and the hands gripping cruelly to hurt. And then the dark sky would have a pale cast with reflected light and the faces open and solicitous, and the hands gentle and trying to help. After a brief but dizzying alteration the second scene won out, you might say, and I was drawn to my feet and supported and patted and told that a doctor had been summoned. Apparently I'd been walking along quite normally, enjoying the view (though one person maintained I'd looked troubled), when I'd suddenly collapsed in a faint or a fit. I offered no explanations, suppressed my agitation and astonishment as well as I could, and waited. I remember looking down from time to time at the diamond pattern of New York's street lights (they looked so *very* far below!) and being greatly reassured by that, so much so that once or twice I almost forgot why I felt so bereaved and forlorn.

I let myself be taken to the hospital, where they couldn't find much of anything wrong with me (except that after a bit I felt very tired) and from which my son retrieved me the next day. After a while I told him the whole story, but he's professed himself no more able than I am to decide between what seem to be the two chief possible explanations: that I suffered an extremely vivid and protracted hallucination, during which I moved through the World Trade Center completely blacked out (and possibly through the subway and Rockefeller Plaza in the same state), or that I actually time-traveled.

And if it were a hallucination, when did it begin? (Or if the other, when did *that* begin?) At the Pool of the Planets? Or even earlier, with my first glimpse of the Girl in Green? Or when I dashed into the express elevator and found it dark (there had been my feeling of breaking through a barrier at that point)? There are endless possibilities.

Did I hallucinate the old Jew, was he completely fabricated from materials in my unconscious? Or was he an intermediate stage in my time travel, belonging to an era somewhere between today and that blackly overwhelmed New York of the future? Or was he completely real, just one more freak at large in today's city?

My tired feeling afterwards convinced me of one thing—that whether an experience is real or hallucinatory (or a dream, for that matter, or even something you write), you always have to put the same amount of work into it, it takes the same energy, it takes as much out of you. Does that say something about outer and inner space? (My son says, "Don't dream so strenuously next time," though of course he says that's entirely my choice.)

If it *was* a hallucination, one thing that has to be explained is when and where I acquired the small and very heavy stylized sculpture of a lioness I had tightly clenched in my left fist at the end of my experience. No one has been able to identify the tawny material composing it, or its style or school, though resemblances have been noted to Bufano's work and to the stitcheries of Martha McElroy. I've experimented with it a bit, I admit, but it appears to have no mystical or weird scientific properties, though I do think it helps my breathing. I carry it as pocket piece now. Might come in handy some day—though I suppose that's a rather foolish thought.

As for the Young Woman in Green, I have a theory about her. I don't think she plunged to her death when she went off the suspension bridge between the two towers—she'd never have leaped off so lightheartedly unless she'd known she had a way of escape. No, I don't mean she sprouted wings or broke out a small jet or levitation unit after she'd fallen out of my sight. But from what the old Jew told me of the Dreck, and from my own observations of it I think it is like soft, powdery new-fallen snow, able to cushion any fall, from no matter how great a height. And I think there are ways of living in it, of moving and breathing, no matter how deeply one is buried. She implied as much when she told me about the additional virtue of my receiver. And she did have her firer with her at the end. I tell myself she survived.

In any case, my feelings about her are such that I would very much like to find her again, even if it were only to begin another hallucination.

Not Much Disorder and Not So Early Sex: An Autobiographic Essay

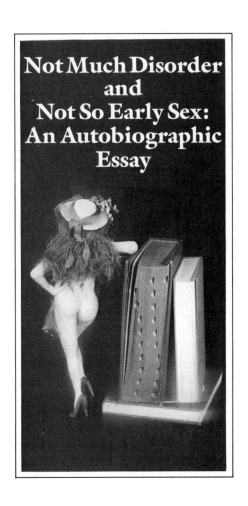

I: I Make a Pilgrimage To A Great Author And Muff It, A Mannheim Cop Tells Me About The Leibers.

revered Thomas Mann and admired his novels and short stories, so that when I burlesque the title of his famous "Disorder and Early Sorrow," I want it understood that I am in no way ridiculing him or his works, but only my own life, which strikes me in many ways as a strange and funny affair.

In fact, I revered Thomas Mann so much that when my dear wife Jonquil, intent on furthering my career as a writer and my growth as a human being, ingeniously arranged for me to visit Mann early in 1943 in his retreat in the Hollywood Hills, I was furious with her for subjecting me to what I was certain was going to be an embarrassing experience and nagged her cruelly about it the whole anxious nervous cat-on-hot-bricks two weeks that intervened between her arranging of the visit and the visit itself.

Often I have to be booted into doing things that are ultimately good for me, and sometimes I've luckily had some long-sufferer like Jonquil on hand to do the booting, though more often not. (When I'm not booted I almost always do the thing by myself anyway, I'm a persistent cuss, but then it's apt to take years and years.)

Finally the hateful day came. Reluctantly I steered my car along many a winding road and up many a wooded lane before I came to the iron gates of the great man's abode, entered with dragging footsteps, hesitantly identified myself to the maid who answered the door, and was ushered into his presence. He was discussing with his secretary a letter in which someone had questioned the use of forks in his *Joseph* novels. After clearly establishing to their mutual satisfaction that the forks in the *Joseph* novels had all been long large ones used to toast meat over fires, not small short ones used to eat with, he dismissed the man and turned to me. (Was this a little scene they habitually staged for neophyte writers, to display a famous writer being thoughtful and careful? If so, a good idea! Excuse me, folks, that's just seventy-one-year-old me being cynical.)

Anyway, I spoke my admiration piece. He gently questioned me, drew me out. After a bit he asked me which of his novels I thought the best.

"The Magic Mountain," I replied.

He said, *"To me, Buddenbrooks,"* and looked at me expectantly.

And, of course, *Buddenbrooks* was the one novel of his I hadn't read. (I still haven't.) And I knew I had to tell him so.

I'd *known* something like this was going to happen! Oh, what a miserable fake admirer and reverer I was not to have read the book he considered his own best novel!

But somehow I got through the rest of the visit, and when I got home I was so relieved the ordeal was over at last that I was no longer angry with Jonquil at all, but instead felt foolish at having got so ridiculously uptight about the whole Mann-visit business, and we had a couple of drinks and I talked her ear off about the interesting things that had happened and I'd noticed, and the fascinating thoughts I'd had about it all, despite the general horror of the day and the shameful exposure of my awful shortcoming while masquerading as a completist Thomas Mann fan.

When my editor, Byron Preiss, asked me to write an essay for this collection of my short stories and explain a bit about my writing career and how I came to be a writer in the first place, the early things that inclined me in that direction, I found that the most difficult aspect of my life to write about, but by all odds the most revealing and certainly the funniest, was sex. (Byron's thoughtful selection of my stories had something to do with this, especially his inclusion of "A Deskful of Girls.") So in what follows I've tended to concentrate on and emphasize sex. I hope no one minds. Myself, I dote on sex and scandal. After all, it's what makes the world go round. And up and down and in and out too. Certainly it's apt to be the thing I'm the most curious about in another person.

Especially another writer. In the second chapter of *In Search of Wonder* Damon Knight writes, "All the great fantasies, I suppose, have been written by emotionally crippled men," and then mentions Howard, Lovecraft, and Merritt. And we all know that emotional crippling is most apt to involve the sex area, which is the one we're least apt to be told about. So I said to myself, well, here's one fantasy writer who will try to give them the straight dope.

In writing about these matters I've discovered that, in view of recent sex liberation and widespread sex education (most certainly a lot of talk about it), we have forgotten the real meaning of words like "repression" and "inhibition" (and young people can hardly know at all), how they aren't just a matter of stuffy old rules but refer to deep and powerful psychological forces that can warp lives and, if we don't watch carefully, even alter memory itself. So I also offer this memoir as a serious contribution to what it was really like, at least for one person, to grow up in this country fifty or so years ago. (Yet despite all seriousness, it stays persistently funny.)

Thomas Mann came to this country from Germany to escape Nazi repression. My paternal grandfather, Albrecht Leiber, came from the same place some eighty years earlier, though whether he did so to escape repression is a toss-up question.

There's a lot in a name. I had a well-meaning grade school teacher argue with me that my name must be Frederick or Friedrich, that Fritz was only a nickname and I should get rid of it, because it was applied in World War I to all German soldiers, the hateful Hun. And I had a high school gym teacher who simply went ahead and called me Fred, wouldn't soil his lips with the other name. Nevertheless, Fritz is the name on my birth certificate, Chicago 1910.

Or Leiber. I'm forever having to explain that it's pronounced LYber, not LEEber, and correspondingly spelled Leiber, not Lieber. "Lieber" is a moderately common German name meaning "dear" or "lover," and frequently, though not always, indicative of its owner being Jewish, while "Leiber" is a relatively uncommon German name with no particular meaning or indications at all ("leib" by itself means "body"). That's all I, or any of our family, knew about my grandfather's last name—that it was rare—and he came from somewhere near Baden-Baden—until about fifteen years ago when a Dr. Rudolf Leiber of Mannheim, West Germany, began to write me about matters genealogical and then in 1971 very kindly sent me a thick volume bound in yellow paper and titled *Leiber-Chronik*. He's in it. So are we, meaning me, my grandfather, father, and son. Since then there have been two subsequent editions, each thicker than and greatly augmented over the last, and more and more profusely illustrated with pictures of very German-looking Germans, in whom I fancy I catch family resemblances. Turns out the scholarly and industrious Rudolf is a high police official (*Polizei-präsident*) in Mannheim, and in fact was something of the same (*Oberkriegsverwaltungerat Bei Militärverwaltung*) in Brussels and Antwerp during World War II. (When I heard that last, I shivered.) His researches have discovered a sizable clutch of Leibers in Swabia and traced them as far back as four or five hundred years, when the name was as often spelled Lieber as Leiber. (My own notion, which I haven't tried to confirm, is that after the German Jews were forced to adopt German names and picked meaningful ones running to precious metals and vegetation but including some "dears," the Leibers became more particular about the spelling. But who knows?)

My grandfather Albrecht belongs to the Möhriger Line of Leibers, while one of the "historic" Leibers was a Robert, who was the secretary of Pope Pius XII during World War II.

So.

So my hat is off to Rudolf Leiber, a hard-working and family-minded cop if there ever was one.

So now let's put the Beethoven *Eroica,* or maybe the *Pathetique* piano sonata, on the turntable, turn the sound up full volume, and have a go at this paternal ancestry business:

II: Albrecht Discovers The Burger War. A Feminist Family. A Shakespearean Marriage. Halley's Comet Flits Again. The Bungalow. I Wet My Pants.

On February 14, St. Valentine's Day, 1836, the year after Halley's Comet made its twenty-seventh observed return plying its seventy-six-year orbit, there was born in the state of Baden-Württemberg in Swabia in Southwest Germany on the edge of the Black Forest, to Joseph Anton Leiber and his wife Josephine Schwab, after three daughters, an only son Albrecht, who in the 1850s immigrated to America, settling in Illinois. Family lore has it that he rebelled against his family's wish that he enter the Catholic priesthood. There is no suggestion of any connection with the revolutions of 1848, but one of his literary idols was Fritz Reuter, sentenced to death in 1833 for his liberal political views, the sentence commuted to life imprisonment, and released in the Prussian amnesty of 1840 to begin his career as a humorous writer of Low German.

It is not surprising that Albrecht became a captain of Union troops during the *Amerikanischen Bürgerkrieg* when one considers that many male German immigrants of that day had had early military training. He commanded a company, first of Irish, then of Blacks, preferring the latter, which roved the Great Plains, fighting Indians, and where during the outdoor nights he studied the stars and laid the foundations for chronic bronchitis.

Returning to Chicago, he employed his mathematical talents in the insurance business and his organizational ability as secretary to the Illinois Secretary of State at Springfield, but was defeated in his attempt to win the latter elective office for himself by the speech impediment of a stammer.

He married a girl named Klett from Stettin in Prussia (now Szczecin in Poland) who died giving birth to their son Albert. Her twin sister Meta crossed the stormy seas to care for the bereaved household, she and Albrecht were in turn married and had first four daughters and then two sons. The girls were named for queens: Dorothea conceivably for Sophia Dorothea of Zell, George I of England's wife when he was elector of Hanover, and by him divorced and lifelong imprisoned for her romantic intrigue with the Swedish adventurer Königsmark; Louise for Napoleon's heroic foe Louise of Prussia; Josephine for Napoleon's first wife; and Marie for Marie Antoinette of France. Despite the traditionalism of this royalistic preoccupation, Albrecht insisted that English be the chief language spoken in the home, although Meta did not follow that rule too well.

The sons were named for writers: the younger for the elegant German poet Emmanuel Geibel (he changed it to Allen as soon as he could); the elder for Fritz Reuter. Fritz was a handsome, competitive, adventurous boy with a long history of childhood accidents and ills. He was born with one foot turned around and wore a corrective metal brace through boyhood. The other foot was almost cut off by a horsedrawn streetcar and required nearly a year in bed for its healing. Another year was devoted to lockjaw, got from jumping on a rusty nail while chief performer in a backyard circus. Also he was hit in the stomach at close range by a sixteen-pound hammer (the athletic sort, whirled on a wire and thrown) and bled internally for a couple of weeks. Nevertheless (or perhaps because of all that, if we follow Alfred Adler's ideas about compensation) he became a notable track and field athlete at Lake View High School, winning in his year the Chicago-wide pentathlon: running broad jump, dash, long race, javelin, and discus.

Albrecht's bronchitis worsened, although it's said he always kept a horse and continued to indulge his interest in astronomy by sleeping on summer nights with his head on the sill of the open bedroom window, and he died in 1896 when Fritz was 14. I've been told that toward the end the only foods he could tolerate were French fried potatoes and champagne, which leads me to speculate that alcoholism may have been involved. His eldest son Albert perished of that illness at a fairly early age.

After high school Fritz became an actor, first with the People's Stock Company on Chicago's west side, then with various touring companies, beginning to specialize in Shakespeare as one of "the American element" in Ben Greet's touring company from England.

Meanwhile, turning the clock back to ten years before the Civil War, a scholarly, serious girl named Flora Holcomb was born in a log cabin in Spring township, Crawford County, in northwestern Pennsylvania on August 24, 1851. The Holcombs were a fairly old American family; some of them were wheelwrights, tracing their line back by way of various Clevelands, Temples, and Lathrops to the Revolution. They also were in the process of moving midwest; they'd try it for a couple of years, suffer losses from disease and ill luck, retreat east for a while, then try again.

Flora was one of the ones who made it to Illinois, Livingston County, by the sometimes seemingly only available female stratagem of school teaching. She learned German to translate the poems of Goethe and Heine. In 1877 she married a farmer named Walter Bronson, who'd done a hitch in the Marines (1869–73) and seen service on a warship in Korea on the first American appearance-making foray to the Hermit Kingdom, having steamed and sailed around Cape Horn to do it.

But despite this fillip of naval adventure, the Bronson-Holcomb marriage became what I think of as a feminist one, shaped by the mind and interests of the female partner. There were one son, who died young, and five daughters: Ella, Edith, Virginia, Mary, and Flora—nurses, an actress, a gym teacher later Christian Science practitioner, and again a nurse, which rather runs the gamut of then acceptable female occupations, since several of the girls did spells of schoolteaching. They had relatively few offspring.

The theatrical season of 1909–10 brought Fritz Leiber and Virginia Bronson together in the Shakespearean repertory company of Robert Mantell, a wild-eyed Irishman with a commanding delivery, growing old, but into, or soon to be into, his fourth marriage, with his young leading lady, Genevieve Hamper. The season for a successful touring company paralleled the academic or school year: the last three or four months of one and the first half of the next with July and August for vacation or, if you wanted to keep busy or needed the bread, a time for summer stock, film making (in those days), vaudeville, or carnival.

The company, with Fritz as leading man, taking parts next in importance to the star, rehearsed at Mantell's half-block, tree-shaded estate in Atlantic Highlands, a pleasant town on the south shore of New York Bay and convenient to the big city during the summer months by the several daily runs of the New Jersey Central Railroad's trim white steamers *Sandy Hook* and *Monmouth*.

Bronnie, as Virginia Bronson came to be known familiarly, joined the company in Chicago, where she'd been attending acting school for a couple of years, supporting herself by proofreading, copy-

My father contemplates his "Hamlet Contemplates Yorick" while other of his Shakespearean self-sculptures look on.

My mother Virginia Bronson Leiber, actress.

holding, and similar jobs, and had auditioned for Mantell the previous season.

That the bachelor leading man and the new ingenue should be mutually attracted was more than youth and good looks. Both were Illinoians, highly ambitious, and adventurous. Bronnie, for instance, at seventeen had taught country school in the wilds of New Mexico to look after her brother George, who'd gone there to treat the tuberculosis which soon afterwards carried him off. And both were self-made versatile actors. Bronnie had won a regional elocutionary contest, Fritz an oratorical competition sponsored by the *Chicago Tribune*. One of Bronnie's earliest roles was the aged nurse in *Romeo and Juliet,* while earlier on in Ben Greet's company Fritz had always played Prospero; the programs read: "PROSPERO: Mr. Greet or Mr. Leiber" and "CALIBAN: Mr. Leiber or Mr. Greet," but the British star, a notoriously poor study, never did get his lines for the much longer part of the elderly sorcerer.

A well-planned tour hit the Coast (which always meant the Pacific coast then) during the coldest months. Bronnie and Fritz tied the knot in Santa Barbara.

1910 was a prodigious and portentous year. Its spring skies were emblazoned by the spectacle of Halley's comet, a more favorable apparition than the one now due in 1986. Mark Twain and Edward VII died, ending an age. On February 8 the Boy Scouts of America was formed. Taft was President. The University of Chicago was building the Annex to its Ryerson Physical Laboratory. On July 9 Harry Otto Fischer was born in Louisville, opening his eyes to the comet's waning beams. (The previous year his oldest friend-to-be Franklin MacKnight had seen light, Peary had reached the North Pole, MI5 (hush! hush!) had been founded in England, while Jonquil Ellen Stephens was already a toddler on her family estate near Merthyr Tidfil in Glamorganshire, Wales.) In the late autumn Robert Falcon Scott was establishing his base camp on McMurdo Sound for his second and ill-fated assault on the South Pole. And on December 24 in an apartment on Chicago's north side the person writing these words first breathed air.

Young Fritz was born healthy and taken good care of, intelligently and sensibly on the whole. His mother's nursing sisters knew about cod liver oil and orange juice and beef juice; dietary science was making giant strides. His mother knew the value of fresh air; she once broke a Pullman car window to get him and her some. One of his ears stuck out; they pinned it back with a bit of surgical tape. And once or twice he was hurried away from outbreaks of polio. Actors and nurses realized that we live in a changing world and can move about and do things about things.

And he was born into the backstage world where he could watch fantasy being created, the spells being woven for the audience in the darkness out front, the mechanics of illusion and illusioning. A world where the need for make-believe is never questioned and the importance, perhaps even necessity, of fantasy in living and thinking is not denied. A world of dressing rooms, backdrops, and wings where clothes were costumes, things were props, faces were make-up, and colors were fascinating curls of gelatin that hued the light. A world through which the lines of Shakespeare reverberated over and over. A world that inclined toward tolerance and progress and that centered in big cities, New York in particular. A world of theaters, hotels, and railway stations.

But he did not stay there long, or at least stay there chiefly. Other environments were being readied.

One was created in his second summer when Fritz, Senior, built the bungalow in Atlantic Highlands. This was a four-room structure, California inspired, set on locust posts, its gently sloping shingled roof rising to a modest peak, near the northwest corner of Highland Avenue and Avenue D, just west across the street from Mantell's larger place, and on the west edge of town. It had a chimney and open fireplace of local peanut stone, a dark sandstone studded with smooth pebbles.

Fritz built the bungalow in a few weeks from knowledge gained, I imagine, watching stage carpenters and other such, and with a fellow actor, John Burke, helping him lay floors. It was the sort of lone wolf project he could accomplish offhandedly, but he lost ten pounds he never did regain, changing him from a smoothly athletic to a more ascetic mien.

There were, or came to be, three big cherry trees in the back yard, one wild, two tame; in front of the front yard the lightning-blasted "stump" of a mighty pine towered forty feet to the grey driftwood nest of an osprey, though those were always called just seahawks locally. While to the west beyond Fritz's property stretched a wide cow pasture that had been quarried for gravel in three broad trenches, so that young Fritz's name for it came to be the cow pits. This battleground-looking expanse ended in a farmhouse that was more often unoccupied than not, and a little scrubby wood that hid a small brackish swamp (the bay shore was riven by narrow creeks full of tall knife-edged sea grass) and then beyond that more open land until the tiny next town began. It was a good area for little Fritz to play in.

And then there was Pontiac, Illinois, where he lived for his first two school years with his grandmother, Flora Bronson, the serious one, while his mother and father were on the road. It was a Bradbury sort of town with wooden sidewalks still on some streets and lots of trees and piles of burning leaves in autumn and a soda fountain called the Spa, although the state reformatory for boys was stashed away on the outskirts somewhere. There was a nice, half-citified farmhouse to live in with kerosene lamps, a well and outhouse outside, a wood stove in the kitchen, and a coalstove with fascinating little isinglass windows in the living room, and two chilly upstairs bedrooms with peaked ceilings.

And finally there was 4353½ North Ashland Avenue on Chicago's north side, a comfortable, six-room, second-story apartment in a big red brick building with windows that looked down on the cross street, Montrose, and on an alley, where Little Fritz, often called Fritzie, lived through all the rest of grammar school (Ravenswood, three short blocks west on Montrose) and all of high school (Lake View, his father's school, but now of course much more hemmed in by dense brick city, four long blocks south on Ashland; and 4353½ continued its influence on Fritzie even beyond high school, as we'll see). He lived with Big Fritz's youngest sister Marie Leiber, a pale, obliging spinster who had a clerical job downtown, and eldest sister Dora Essenpreis, a motherly though childless housewife who was a very good cook, and the latter's second husband Edwin, of Swiss extraction, who worked at a big jeweler's down in the Loop, the literal chessboard of Chicago's centralmost downtown, eight big blocks by eight, sixty-four big square blocks in all with the southmost forty-eight of them bounded by the four-cornered loop of high steel tracks that was the heart of Chicago's Elevated transport system, the "El."

Ashland and Montrose was a still respectable area of Chicago's preferred north side that was deteriorating very slowly, wearing out very, very gradually, you could say. In a changing world it was a spot that wasn't changing much for quite a long while—a mixture of two- and three-story apartment buildings with rather close-set houses with small front yards that were kept up, making allowance for Chicago's coal smoke which dinged everything. A few trees still. No highrises. A few small stores on Montrose, which had a streetcar. A block and a half beyond the grammar school, just the other side of the Ravenswood elevated line, there was a small movie house,

Little Fritzie strikes a pose in front of the Bungalow.

the Rosewood, while if you walked ten short blocks east on Montrose, skirting the north end of huge Graceland cemetery, you came to the main north-south elevated line and a couple of busier streets and a small clutch of taller buildings and two big movie houses, one having five or six acts of vaudeville in addition to the film. And a few blocks beyond all that Lake Michigan, but that was getting very far away from home. Such was 4353½.

But what was Little Fritzie doing in these three environments, what was happening inside him, what was his awareness like, how did he feel about them and their chief inhabitants? It's one thing to describe places you've been as clearly and accurately as you can remember them, but quite another to answer questions like those. Memory's a tricky thing, and while a little child has the words for objects and their shapes and colors and motions, he hasn't the words for feelings, or at least not many, and what you can put into words at the time it happened is best remembered. It's a matter of an adult trying to recall what at the time he had no words for, getting flashes of what he's after, trying to get the flavor of it, and then trying to fit feeling-words to it that the child didn't have at the time.

For instance, I remember being in a hotel bedroom with my father and mother, and my father crying because he had just got a telegram that his mother Meta had died, and being much struck with this because as a rule my father didn't cry. I didn't feel grief myself, I think, but I sure knew that he did because he was crying.

Or being in a theater with a lot of excited people (lobby? audience? backstage? I'm not sure) and a crowd making noise outside because of something to do with a war. First World War, of course. It must have been the armistice, or false armistice, because the crowd outside was cheering. But I'd have been almost eight by then and I don't recall feeling that old. Could the crowd have been cheering the re-election of Wilson because "he kept us out of war"? But did New York crowds cheer that? Memory and its interpretation can be very tricky.

Or the strong feeling of comfort and relief I got from urinating down my leg in my seat in a first grade or kindergarten classroom in Pontiac with warm sunlight in the room. I knew I was doing something bad or at least reprehendable (that is, I think I remember so) but at the time it was a rich dreamy feeling. About the same time I remember hiding tiny cardboard boxes of my own urine behind the upright piano in the living room of my grandmother's home; I haven't the faintest idea why, but it seemed necessary and very important.

Certainly childhood memories do seem to center around things that surprised, awed, scared, or delighted us, especially things that got the big people excited too. But it was the things that happened more than what we felt about them. We were just observers and the things took hold of us.

I remember the little woods beyond the cow pits backgrounded by black sky laced with distant red fireworks and the sound of irregular far-off explosions, just as though I were on the edge of a battlefield. Which wasn't too far from the truth because it was the munitions plant of Morgan Station seven miles away exploding section by section and taking most of the night doing it, keeping up a steady drumfire with occasional big bursts. It happened the evening of October 4, 1918, one of the more notable engagements on American soil that occurred during that conflict. The shells discharged themselves without being loaded in guns, the workers lost heavily to the first volleys (sixty-four fell in all) and retreated in dazed confusion. I remember how there'd be an especially big red flash and then how forty seconds later we'd get a deep *boom* and the bungalow windows, which hinged at the top, would lift and drop back with a slam.

And I remember at Pontiac scrunching up balls of tinfoil for the war effort. And something about war savings stamps.

And I think it was at Pontiac that I composed my first two poems. They were pithy, at least, though disgustingly cute: "Little chap, Eat pe' ap'," the last two contractions being my childish rendering of "peeled apple." The other: "Get in the 'bile, And turn the wheel." "Automobile," of course. My family's first was an Overland touring car. Then an Essex, same style, with sheet metal like armor plate. By the time of the Buick coupe I was grown up.

But that's getting into the sort of memories one is told about rather than actually remembering: the "cute" things you said or did; or the naughty things, like when I poured a glass of water over my uncle Dudie's (nickname for Allen, "the Dude") new pressed pants.

And it doesn't get us much nearer what was going on inside Little Fritz's head, the texture of his consciousness. I think I was primarily an observer and enjoyer. I was seldom given work or chores to do. Neither my father nor my mother were the sort of people who needed or wanted helpers. Most good actors, good troupers, have a touch of the lone wolf. Besides, the summertimes we spent together were looked upon as vacation by all three of us, a time for them to make up to me (and I to them?) for the long separations enforced by their jobs in the theater. I was well taken care of and, imitatively, I spent considerable time taking good care of myself, maybe to compensate for my father's mess of childhood accidents. And time devoted to eating and drinking, although I wasn't a fat boy then. I had a passion for carbonated beverages, especially plain carbonated water, soda water; it had the thrilling effect I craved, unconfused by sweet or sweet-sour taste. In the drug store at Atlantic Highlands, which had mysterious globes of red and green fluid in its show window, I once got so avid about this that I bit the rim off a glass of the stuff I was guzzling. I remember looking down in astonishment at the spill and fragments on the small round wire-legged table as I sat on my wire-legged, wire-backed chair.

I remember during those early summers at the Bungalow thinking that my father read an awful lot, when he wasn't doing carpentering or bricklaying, that is, or offhandedly making lamps of beaten sheet copper and brass paneled with transparent copies he'd painted of Howard Pyle's Arthurian illustrations. He bought books seriously, by sets, like the young hero of *All Quiet on the Western Front,* and would concentrate on a different author each summer, trying to read all of him or at least a lot. That way he got through Dumas, Hugo, de Maupassant, Balzac, Dickens, Thackeray (he was disappointed in Thackeray), and Conrad. (Oh yes, and I remember he got disgusted with Cooper, because of the sheer physical impossibility of some of the feats attributed to the heroes—he had the athlete's and builder's judgment of what you could make bodies and objects do and what you couldn't.) He extended the living room six feet at its library end to hold the books. I imagine now that during those long reading sessions he was also planning his own productions of Shakespeare, sets, lighting, costumes, etc., in anticipation of the time he would start his own company. And testing out his own theories of acting and human character against a half dozen of the world's psychologists and showmen.

And then there was playing by myself and with other children, but playing can be a serious matter. I remember once Bruce Mantell and an older boy who was his confederate threatening to shoot me with a BB gun. I was terrified. The suspense was awful. They lay in wait for me and shot me from ambush once or twice and it stung. There didn't seem to be anything I could do about it. Maybe it was in the nature of things and company matters that the star's son could shoot the son of the leading man.

I recall that in Pontiac there were rather more children to play

Mary Catherine (my first anima?) and Little Fritzie on the front steps in Pontiac.

with, and girls as well as boys. I have a 1915 snapshot of myself and Mary Catherine, the girl next door, sitting side by side on the top step of a wooden porch, staring intently at the camera with happy faces. She is holding a small cat toy on her lap, I an equally tiny airplane. But the only memory I have of her is a flash of the two of us in the stable behind her house (the Bronsons had a red barn behind theirs). I'm on the ground looking up. She's standing in the driving seat of a buggy brandishing a buggy whip with a beautiful fierce expression on her face. Then nothing of what happened after that—just the one flash. Was this the first appearance of my notorious Anima? I am inclined to believe so.

As things turned out, she was the last girl I played with for a long, long while. Or remember playing with, at any rate, and if a single flash counts as remembering. I recall girls playing jacks and hopscotch and being much impressed with their abstruse knowledge and recondite skills. They could jump and dance about, while I moved more sluggishly.

III: 4353½ Takes Over. A Good and Law-Abiding Family. Punching King George in the Snoot. An Aunt's Adventures. Realists & Illusioners.

Pontiac, where I went through the first two school grades and attended Methodist Sunday school, ended abruptly as an environment for me when my grandmother Flora moved to an apartment on Chicago's west side, to be near her youngest daughter who was training at the Presbyterian hospital there to become a registered nurse. I went with her to begin with and started third grade (those multiplication tables!) at a public school in that neighborhood, but after two or three months it was decided that it would be best for all concerned if I went up and lived with my paternal aunts on the north side, transferring to the Ravenswood public school. They were younger women, there were two of them, and the north side was more respectable, or at least safer, at any rate. (As for the south side that was beyond the pale; it held the dreaded Black Belt, and it was ten years before I got there once, although my destiny turned out to lie in that direction. No east side to Chicago but Lake Michigan.)

I was delighted with the change of residence. My north side aunts catered to my comfort more, kept their apartment warmer, made more of food, talked with me more comfortably, took me to movies. I bade farewell to my somewhat austere maternal grandmother, who had called my attention to prehistoric monsters, dinosaurs, and, I think, rocks and the stars.

And so the place and pattern of my growing up were set. For ten months of the year my two aunts (and my uncle-in-law) were in charge of, or more precisely, especially as they interpreted the relationship, responsible for me. For the two months of summer vacation and sometimes at Christmas and at other special times I was with my parents, getting some glimpses of their magic world of the theater and backstage that had entranced and occupied my infancy and preschool childhood (for instance, I'm told, I learned the huge part of Hamlet at four while listening to my father get it up in hotel bedrooms for a special performance while he was still in Mantell's company, and I still know most of *Macbeth* by heart, the whole play).

That was the basic set-up. Later on by gradual stages I came at times to resent bitterly being shut out of the wonder world of the theater and spent long dark minutes while getting to sleep longing romantically to be with my father and mother. But really the idea was unrealistic. Laws were strict about actors' children getting regular schooling. My parents were in no position to arrange for special tutoring and such—why, when the 4353½ set-up was made they didn't even have their own company yet. And I didn't like being baby-sat in hotel bedrooms by actors' wives, or sitting up forever doing nothing at grownup parties. No, in those dark (and often scary) bedtime minutes I was nursing an impossible dream of union with glory.

Besides, during those first two or three years with my father's sisters, I didn't resent at all what I later came to think of as the dull life of a respectable north side apartment. I wasn't bored by it then. I ate it up! After a good supper with some favorite dessert I'd sit around the living room like a little adult listening to the adventures with watches and diamond rings my Uncle Ed had had that day behind the counter at Juergens and Andersen's and that my Aunt Marie had had in the office of a big clothier's, hear a little almost always approving and celebratory talk about relatives, harken to their sage remarks about the stories in *The Chicago Tribune* (I doted on its comics: The Gumps, Gasoline Alley, Dick Tracy, Moon Mullins, Winnie Winkle, Little Orphan Annie), and occasionally interject a carefully thought-out observation of my own, which they thoughtfully absorbed in turn. I always was a good and receptive listener. That and a spot of homework left over from afternoon easily used up the time until bed, which came early for all of us. Ed and Marie, who were nothing if not dutiful and conscientious employees, vied with each other, surreptitiously setting the communal alarm clock ten minutes ahead, so there'd be absolutely no chance of either of them being late to work. Sometimes this way they'd get it more than an hour fast, generating a certain amount of wonder and astonishment and occasional mutual protestations in the predawn darkness.

Via the *Tribune* and various people I met, including my other north side relatives (more of them later) I was exposed to various fixed ideas and prejudices that I came to think of as typically north side—that Blacks were dangerous though stupid animals (there'd been "Race Riots" in Chicago just after World War I), that Jews were out to get you financially (they were such criminally good businessmen and could live on nothing), and that the British were trying to reconquer or suborn the United States by way of the effete and snobbish East. That last was the *Trib*'s particular pet, designed to appeal to the large Irish and German element in its readership;

they enjoyed repeating the threats of Big Bill Thompson, Chicago's Republican mayor then for two terms, to "punch King George in the snoot," should he ever seek to visit the Windy City. Some of this nonsense had rubbed off on my aunts and uncle, but not much; they were too subserviently law-abiding and pacific to harbor strong hostilities of any sort; besides, the clothiers Marie worked for were Jewish. And I must say that the more I heard of such stuff over the years, the more it began to have a reverse effect on me, especially as regards the British and Jews. They just *couldn't* be as bad as painted. I hadn't suffered at their hands. Besides, there were lots of British and Jewish and even Negro actors, weren't there? Yet I don't recall voicing these revolutionary opinions out loud. I was absorbing the views around me, all right, even when I was questioning and privately ridiculing them.

And then on weekends there were the movies. I gratefully accepted at first my Aunt Dora's escort to the Saturday afternoon bill at the Rosewood: the feature, the comedy, the newsreel, and the shout-eliciting serial with Pearl White or Ruth Roland or about *Elmo the Mighty,* my hero then. It didn't seem quite safe to her to let me go alone; after all, I was her brother's treasured only child, and besides, she loved movies herself. The serial *The Million-Dollar Mystery* had made a great impression on her before my time. On Sunday afternoons I was happy to walk with my younger Aunt Marie the longer distance east to the Riviera or Uptown. We liked to talk about movies and the stage. Her favorite star later was Jeanette MacDonald; she saw some of her films as many as eighteen times.

Sunday mornings I went to Sunday school, at the Congregational Church because that was closest, or perhaps my parents had had a hand in its selection. My Chicago caretakers had long fallen out of the habit of going to church themselves, as had my parents, but they (and my parents) thought Sunday school was good for children. I accepted it as something dull but apparently necessary, not very important. At no time in my youth did I encounter the problem of coping with religious fanatics. (I'd probably have agreed with them politely and then gone my own murky way, my usual tactic.)

Occasionally my Uncle Ed would hold forth with minor zest on something he recalled from one of Robert Ingersoll's lectures—how when we died our bodies were reduced to atoms which then went on making up other beings, and so on *ad infinitum.* My aunts would look a little worried when he said things like that, and motion their heads toward me, but voice no protest.

I had hardly any playmates, but that didn't bother me at first. Mostly it was a lot easier to stay in and read, or talk with my Aunt Dora, or watch her cook, than to go out and try to play, anyway, in the great city. With my Aunt Dora I had a special relationship. I came to recognize that there was a sense in which she was a lot closer to the real world and willing to talk about it than my Aunt Marie, say.

My paternal Grandmother Meta, Albrecht's wife, I gradually found out from talking with Dora, had been a rather nervous and hysterical woman, romantic and impractical, not very competent as a house-wife, so that after my aunt Dora had finished fourth grade, she had stayed home to look after the younger children and the household generally.

This solved the entire home problem, I gather. So long as Dora stayed home and did housework and helped cook and looked after things and made practical arrangements when needed, her three younger sisters were able to continue school, even go to a fancy finishing school to learn a little French, music, European culture, and deportment; the boys could hitch rides on horsecars, walk tightropes, and jump off roofs on dares; Meta could go to the opera and have her occasional indignations and raptures and vagaries and hysterical fits and collapses; while Albrecht, I suppose, could ride home from the railway station on his horse after being away in Springfield or downtown Chicago, note with approval and perhaps a certain wonder that his home hadn't come apart in his absence, maybe take a few drinks, and stick his head out the bedroom window and go to sleep.

At seventeen the little mother and household drudge and realist married a handsome young farmer and went with him to Nebraska or South Dakota, somewhere way out there, and lived in a small farmhouse with him and his old mother, who smoked a pipe, the three of them subsisting solely on potatoes and on blackbirds he shot. The only book in the place was, somewhat strangely, a col-lected Shakespeare which the old lady read habitually and quoted exactly as if it were the Bible.

After a year of this, along with all the wonders and delights of love and marriage, Dora pulled out and returned to Chicago, coping some more for her family, but also getting jobs such as nursing assistant to various homeopathic doctors, things like that, and finally marrying Ed Essenpreis, who at least had a civilized job, exuded regularity, and didn't look the type to take off for the wide open spaces and hit the blackbird trail.

Anyway, Dora seemed to know a lot about physical things and could talk interestingly about jobs and animals (once she and Ed had run a chicken farm) and birth and death and disease and operations; once she'd had an immense benign tumor removed from her abdomen and she'd watched them take out her intestines and lay them to one side on a warm towel, laying a fold of it over them, just to make room inside her to work in—fascinating!

(A few years later there were certain terribly simple questions about the human body, male and female, I was desperate to know the answers to, but by then we'd lost our special rapport; or despite her realism I didn't think they were questions I could take to her.)

Anyhow, those were just the sort of things you couldn't talk to my Aunt Marie about, at least not in the same way, animated solely by the naive desire to know and tell what things looked like and how they felt and how they fitted together. Marie liked to talk about nice things, how rich people lived, wonderful places to go to, the best restaurants, flowers, Jeanette MacDonald and Nelson Eddy—not unpleasant stuff. Why, Marie couldn't bear the smell or taste of onions, and as for garlic—that was an Italian nastiness, a French aberration. Once or twice Dora put finely chopped onions in chicken stuffing to prove that Marie liked them when she didn't know she was eating them, but even Dora never tried any tricks with garlic—at least (come to think of it) not that I knew of.

If Dora was a realist, Marie was—how does one say it?—romantic says too much. No, Marie was an illusioner.

Of course it was many years before I got a glimmering that ninety per cent of the talk we made after dinner, most of all talk, was illusioning. Things said to make dull lives sound exciting, uninteresting jobs bearable, to make us feel that the powers that be were always well intentioned and working for our good, that our fears were all sensible and helpful, and that everything was working out okay.

And I, as a small boy, went along with the gag mostly because I liked to feel safe and comfortable. I spent, it seems to me now, an inordinate amount of time cossetting myself, making myself comfortable in chair or bed, drinking and nibbling and sucking as I read my book, or thought my curious slow thoughts, or simply waited for something to happen in the day's grey expanse—I'm still doing it! sipping coffee continuously and smoking one cigarette after another as I type these words in 1982, though I have given up for the time being uninhibiting alcohol and blessed consciousness-blotting barbiturates (though they seem to rule out the deepest and most healing levels of sleep—yes, I've heard about that).

But what am I doing and saying? I've been attacking illusioning, and yet I've devoted my whole life, more than anything else, to one form of illusioning, to fantasy. Why, back in the late 1940s I wrote a prose poem called "Fantasy on the March" for the *Arkham Sampler* that pictured us devotees of fantasy as tramping off in our own wild direction to a sweetly sinister different drumming and treasuring werewolves, hamadryads, and the mysteries that lie beyond the farthest stars above all else. Retitling it "In Defense of Werewolves," I put it in *The Second Book of Fritz Leiber*. Certainly if I have faith in anything in this world, it's in Mystery and Fantasy. It's by no means a certain faith; it has an element of desperation and lost cause about it, but it is a faith nonetheless. Yes, a faith in Fantasy and a loyalty to Science, that about sums me up.

But if I go on like this, dredging up so much autobiographic detail and analyzing, even psychoanalyzing, long gone moods and, so help me, even starting dialogues between my nine-year-old self and my present seventy-one-year-old one, I'll be forever writing this piece! and as it happens, I have a deadline for it, time's a-wasting, and I've just got to get back to writing fiction—Fantasy—which is my real life.

So from now on we'll just hit the high spots. We'll do a speed job on the further development of that thwarted child of the theater, that conservative little boy who sat around in 4353½ doing as he was told, reading and musing, swotting at his homework religiously, not going out and seeking play adventures because it would worry his aunts, who were responsible for him (and it would have), but really more because he was scared and lazy and lacking in initiative when it came to approaching other children (he built numerous shells around him).

And hopefully we'll do something to justify and explain that bravado prologue in which I had Halley's Comet foreshadowing the birth of my parental grandfather and seventy-four years later blazoning my own birth and that of my late wife Jonquil and my friends Harry and Mac.

And say a word or two about chess and cats and dice, and romance and girls and sex, and ghosts and the stage and Shakespeare, and tall buildings and the stars and Chicago's El and witchcraft—and anything else that may seem necessary and noteworthy.

IV: The Big Flu. A Homeopathic Teaspoon. The Fritz Leiber Company. A Reckless Feckless Friend. I Tearfully Learn Chess. A Competitive Papa.

Although 4353½ did indeed become a sort of supersafe fortress (and prison) for me, my sojourn there began with a whiff of disaster and mortality. I got the big bad 'flu in the epidemic of 1918 that slew its half million in the U.S.A. I was abed three weeks, up for a day, relapsed for a considerably worse-feeling three weeks, and then had to practice walking for a while before I got the hang of it again. I recall the tasteless homeopathic medicines given me in doses so tiny that I now know (well, believe) couldn't have hurt, or helped, a kitten. They were in two glasses of water standing in saucers on my bedside table and that looked exactly alike except for a teaspoon atop one of them. I'd get a teaspoon of that one, and it would be laid atop the other glass. Next time I'd get a teaspoon of fluid from *that* glass, and so on alternating. I recall one dismal afternoon during the second half of my siege when I was trying to read *The Wizard of Oz* and finding the story pretty unhappy and peculiar, especially with that wet burnt linen smell around that always seemed to go with the 'flu. My Aunt Dora was taking my temperature more often than usual (I was told later it was 104.5), and when the doctor came they stood in the doorway looking solemn and whispering, while I felt quite grim.

Next day Dora brightened up and everything turned out okay, but ever since then the original illustrations for *The Wizard of Oz* have seemed slightly sinister to me and the book itself faintly nightmarish.

And every winter after that for the next twelve years, about the same time each year, I got a case of 'flu, though nowhere near as severe. It seemed that each year the fever got less, but lasted a little longer. The last year (I was in college by then) the low fever hung on for weeks. On my (still homeopathic) doctor's advice I finally just ignored it, got up, and went about my business. The cure worked perfectly. (Much later on I discovered that somehow during my life I'd got some tubercular scarring on my lungs. One can only surmise.)

Anyhow, that 'flu (knock on wood) was the only disease I ever had that amounted to anything, except of course for alcoholism, which I'll go along with the A.M.A. in calling a disease though it sure has its psychological angles—about ten million of them!—

though I wouldn't exactly call it psychosomatic either, even if its symptoms can be counterfeited to some small degree by temper tantrums, laughing fits, and crawl-into-a-hole depressions.

One more thing about my 'flu. After it I began to put on weight, so that through the last grammar grades and the first year or two of high school I was medium plump. Of course this was in part Dora's good cooking plus the sedentary habits I acquired at 4353½.

I hadn't been living there and going to Ravenswood for more than a couple of years when my father and mother left Mantell, and Fritz, Senior, launched his own rival Shakespearean company. This was another of his lone wolf projects, his life's chiefest one, and thoughtfully envisioned and prepared. Most American productions of Shakespeare at that time were encumbered by elaborate realistic scenery, a la grand opera, which in turn enforced long waits between scenes, breaking the flow of the play. He designed and built, mostly by himself, sets which were atmospheric and simple, suggesting the scene rather than giving it realistically, so that waits between scenes were cut to a few seconds literally, never so much as a minute. As he finally developed it, the scenery became a good panoramic backdrop, adjustable drapes that could break the stage into several acting areas, platforms, and a very few suggestive set pieces, with changes in lighting doing much of the work—the sort of functional setting that has become a commonplace in the modern theater.

He also favored a more natural style of acting and delivery of even the most "exalted" lines, colloquial rather than elocutionary; his actors were told to react, not to "act"—again essentially the modern thing.

He also supervised the design and cut the materials for his company's costumes, employing a local Atlantic Highlands seamstress to finish them, a rangy and dour New England type woman.

Of course that was a very exciting summer for me. The Bungalow and its surrounds were a hive of activity. It particularly fascinated me to watch my father make "props," stage swords and daggers, scepters, thrones, and Roman helmets, and weave Richard III chain armor out of heavy cord that was later silvered.

Naturally a main reason for doing so much of the work himself (with the directing and acting still to come!) was simply to save money, cut expenses, make sure there were enough funds left over to get the show on the road. He wasn't a lone wolf when he didn't have to be. Not always.

It was an extra treat for me to be able to watch the first rehearsals before I had to head back for Chicago and school. A couple of the actors I knew from Mantell's company; others were new.

And later that autumn I had the excitement and thrill of being in the audience for their first performance in Chicago. And pride—they were getting good notices on the whole and tickets were selling. It looked as if the company was going to be successful.

There was one very minor blot on all this fun. During the third or fourth day of their Chicago run I fell asleep one afternoon in class, and I think my parents were very gently rebuked about this. Everyone was very understanding, but thereafter my attendance at evening performances was curtailed. Gee, the stage and school just didn't seem to mix, I thought unhappily. Why couldn't there be time for both, or different sorts of time for each?

The tour continued to its end, months and months of playing Shakespeare around the country (with me hearing a little about it in letters and writing my eight-liners back that began, "Dear Pa and Ma, I am having a fine time in Chicago"), and it was repeated, with variations, during almost every theatrical season of the 1920s. That was real proof of success, that you could keep coming back.

My father became a figure very much to be reckoned with in the theater: actor, director, producer—or, as they tended to put it then: actor-manager, one of the real stars. Not that he was all that much in love with the star system (though of course in another sense, I'm sure, he ate it up!). For instance, from the start he never did like to play Romeo; he sensibly considered himself too old for it, and more than once had the youngest juvenile play it, and the ingenue play Juliet rather than my mother, the leading lady; but then a surprising number of complaints would come back from the audience: "Why weren't the stars playing the star parts?" It seemed to be considered a sort of cheating, perhaps sheer laziness.

No, the star system was hard to deviate from, and not just because of the egotism of the stars. Mantell played Romeo into his seventies (ahem! that's me, too, folks, your writer), carrying a pilgrim's staff to support and smooth his hobbling footsteps; at least it looked more romantic than a cane.

My father played in other stuff than Shakespeare from time to time. He created the title role in Paul Green's *The Field God* and played John Knox in *Mary of Scotland* with Helen Hayes, bowing out when he didn't get the equal billing he'd been promised. And got money for doing Ponce de Leon in an ill-starred Broadway production of Eugene O'Neill's *The Fountain* that didn't make it to opening night. He added the last play to his repertory.

How was the first Fritz Leiber Company financed? Well, to start with, his own money, all he'd been able to save up; I'm sure that was the main reason he'd just done two star parts in two big films shot in Hollywood during summertimes: Caesar in Theda Bara's *Cleopatra* and Solomon in the first *Queen of Sheba* with Betty Blythe; in the latter film the female star's state of undress was cause for considerable religious consternation throughout our fair land; at some Sunday schools, I've been told, children (boys especially) weren't allowed to go home until they'd sworn on a Bible not to see it.

The balance of the money came from a few people willing to take a risk on the company's success, principally William L. Wallen, a very German German-American businessman who'd married Fritz's sister Louise (Aunt Lulu) and had a talent for promotion and a look of smoothly settled prosperity about him; even his German accent added to his air of authority and made you trust his judgment. Although in the end he made most of his money from real estate, he'd launched a variety of commercial ventures including a downtown Chicago restaurant called The Shakespeare, so he probably had the rather common German enthusiasm for the Bard, along with his devotion to Wagner's Ring operas and what he called the Laws of Nature.

Fritz's remaining sister Josephine (Aunt Josie) was married to a man who was equally successful in the end, though he had to fight for it longer and hang onto it harder: Lester A. Wheeler, a tough and hard-headed athletic coach and physical education teacher who was deep into local Republican politics, especially during the mayoralty of Big Bill Thompson, and who was, I believe, for a time, Superintendent of Lincoln Park, Chicago's biggest. "Aces-back-to-back Wheeler," they called him in the stud poker circles where he regularly supplemented his hard-won income by his ultraconservative realistic play. There was a rapport between him and my father because they were both big men and deep into athletics in their ways. Once, I'm told, they halted a riot in a streetcar simply by wading in and pitching the battlers off it four at a time.

The Wallens had three children and the Wheelers four, so when the families got together for Christmas or some other celebration I found myself surrounded by cousins, though they were all enough older than I was to put them out of the possible-playmate class even if we had lived nearer together or met more frequently.

Rather late one Christmas evening, when I was supposed to be dozing, but wasn't, after the big dinner Aunt Dora had cooked (mashed potatoes and gravy and candied sweet potatoes too!) one of my cousins voiced an opinion of me that stung at the time but that I realized later had much truth in it (and now I believe it wasn't the cousin's own opinion but repetition of one heard from a shrewd parent).

What the cousin said was: "You know, there's one thing about Fritzie, he's bright enough but you always have to tell him. If you told him, 'Be a banker, Fritzie,' he'd go and be a good banker. If you said, 'Fritzie, be a janitor,' then he'd be a good janitor. But you always have to tell him."

Yes, that did say something about my character, something that my long sojourn at 4353½ was intensifying.

The existence of the Fritz Leiber Company resulted in some changes in the Bungalow's surrounds. My father built a rehearsal hall in the backyard beyond the tall cherry trees, this time with a little professional help, that had a two-story section at one end for storage of the Company's scenery between seasons.

I remember the kids I played with at that time in Atlantic Highlands as being a rather unexceptional and dopey lot...until there appeared among them one Eddie Smith. He came from a broken home, wore jeans, had a disreputable grin and the reputation of being a bad boy in school, but somehow our imaginations meshed, and he and I played endless games and had adventures together. I remember my father cottoned to him because of his daredeviltry and Huck Finn look. His bad-boy reputation consisted of things like this: Assigned by his teacher to write two hundred words on a given topic, he'd copy exactly the first two hundred words from the encyclopedia article on the topic, ending in midsentence, and hand it in. He had style.

You know, it's hard to believe but I can't recall now exactly what those games and adventures were. Maybe now that I've recognized that gap, my subconscious will work to fill it. I don't think there can have been any great risks and rulebreaking involved. If he was Huck Finn, I was more Sid Sawyer than Tom, or at least my 4353½ self was. And yet there was a glow about our relation; we laughed a lot; looking back now it seems like my first intimation of Fafhrd and the Gray Mouser.

Of course we could only see each other in summertime, and not always then. Eddie's roughneck mother (as I remember her) moved around a lot.

One exception to that. One winter Eddie sent me in Chicago two copies of *Weird Tales* and *The Insidious Dr. Fu Manchu,* noting that he thought I'd like them. It was the sort of simple act I'd never have thought of doing myself then. And believe it or not, I didn't much care for them then, too many spiders and centipedes, too much death and strange diseases. Later, of course, I'd go for them.

Our friendship ended when Eddie and his mother moved away from Atlantic Highlands permanently.

Several years later he paid me one last visit there, but we found ourselves uncomfortable with each other. I was aware of how differently we dressed. I took him to play golf, which I'd taken up in imitation of my father doing so himself in mid-life. I realized Eddie was guarding his speech with me, watching the words and expressions he used, while the longer we went on, the more I felt dandyfied, sissified, over-refined, artificial. It was a bad business.

Much later on I heard how his life ended—very characteristically and very much in style. He got married and became a structural steel worker, one of the daredevils of the high iron, and was very good at it. The day he was due to come down at last and transfer to a job on the ground, he was in especially high spirits. After lunch he put on one of his exhibitions of skylarking, went through his whole repertoire...and took his first tumble.

A few times during Christmas holidays I'd entrain with my Aunt Marie or one of my mother's sisters, and we'd join the Company on tour for a couple of weeks—delightful! Once it was in Minneapolis. There was a blizzard and next morning the shoveled-aside snow outside the hotel was higher than my head. While the air was so cold and dry you could generate a big static charge walking down a hotel hall, especially if you shuffled, and discharge a mighty spark on the doorknob or elevator or on another person. We had a scary but exciting game of sparking each other.

Another time, Denver. I'd just turned twelve. This visit was especially memorable because during it I was taught how to play chess by Alexander Andre, an actor with a commanding brow and steely gaze and Slavic mien; I think he played Caesar sometimes. Later I noted the minor similarity of his name to that of Alexander Alekhine, soon to become one of the world's more eccentric (but they're most of them that) chess champions. Such was my introduction to the maddening game that has since taken up a good slice of my spare time during several periods of my life (during others I've foresworn it).

There was a fly in that ointment, though. My father picked up the game by watching me learn it, and beat me in our first encounter. I was reduced to tears, literally. My father was terribly good at picking things up that way, and a tireless competitor. I've mentioned golf. He went out for his introductory game with a couple of actors in his company who played it, and shot his first nine holes in under fifty even though he held the club cross-handed, just as he'd batted in baseball. Oddly he never got much better than that at golf although he played for years and eventually adopted the conventional grip. At golf, and at tennis too, he hit the ball just like he hammered a nail.

Would you believe that when I first began writing stories and submitting them to magazines, my father immediately started doing the same thing? He actually ground out three or four, I think, and he showed a couple of them to me. One of them was that "The Adventures of a Penny" story that I imagine every budding author *thinks* of writing, and maybe one in fifty of them actually writes (the adventures of a penny, a two-dollar bill, a wig, a ring, a sword, a gun, a flag, a car, a space probe—I recall a fellow alcoholic showing me a story he'd just knocked out about the adventures of a beer can) and that maybe sells once in ten million times.

The other story was a bull fight told from the viewpoint of the bull. He'd just been in Mexico doing a picture, and been taken to his first (and last) bullfight, and was disgusted by how the fight was rigged, the way he saw it, for the matador to win. This story had considerable pathos and indignation and strong feeling in it, but not much of a plot.

I'm not sure my father actually submitted any of his stories; I don't recall him showing me any rejection slips, but I shudder to think how I'd have felt if one of his stories had really sold, because then it was two or three years before the first of my own stories got accepted!

V: "Midnight By The Morphy Watch". Chess At The University. A Fateful Game and Friendship.

But speaking of stories, one of the reasons I'm writing this is to show how the stories in this collection got written, when and how their themes became part of my life, what triggered them off, and any other connections and synchronicities that seem interesting.

The stories in this book were selected because the editor liked them best, but they also happen to represent most of my chief interests in life, the things that have fascinated me persistently and made me study them.

"Midnight by the Morphy Watch" is a story about wild talents and chess and San Francisco, my present home, and a strange historical object that actually existed and may still exist: a gold watch with its dial circled by the symbols for chess pieces instead of the usual hour numerals.

I've already told you how I learned chess and how it was marked (and marred?) by a father-rivalry, as has been suggested was the case with the ultimately psychotic Paul Morphy, "the pride and sorrow of American chess," who was astounding the world with his precocious genius back in the 1850s, the decade when my maternal grandmother was a little girl and my paternal grandfather was getting a toehold in America.

My interest in chess and my ability to play it with any small degree of mastery developed very slowly, as has been true of all my approaches to most if not all of my big interests in life. I played it a little during the rest of grammar school and a little more in Lake View High School, where I joined the Chess Club, but it wasn't until I got to the University of Chicago (fifty to sixty blocks deep in the early abhorred south side!) and met the players in its Reynolds Club that I got really hooked and read up some on the fascinating history of the game and began to dream romantically of becoming a chess master (and a great mathematician, I told myself for a year or so).

I should explain here that my 4353½ environment continued to enfold or at least loom about me; through my four years of college I was still with Dora and Marie and Ed. We'd all just moved to a very similar apartment twenty-four blocks north of the old one but still close to Ashland, on Wallen Avenue, a short street named for my uncle-in-law the real-estate entrepeneur and enthusiast for nature and German culture, at whose office a short distance away Marie now worked.

For my first year at the University of Chicago I lived at home on Wallen and commuted to college, though it meant traveling almost from one end of Chicago's el system to the other twice a day, which took almost three hours in all. On chilly winter mornings I'd see the stars while waiting on the Loyola el platform, not knowing how much they'd someday mean to me—another very slowly developing interest. But I can't grudge the time spent on those long el rides at dawn and dusk. They introduced and wedded me to Chicago's lonely and dismal world of roofs and some fifteen years later gave me "Smoke Ghost," my first strong supernatural story.

That daily elevated trek at the third-story level of the city's grey roof-world only went on for my freshman year and an odd month or two of the next. Thereafter I domiciled in one of the men's dormitories, Hitchcock Hall, at first by my lonely self in a rather narrow north-wall room that looked out on the Gothic-styled grey Indiana limestone of the Anatomy Building with a griffin crawling down the roof's steep angle as if about to launch into space (he, merged with other grey beasties from the gatetops and roofpeaks and from under the eaves all around, became years later the original of the one in my novel *Conjure Wife),* but during my junior and senior years in the adjacent, larger, northwest room which I shared with Charles L. Hopkins, who became my lifelong friend. During this period I quite often journeyed up to the north side for Sunday dinner and perhaps a movie with Marie, and of course that's where I was bedded down when I had that month or so of low fever, that last aftermath of the 'flu, in my junior year at the U. of C.

But before that, during my first year at U. of C., while playing chess at the University's Reynolds Club below the limestone-toothed spirelets and crenelated towerlets of Mitchell Tower in the quadrangle a block east of Hitchcock, I made my first friendship based on similar tastes and interests, life patterns and temperaments, a friendship that's endured throughout my life. I'm sure that during the first twenty or so moves of our first game together Franklin MacKnight and I sensed we were kindred spirits; we both hated obvious moves, liked to find "mysterious" ones and surprise each other with complications. Later, away from the chess board, we began to explore the areas of kinship. We both liked supernatural horror stories and were attracted by all manner of strange weird happenings—the sort of taste catered to, rather crudely, by Hearst's *American Weekly;* ours had a wider range and involved greater subtleties—those were the biggest things. A love of and search for the weird, fantastic, and mysterious. (By contrast, my friendship with Charles Hopkins, begun a bit later, lacked this one element, though in other ways was as deep or deeper.) Mac and I both were majoring in psychology, but we were attracted to all the sciences and read science fiction and fantasy. We were both solitaries, unaggressive, sensitive, and socially unpracticed, yet willing to talk honestly when the barriers were down. Mac was a great devotee of literal truth, I soon found out. It was all a revelation to me.

Yet all this came from a game of chess.

And Mac a little later on led to other things. He led me to read the supernatural horror stories of H. P. Lovecraft, who gave an enduring set to my life ways and to my writing ambitions. And

Mac introduced me to his hometown (Louisville, Kentucky) friend, Harry Fischer, who both invented and became the Gray Mouser. (I tell more about those things in my essays, "Terror, Mystery, Wonder" in *World Fantasy Awards: Volume Two* and "Fafhrd and Me" in *The Second Book of Fritz Leiber*.)

All that too from a game of chess.

But I mustn't stretch this point too far, build too high and mysterious a silver pinnacle for chess in the dark lonely world, pile all of this on too thickly.

Mac and I got deeper into chess, played on a Reynolds Club team or two; then about the time I got married I gave it up, figuring it was too dangerous, that it could steal away too much time, especially from a writer. Gave up serious tournament, match, and team chess, that is. And as for the other kind, "skittles," playing for fun, I never cared for that much. Chess seemed to me too important a game to be trifled with.

Then about twenty years after that, after an alcoholic midlife crisis, I took up serious chess again, reading up on it and studying it some more, self-training regularly, and playing in three or four tournaments a year. I figured I was too old and my writing drives too deeply established to be much endangered by it. Also I deserved some sort of reward, I thought, for giving up booze. I kept this up for about five years, enough to achieve Expert rating (above an A player, below a Master) and wrote the novelette "The Sixty Four Square Madhouse" about the first tournament in which a computer programmed for chess played on an equal basis with the world's leading international masters.

Then I gave up chess again, or it gave me up, when I began to drink again, and struggle against drinking, and then quit again and drink again, in an on and off pattern.

After the death of my wife and after what I guess you could call an alcoholic old age crisis, I played in one last tournament in San Francisco, a rather slapdash, happy-go-lucky, unimportant, unrated contest promoted by a restaurant man who was inspired by the goddess Caissa, or else nutty about chess, depending on how you feel about such things. And that experience led me to write "Midnight by the Morphy Watch." Rasputin and the Czarina in that story were real people, real contestants in the tournament, and I invented those private nicknames for them before I conceived the story. But I never did happen on that wonderful antique store and its eccentric proprietor, alas.

As for the actual tournament in Paoli's Corner House restaurant on Commercial Street, I didn't win it. Rasputin did, just ahead of the Czarina.

I guess you can see from this backgrounding I've been doing of the Morphy watch story how it necessitated jumping around in time, fitting in autobiographic bits when they seemed helpful. Some of these different Fritz Leibers (Fritz Leiber, Juniors, until my father died in 1949) seemed quite familiar to me, others rather strange, but all of them were working together in a sense, gathering material for stories yet unwritten and undreamed of.

VI: "Four Ghosts in Hamlet". I Discover Science & Become a Grind. The Chicago Civic Shakespeare Society. Tyrone Power, Sr. & Jr.

"Four Ghosts in Hamlet" was the first story in which I made direct use of experience I gained from years of watching and hearing about the operations of the Fritz Leiber Shakespearean Repertory Company. I changed the names, of course, and shaped and fitted the incidents together differently, drawing on the events of several seasons and inventing a couple from whole cloth, and then finally setting the whole thing in England. But under all this costuming, there were real people and things I'd been told, or witnessed as a privileged backstage observer, or even participated in as a full-fledged member of the Company!

For, no, the melancholy child of the theater immured at 4353½ did not stay thwarted always. He got two good cracks at acting in the Company, once for the last half of a regular season and again some five or six years later for all of a rather short season, my father's and the Company's last.

The earlier opportunity came when I got my diploma from Lake View High School in January 1928 when I'd just turned seventeen. It seemed reasonable to delay my college entry until September to give me a taste of the theater. This was partly a reward for having got top grades and the leading male role in the senior play (though my performance was marred by a dreadful onstage failure of nerve which you'll hear about when we discuss "A Deskful of Girls") and for having finished in a complicated three-way tie with two chums for the highest grades in our graduating class.

Yes, my first school friendships were based squarely on academic competition, the prosaic pursuit and capture of "Excellents" and "Superiors." From our sophomore year on we knew we were a small elite of rival grinds, though one of us affected seldom to crack a book outside of school—until his mother blurted out innocently, "Oh, ———, he's always studying."

There were two other Germanic youths, the portly young-old-looking Edward Haenisch and the Prussian-slender Clifford Heimbucher. And trailing just behind us (in grades, of course), Willard Sproul, but he was important to my life in a way because his father ran a Presbyterian institution halfway between 4353½ and the Loop and going to Presbyterian Sunday school there was my first regular excuse for taking el trips alone.

Edward was another only child and lived with a clutch of aunts larger than mine, four I believe, while Clifford had a younger sister. We never exactly played together as I recall, we were too serious for that, and none of us were athletic, though summertimes I was getting into tennis by then (more of that later). And we didn't seem to have any great intellectual life either; high grades were the thing, not ideas, though we were all stirred mentally by the sciences—chemistry, physics, and mathematics especially—where Lake View still had an unusually fine faculty. And we did joke together in a way that now seems to me Germanic—bumptious, satirical, and mocking.

Anyhow, the three of us ended high school in a dead heat of sorts. There were two systems for totalling grades. By one Edward was first, I second, and Clifford third; by the other Clifford was first and Edward third, while I held at second. Perhaps the first system was the most important because Edward was chosen valedictorian, but I didn't envy him having to write and deliver an address.

So there I was, touring with the Company at last, and do you know, it wasn't all that much of a big deal? I stayed at the same hotels my parents did, generally in the next room. I played such tiny parts befitting my youth and inexperience as I could be fitted into at midseason without upsetting the rest of the Company, generally a part someone else had been doubling or the stray woman doing, and that I could be trusted to handle without a lot of rehearsing. The longest and most important of those was Fabian in *Twelfth Night,* a mere hanger-on of the mischievous revelers, and what I most remember about him is that at one performance I garbled the speech, "Hold, Sir Toby, here come the officers" by reading the last word as "ossifers"—bone collectors, perchance?

In *Macbeth* I recall being an apparition in the Witches' Cauldron Scene and also Donalbain, King Duncan's less important son, while in *The Merchant of Venice* I was probably one of the hanger-on "Sally" characters—Salanio, Salarino, and Salerio (to whom the Canadian humorist Stephen Leacock added a memorable fourth, Saloonio). The rest of the plays are a blur so far as what I did in them is concerned—oh, come to think of it, I must have been Francisco in *Hamlet*, the least important soldier, even though he helps start the play, and also one of the Players, though possibly one without lines. And one of the Roman mob in *Julius Caesar*, of course, and various speechless Attendant Gentlemen. It was all I could reasonably expect.

The tour took us into New England as far as a week in Boston by way of three nights in Hartford, Connecticut. In Boston I remember the curving downtown streets, so unlike Chicago's graph-paper grid, and going by myself to a daring Clara Bow movie where she ripped off an evening gown and dove into a fountain or pool in her underwear. While in Hartford I went into the courthouse and listened to a couple hours of a racy murder trial, typical daytime entertainment for a traveling actor; I recall several references to "the trombone player's evidence," which the jury had heard the day before and sounded as if it had been interestingly shocking.

Later the tour went south, where I recall we played Chapel Hill, because the University of North Carolina was there, and Nashville, where my father and Shakespeare were very popular, and surely Atlanta, "the Athens of the South."

What stands out most in my memory about that tour is the railway trips between cities: the early morning gathering in the railroad station, the suspenseful making sure no one was missing, and then the trip itself through the bright mornings and long afternoons. We'd often have a whole coach to ourselves while the scenery and trunks would travel in the Company baggage car. Generally four of the actors would play bridge, abetted by the odd Englishman in the Company, while the stagehands would engage in their inevitable pinochle game, in which my father sometimes joined. I'd listen, if I were lucky, to various older actors reminisce and hold forth. I remember the juvenile (Romeo, Sebastian, Roderigo, Osric, Lorenzo) once generously broadened my high school culture by giving me a rundown on Rabelais' *Gargantua*, which he was reading, and often I'd just sit and dream and soak in the sense of being a member of the Company.

One reason that tour wasn't such a big thing was that I knew I'd be going to college in the fall. Back when I'd entered high school my father and mother had talked of sending me to an eastern college and I'd dreamed romantically and a bit apprehensively of Yale, Harvard, Princeton, and Dartmouth, as if it were something happening in a *Rover Boys* book (I'd also read *Tom Swift* assiduously). Dartmouth won out by a hair for some Rover Boy reason (the smallest college? and so the underdog?) with Princeton second. I recall being a bit worried about that because Dartmouth was alone in requiring a year of Greek in addition to Latin and that was the only college prerequisite my Lake View courses hadn't been able to supply.

But my heart couldn't have been set too fondly on Dartmouth, because I never did anything about getting the Greek, and when the fateful day did arrive it turned out that the family exchequer was at a low ebb and I'd have to be satisfied with the University of Chicago and not living in a dormitory. Such low ebbs did happen between seasons a couple of times, though this wasn't the occasion my father had had to do Antony's oration six weeks in vaudeville to make ends meet and assure funds for the Company reopening next season. (That had been a successful though very grueling venture; my mother appeared in it as Clio, the muse of history, and instituted proceedings by announcing impressively while looking out at the audience over a big book or scroll, "Time? A word! Two thousand years? A thought! We turn the page and let the years roll back. Rome! Eternal city! Rome!")

I was a bit disappointed but also secretly relieved at the way things turned out. I'd be able to stay on at safe old 4353½ a bit longer, though now at an address farther north, farther from the U. of C., while Ed Haenisch and Willard Sproul were also going to Chicago!

In fact, they'd entered immediately after graduating from Lake View and so were a semester ahead of me. I palled around with them a while; at least we often had lunch together in huge and lofty Hutchinson Commons, long enough to get a kick out of one more typical bit of Haenisch (heinous?) behavior. It seems the university doctors had taken a look at Edward's portliness and put him on a high-protein diet, then very new. The first day of Ed's diet they'd had beef stew for dinner at his home. Ed got out his chemist's scales, and when he'd done weighing things, he got all the meat while his aunts had to make do with the gravy.

But now he was in college, Ed was twice as serious about things as he'd been in high school. I think by the end of the year he was living at Snell Hall and studying physics and chemistry like fury, while I was already hedging just a bit on my ambitions to become a great scientist. Laboratory physics or chemistry in addition to mathematics and the first semester of a two-year science survey course sounded too much to me, and so I put off taking those courses and finally never did, making do with two years of human physiology instead and finally majoring in psychology, the dubious science that has meant so many different things to so many scholars, but one in which I could get high grades without working hard— an insidious attraction.

The flame of exact precision science continued to burn strongly in Ed and he became a distinguished chemist. But I inevitably drifted away from him—and from Willard too. I was done with Sunday schools and religion (or so I thought).

Before the next academic (and theatrical) season came round, a great, miraculous-seeming change had been worked in the fortunes of the Fritz Leiber Shakespearean Company (they spelled him Shaxpur in the U. of C. catalogue, by the by, for arcane English Department reasons, but the style never caught on), a change that would make the Great Depression, which was lying in ambush just ahead, almost a good time for my father and cushion him from its worst effects.

A utilities magnate named Harley Clark was moved to become the chief backer, to the extent of a quarter of a million dollars, of what was called the Chicago Civic Shakespeare Society. Chicago Grand Opera, glory of its high society, was moving into an impressive new theater that had just been built for it at the south end of a brave new building on Wacker Drive on the Chicago River and west boundary of the Loop. At the north end of the same building, fused to the opera house by a pillared portico, was a small theater, equally new and impressive. This became the new home of the Company, now that of the Chicago Civic Shakespeare Society, my father its director and star. They would play ten or twelve weeks in Chicago, then tour elsewhere much as usual.

Harley Clark had social as well as cultural and civic aspirations. Bringing the productions of Chicago's leading Shakespearean actor back to the city of his birth seemed the way to achieve them. Clark had a vision of Civic Grand Opera and Civic Shakespeare promenading side by side with much social pomp and flurry.

The venture was successfully launched in the autumn of 1929, ironically about the same time as the Wall Street stock market collapsed and the Great Depression got under way, but it was done with my father's customary care and economy, and with any luck could have become a Chicago institution or at least lasted a half dozen years—and for the first two seasons things did go very well on the whole. I profited from it, of course. During the Company's Chicago season I stayed with my parents at a near north side hotel, and when it went on the road (as the Chicago Civic, naturally) there was no question for me about the funds to live at Hitchcock Hall. At college I reflected my father's and the Company's glory somewhat and became a campus personality of some distinction without being aware of it, so that, for example, I got parts in the productions of the U. of C. Dramatic Association without trying very hard. Years later I discovered that my diffidence at that time was generally seen as snobbishness, and that whereas I thought I was lonely, many of those around me imagined I was spending half my time on some glamorous secret off-campus existence that I was very selfish about. Nature and the osmotic influence of the stage had given me height, some good looks, grace, poise, and restraint, and college observers tailored for me a wholly fabulous personality and inner life to match the outward show. Such are the crazy shells we build around us without knowing it!

During my junior year (and the second season of the Chicago Civic) my father generously arranged for me to play the romantic part of the Prince of Morocco in a special performance of *The Merchant of Venice*, which added to my rubbed-off glamor. The same season my father sought to strengthen the Company by adding to it a couple of fairly big names, one being that of the veteran Canadian Shakespearean and also film actor Tyrone Power, Sr. This experiment was not altogether successful, but since the attendant events supply much of the story of "Four Ghosts in Hamlet," I'll not repeat them here.

Yet one thing must be said in the interests of truth. When some five or so years later the promotion department of the studio that was grooming Tyrone Power, Jr., for superstardom garbled the latter's reminiscences about his father and himself into a heroic tale of how young Ty was accidentally stabbed by *my* father on stage during a performance of *The Merchant of Venice*, yet courageously continued acting the scene to its end despite his wound, they were doing just that: fabricating an exciting piece of theatrical history for a young actor who essentially had none. Let it be recorded: Tyrone Power, Sr., acted for a season in the Chicago Civic Shakespeare Company; young Ty never did, though he was present backstage several times that year during its Chicago run, and may have gone on as an extra.

I bring up this incident because it's gotten into at least one of

Power's biographies (oddly, he died during a remake of *The Queen of Sheba,* the film my father had starred in as a silent) and because my father could never have been as clumsy and irresponsible as that on stage. He had the worrisome imagination for possible accidents, especially to other people, that I've seen in more than one older athlete who took big chances in his youth.

VII: High Society. Chicago Civic's Great Debacle. I Unexpectedly Turn Religious And Run Two Churches. Last Shakespeare Season. On To Hollywood!

During the third session of the Chicago Civic (corresponding to my senior college year) its backers went crazy, falling victim to what you could call a Burst of Glory mania or an attack of Think Big...and Bigger. (Those were nervous, uncertain, catastrophic-seeming, suicidal times, remember?) Their Shakespearean venture had been successful, but not successful enough, and while there had been some social flurry, it hadn't equalled that of Grand Opera. Though Heaven knows it had seemed big enough to me—why, I remember now! it had even got me my first dress suit (the tuxedo sort; I never did graduate to white tie and tails) which I wore to several openings and civic affairs and parties given by wealthy people.

I remember in particular the Steinbrechers. Paul was a high school crony of my father's, or at any rate had known him way back when, a genial, witty, plump little man who had a handsome narrow stone three-story house on exclusive East Schiller Street on the near north side by the lake, where he lived with his statuesque energetic wife and two charming daughters a little younger than myself and a dazzling, sumptuous library of the books he'd collected and often had rebound. He was also a member of a very small informal club of wealthy collectors called the Skeeters. And now that I come to think of it, the Skeeters and Paul must have been the link between my father and Harley Clark. I don't know to what extent any of them were financially involved in the Chicago Civic, though I imagine they must have been, but they were certainly a very pleasant, mildly worldly group. One of them had a leading collection of Lincolniana, and it was at one of their little dos that I first heard Carl Sandburg read his poetry and strum the guitar, or was it a banjo?

And it was at a Chicago Civic performance that I first met Celeste Holm, an exquisite but lively twelve-year-old with long fine blonde hair and big gold braces on her teeth. She lived on the near north side too, with her father Theodor, a Norwegian shipping official, and her mother, the artist, poet, writer, and mystic Jean Parke, both of them keenly intelligent and beautiful gentle people.

In fact, I almost got used to wearing my evening suit, though not quite. My chief memory there is still of gracious elderly ladies coming up to me with a thoughtful smile and putting their arms around my neck to adjust my bow tie which I'd forgotten to tuck down in back or put through the little white loop there.

And if all this suggests someone bobbing up from time to time into a bright frothy surface-of-society world and looking around curiously and eagerly but with a certain uneasiness and then ducking back down with relief into a middle (or upper middle) class tunnel lined with 4353½ drab or at best U. of C. gothic grey, then I'm conveying the impression I want to.

I also recall from about this time how as a result of the University and my new social contacts, those north side prejudices in which I'd never quite believed were fading away, especially those against Jews. I remember one evening on the Midway parting from a companion in a heavy overcoat with whom I'd been having some sort of intellectual discussion and thinking to myself with an air of great wonder: "I have a Jew for a friend," as if to say, "Who'd ever thought that would come to pass?" I think the person was a Paul Rosenfeld, who'd decided to devote his entire young life to investigating the causes of World War I.

But I was telling you about the madness that seized the Chicago Civic Shakespeare Society that third season. To begin with, the backers thought Fritz needed assistance and assistants, especially someone to direct while he concentrated on his own acting; an ingratiating Englishman, Lawrence Cecil, got that job. This is something that happens to most lone wolf types when they're very successful, and it's extremely difficult for a lone wolf to cope with. And since the Big Names policy had been only a qualified success the second season the cure for that was obviously to get still more Big and Bigger names, Pedro de Cordoba, Helen Mencken, Whitford Kane, etc. And the Chicago Civic Theater out by the opera house was too small; they must move to a big one in the center of the Loop. And charge higher prices!—even if it did mean mostly thwarting the school audiences who'd previously been a mainstay. And finally after the Chicago run they mustn't head down south or some other region where the name "Fritz Leiber" really meant ticket sale, but go straight to New York and Broadway and have a second big run there!

Well, any damn fool can see now where a policy like that was going to lead in the third year of the Great Depression. In fact, I think it's a prize example of the hysterical lemming-like rush deeper and deeper into destruction that was going on then (we'll get back to this moment and mood once more at least, when we discuss alcoholism and "Gonna Roll the Bones"), while, artistically speaking, you can't departmentalize a lone wolf creation without the most careful thought and preparation, or expect to super-improve a good show by hurriedly dumping Big Names into it, no matter how well they can act.

The best thing you can say about the crash of the Chicago Civic was that they didn't have to borrow money or go bankrupt to do it. They simply blew capital that should have lasted a couple more years at least in one grandiose burst, and that was that.

My father saved out of this debacle enough of his salary to cushion us during the next few years, which was a pretty damned good outcome, as outcomes were going at that time, though of course it was a bitter disappointment to his Shakespearean aspirations for the Midwest. No wonder he retired to the Bungalow with Bronnie for the next couple of years to lick his wounds and get the feel of the cold new winds that were galing across the economic landscape before venturing out again. Providentially he'd just winterized the Bungalow by digging a cellar for a furnace under the kitchen and building a big bedroom over that corner of the house, and a steeper roof over the gentler one while leaving most of the latter in place, which helped the insulation considerably. Taken all in all, he was a pretty prudent and resourceful man, you know.

Meanwhile during all this commotion and excitement, I'd got my bachelor's degree. I'd made third year Phi Beta Kappa (boast, boast!) mostly because the high-grades compulsion of high school had continued despite the theater's rival attractions, and in my fourth year won a full graduate scholarship. In philosophy, of all things. Psychology had gotten me interested in metaphysics, you see, and there was a good dreamy professor named Charles Hartshorn who taught that, and an equally fascinating one named Eustace Haydon who had a tiny Department of Comparative Religion all his own, in which he promulgated a brand of anthropological liberal humanism that intrigued me and inspired my noble "do-gooder" side. (It derived from Ethical Culture, I found out later, though I didn't know about that then.)

Of course I didn't have a single realistic thought about the practical consequences of all this, as the foregoing may already have suggested to the astute reader. I didn't have the faintest notion, then, that studying philosophy would have prepared me for teaching philosophy, period. Or maybe get me ready for a political career, furthest thing from my thoughts. No, I thought then that in the university you simply followed your changing tastes and interests, accumulating all sorts and varieties of knowledge, and that finally the pressure of all that wisdom (especially if you kept getting high grades) automatically launched you into some nicely paying job. Emotionally I was still pretty much a baby, though quite a savvy-seeming guy in several areas. (Again, the wondrous shells we build around us, the amazing camouflages! And also around the world and the life we think we're facing. And that other people fabricate around us.)

Well, with me drunk on that sort of brew, and with my parents looking around at their own fractured careers and wondering what to do about their bright, studious, but most unworldly son now that the theater was out for a while, is it any wonder that when an extremely able, modern-thinking, but utterly theater-struck Episcopalian priest of a parish neighboring Atlantic Highlands (and who also ran a New York advertising agency on the side) seriously suggested to us that I enter the ministry, and provided practical means for my doing so, we should all three of us have taken this fantastic suggestion seriously and ended by deciding it was a bonzer idea or at least the best available solution of all the problems of Young Fritz?

You think not? Well, you've got to remember we were all three actors, and to an actor a priest is just one more role or part, a particularly easy one because a priest himself is just a sort of actor who puts on shows in churches and delivers long orations or soliloquies called sermons. This thing gets pretty deep if you pursue it because the first actors in classical Greece were indeed religious celebrants, minor priests of a sort, who put on dramas to honor gods. And to me in my scholastic dream world after watching my interests veer from physics and chemistry to mathematics and psychology and from those to philosophy and metaphysics, it seemed most logical that they should take the next step into theology, at least to feel out the ground there. Also you've got to keep in mind that these were Depression times, when no job offer of any sort was to be cast aside lightly. I know it impressed me mightily that I'd be *paid* a little for taking this bizarre vocational plunge and supported fully while attending the General Theological Seminary in downtown Manhattan on weekdays and eating there and sleeping there weeknights.

Of course there was the matter of belief, belief in God, to be considered. It seemed to me that was, or might become, important. (Score one for my budding realism.) I asked the Reverend Ernest W. Mandeville ("Beezie" for short; he'd gone bald young, reminded me of Daddy Warbucks) about it. He looked me in the eye and said, "Think of it as social service." That's why I described him as "modern thinking."

So I got rather hurriedly baptized and confirmed and to wrap it all up Beezie staged a little promotional gag (he ran an advertising agency on the side, remember?—and was theater-struck) in which my father garbed as Shylock (and representing the Old Testament, you could suppose) gave away or dedicated handsome me in cassock and surplice (the New Testament?) to Beezie in full priestly regalia (Episcopal Christendom?) on the front steps of Beezie's church in Middletown, New Jersey. Made *The New York Times* too, picture and all.

Which seems to confirm the popular belief that actors will do anything for publicity and also my point that priests aren't so different from actors, after all, when you get down to the nitty-gritty.

When my University of Chicago friends and acquaintances saw the news, they naturally thought I must have gone ga-ga for God, completely bonkers. After all, they knew I never went to church or showed any interest in religion. But that information was slow in filtering back to me. And I had lots of new things to occupy me.

If you took seriously my cousin's opinion that I could be a good anything *if* I were instructed to do so, you won't be surprised to hear that I got high grades at the Theological Seminary the first semester and that on weekends I functioned okay as minister and lay reader at my two little previously failed Episcopal churches in Atlantic Highlands and nearby Highlands. I put on a pretty good show at morning prayer, I preached adequate very short sermons, I visited parishioners dutifully, attendance revived, and once a month Beezie turned up to bless 'em and pass out the wine and wafers. He conducted marriages; I handled baptisms and funerals; while my father got the opportunity to put his stage carpentry skills to various good uses and even built a new altar and painted a new triptych for Highlands. (Oh, he was indeed a Renaissance man, I really mean it!)

And if you've given some thought to the vagaries of my psychology, you probably won't be surprised to learn that the second semester I was consumed with doubts about the whole business (I had discovered that, contrary to what I'd been told, social service had no Belief in God department.) I stayed to the end of the season, as any good trouper would, and then bowed out, feeling embarrassed and very foolish, but extremely firm about my decision.

Nor will you be startled to discover that next season my ploy was to rebound to the University of Chicago and try to take advantage of that scholarship I'd passed up. Turned out they'd only give me a third of it, but that was better than nothing, and there were still my father's dwindling Chicago Civic savings to cushion me.

This time I shared an off-campus apartment with two other guys (economy *was* becoming important) but as far as my scholarly ambitions went, my intent to compass the universe by way of philosophy, I discovered at long last that I was getting a bit disorganized, emotional and vocational and sexual problems (we'll explore those when we talk about "A Deskful of Girls") were beginning seriously to interfere with my work, and I ended the season with five incompletes that never did get completed and a couple of short papers on metaphysics that read like notes for future papers as yet unwritten.

Pretty discouraging, all right. It looked as if the University of Chicago no longer held any more future for me than the General Theological Seminary had. So when early that summer, back at the Bungalow, I discovered that my father after lying low and mulling things over for two years had *a plan* for himself and Bronnie, and that the plan included me, you can bet that I lifted up my ears.

We were five years into the Great Depression now. Most of the theaters all across the country were dark. Only a clutch in New York and a random few in other big cities were operating, and some of those only sporadically. The state of the stage was lousy.

And so my father was planning a tour. The Fritz Leiber Shakespearean Company was going to challenge all that Depression darkness and dare the road again, and I was going to be acting in it. We'd only be doing five plays, most of them biggies: *Hamlet, Macbeth, King Lear, Julius Caesar, The Merchant of Venice*. And I'd be playing some decent parts at last, best of them all the madness-feigning Edgar, who has to create fantasy worlds on stage, in *King Lear*, a play for which I'd actually helped my father prepare a new acting version at the Chicago Civic, one that restored the scene in which old Gloster has his eyes poached out on stage—a scene

Myself as Edgar in King Lear, *an oil by Francois de Brovillette.*

which, Charles Lamb to the contrary, was *not* put in just to titillate the groundlings, but also to discharge some of the hellish emotional pressures built up in the drama, make the audience live the horror and share the guilt and remorse. I'd be playing under the name of Francis Lathrop, a real chance to prove myself, and not as a "Jr." And we'd be using the good simple scenery and some of the actors from the old company, but also new ones—time had passed— including an Arnold Robertson I'd gotten to know at a semi-amateur production of *Hamlet* by Harry Thornton Moore I'd helped with (not much really—I'd offered to make up Robertson for the

King and botched the job) at the University of Chicago. We'd rehearse at Atlantic Highlands, open in Newark or Jersey City, and then head for the Midwest.

This plan wasn't the suicidal foray it sounds like; my father hadn't succumbed to Burst of Glory mania or an attack of the Forward, All Lost Causes! The plan contained a concealed secondary stage, a secret escape hatch, but I can't tell you about that right away without spoiling the suspense. Nor could my father have told any of us at the time without ruining our dramatic concentration.

And it *was* a great intensifier of things, a great shot in the arm for all concerned, to get going on that wonderful season. I won't tell you about it in any detail, because again I'd be duplicating things in "Four Ghosts in Hamlet" (you can figure me as the young narrator there and make guesses). Except that I did get a genuine season in Shakespeare, and although I hadn't had nearly the acting training and experience I should have had by then, and had my lonely emotional problems to cope with besides, I did pretty well according to the notices, well enough so that by the end of the season I was acting under my own name.

There was even a funny little bonus to start with. By now I was sure that whatever I became I was going to be some kind of writer on the side (tell you more about that later). So when my father decided this season to have souvenir programs (a dollar extra) I got to use my university wisdom in emulating Lamb by writing the stories of the five plays. Also at the same time I was writing children's stories for *The Churchman*, a most respectable Episcopalian journal edited by the Rev. E. W. Mandeville, another of his side jobs. Beezie wasn't one to bear a grudge. I'd failed him as the young assistant priest with soulful eyes and a marvelous stage presence he'd hoped for, but he was happy to give me a hand on *my* new sideline. I've really gotten lots of screwy assists in life!

But about the season. We opened briefly in the East and headed for the Midwest fast, not even dipping into the possibly still sympathetic South. And we didn't linger near Chicago either; in fact, we played Milwaukee instead. Before we knew it we were in Denver, where I'd Christmas-visited my folks as a boy and got included in a panoramic picture of the 1923 Fritz Leiber Company. Then, in rapid succession: Pocatello, Idaho; Walla Walla, Washington; Seattle; and Vancouver, B.C., where we'd have done great business if there hadn't been a thick four-day fog.

Next a week in San Francisco, where I remember staying at the then-new El Cortez Hotel, just across the street from where I'm living now. That week was really a final tune-up for the secondary stage of the plan, though I still didn't suspect what was going on—I'm slow on the uptake—in fact, I was furiously studying the part of Cassius, which I'd taken a great fancy to and hoped to persuade my father to let me play *once* this season, in some unimportant city.

But this wasn't the time for any such minor vanities. The moment was upon us. We played two weeks in Los Angeles and we played well, we got good notices and the attendance was good; a couple nights we sold out. Presto! Mission accomplished—although I *still* didn't see it; I so wanted to play Cassius.

Oh, after that we played three nights in Tucson, Arizona, but that was just for the sake of appearances. Wouldn't have looked right to have *closed* in Los Angeles.

But in Tucson Big Fritz did close the company, shipped off the scenery, and gave the other actors and the three company stagehands their tickets back to New York.

But he and Bronnie and I returned to Los Angeles, not to the Biltmore, where they'd stayed during our little run, nor I to the cheaper nearby hotel where I'd had a room.

No, we were shortly to be seen ensconced on the rustic front porch of the resort-like old Hollywood Hotel at Hollywood and Highland, three blocks east of Grauman's Chinese and a half dozen west of Hollywood and Vine, right in the heart of filmland. The second stage of Big Fritz's plan was under way.

Oh, it took patience and a good agent and some holding out but the plan worked out reasonably well in the end. In a few months on the strength of his general reputation and that last smashing appearance he was getting the parts that would maintain him and his during the next fifteen years and one penultimate heart attack: a series of Frenchmen, priests, doctors, German spies, and Indian chiefs, most of them in big pictures, though he never became the star again he'd been in the silents. Now *all* the stage actors were in Hollywood.

By an un-odd coincidence, the Abbey Players from Ireland were doing much the same thing at the same time. On the strength of a good Los Angeles run, or partly for that reason at least, a half dozen of them made Hollywood careers for themselves, among them Barry Fitzgerald and his even more talented but less photogenic brother, Arthur Shields.

Even a couple of actors in Fritz's company took his cue, stayed on the Coast and made it out there, including my friend Robertson, who did well in radio, too.

*Playing grave-robber and mad doctor. Photograph by Walt Daugher-
ty. The head's from the film* Spartacus.

To glance ahead, my father located permanently on the West Coast. He and Bronnie never went back to the Bungalow, except to sell it after World War II. Before his death in 1949 he'd been in more than fifty films, including substantial roles in *The Story of Louis Pasteur, Anthony Adverse, Monsieur Verdoux, The Prince and the Pauper, The Hunchback of Notre Dame, Champagne Waltz, The Thief of Paris,* and *Devil's Doorway,* his last.

That leaves to explain why ever did I set "Four Ghosts in Hamlet" in England instead of the country I knew a little about. Easy. The year I wrote the story was 1964, the quatercentenary of Shakespeare's birth. To celebrate it, the *London Argosy* put up a prize of one thousand pounds for the best short story that had Shakespeare as a character. My attention was directed to this offer by Theodore Sturgeon, who'd won an earlier *London Argosy* story contest and knew that Shakespeare was one of my things—another of those screwy assists I've gotten from generous imaginative people now and again.

When Ted slipped me the news the contest deadline was close at hand, I wrote the story in four days and air-mailed it off. I'd been goosed, you might say, into writing a story about my own experiences and those of other real people, disguisedly of course, in an area I'd never ventured into before. If I'd had more time in which to weigh and consider I might have lost my nerve, had second thoughts.

Since a British magazine was running the contest, I thought it might improve the story's winning chances if I set it in England. I can be surprisingly meretricious when it comes to selling a story. So I made my father a British touring star like Greet or Benson and tried to make the narrator sound British. And I laid the crucial scenes in an imaginary Wolverton rather than a real Wolverhampton because I was afraid of making mistakes if I set them in a real city I'd never visited.

All probably quite unnecessary, and my story didn't win in any case, but as soon as "Four Ghosts in Hamlet" came back from London I shipped it off to *The Magazine of Fantasy and Science Fiction,* and they liked it well enough to buy it, which soothed my disappointment.

VIII: "A Deskful Of Girls". Sex Lifts Her Loverly Face. The Movies. Love At A Distance.

And so we arrive at "A Deskful of Girls," which I've been hinting I'd talk about, even dropping the word "sex" as bait.

But you know, when I sat down late last night with "Deskful" to read it carefully word by word, I had to fight resistance every inch of the way to make myself finish it.

Whenever I read anything I've written about sex a few years ago, let alone almost twenty-five, I cringe in expectation of finding it unbelievably ignorant, shamefully naive. That's a measure of how uptight I can still get about sex, what a forbidden topic it was for me, a fortress of dark secrets guarded by monsters and furies, and how concerned, even obsessed, I am with understanding it and speaking and writing honestly about it, and for that matter in acquitting myself honorably in the exercise of it, no matter to how small a degree....

But let's hold up a minute before getting in so deep. There's still my reactions to re-reading "Deskful" twenty-four years later to be discussed.

Well, pretty soon, as I kept reading along, pushing myself, I noticed that my villain, Dr. Slyker, was supposed to be incredibly knowledgeable about sex. What a laugh, I thought, me trying to put that over on the reading public. Still, I told myself, in fashioning any story you have to be willing to be all things in it, even if you have to fake like hell; it's part of the fiction writer's job.

I also saw that I was writing what Kingsley Amis in his amusing book about James Bond, "that damned elusive 007," has described as an essential scene in any Bond book: the one in which the supervillain—Dr. No, Blofeld, Mr. Big—gets Bond completely in his power and then proceeds to lecture him on how clever he, the villain, is and how stupid and childish Bond is, and how after the lecture he's going to kill him in an exquisite manner yet fully to be determined. The scene in the headmaster's study, Amis called it.

But then I remembered that when I wrote "Deskful" I hadn't read a word by Ian Fleming. It would be five years before I succumbed to the urgings of Jack Pocsik and discovered the genteel pleasures of Bond. So I'd hit on the scene without Fleming's assistance. Not that that was any particular achievement. Other writers had done it still earlier, notably Sax Rohmer.

I also realized that my heroine was obviously inspired by Marilyn

Monroe. Yes, I remembered, by 1957 I'd come fully under her delicious spell. But why among earlier cinema sex goddesses hadn't I mentioned Jean Harlow? Oh, yes (I discovered on the next page), because my heroine was going to star in *The Jean Harlow Story.* Well, I'd been accurate there, I congratulated myself. Marilyn Monroe *could* have played Jean Harlow, I'm certain. She'd just have had to stiffen her chin and be a mite hard-boiled. Who knows? It might have done her good, poor kid.

Pretty soon I'd turned the last page and discovered to my relief that it was a pretty feminist story, after all, despite all the pseudo-macho and voyeurism in it, and perhaps not too bad a try at making scientifically plausible, or at least pseudo-scientifically plausible, a very far-out idea.

But then that's true of all the most exciting science fiction and science fantasy stories. They use good honest science in the service of really wild speculations.

And now I remembered something about "Deskful." Along with "Try and Change the Past," it was a spinoff from my novel *The Big Time.* In fact, those two short stories were published, in *MSFS* and *Astounding,* respectively, the same months (March, April 1958) that *The Big Time* ran as a two-part serial in *Galaxy.* I'd sold pieces of the same idea to three rival publishers at once—maybe not too smart a procedure.

Now *The Big Time* was—in fact, in a sense *had to be*—a very rich novel simply because I hadn't written *anything* for three years (1954, 1955, 1956), and new raw material was accumulating in my subconscious all that while. The reason I hadn't written anything was that I was going through my first and most severe alcoholic crisis, and between drinking and fighting drinking there was no time for anything else. Nor the capacity for doing anything creative, of course.

But when I finally did get off the booze and squared away (it took four months, there were complications, I had to get off sleeping pills too) I wrote *The Big Time* in exactly one hundred days from first conscious conception to sending off the manuscript, which I'd laid out lovingly and handsomely and final-typed myself. Very rich with all the stuff of my galloping alcoholism and its eventual remission, fictionally transmuted of course. My typewriter was *hot.* I have that on the testimony of no less than Horace Gold, editor of *Galaxy.* (He changed his mind about that, of course, as soon as I sent him a story he didn't like, in fact.) But at the time he said so, and it was true, my typewriter really was hot, and some things spun off it almost automatically.

In *The Big Time* I never explained in so many words the metaphysics underlying the Change War that was going on in it. So I explained that in "Try and Change the Past," the first spinoff.

And then in the same novel I'd invented these fascinating creatures called ghostgirls. Ordinarily they hung on racks in the storeroom, like theatrical costumes between seasons. But when you needed them to comfort the soldiers in the time-traveling rehabilitation station that was the scene of *The Big Time,* you took them down and animated them. You could use up a lot of girls that way— ghostgirls, I mean, nothing sexist intended.

Now in *The Big Time* it was assumed that the psychomedical unit running the rehabilitation station had access to all sorts of gadgets and devices of far future science, so I didn't have to explain there in detail exactly how the ghostgirls worked. Yet I, as their inventor and writer, got more and more fascinated with them, thinking of them hanging on their racks in the dark storeroom like long veils of flesh-colored silk streaked with wisps of fine black and platinum hair and very faintly shimmering (yet how *real* they seemed in a suave mindless way when animated). I guess I fell in love with them in a way, and I began to wonder: *Could there possibly be anything like them in the real world? in the real world of today where I might meet one? Think now, could there?* and so "A Deskful of Girls" spun off. Any erotic zing that story has goes back to this wondering of mine about ghostgirls in the dark, trying to make them stir and fill out and swim around, luxuriating generally, and come to life.

One last detail: Both *The Big Time* and "A Deskful of Girls" were written to music; the only other story on which I ever used that technique successfully was the novella "Ship of Shadows," but it can be stimulating and good discipline. I'd started each writing session by putting on the record of the music that I'd picked to go with that story, and before it was done I'd have begun typing. For *The Big Time* it was Beethoven's piano sonata, *The Pathetique,* and Schubert's *The Unfinished Symphony,* while for "Deskful" it was of course Tchaikovsky's *Nutcracker Suite,* which figures in the story, especially the wholly imaginary "Ghostgirls' Pavan," which I took the liberty of adding to it. (And for "Ship of Shadows," Holst's *The Planets.)*

In writing about the sexual aspects of my growing up, insofar as I ever did, I'll be doing a lot of time-traveling up and down my own lifeline. If some of Little Fritzie's memory flashes sound like

Victorian curiosa, remember that a lot of the so-called sex liberation of the 1920s was superficial, a matter of the big cities, the arty upper crust, and college fads, that it was also a decade of strict censorship, reactionary government, the rule of taboo—why, my God, they had *Prohibition*—and that deeper liberation didn't really get under way until the movements of the 1960s and 1970s. And

although I've stressed, maybe even exaggerated, the liberalizing influence of the theater, remember my parents were first-generation actors with conventional conservative childhoods which on the whole they tried to pass on to me. Also keep in mind that all my life I've been a writer, not a doer, and so my intellectual liberation was *far* ahead of my emotional and behavioral ones, and even so had many curious blind spots.

My earliest awareness of the difference between the sexes was a strictly above-the-waist business. I have this memory flash of asking my mother what those bumps on her chest were. She drew back her shoulders proudly, got a bright dramatic light in her eyes, and responded, "Wings!"

Well, certainly no one can complain about an incident like that. Though of course she might have gone on to say "Milk glands," and in fact she probably did; it just didn't get into my memory flash. I think her answer struck a happy note, putting her breasts' decorative and recreational functions ahead of their utilitarian one. Suppose like Carrie's mother she'd said, "Dirty-pillows"—ugh! It doesn't bear to be thought of! But I've already told you my childhood wasn't troubled by religious fanatics or sexual morality nuts. No, it was more by way of things I wasn't told and didn't investigate or ask questions about that difficulties in this area began to accumulate for me. Remember, Little Fritzie didn't take the initiative; you had to tell him.

Perhaps that early memory flash was a first indication that breasts would become for me the focus of erotic attraction and female beauty.

All my later life it's been an unending amazement to me how much of my thought and feeling has been wrapped up in so limited an area of the female body. Why so much of the exquisite, the poignant gently folded into that crucial area? Why that particular concatenation of shapes? I can go at it geometrically and say, "Two conoids embedded in a flattened cylinder" or, somewhat more aptly, "Adjacent twin conoids of a height about one third their diameter, their apices small hemispheres, smoothly set their own diameter apart and slightly divergent in the broader face of a somewhat flattened cylinder," and yet geometry can be at best only a part of the explanation; the whole thing's maddening.

And yet when I first became aware of a romantic attraction toward girls, it was their faces in which it centered, not their bodies at all, or at least not for a while yet, and then not the whole body but the upper half.

But before I get into that, I want to set down another memory flash, the time being about my last year of grammar school, warning you in advance that I can offer no clever explanation for it. I've begun to have wet dreams, nocturnal emissions, a strange phenomenon I mention to no one. I'm in my inner temple of privacy, the white-tiled bathroom of 4353½. I'm naked, I've just taken a bath, and I'm anxiously studying my fattening torso and breasts in the mirror over the washbowl and wondering somewhat fearfully if I am turning into a girl. That's all, period.

The situation reeks of narcissism, of course, but that's an afterwards thought, a judgment by me here and now. I don't recall having any simultaneous fears then that my penis was shrinking, or my testicles retreating back into my body, but such fears may have been there—though that last's unlikely, I hadn't the anatomical knowledge. Was it anything like the crisis of identity transsexuals have? A fleeting attack of transsexuality, so to speak? No levity intended. For somehow this fear (if it was wholly that) faded out and I recall no more of it.

But it does remind me to tell you that at about this time I ceased forever to sleep in the same bed as my virginal Aunt Marie. I'd never done that regularly or even often, but I had terrible night fears, as when after seeing the play *The Cat and the Canary* I lived in terror of a small panel opening at the head of my bed and a skinny clawed green arm come snaking out and sink its talons in me, and at the worst of such times I couldn't get to sleep alone. My aunt and I would sleep on opposite sides of the bed, when we did, there was no touching, and we did not undress in the same room, or at least watch each other undressing and putting on pyjamas or nightgown, though I recall on one occasion pretending to be asleep before her and slitting my eyes open and glimpsing her small flat white unsagging breasts. My night fears were banished by the knowledge that there was someone within touching distance, or just in the same room. At such times there were no thoughts of primary sex organs, of bodies below the waist, and as for sex acts, I didn't know what those were. For that matter there was very little physical contact between us at any time. Handshakes and an occasional formal light kiss on the cheek, her hand on my arm as we walked, my hand holding her elbow when we crossed a street. And then one day I overheard a short whispered altercation between her and my Aunt Dora (the realist) with my Aunt Dora saying we couldn't go on doing it any more, it wasn't right, and my Aunt Marie agreeing after a moment of breathy protestation. And that was that, we never did it again. I recall very little more about it, really, except how still I lay on my back in my aunt's bed and watched the ceiling. I suppose now that we must have got a lot of practice at restraint that way—it was a sort of "sword between us" testing—and deepened our inhibitions against body contact.

Back to faces. I believe I know where their romantic attraction began for me—in the movies! The romantic parts of movies weren't as interesting or exciting to me as the adventure parts, but practically all movies had them, and one way you could pass time during them, keep your mind occupied, was in deciding which young actresses you liked most, which were your favorites. And since the bodies were all pretty much alike, as far as you could tell, you went almost entirely by faces, to which the camera paid the most attention anyhow. I recall a certain wonder at how different two faces could be, yet both be very attractive: Colleen Moore, say, and Laura La Plante, both were favorites of mine. And then of course there was your arch-favorite, the one with whom you were, in a way, "in love." For me, Alice Terry first, then Garbo. And then, though she never quite supplanted Garbo in turn, Jean Harlow—but that's going ahead too fast, by that time I was into breasts (and oh, the wonderful peekaboo games she and her camera played with them! In *Hell's Angels,* say, the evening dress scene—the dogfights were a minor attraction by comparison; and then Marilyn Monroe carried on her great tradition in the crucial area most charmingly).

Perhaps I should say here, though it seems obvious to me, that I did not "mentally undress" any of these young actresses—except Harlow, of course (or should I say Jean?) and she came later. I'd never seen a real girl do it. And I wouldn't have thought about a real girl in that way, then.

No, at the time I'm talking about, second year high school, I surreptitiously studied the girls in my new homeroom 108 for several days and finally picked the one I was "in love" with. I don't recall her name, while her dear face is mostly pale blur across the room inside my mind today, pale blur within bobbed pale brown hair, with wide-set eyes and serious expression. I don't recall talking to her except in the course of schoolroom business; I don't recall trying to. Outside 108 I sometimes followed her around at a distance for short stretches, but I never got to know where she lived or much of anything else about her. And then after a while she faded.

I don't recall that this notable lack of success bothered me much. It seemed in the nature of "love." You didn't get to know movie actresses, did you? (Actually, some fifteen years later, I played the tiny but screen-credited part of Valentine in *Camille;* my one scene was with Robert Taylor in a garden standing behind a buffet wedding breakfast table, with me standing in a hole so as not to look taller as well as handsomer; I never did meet Garbo in the flesh.)

I recall the number of the room because when the sophomore class, divided over several homerooms, elected its officers, we voters were encouraged to electioneer for our mates. I noted that there was a candidate for each office in our homeroom and created the rhyming poster, "Vote the Straight, 108." Which indicated two things: that my poetic talents had not grown noticeably since infancy and that I was no shrewd politico. Wiser roommates voted against my poster's display because of its cliquism and the offense it would give voters in other homerooms.

I did not cut much of a figure in 108. The grades chase had not yet attracted much attention and I was still quite plump. But by the next year, fortunately, an increased growth rate and tennis had begun to take care of my overweight.

One final sidelight on my romanticism of this period, my lukewarm devotion to "love at a distance." A friend of mine whose views I value highly—she's someone very special—is Myna Lockwood, Manhattan friend of my mother and father, successful commercial artist and author of children's stories and the grown-up novel, *A Mouse Is Miracle Enough,* whose husband Walter was a Midwestern crony of my father, New York advertising man, and occasional fantasy author for *Bluebook* and such. Now, at age ninety-four, she is busily setting down (solely for her own amusement, she assures me) her recollections of folks past and gone under the general title "Specks of Dust." Lately she wrote me: "Whatever else is crumbling of me because of age, my memory remains intact. It seems to be a veritable attic of put-away odds and ends, this and that. You'd be astonished to know what there is in that attic of records of you and trivial incidents. For instance I have one odd bit about a very tall girl you became acquainted with as you were both trying on shoes in a store. Later she went off to Europe on some ocean liner and you told me you went down to the Battery and watched the ship depart until it was a mere speck of light in the far far distance. You told me, 'I thought how strange it was that such a very tall girl with big feet could be in that speck of light.'"

IX: "Deskful" Part Two. Tennis To The Rescue! Sex Puckers Up, I Panic. A Dreadful Midnight Kitchen Scene. Emotional Crimes. The Electric Kiss.

But on to tennis!—which was very much a summer thing, a Bungalow thing, my mother its chief instigator, although she never cut much of a figure at it herself or tried to. Looking back now I think she supported tennis strongly because she thought it might have a good socializing influence on me, especially where girls were concerned.

My father was always easy to interest in anything athletic, and he must have thought the exercise would be good for me, but like the stubborn and somewhat reclusive lone wolf he was, his inevitable first response was not to join the local tennis club, which I think my mother had intended, but to lay out a lawn tennis court of our own, there being just room enough to squeeze one in between the Bungalow and the Cow Pits.

Learning tennis, however, led us to get in the Essex and drive over more than once to look at the August tournament of the exclusive Sea Bright Lawn Tennis Club, a staid and toney institution not above selling the hoi polloi tickets to their meet, which was one of the three or four big Eastern tournaments building up to the national championships at Forest Hills. The spotless white buildings with shaded porches, the white-lined green courts, the temporary grandstands, the dashing players all in trim white garb, the white-clad scurrying ball boys and striding officials combined in the hot sunlight and cool sea breezes to create an air of aristocratic theatricality which captivated us: Suzanne Lenglen, Helen Wills, dashing Dick Williams, the "Three Musketeers" Lacosta, Cochet, and Borotra ("four" if you count Brugnon), above all the fantastic and ever gentlemanly gay Big Bill Tilden, theatrical and theater-mad (he played Count Dracula in a road company), his life headed for a woeful comic tragedy ending that was his era's fault, not his— they were all of them like nothing before or since.

Next summer my father relented and we joined the Atlantic Highlands Tennis Club, which boasted five clay courts overlooking the

Bay from atop the palisades at the east end of town on the road to Highlands; for secretary it had a skinny nat-brown Anglo-Indian, Mr. Syer, whose favorite phrase was the flatteringly conspiratorial: "Those in the know..." I don't recall being much socialized by the club, or getting to know girls any better, but my family slowly acquired a new circle of friends, most of them with New York ties and some of whom went in for fairly serious drinking; I remember driving with my father into the backwoods a little ways to buy some illicit applejack at a farm (Prohibition days, remember?). And I got to know a youth who worshipped R.O.T.C. and Eastern colleges and systems and being "in the know"—later during my season at the General Theological Seminary he became my chief Manhattan friend.

Over the years my own tennis improved to the point where I played once or twice on the club team, no more than that, but I read a lot of books on the game and got more enamored of it and practiced quite a lot, banging the ball against the fifth court backstop with the white line on it or against the Bungalow garage door, and had my mild dreams of developing my will power like Lacosta by Dr. Coue's system of autosuggestion and becoming a Sea Bright star.

And because of his imaginative and logistic talents my father eventually got saddled (quite willingly) with the job of laying out and semi-supervising a couple of treasure hunts to raise money for the club. This pleasant nonsense, which involved clues laid across the near countryside and much racing about in automobiles, was rather like carefree war games and quite characteristic of the late 1920s and early 1930s (see the movie *My Man Godfrey*). I, being in the know, felt suspended between excitement and boredom.

Starting my senior year back at Lake View High, I deviated from the college entrance grades-chase just enough to take one course in drama from a Miss Easton (or Weston?), whose rather mod, vaunting credo was that we should all try to be sulphides, not stuffy old bromides, and this did involve me to a limited extent with girls, mostly one girl. We put on a classroom production of Edna St. Vincent Millay's *The King' Henchman* (see, Miss Easton *was* mod), and being my father's son, slimmed now by tennis, I fell into the male lead part, while the female lead was enacted by a tall, rakish and ravishing brunette, Elizabeth Craig Nelson. In *Henchman* she discovers me asleep in a forest glade and instantly falls in love with me; really, there's a lot of deep humor in that if you think about it properly: me, the 4353½ virgin, as Sleeping Beauty.

Because it was just a classroom production, a sort of work or exercise rather than entertainment, the closer embraces and kisses were omitted, not wisely as it turned out, but there was a lot of rehearsing and staring deep, deep into each other's eyes. Hers were prominent and brown.

Now you'd think with a situation like that, there'd have been a lot of running around together and getting acquainted by us two, but I honestly don't recall so. There was some talking at school, having lunch there together, nothing else. One gets the impression this Fritz Leiber was a standoffish guy, slow to talk honestly about himself, hard to get to know. Yet Miss Nelson was a bright girl, already better educated than I in a general way. I recall she recommended I read *Jean Christophe* by Romain Rolland, a pacifist hero of World War I, which should have been just right for me the way I was going to develop, but I didn't consider having a go at it. I had no use then for books that weren't either class assignments or adventure stories; the one exception I made to that was H. G. Wells, and after all his scientific romances were mostly adventure story, though they had their serious spots.

No, it wasn't until we got cast for the leads in the senior play that Miss Nelson, sensible soul, took matters into her own hands and insisted that I go on a date with her.

Now this was my very first date with a girl, believe it or not, and only a Sunday afternoon date at that (I to pick her up at her home, we to go over to some friends of hers), and yet it was marred, or at least encumbered, heavily weighted down, by a typical 4353½ confusion.

I didn't know, you see, whether I'd been invited to Sunday dinner or not, and if so where? Why I did not call up and find out I do not know. Maybe I tried to and they were out. Anyway, 4353½ took counsel and I ate Sunday dinner at home, feeding a little lightly, but not much. Arriving at the Nelson house I found another Sunday dinner awaiting me. It filled the gaps left by my light feeding and then some. Somewhat uncomfortably distended, I accompanied Elizabeth to her friends' flat where (somewhat to *her* surprise also, I think) a third Sunday dinner awaited me. My impressions of our visit are chiefly of trying piece by piece to conceal two thirds of a large helping of chicken salad beneath a piece of lettuce on my plate, while time moved with nightmarish slowness. Not much talking got done that I recall, I believe some records were played, Elizabeth and I learned little of each other, we were hardly in a mood to, and I got back to 4353½ in the early evening, which was just as well, since Dora, Marie, and

Ed had begun to worry about me (prefiguring a second disaster that was to follow hard on the heels of my Senior play boo-boo).

The senior play was *Pygmalion and Galatea,* not the thing by Shaw, but a play in a paperback acting edition put out by French about a modern sculptor whose statue of a beautiful nymph comes to life. And it was well rehearsed, all but the final embrace and kiss of the two title characters, actions which, I suppose, were supposed to come naturally on performance night.

I have known of companies where there's a tradition of never speaking the final line of the play being produced until opening night, or dress rehearsal at any rate. I cannot recommend any such practice.

And I have sometimes wondered if there is an unspoken belief that the climactic kiss of the heroine and hero of the high school senior play is symbolic of a declaration of liberation by the whole class. Perhaps. But for me that is a grim thought.

For on performance night of *Pygmalion and Galatea* in the vast auditorium of Lake View High School, I flinched. My memory somehow sees this from two viewpoints. In one I'm on the stage in my own body. In the other I'm watching from an imaginary balcony. But for both the sequence of actions is the same. His arms enclose hers, their faces tip together, closer and closer, and then to the great surprise of all concerned his lips dodge past hers, as though he were a vampire seeking the neck bite, but then his face prematurely comes to rest against hers, cheek to cheek. A few startled laughs grow into a moderate roar of mirth which dies out rather suddenly because of embarrassment or a belated show of consideration for my feelings.

There memory and my double vision break off. I do not know for sure if anything more was said about my disgusting omission afterwards, but I do not think so.

A couple of days later I am invited with Clifford Heimbucher to a sort of surprise graduation party at Edward Haenisch's. 4353½ is dubious about this. It involves an el trip and I am seldom out at night. But I assure them I'll be home early and go off.

It's a surprise party, all right. There are girls. For Clifford, Margaret Koch, who lives near Ravenswood Grammar School. For me, Elizabeth. I am having my first night date with a girl and 4353½ doesn't know about it.

I don't know why I don't just call them up and tell them about the changed situation. Perhaps I despair of explaining it to them, or of making them understand that girls have to be taken home after parties, or just that some people stay up late sometimes, somewhere. Perhaps I think that if I so much as contact 4353½ my aunts will make a magic that will draw me home instantly and irresistibly. Anyhow, I don't.

I recall almost nothing of what happened at that party and at its continuation when Clifford and Elizabeth and I have taken Miss Koch home and been invited in for another round of refreshments. I only know that time is hurrying, hurrying, the hour getting later and later, past twelve, past one, and that at 4353½ they are worrying, worrying. And that there still remains Elizabeth, my date, to be taken home.

Do I really think that 4353½ can do nothing but worry about me? I guess so. Can't it spare one pang for Elizabeth who has to get home too? I guess not.

I am aware of darkness and a pressure that keeps growing.

As Clifford, Elizabeth, and I am waiting on Rosewood for a streetcar that isn't yet in sight, my resistance snaps. Before I have completed my blurted-out explanation I am running home like the wind. Without my contacting it electrically, by phone, the magic of 4353½ has worked. And Clifford, my fellow grades-maniac, but seemingly having other talents as well, emerges as the surprise hero of the night.

I try to steal in by way of the back door, but the three pale pitiful masks of horror are there in the glare of the overhead kitchen light, all of them stricken and outraged, two of them tearful, just as I've been imagining them all evening. The flood of expostulations and reproaches descends. They are all talking at once, Ed would like to be able to threaten physical violence, but is headed off, I attempt explanations, but can't talk fast enough, it goes on and on. It is like being beaten severely in the face with invisible pillows. But of course what I find most unbearable is the thought of the agony I've caused them, of which their working white faces and near hysterical babble are living testimonials: I have almost worried them to death.

Eventually the tumult dies away, a point of resolution is found which allows life to go on, faces become relatively composed, and I slink off to bed.

Now, of course, I must have known even then that I hadn't actually damaged my aunts and uncle, and that I wasn't feeling so much pain at the emotional hurts I'd done them, as unhappiness at the embarrassment they'd caused me. At some level I must have thought they were just being stupid, "dumb."

At the same time I couldn't honestly accuse them of "putting on an act" to make me feel bad and guilty. No, they were simple folk, they felt acutely responsible for me to my parents, they did worry, and the fact is I had never done anything remotely like this before, never stayed out until anything like 2 A.M., let alone without any prior warning.

No, what had broken down in the face of senior high school social realities was my system of avoiding reproaches and the demand for explanations simply by never doing anything that would bring them on. I'd gotten into the habit of expecting complete approval from everyone for anything I did. I'd had no experience whatever of operating against disapproval, even from one person only, let alone a group. Explanations were a bother, I was lazy, I'd always expected a calm innocent front to get me by anything. And this time it hadn't.

So is it any wonder if at a deeper, less conscious level inside me, strong resentments were building up not only against my aunts and uncle, but also against the plotting schoolfriends and innocent (?) girls who had been the immediate cause of my troubles?

And yet the only person who seems to me now to have come off well from this deplorable and utterly ridiculous incident was Elizabeth. Because two days later my Aunt Dora (the realist) informed 4353½ that Miss Nelson had called on her in the daytime, was a very nice girl, and had explained everything perfectly. (Only why hadn't I somehow managed to do the same beforehand?)

I was grateful to have been gotten off the hook this way, though probably a little miffed not to have done it myself, to have needed a girl's help, and yet I probably departed on my first tour with my father's company in a better frame of mind on account of it. But I think the important point here is that Elizabeth's friendly action did not result in any rush of communication between the two of us. I don't recall thanking her or writing letters to her while I was on tour.

The original horrendous-silly incident did, however, have two definite consequences of different sorts which were a long time coming, quite slow in building up. The second was a single incident and action, to be described in due course.

The first was a theory or concept about social life, an important weapon in my mental armory, indeed in a way the *first* weapon in that armory, certainly the only one I'd forged for myself.

It was the notion that there are "emotional crimes" quite as serious and deserving of punishment as physical crimes. A typical emotional crime, probably the *most* typical, would be forcing a person to do something, or refrain from doing something, by telling them you'd be terribly worried if they didn't, or did, do it. There were other forms of emotional coercion, of course, but they all tended to reduce to this basic one.

I believe I got so far as once or twice to write down a couple of pages of prospectus for this concept. I don't believe I ever got around to considering what the appropriate *punishment* for emotional crimes would be. But I did know that the defense that your victim didn't *have* to do, or not do, what you'd told him you were terribly worried about, didn't hold up in my law courts!

This grotesque monument to human hypersensitivity, this placebo for victim types, this message of great comfort to people who can't resist emotional pressuring of any sort, this inflated metaphor actually figured in my serious thinking during my college years and after, and only gradually faded down to a general belief that parents and husbands and wives shouldn't be "possessive," that propaganda of any sort is dubious, and to a weakness for Freud, Adler, and (especially!), when it came along, non-directive therapy, which is an obvious distant relative of my own overblown-to-bursting notion.

The second consequence of the "traumas" attendant on my graduation from Lake View High School was that at some time during my freshman year at the University of Chicago I called up Elizabeth and made a date with her for the sole or at least chief purpose of (though I didn't tell her this over the phone) kissing her once. Here we arrive at the second great insight into Little Fritzie's character after, "You got to tell him," namely: "Once he gets hold of an idea, he's stubborn about it, he hangs onto it."

I don't remember what we did or talked about on the date (I guess we went to the movies and ate something somewhere), I was so busy watching for and being sure not to miss my opportunity. It finally came when we parted on her front porch. I resolutely pressed my lips against hers and, do you know? I got a definite, in fact quite strong electric shock! And, thank God, I didn't flinch away! No, I just smiled at her wonderingly and haltingly, suppressing the impulse to touch my fingers to my lips, and said good night and thanks for the date, and backed away from her down the steps and went off, looking over my shoulder at her from time to time and saying to myself, "I've done it, I've done it! Amazing!"

First, about the electric shock. Only once in my life have I experienced anything quite like it, and that happened a couple of years later in the course of a psychology experiment, in which I was a guinea pig, that a graduate student was doing for his doctor's thesis. The experiment was typical of the dumb behaviorist (only they called it "functionalist") clique that was in power in the U. of C. psychology department at that time. The subject was given a learning task and then at a point when he couldn't possibly have finished it, was told that the average intelligent person should have finished it by now.

The idea was to see how much this bad news ruined his subsequent performance. I fooled 'em on the first task, a stylus-and-groove maze, by running it right on the first try—I think I'd learned that particular maze in a previous experiment. But on the second—learning a list of nonsense syllables—I got shaken to my shoes just as they'd expected. While I was trying to recoup myself and at least score as an imbecile rather than an idiot, my face and fingers began to tingle as if I were getting little electric shocks there, I was so agitated and keyed up. So I guess there was a similar explanation for the strange and marvelous quality of my first serious kiss. Too bad in a way. If girls, like the eel *Electrophorus electricus,* could at will administer mild to moderate shocks with their lips it would certainly add spice and surprise to their lovemaking. (While if they, or at any rate an occasional girl, could deliver killing charges that way, it would at least make a nice feminist vengeance fantasy. "The Electric Chair Kiss," "Lightningbolt Lucille." Or just "Hot Lips.")

Second, was I using Elizabeth as a sex object rather than as a complete human being in her own right? The answer to that question is, well, certainly I was—with the proviso that "kissing object" would have expressed it much better since I still didn't know then what the sex act was. I wanted a girl, or girls, to practice kissing on. But this didn't mean I denigrated Miss Nelson and put her down. No, quite the opposite. I looked up to her and admired her cool easy mystery in an area that was a lot more abstruse than jacks and hopscotch, and I was grateful to her for her generosity. In fact I believe I thought that she was rather too advanced for me. To tell the truth, I think she managed to convey to me during our date that she was going with a guy a little older and more advanced than I. I didn't ask her for another date, or if I did it was to discover about this prior involvement. I know I never had another date with her. Yet I went away from her that night feeling respect and gratitude toward her, and with the firm knowledge that I had taken an important step forward and when another opportunity came for osculatory contact I would not bungle it. Her friendly smile and speculative gaze followed me away.

And after all, I told myself, she wasn't going to the University of Chicago. Hopefully there'd be a more convenient girl, or girls, there to practice kissing on. And in any case now there'd be lots of time for that and for contemplating, planning, and achieving further advances in the girls area. This might be formulated as a third great insight into Fritzie's character. "He always figures he'll have lots of time to work things out."

X: More "Girls". Sex Toys With Her Blouse Buttons. *Spicy Stories*. Cast in Romantic Roles. Cinnamon Toast. Utterly Titstruck. An Outraged Virgin.

At the University of Chicago I eventually became closely acquainted with people who, I found, were, like Elizabeth, more advanced than I, yet I did not resent this in them or feel it spoiled our relationship. Like my roommate Charles Hopkins and my new chess-and-weirdities friend MacKnight. When in the fascinating course of exchanging peculiar experiences, strange dreams, and future ambitions with each other, "Mac" ventured to tell me a little about the girl he hoped to marry and how he'd come to that important decision, my reaction was chiefly, thank goodness! it would be a long time before I had to cope with any problems like *that!* Yet I was as much interested in this information and eager to understand it fully as any other stuff he told me. I was back in something like the situation where as a boy I'd listened to my Aunt Dora talk honestly about operations, diseases, animals, jobs, and such, tried to understand it, fit it all together, and then replied honestly to her. And I discovered that if I put my mind to it and used my imagination, I could make intelligent points and on rare occasions helpful suggestions in areas that were ahead of my own experience. I began the process of discovering that there seemed to be no area in human experience so alien that you couldn't empathize with it if you tried, so that eventually I began to think of myself as a peculiarly sympathetic listener, indeed a budding psychiatrist. And if I played doctor this way, I could get to feeling close to a friend without having to tell him so much about myself, at least the more naive and embarrassing things; maybe, if I played wise this way, I'd eventually get told everything I wanted to know about sex, etc., without having had to ask any questions at all. And of course it was a lot easier to work out other people's problems than my own; perhaps sharing other people's feelings was a step toward developing feelings of my own, while my talent for comforting rationalizations such as my "emotional crimes" theory doubtless helped me here too. Even rigorous logicians and devotees of literal truth, when they are emotionally disturbed, are suckers for comforting rationalizations.

And so my ego was boosted a bit. It also got some assists, as I earlier started to tell you, from my father heading his Chicago Civic Shakespeare Society company downtown and from the parts I got in plays put on by the Dramatic Association:

1. A mature (hair streaked with grey) British aristocrat (my new dress suit) in a play called, I think, *To Meet the Prince*. This play made me a smoker—no question, the stage is the instructress of all vices. You see, the script called for me to light a cigarette, so what could I do? I picked Kools to learn on because they didn't taste so purely vile, and now after a lifetime mostly of Philip Morris and Pall Malls I've regressed back to Kools in my old age.

2. Mr. Trevilla, the nominally elderly (grey-streaked hair again) but really romantic guardian of Elsie Dinsmore in a comedy sequence about that prehistoric soap opera heroine in a *Mirror* production, the University women's annual contribution to the theater. The men's, *Blackfriars,* I never had anything to do with. Even then, my destiny was linked with that of the females. The role of Mr. Trevilla would suit my present-day persona better, an aged vampire eking out a precarious existence by small transfusions of romantic élan vital from hypnotized exceptional young women, but even then it wasn't a bad role, nor I unattractive in it.

3. Simon Legree in *Uncle Tom's Cabin*. White tropical suit and hat, slinky mustache, wielding a long bullwhip, and gunned down at the end by his half-caste paramour Cassie—this was a first-class sex symbol role with SM aura, all right, though I certainly didn't think of it as such then.

Well, anyhow, with all these little pluses, and with a certain superficial sophistication imparted by elementary readings in psychology even if in a stuffy behaviorist department where Köhler's Gestalt psychology was looked askance at and psychoanalysis beyond the pale (my apologies to you, John Bogardus Watson!), I was emboldened to turn my attention to girls, the focus of my most intense interest gingerly descending from face and lips to breasts though not yet venturing below the waist, an area I quite literally kept my hands and eyes and even my thoughts off.

Now I know it's hard to credit that someone in third and fourth year college at a top university with great science departments (except maybe psychology) who's taking courses in human physiology and grown up partly in the theater, who's had and has at least a few intelligent teachers and friends, should still be unclear about the nature of the sex act and still entertain a vague notion that babies are born by some sort of surgical section or dimensional magic in the area of the high abdomen, almost between the breasts, but that's the way it was with me back around 1930, fifty years ago. And I wouldn't be telling you all this and making myself out to have been such an incredible dummy (and there's more of that coming!) except I'm convinced that such cases of protracted weird ignorance in the sex area still occur from time to time in this age of sex education, and wanting to let such individuals know another has shared what they're going through. (And in a way I'm looking for company, companions in my bizarre deficiency.)

That's my "noblest" motive, you might say, for writing this sex stuff. Also, I've had these embarrassing incidents knocking around in my mind for fifty years, and it's a relief to get them written down straight for once; so self-therapy is involved too; by writing it out as if I were a character in a story, trying to live (or, in this case, re-live) and feel everything as fully as possible as it happens (or re-happens), I'm discovering new things about myself; I think I get closest to real truth that way. And finally I plain find sex to be endlessly interesting and often amusing, as well as highly revealing both of personality-quirks and culture-changes, and fun to write about, to boot, so I'll keep on for a bit with this Comedy of Ignorance, Curiosity, and Vanity, even though I'll have to leave some of the actors nameless.

Anyway, I recall that my interests in breasts took a rise when I attended with my father and mother a performance of Ziegfeld's *Follies* or Earl Carroll's *Vanities,* both of which shows were considerably built around revelations in the pectoral area. My reactions to a gag and a song are indicative of my then-knowledge. An old-fashioned bellows type camera on a tripod viewed the girls from time to time. If they were sexy or scantily clad or especially if a shoulder strap broke or a low neckline unexpectedly dropped a couple more inches or a plunging one widened inadvertently, then the slack bellows would stand to attention appreciatively, the degree of stiffening dependent on the extent and pulchritude of the revelation—I got the analogy they were making there all right: I'd noticed that below-the-waist phenomenon in myself. On the other hand, it was several years before I got the point of a song, "Hammacher-Schlemmer, I love you," about a hardware manufacturer whose chief product was screws. My bawdy vocabulary was extremely limited. In response to my parents' comments and faintly curious questions I played it cool and noncommittal, of course.

Later on I went occasionally to the Rialto, Chicago's last burlesque house, always alone and never mentioning it to anyone. The form of the show was the old elaborate one interspersed with four strips which I'd have liked better if the undressing had been less ritualized and more naturalistic, and the young women better actors.

I enjoyed having erections, you see, but had never masturbated. My policy toward my penis was strictly non-directive—hands off!

This strangely restrained attitude even survived my reading *Spicy Stories,* a now rather infantile-seeming magazine which with great trepidation I bought under the counter from a stand under the elevated on Sixth Avenue in New York, and which contributed considerably to my breast-centeredness and even introduced me guardedly to sado-masochism. I especially recall one cover of a girl leaning forward so you could look down her neck—utterly delicious!

Spicy, you know, at that time followed in its stories something like my own policy of above the waist, okay; below, nix! They could get away with describing breasts and the act of caressing them, but anything about the major genital organs had to be got at indirectly. Their descriptions of breasts were, well, heroic. I didn't believe nipples could literally get hard as diamonds, rubies, and other precious gems, but metaphorically such statements struck me being on very firm ground. ("Chiefest jewels in a girl's treasure *chest,*" which is *my* extravagant language, not *Spicy's.)*

Here's a *Spicy* plot that sticks in my memory. A girl plans to wear a low-cut evening dress to a dance. Her stern mother makes her wear a cotton brassiere. On her way out the girl stuffs the brassiere in the umbrella stand. She falls in love with a wonderful guy at the dance and necks with him. Her lovely globes are fondled. Coming home, her mother has discovered the abandoned brassiere and takes her over her knee and lifts her skirt and spanks her on her panties. Defiantly, next night the girl goes on a date with the wonderful guy and their petting goes an (unspecified) degree further. This time her mother, lifting up her skirt to spank her, discovers she isn't wearing any panties either, so she spanks her with a hairbrush, first with the wood side, then *with the bristles side down,* which is supposed to be unbearably excruciating, utterly fiendish. The hero busts in, rescues her, and they go off into the night. End of story.

A few observations. One: The beginning of this plot they could have got away with in the movies and I believe did. Two: The spankings are not only there to excite the reader directly, they are also a way of saying that intense sensations below the waist are possible, they stand for the act of intercourse that has taken place on at least the second date, but not been described. Three: Yet the sexual connotations of the spankings are disguised, "softened," by having them administered by a woman, a mother, at that! Four: It is my further suspicion that similar considerations underlie the belief of many males that lesbians habitually go in for orgies of mutual sadism, and even in part the singular fascination the role of dominatrix has for them; she's a sort of mother figure, making everything all right; they can enjoy scenes of girls whipping girls, while if males were brought into the act, unpleasant guilts and jealousies would arise. *(Cf.* the pornography in R. E. Howard's "The Slithering Shadow" and "Red Nails.")

Anyhow, as I started to say a couple of pages ago, I cautiously turned my attention to girls, approaching the ones who struck my fancy and trying to win their interest by saying clever, perceptive, or just bizarre things, giving them compliments, walking with them between classes, carrying their books, and taking them to the University coffee shop—most of them were crazy for cinnamon toast, somehow. Being an actor, I even sought to dress romantically; I recall being bucked up when Harry Fischer complimented me on the studied carelessness of my attire; I'd been trying for it, all right!

Then if things seemed to be working out and they continued to attract you, you could invite the girls for walks or to the movies, write them a poem (I'd got a little beyond the "pe' ap'" stage, things about grey eyes and grey seas and meltings into), try holding hands, venture a kiss or two (thank you again, Elizabeth), even take them to a show downtown, when a taxi ride back offered ideal opportunity for steamier kissing and gentle assault on, conceivably even penetration of, the sleek fabric defenses of the high frontal area that was always the ultimate target, the great desideratum. Oh, how I loved those old taxi cabs where the driver was shut off from you—and not for the then-undreamed reason of his safety. Cabs lost ninety per cent of their calm for me when the disgusting democratic practice came in of having the driver share your air and sound space.

I didn't approach too many girls this way before I found favor in the eyes of one who was a fellow psychology major and whose twin thoracic embellishments were simply wonderful—nothing extravagant or excessive, just the highest style. I was indeed a fortunate youth. My psychology girl lived at home close to the university, just right for a walk and farewell hug and kiss, was good-natured and merry, and had a good store of coffee shop talk and fun, where she was a leading cinnamon toast addict, of course.

My own addiction to her bosom was pretty excessive. One Sunday she drove me and two other couples down to the Dunes State Park in Indiana. I was sitting beside her in front. Some mild necking was going on behind us, and this emboldened me to thrust my hand around her neck inside her blouse and brassiere. Memory of this gaucherie still makes me wince, but she just reached in and lifted my hand out (while continuing to drive with her other hand;

we were going quite fast, incidentally) and placed it, giving its back an admonitory little slap, against her breast *outside* her blouse.

I mention this little lesson in manners she gave me to show how socially naive I still was and ignorant of gradations in permissible sexual behavior, not at all hip really, just pursuing my obsession down a very narrow avenue of new and clumsy freedom.

I lived in a state of mammary-contact exaltation for several months and even wrote a couple of sonnets to the vehicle of my fetish, but then as graduation neared (perhaps that should have warned me) I was handed another "trauma" out of the blue. I was on an ordinary date with my psychology girl when she decided we should end it an hour or so earlier than usual. This miffed me a bit, but then I found I was not taking her home but to the apartment of a friend of hers, an older woman, who was away for the night.

We had some refreshments and some nice caressings of the usual sort, but something was making me puzzled and uneasy, and this feeling wasn't dispelled when she excused herself and went through the bedroom door, which she shut behind her.

She returned in a few minutes wearing a nightdress, dressing gown, and slippers, rather like my Aunt Marie, come to think of it, and this time leaving open the door, which showed a bed turned down. I can't be sure of all the events of the next few minutes, or their sequence. Memory blurs here. I fancy that a lot of that special electricity was blowing up and down me and maybe leaking into my brain. I know I had my shirt off and maybe my shoes. At one point I think she maneuvered me onto the bed, but I wasn't going to take off my pants and nothing could make me. All my previous love music had been pitched in the upper register, I knew nothing whatever of the bass clef, especially in a girl (maybe that's why I tend to misspell it "cleft"), nothing of fundamentals. Talk about your shy virgins! I gave a star performance in that role.

There were no tears or loud talk or emotional outbursts from either of us, though I think both of us were quite angry with each other for different reasons. Fortunately, she was always a very steady girl, with good nerves, not at all hysterical. There was no dia-grammed-specifics talk about the sex act, either, I'm sure. Now I can imagine, I think, her puzzlement at a guy who had been so eager in taxicabs (and played Simon Legree, my God) freezing up so strangely in the bedroom.

Then we were going out of the Gaylord apartment building, I still quite huffy and upset. (By a synchronicity I can't resist men-tioning, the building was next door to the big white house of the girl I eventually married, though I hardly knew her at the time, and certainly not where she lived.)

XI: Still More "Girls". Silver Nitrate. Religion Takes a Hand...and Alcohol. The Poli-Sci Girl, Or What Else Have You Planned For A Romantic Weekend? The Road Again. Wrapping Up "Deskful".

So. I had had an acute and "traumatic" failure of nerve just about exactly four years after the ones that had made memorable my high school graduation, and like those earlier ones, alas, it was not followed by any rush of communication between myself and the girl involved, but likewise it had two definite consequences which I will now relate.

First, the actor in our tragi-comedy went for the first time to the rare book room of Harper Library, asked for the book *Ideal Marriage* by the Dutch gynecologist T. H. Van de Velde, which of course could not be taken out, and read it in two afternoon sessions.

Second, returning to the Bungalow that summer (which was the one that ended with him entering the service of the Episcopal Church, you'll recall) in a fit of despondency and desperation he masturbated to climax in the bathroom, a violent and altogether unjoyous act which left him gasping on the floor, his spurted semen seeming to him like the noxious discharge of some dread sickness.

From our present vantage point we may ponder how much more wholesome and even pleasurable those lonely and shocking convulsions could have been if undergone in friendly company back at the Gaylord, when at least there would have been someone at hand with whom to talk about a *shared* experience.

Hunting for sex books in the Bungalow's diverse library, I discovered racy bits in de Maupassant and also an Army field manual from the Spanish-American War which contained directions for hygienic treatment of soldiers returning after contact with native women by irrigating their urethras with a silver nitrate solution— a sort of companion volume to *Ideal Marriage,* you might say. In a letter to a university friend (not Mac) I jauntily dropped in the information about silver nitrate, saying it was a good thing to know if one should visit a prostitute. I think I just wanted to talk about sex with *someone,* but didn't know how to go about it, for in his reply my friend scored off my silver nitrate paragraph as crude, offensive, and uncalled for; about twenty years later I discovered he'd always had a gay inclination, which could have made my remarks doubly inappropriate and disgusting.

That summer I was introduced to getting drunk by my R.O.T.C. tennis club friend, who served me up martinis made of grain alcohol, water, and juniper extract in an atmosphere of eye-winking secrecy. Now *he,* I know now, with his military enthusiasms, wouldn't have been offended by my silver nitrate data, but I didn't think I knew him well enough then to talk about sex at all, even though I knew he was soon to be married, which would have been another way into the topic.

My own lonely preoccupation with it continued into and was given a medieval flavor by my year at the General Theological Seminary, a walled Gothic enclave just north of Fourteenth Street in Manhattan's not too savory lower West Side. We students wore black cassocks to classes and chapel. After evening prayers we'd pour from the chapel and stroll through the winter twilight toward the refectory. For a stretch of a couple of weeks there'd be this woman who would appear at a lighted third-story window across the street and just when the throng was at its thickest whip off her dress over her head and wiggle in her underwear. It always struck me that that combination of grey ecclesiastical stone buildings, robed theology students, and woman flaunting her nakedness was peculiarly medieval, or Reformation at any rate, Bergmanesque.

Broadway being at hand, I saw a few plays, including British Shakespearean productions for the first time. Gielgud's Hamlet still seems to me by a shade the best I've ever seen, definitely superior to Olivier, Barrymore, and Burton, while Richardson's Macbeth is the only one that came anywhere near my father's.

And I spent one nostalgic evening enjoying the hospitality of the nearby Marshall Chess Club.

And once I attended a public confession by the Oxford Groups people, the Buchmanites, whom wicked rumor said held wild weekend parties out in Long Island so as to be able to have things to confess at meetings, but I only heard a guy baring his soul about how he had been enabled to conquer the tobacco habit, and I little dreamed of the crucial assistance their AA offspring would render me twenty-five years later.

My only other diversion was little cocktail parties in the upper West Side apartment of my tennis club friend and his plump blonde bride, a real charmer. There'd generally be just one other girl present, a skinny brunette, and after we all got woozy she and he (skinny brunette and husband of plump bride) would take to vanishing into the bedroom with little squeals and giggles, while the bride would grin apologetically at me and wrinkle her delectable nose or shrug her creamy shoulders. Now I think she probably thought her husband's naughtiness was pretty damn silly. Eventually I caught on to what seemed to be happening, and once I and the bride tried to do something back at them, but I was impotent. Fortunately this new failure of mine didn't seem so important in the who-cares-anyway world of alcohol. She just gave me another cute smile-and-moue, and so I didn't feel so terribly wounded. I still had a considerable buzz on. I took the New York el back downtown, the same one the folks were riding on when King Kong wrecked 'em. I love all els—alas for the vanished Manhattan ones!—and I felt medievally wicked as I passed the monitor's scrutiny a few minutes before midnight and got back safely to my monastic cell, which even had a fireplace of its own, by the by. I guess the Seminary hadn't heard about silver nitrate, though there was a rumor that they added saltpeter to the diet.

Back at the University of Chicago next season, I found that the psychology girl had got married, but on the plus side Prohibition was ending. No more juniper extract, etherized beer, or bourbon tasting faintly of the corpses of hijackers who'd been pickled in it. While the bartenders were coming out of their beer flats and appearing all smiles behind the spigots of legitimate drinking places reopening on Fifty-fifth Street, some of both sorts of establishments, incidentally, being on University-owned property.

This didn't happen all at once. Prohibition didn't end until December fifth, and then only by stages. First they legalized three-point-two beer; next, after a few weeks, stronger beers and wine; and finally, when the drinkers presumably had had sufficient practice and were up to coping with it, hard liquor. And of course I was no daily drinker then; the only thing I cared about was serious drinking parties where you got enough alcohol so your mind began working in wonderful new ways and the whole thing could be looked upon as legitimate metaphysical research.

And after a few months I had a group of colleagues, you might call them, in this worthy philosophical endeavor, all of them brilliant. There was a wise old professor who'd always loved drinking, but given it up during Prohibition as a matter of principle, and was now making up for lost time and lost inspiration. And a stalwart poetical young enthusiast for all things German from *Weltanschauung* to *Weltschmerz* to *Weltkrieg* (well, soldierly drinking songs anyhow). And several of the superbright youths (one of whom,

Georg Mann, a budding sardonic essayist, became a lifelong friend) and maidens who were coming up under President Robert Maynard ("Great Books") Hutchins' New Plan, whereby if you had what it takes, you could get a degree in practically no time at all. And why not, with President Roosevelt's New Deal going off like fireworks all around us, its Blue Eagle terrifying Republican millionaires? One of the maidens, the drinking party's reigning nymph in a way, the inspirational feminine glow at the punch bowl's center, I'll call the Poli-Sci girl—but those days everyone was getting into political science and revolution of one sort or another.

Not me, so much, on those last two, though I loved to watch the witches' cauldron brewing up, and still do. No, I was mostly mooning about metaphysics and even reading it a little and writing a paper for Haydon on how Ibsen in his plays anticipated almost all of psychoanalysis (he did, too!) and all the while working, working, working (very indirectly and mostly, I now think, on a fantasy level) at getting *some* kind of sex life going for myself.

After the old cinnamon-toast approach, I eventually got the Poli-Sci girl to agree to a weekend date, which was biting off too much. Some of my preparations for this stupendous event were fantastically paranoid. See, for a weekend date you had to rent a room, which meant passing the scrutiny of a desk clerk, which meant you had to have a fake name and address that would stand up, which meant you had to have some sort of concrete evidence for those. Now you couldn't just invent any old address, because the desk clerk might just happen to have come from that city or town and know there wasn't a street of that name in the place, and even if you used a real street and number, the desk clerk might just happen to come from that very address himself, or know someone who did.

I've never trusted the laws of chance and probability to protect me one damn bit in a crunch, you see, no matter how huge the odds in my favor. Safety in numbers is a myth.

So I picked the name of Alexander Temple and the exact street address of some cousins of mine down in Pontiac. (It didn't occur to me then, I have to admit, that by doing so I was giving enemy agents a line on my real background and associates, leading them to me even.)

But what about the concrete evidence? Ah! I mailed a couple of letters to myself addressed rather faintly in lead pencil. Then when they were delivered it was easy to erase those addresses with art gum and write or type in my fake Pontiac name and address. That way I had postmarked mail proving my fake identity to carry around in my breast pocket. (This was before Social Security and credit cards, you have to remember.) Then to further strengthen my cover I wrote myself a couple of letters to the north side apartment hotel that was to be the scene of the weekend of mad bliss.

You know, considering my obvious great talent for it, it's pretty amazing that I've never once in my life worked in intelligence. But perhaps the CIA is better off without me.

Well, the Poli-Sci girl and I arrived at our fateful destination per schedule and by some miracle of chance the desk clerk did *not* turn out to be one of my Pontiac relatives. He handed me my two self-addressed letters—ahem!—and I never had to show him the post-marked envelopes in my breast pocket!

I said something about biting off too much. I meant a weekend's a pretty long time, and it's just as well to have some activities planned besides in-bed lovemaking, particularly if it turns out, as it did to me, that you've suddenly developed the problem of premature ejac-ulation, which adds to the amount of available weekend time that has to be filled up in other ways.

Now it seems to me not so surprising that one who spent so much time *visualizing* things in advance should develop *voyeurism* and be brought to climax by the sight of the crucial areas in his partner's anatomy, but then it was a dismal and self-debasing shock.

And now I'd be apt to tell myself that sex is just one aspect of *pairing,* a very important concept in human relations, and that sex itself has many expressions besides the in-bed one, and also many in-bed expressions besides the phallic one. I'd also say that after years of not even letting your thoughts go below the waist, it takes a period of appreciation of the crucial area there, of cossetting and worshipping, of close visual as well as tactile familiarization, before that area becomes fully as beautiful as breasts. (Indeed it's something worth a lifetime of compulsive devotion.) But then my premature response seemed to be an unforgivable failure of my physiological apparatus, the very end. And I couldn't lighten the gloom with humor. I was too close to it. Besides, the Poli-Sci girl had told me I was just no good at telling jokes and stories that turned on sex (and thirty years later a British reviewer was still making the same criticism of my writing in my novel *The Wanderer)*. It was just as well for both of us that I had brought a bottle along.

I'll tell just two more things about that weekend. It was financed by twenty-five dollars borrowed from (and never repaid to) my Aunt Marie, who was still working in the Wallen real estate office. Men exploit mercilessly those fond of them, past flames. And I later discovered that the apartment hotel, though twenty blocks away, was then owned by Wallen. So much for secrecy!

A couple of months later the Poli-Sci girl and I tried it again in a humbler caravanserai near the University (my paranoia was ebbing), and things went a bit better, though only a bit. I think what made the difference was that the second time we were listening to live radio reports of a big fire raging at the stockyards, and the reporters got out of hand and had it jumping ahead a building at a time, then a block, then ten blocks—oh, it was pretty scaly for a couple of minutes! (And that sort of reporting still goes on. Last year we burned down San Francisco the same way, at least judging by TV impressions my friends Harry and Martha Fischer were getting in Clarksburg, W.V.) But I really do think catastrophes conduce toward sex, which was one thing I was saying in *The Wanderer*.

I was groping and fumbling a lot with sex then and not in the rumble seats of Stutz Bearcats either, which would have been more to the point. And every step I took I stumbled, made some horrendous *faux pas*. For instance, just after they legalized wine I gave a party and invited to it *three* girls in whom I was interested to varying degrees and for various reasons. Was it my vanity that was colossal or my naivete? Some thought both. I thought I was... just trying things on.

One of the girls was Margaret Koch, Clifford's date on that fateful high school night. The link there was the theater. She was a professional dancer; even back in high school she had been running two dancing studios with her mother managing. Then there was a little girl who was president of the University poetry club, Jonquil Stephens, who'd been persuaded by a girl friend to see me as Simon Legree in *Uncle Tom's Cabin*. And the Poli-Sci girl. No wonder the latter had a rock-bottom opinion of my *savoir faire!*

She got a bum deal from me all the way round. Next autumn when I was touring with my father's company and we played Milwaukee instead of Chicago, I was feeling pretty lonely and low, so I set up a date with her for late, late Saturday night. After the Saturday night Shakespeare performance I'd catch the midnight electric interurban down to Chi and be back via the same route in time for the Sunday show. But on Friday, the night before that, I walked the Company's New Ingenue, a pale, skinny blonde, back to her hotel after the show, thinking to lay the foundation for possible romantic developments later on, and was vastly taken aback when after little more than a kiss she proposed coolly that we set up housekeeping, as it were, for the season; she'd made a lot of trouble for herself on her last tour, she told me, by not getting her love relationships worked out right (finalized, as it were) at the very start. The prospect of carrying on a love affair under the eyes of my father and mother daunted me, just the idea of committing myself to day-to-day arrangements in the sex area was something new to me that wanted lots of thinking about (I wasn't sure I could manage the sex act decently even once, let alone on a daily or whatever basis), and I backed off hurriedly, seeking to temporize. Alas, I was in the process of discovering that in the erotic area there are opportunities that must be seized, or at least swiftly decided on, or else forgone, and that there are people to whom sex is a regular activity rather than a rare delight. I became further depressed, and as I acted my way through Saturday's matinee and soiree, getting tireder and tireder (about forty-five years later I discovered that the young schoolboy, Robert Bloch, had been in the audience that weekend), I got cold feet about my late, late date. I told myself that with the two-hour interurban trip and two hours back I wouldn't get any sleep at all, someone would find out about my absence from Milwaukee (my betrayal of the Company!), my father would disapprove, there was bound to be trouble (maybe my Friday night retreat was hypnotizing me into making another one)—anyhow, I called up the Poli-Sci girl and cancelled the whole thing. God, but I was a cowardly self-frustrator back in those days.

So the whole short season had a self-added note of lonely gloom for me, and I had time to write a couple of my *Churchman* children's stories and even work on a Mayan "lost civilization" adventure novel that I never got far with. Toward the end of the season the second juvenile embarrassedly thanked me for "stepping out of the way for him," as it were, and in that way I discovered that the new ingenue's love life hadn't suffered greatly because of me. I managed a brave smile.

In Hollywood my mood of unrestful depression continued, interspersed with forays at writing (Robert Graves' *I, Claudius* had just been published, a writer and book that have influenced me vastly ever since, and I was trying to work Fafhrd and the Gray Mouser into the stuttering emperor's loony household), and after a few months, as spring moved toward summer, I persuaded my father to let me go back to the University for a bit "to straighten things out about my incompletes." My unspoken grim intention was to somehow "solve my sex problems," which gives me a laugh now, "grim"—or even "serious" for that matter—being about the stupidest way of approaching sex, "lighthearted" and "carefree," even "reckless" being the right watchwords.

Back in Chicago I rented a cheap one-room apartment south of the Midway in the same area where my friend MacKnight had used to pitch his tent. (But Mac was back in Louisville now, married and teaching school, though later he'd return to Chicago with his wife Esther to get a doctor's degree in geology.) God knows my apartment was "grim" enough, I don't think I ever invited a soul up to it. It was the most dismal abode I ever bivouaced in (except maybe for a tiny YMCA bedroom I occupied for one night in the 1950s when I was trying to stop drinking, and spent hours taking a cheap watch to pieces "because I'd never done that like other boys when I was a child").

I didn't do anything. I just hung around the University through the thin summer term and felt desperate and sometimes solaced myself with beer, or rum and Coke, or a bottle of burgundy with peanut butter sandwiches on darkest pumpernickel.

Now you might say I was just loafing and looking for trouble, manufacturing a lot of frivolous worries and going through a lot of antics about sex, etc., and if my father had just quit supporting me and I'd had to get a job and work for a living, I'd have straightened out, and you may be right though it *was* the Depression. Anyhow that's the way it was with me.

Of course I tried to get things going again, if you can call it that, with the Poli-Sci girl, but she quite understandably wasn't having any. She said I was unstable and she was right. One trouble was there were so few people I knew around during the summer term, which was mostly inhabited by high school teachers trying to improve themselves. One exception to that was a psychology major I'd known at Hitchcock who was working hard for his master's degree, a baby-faced chap who laughed a lot and seemed to take life lightly and always saw the bright side of things.

I remember one superhot summer night when it was impossible to sleep and he and I were listlessly walking around the Midway hunting a breeze, I broke down and asked him just *how* did a guy go about getting a girl to have sex with without going through months of the cinnamon toast and small talk and compliments and presents routine. (And if you think my antics then are a splendid argument for sex education and no-nonsense sex therapy, I agree with you heartily.) Anyway, he laughed and laughed and laughed and finally said it was very funny I should ask him that question because, he now confessed lightly, he liked boys more than girls.

This didn't shock me greatly—you get to know about homosexuals in the theater—though it did disappoint me at the time, as I'd been counting on him to tell me the great girls secret. I think I appreciated something of the courage his confession took and some of the friendliness it showed back in those days when so many gays were still in the closet. On the light side he told me a joke about a homosexual who said defensively, "I'm not one of the ones who go screaming and swishing down Michigan Boulevard," and on the more serious side he recommended *Twilight Men* to me and I read it and was further edified. And then about four years later, just after the Hitlerian War got started, I read in the paper that the man who was forever laughing had hung himself, leaving a note explaining that the world was becoming too evil for him to bear.

You might begin to wonder about my own gender, noting my tendency to take my sex questions and comments to gays I didn't know were such. I think it was simply because they were more sensitive because of their own secret lives and socially disapproved desires, more apt to respond courteously and considerately to any sex questions rather than make some standard flip or macho come-back, as most "straight" young men tended to do, either because of their own sex experience or total lack of it.

Then people I knew were coming back for the autumn semester and it wasn't so lonely. I arranged to share with an archeology student, Frank Allen, his comfortable low-eaved tree-guarded apartment called the Mews, a living room and two bedrooms over a stable-turned-garage behind one of the fine old houses near the University—which incidentally was getting a little more political all the time. I wasn't political at all, except for thinking of myself as a devoted pacifist, yet I dearly enjoyed the behind-the-scenes and in-the-know feeling of doing my late night drinking with a brilliant Trotskyite couple and a sharp and shifty young Communist who'd been expelled from Oxford and England because of it, and who let you know about that, and a mysterious German archeologist who'd dug in Turkey and had an unhealing high neck wound got in the last days of World War I when he was a boy soldier for the Kaiser (a cranial nerve was severed, so he couldn't taste anything, only feel the chemical bite of proof alcohol and red pepper). They'd comment sardonically on the day's politicking, leak information and red herrings to each other, rove their eyes around, while I'd lap it all up and occasionally shout down a comment from my ivory tower, just as if I really were a wise old muezzin. (Much later on, the Trotskyites wrote books, the Communist did a Whitaker Chambers, and the mystery German returned to Turkey, got picked up as a Nazi agent the day that country went belligerous, and was nevermore heard from.)

I still hadn't done a damn thing about my incompletes, but I whacked out some more pages on my abortive Mayan thriller and started a long story with the abstruse title, "Adept's Gambit," set in Seleucia in Alexandrian times, about two guys named the Gray Mouser and Fafhrd whose girls kept turning into pigs and giant snails.

And now I'm going to leave our unenterprising Candide in suspension for a bit, and the reader in suspense (of sorts), and get back to "A Deskful of Girls" and then on to backgrounding another story. He's no nearer to solving his sex problem than he was in Hollywood, the desperate gnawing predicament he's in, or likes to think he's in for some peculiar reason. Is he afraid of girls? Is he a latent homosexual? Transsexual? Is it that no one's told him, "Fritzie, go get a girl and get her out of her clothes and make love to her!" like they told him to go be a minister and he did? Does he want it all diagrammed beforehand? (*That* I'm sure he'd appreciate.) Is he scared of doing much of anything without general approval? Does he want the luxury of being able to say "No," and then have someone (the girl, say) argue him around? Or is he just terribly lazy? What a character! Well, at least we know we're leaving him in more comfortable and romantic surroundings than he was south of the Midway—the Mews, the place of hawks. I have it! We'll pick him up again (long enough to see him out of his plight, and then continue his history at a much, *much* faster rate) when I come to my cat story and one *mews*.

Wrapping up "A Deskful of Girls" should only take a minute, a matter of making a couple of points, or maybe three. Point one: The hero, though introduced as a detective and talking as if he belongs to the hard-boiled school, spends most of the story tied up securely and forced to listen to a lecture and then watch a little show about sex. Parallels the frustrating incapacity to take any action about sex which I felt at that time in my life.

Point two: If the hero (or the reader, for that matter) experiences any sexual excitement during the story, it has to be voyeuristic, because he can't do anything, he can just see. He can't even masturbate, supposing he wanted to, because he's immobly bound. So he, and hopefully the reader, needn't feel guilty about any voyeuristic pleasure experienced.

Voyeurism goes deep. A Chicago friend once told me, "You're

not really into voyeurism until you've done things like put a photograph of a naked girl in a glass cabinet, lit it by candlelight, and then spied on it from behind a chair across the room with a telescope."

Point three: It may be significant that the hero is released from his plight by a woman's *hand,* a woman's *finger* pressing a button.

XII: "Space-Time For Springers". The Real Gummitch. Enter Our Heroine. Lifetime Anglo-Feline Alliance. Wed In A Blizzard. To Hollywood Again And Back. My First Sale.

"Space-Time for Springers," my cat story in this collection, is an ultra-realistic story in a sense. Except for the central and climactic incident, it's pretty much an account of things that actually happened. I'm Old Horsemeat; my wife Jonquil is Kitty-Come-Here. Gummitch was a real cat with the same name and was indeed rescued by Jonquil and went through kittenhood as described. The time was the winter and spring of 1957. I'd just finished *The Big Time* and "A Deskful of Girls." We were living at 5447 Ridgewood Court near the University of Chicago and had been living there for ten years, the only house she and I ever owned outright, and for all of those ten years I'd been working at an office on the near north side as associate editor of *Science Digest* magazine—until I'd quit that job the year before during my alcoholic crisis.

The two children of the story, the baby and the toddler, and their respective perils and deviltries, are *not* real, but pure invention—that is, as pure as invention ever gets. Actually our only son, Justin, was about eighteen at the time, had recently declared his independence of 5447 and us, was living in an apartment in the neighborhood in exchange for housework, eating oatmeal and beef heart cooked on a radiator, regularly picking up extra money by making a fourth at bridge at the Hamilton Hotel down in the Loop, and continuing to attend the University of Chicago in pursuit of his bachelor's degree—while 5447 was temporarily a boarding house for female University of Chicago students (four maximum capacity), a transformation Jonquil had resourcefully effected to help support us, while she and I occupied a bedroom extemporized in the back basement. (I did my writing up in the dining room, however; likewise my solacing of kitten waif Gummitch in a fold of my bathrobe.)

Actually the kitten-rescue and boarding house capers are a good

I'm looking east from 5447 Ridgewood Court.

way of introducing Jonquil into this narrative, for she was quite like a kitten when I met her and in some ways managed to continue so until her end about thirty-five years later. She was small (four foot ten; best weight, ninety pounds), had bright blue eyes that were at times violet; she was fast (at Cyfartha Castle school in Wales she'd been a great scorer in field hockey; her method: get the ball and dodge your way to the enemy goal, no teamwork needed—you can always dodge big girls) and a good apache dancer; she had natural grace and artistry (early on she'd done illuminated manuscripts just as had the hero of Machen's *The Hill of Dreams);* in America she posed for silk stocking advertisements; she was a great party planner and giver, a gifted fortuneteller, enthusiastic, and friendly, but capable of sudden vast dignified reserves, again just like a kitten.

Her English background was pure *Upstairs, Downstairs:* one of those wealthy families like the Bellamys—country estate in wild and witchy Wales, town house in fashionable London, summer place on the South Coast—that managed to work their way to financial ruin ("The consols have dropped to nothing somehow") between the two World Wars. A charmin' but somewhat weak semi-invalid father (results of a fall in youth got jumpin' between roofs at Oxford), a strong ridin', shootin', and spendin' mother (always ordered white kid gloves a dozen pairs at a time) with a taste for Spartan discipline, a parcel of big manly half-brothers (mother's first marriage) all killed in World War I, three full sisters and one full brother (who was shot dead at age four in Ireland—they had another place there too, worse luck—while on an imprudent country ramble with his sister Jonquil, age six, who boasted a bullet scar in her forehead from it).

The downstairs part came from liking the life there, the warmer rooms, the kitchen fire, the gossip, the sensational stories in *News of the World,* and from being kidnapped for a month or so without it being very much noticed upstairs, by a disgruntled maid, and taught the rudiments of street begging in Limehouse and finally retrieved by police when they came to arrest the maid's brother for murder (she wrote the story "Nellie Norbree" about it).

Brilliant school record, writing talent, intellectual tastes, year at Oxford, then on account of family frictions and omens of approaching ruin shipped to Chicago to live with a wealthy female cousin ("aunt" by courtesy) who wanted a companion; classes at U. of C., didn't take American colleges too seriously though relishing their freer social life.

Anyhow, when Jonquil and I met again while I was living at the Mews, it seemed very much to me as if I were being rushed by a bright kitten determined to make friends—though she wasn't at all forward, in fact capable of retreats and hidings. All my previous girls or would-be girls (except the one in 108) had been tall, and a small quick one was fascinating. When we started to date we found we were both on the rebound, I from the Poli-Sci girl and she from a brilliant Louisville bloke at the U. of C. (no connection with Mac) who was so winning and talented he sort of traveled with a cheering section of straight male admirers and hangers-on. And on account of that, we were both so busy sympathizing and being gentle with each other that there was no time to be huffy or scared. We both easily got caught up romantically in the idea of somehow rescuing each other, she me from my loneliness, I her from her somewhat devouring aunt. We romanticized each other: the solitary knight on a quest, the princess imprisoned in the tower. At the same time we began to discover the joy and relief of having someone you could safely tell everything, or almost everything. And we shared a delight in romantic poetry—Keats, Millay, and such— and ghost tales from *The Duchess of Malfi* to moderns like Wakefield and James. We had a couple of rendezvous at the naturally conspiratorial Mews with me setting forth wine and cookies (no cinnamon toast this time!), and somehow we weren't shy of touching each other and where her helping hands went. So that when in the back of a taxicab she brought up the topic of marriage, I considered the idea for a long moment (it did seem a momentous decision to make, just like that) but I couldn't think of one good argument against it, and after all it did appear to be what I'd come charging all the way from Hollywood to do, it really did, didn't it?—and finally it seemed such a beautifully final response to all that north side anti-British prejudice I'd got in childhood, that I answered, "Yes, let's do it."

Neither of our immediate families evinced vast initial enthusiasm at our decision, but as I've said, Jonquil was a great party planner and giver and I was a good back-up for her, being very stubborn about any idea once I'd got hold of it, so preparations went forward with a rush for a big wedding with all the fixings. I had my father's old Buick coupe from Atlantic Highlands (somehow it had got driven to Chicago during the interim) and that was a help. My spare time I spent finishing "Adept's Gambit," so we'd have something to live on when Jonquil's money ran out. And we rented a gloomy little back apartment on Fifty-fifth Street for after the wedding, economy being a consideration.

So on the cold evening of January 18, 1936, under the Sign of Capricorn with a thick snow falling, we got married at the University's Bond Chapel in a sparkling Episcopalian evening-dress ceremony. Jonquil's aunt had had a terrible temporary heart attack that morning, but we'd arranged for Celeste's father Theodor Holm to give the bride away, and they made a strikingly aristocratic couple. Immediately afterwards we hosted a dinner party for the bridesmaids, best man (my Hutchins New Plan friend Georg), and their dates. I'd even had a bang-up stag party the night before in a weird old Victorian mansion belonging to friends of Jonquil. After the dinner party, which involved considerable wine bibing from huge goblets, we had to ferry back to her abode the chief bridesmaid, whose date didn't have wheels, in my trusty old Buick, which fortunately had a wonderful exhaust heater, for the snow was a blizzard now. We finally arrived at our dark little apartment, quite worn out from stage-managing our own nuptials.

That was the coldest winter I ever knew in Chicago; the temperature hovered a few degrees above zero for days on end. Windows froze shut. Once we were almost asphyxiated by the oven we kept going to supplement the inadequate radiator—the same sort of trouble Admiral Byrd was going through at about the same time alone at his advance base in Little America. I read Jonquil all of H. P. Lovecraft's novel, *At the Mountains of Madness* (the Antarctic again!) from *Astounding Stories,* where it was appearing as a serial.

I'd finished "Adept's Gambit" on schedule, but, alas, it did not appeal as a novella to any of the book publishers to whom it was offered (nor did it find one for eleven years; actually, I was still three years away from my first short story sale to a magazine). As the weather reluctantly moderated, the writing on the wall became clear. We'd have to traipse out to California and live a while with my parents and I would try to find work, as my father had, in the movies. Happily they were willing, even eager, to help finance this operation. (Decades later I discovered that they'd had Jonquil investigated by a private detective agency, which made no earth-shaking discoveries; at least she wasn't a British agent, we good Chicagoans hoped, though she did become one of sorts when World War II came moseying along.)

So in the midst of an unseasonal April snowstorm we set out south in the old Buick on a belated cross-country honeymoon. Our first stop was Louisville, where we divided our time between Jonquil's amiable last year's beau, the man from whom she'd rebounded to me, and my friend Harry Fischer (more of him when we get to "Baazar of the Bizarre") and *his* new wife and fellow-puppeteer Martha, who'd just spent the Fimbul-winter together in a small house trailer. They drove us out into the greening countryside where Harry's folks had a snug cabin and where at a nearby farm our souls were enravished by two kittens who, as Murphet and Grayface, became the companions of our tender voyaging, and whose cosseting at motels and smuggling into a couple of stuffy hotels were among its incidents of note. Next stop, for weirdness' sake, Mammoth Cave, where we took the short trip. (Years later, Jonquil told me she'd been terrified the whole time underground.) Next Memphis and Houston, where we partied a week with the chief bridesmaid and her family and visited Gulf-dreamy Galveston. Then San Antonio, where we stayed at a raw ultramodern hotel, one of the stuffy-about-cats ones, that had electric doors that hit you in the face and ice cold air-conditioning along with wasps. In search of Mission atmosphere, we found a sign, "Immaculate Conception, ten cents." Thereafter Ft. Stockton with its cool gently bubbling springs, where it hadn't rained for three years though they had a regular late afternoon lightning storm daily, and then by way of El Paso, Phoenix, the Mohave's furnace heat, and Azusa ("Everything from A to Z in the U.S.A.") to my parents' duplex in Beverly Hills, where we arrived with desert throats and fevers, but the kittens soon chipper.

There followed what was, particularly from my point of view, a pretty stupid year that left me with a deep hatred of Hollywood that's been a lifetime easing. I went through the motions of making myself glamorous, "getting publicity," hunting a movie job (and I did get that part in *Camille* and one in *The Great Garrick* that ended up on the cutting room floor), but all I was really trying to do was write a story that would sell, especially a supernatural horror story such as Lovecraft wrote, though not necessarily in the same style. Jonquil, knowing my deep interest in his work, had the gumption to write him and as a result we both conducted long and rewarding correspondences with him during the four months preceding his death. Mine influenced my whole life. *That* was our only significant achievement during our year on the Coast; and then, after Lovecraft's death, but through him, we met Henry Kuttner and Robert Bloch, the latter on a visit from his home in Milwaukee. There were a number of good parties with film folk, but my heart wasn't in them, and Jonquil charmed a number of important movie people, including John Barrymore and Jeanette MacDonald, but everyone's

Jonquil and Fritzie with their cat Murphet on the back stairs in Beverly Hills.

a charmer in Hollywood, so the quality's no automatic passport to a job.

Then there was the fun of watching the two kittens grow up. Murphet developed a remarkable talent for fetching ivory slave bracelets. He looked most barbaric as he returned to you with one swinging from his lower jaw, where it was securely caught behind his canines. But we were green about cats. After almost a year of fun and games Grayface died of the great cat pandemic, feline enteritis. We didn't know about shots, which I think were just being developed for it about then, anyway. And a couple of months after that Murphet got run over one evening. I found him flattened and dying and finished him off by smashing his skull in with a brick, a surprisingly hard job. I wouldn't handle that situation the same way today. It was a measure of the bitter and marginally desperate mood I was in.

I effected our escape from the Celluloid Capital by persuading my long-suffering father to finance us back to Louisville on the feeble but honest pretext that I'd be better able to write there. On the train back (the Buick had been sold) in the Pullman car Jonquil told me she wanted to make a baby, and I understood and agreed with at least part of her motive—anything to make us more a family of our own rather than some appendage of a film baronetcy. So we went ahead with that; desperate measures seemed called for.

In Louisville we rented a small apartment in a cut-up old mansion with fourteen-foot ceilings where they'd kept the feeble-minded sister in the attic for a couple dozen (or hundred?) years. That weird touch came out when I was asked to carry her downstairs to an ambulance and did. We got a few weeks of magically hazy Ohio Valley autumn weather and taking long walks and writing away and devising a Lankhmar war game with Harry, our wives helping, and shopping for marvelous cheap foodstuff such as pepper-cured bacon and country cheeses and loin of pork roasts (remember, Depression times still) in the farmers' market down toward the Ohio River. And then my friend Georg Mann wrote me about a thirty-dollar-a-week writing job I could get at an outfit called Consolidated Book Publishers who were getting out a set of new books called *The University of Knowledge* for sale through newspapers. They were hiring a lot of University of Chicago graduates to do the job for them and a number of academic names to sign the books and in rare cases even write or help write them. So Jonquil and I headed north pronto, and I found myself back in another Chicago winter, only this time I was commuting to a job that was like being back in grammar school, only worse. You were shut up in a big room with a lot of other people your same size. You had to sit at a desk and be busy or pretend to. Only instead of getting out at three or three-thirty, you had to stay until five, and work a full Saturday too! But at least it was a writing job.

At first we stayed at my Aunt Marie's on the north side, sleeping on the pull-out couch in the living room; she had an apartment of her own now that Dora had died. But pretty soon Jonquil found us a south side apartment in the University neighborhood and redecorated it and laid some linoleum and got some furniture, and we moved in and got along okay, since I still was getting a little money from time to time from my father. Evenings and Sunday mornings I'd write stories and afterwards we'd sometimes drink beer, and Saturday nights have a beer bash with Georg Mann and *his* wife Downing, and afternoons maybe go for a walk in Jackson or even Washington Park, which bordered the Black Belt. Come summer Jonquil had our son Justin at the Chicago Lying In Hospital at the University, and I began to talk about theories of raising children (among other things, you had to teach them yourself the Facts of Science, the Lies of Religion, and the Great Truths of Life, which last I guess you thought up for yourself). And then come winter again I had my story, "The Automatic Pistol," accepted by *Weird Tales*, we both peed our pants a little, we got so excited, and then a couple of months later John Campbell, editor of *Astounding Stories,* paid me one hundred and twenty-five dollars (almost a month's Consolidated salary—I'd been raised to thirty-five dollars in the interim) for my novelette "Two Sought Adventure," to be published in his new second magazine, *Unknown,* and since that was another Fafhrd-Mouser story like "Adept's Gambit," this seems an especially good time to break off with cats and get into the next tale.

XIII: "Bazaar Of The Bizarre". Gray Mouser And Fafhrd. Explosion On A Suspension Bridge. On (Yet Again) To Hollywood. I Teach Speech And Hate It.

"Bazaar of the Bizarre," yet another Fafhrd-Mouser story and one of my personal favorites, belongs to what you might call (ahem!) my late middle period, was written in 1963, a year or so before "Four Ghosts in Hamlet," when Jonquil and I (next year we moved to Santa Barbara for a time) were with my mother in her house in Pacific Palisades (part of the city of Los Angeles) about fourteen years after my father's death. But surrounded by the mementos of his filmic career, my old hatred of Hollywood was refired, and I determined to make it the villain of my tale, a ubiquitous organization known as the Devourers that prided itself on selling junk at high prices; the shittier the junk, the higher the price, would be their motto. I knew before I began the story, you see, that it would have to feature a fantastic store or shop of some sort, for the cover sketch Cele Goldsmith, gifted editor of *Fantastic,* had sent me to write a story around, showed the façade of such a place with a crazy Arab sweeping up in front and a harem girl sitting on a velvet cushion in a suspended golden cage inside; even the story title was on the cover, Cele's invention rather than my own.

In the last few stories of the Twain I'd written there'd been no mention of either of their wizardly mentors, Fafhrd's Ningauble of the Seven Eyes and the Mouser's Sheelba of the Eyeless Face, so they should be in this story, I decided, lest the readers begin to forget all about them. Also in one of those recent stories I'd had Fafhrd behave like a terrible self-infatuated lovesick klutz whom the Mouser had had to rescue from the fix his amorous stupidity got him in, so this time to balance things I'd turn that situation around and have Fafhrd rescue the Mouser. Mustn't let readers get thinking of the two as that stereotype adventure-pair of the big dumb brawny barbarian and the smart little crook who's his brains. Where set it? Why, Lankhmar, of course, that exotic prototype of cult-ridden money-hungry Los Angeles wherein Hollywood Boulevard is the Street of the Gods. And where especially in Lankhmar? Well, the Plaza of Dark Delights sounded enticing, and so a whole new zone of the ancient and depraved metropolis arose overnight, as though built by genies! There are your story elements.

So how did I ever come to write about these two guys in the first place? And what aspect of my life, what theme, should we look at in connection with this large clutch of adventure tales of the heroic-fantasy or sword-and-sorcery sort? The answer to the second of those two questions is obvious. Why, comradeship, of course, male friendship. We've been looking at girls an awful lot in connection with the last two stories; it's time we turned our attention to the weaker sex. And then along with comradeship, its characteristic activities: fighting, adventuring of all other sorts, sailing, mountain climbing, wars, treasure hunting, mischief hunting, business ventures and opportunities.

As for the first question, I've answered it more than twice, though especially in my essay "Fafhrd and Me" and in my introduction to my first book, *Night's Black Agents,* how Harry Fischer got me writing long letters and playing fiction games in the course of them and how he came up with this seed-fragment about the Twain and I took him up on it in my reply and the thing grew and grew, which I'm tired of explaining and don't want to go all over again. So let's take a fast look at the comradeship-adventure-fighting thing in my early life and then a closer one at Harry and me when Harry comes on stage at his appointed time.

I remember when I was a little kid at the Bungalow I had this adventure situation I used to put myself to sleep with, or else keep myself awake with, or maybe I wore myself out with anxieties about it and so went to sleep from emotional exhaustion. There was this rather deep chasm with a tropical river and alligators or crocodiles at its bottom, and across it went a crude suspension bridge made of slats and rope or woven vines. On one side of the river atop the cliffs were hungry lions, on the other side bloodthirsty natives with long sharp spears. Attached to the middle of the bridge, or sometimes at one end of it or both, there was a time bomb powerful enough to sever the ropes or vines holding up the bridge when it exploded. And you were somewhere on the bridge, without a gun, of course, and had to figure out what to do. Not a very imaginative situation and almost certainly derived from the movies; the serials were full of perils just like that, which you saw recently all over again in *Raiders of the Lost Ark*. And rather hopeless at first sight, but there were ways out if you put your mind to it. Like, if you had a hatchet you could cut the bridge yourself in the middle with the time bomb *on your side* (that took courage, all right) and then hold on tight to your side of the bridge when it swung down so that you and the bomb were dangling a couple of feet above the water and the snapping alligators. Then you rapidly climbed the bridge as if it were a rope ladder out of range of the bomb (all this took very precise timing, of course) and then the bomb went off, killing a lot of the alligators and scaring the rest, and you could come down and at least start your escape by way of the river.

I imagine the bridge problem was one that Eddie Smith and I worked over and that made us grin at each other as we scored points on the lions or natives or thought of new ways we could be doomed. (Remember that bridge; it returns with the last story I discuss here.)

Unfortunately I never found another Eddie Smith at Ravenswood Grammar School, maybe because my father wasn't there to be a magnet for other imaginative kids with his carpentry and stuff, for during the first year there I was pursued on the way home from school by some bully and his henchmen who threatened the actual physical insult of pinching my arms, especially my biceps, while chanting some hateful little ditty about my "muscular mellows," whatever those were. It was just one of those things from which there seemed to be no escape that terrified you for weeks and months and then faded off. Once during recess I got mad enough to turn on one of the henchmen and a cry went up and a ring started to form, but before any blows of consequence were exchanged the gong went off for the end of recess and I was saved by it (or maybe redoomed?) and maybe my opponent was saved. I don't recall that he looked terribly enthusiastic.

I wasn't any good at team sports, of course, and that didn't help. I recall being rather proud of a football poster I'd drawn or done with montages of colored paper, and then one of my athlete class-mates pointed out that the players in my poster were breaking the rules, like one guy tackling the other below the knees, and so it couldn't be put up. That was probably one of the things that soured me on art and made me opt for mechanical drawing in high school (that and a kind of science enthusiasm that made me favor anything that could be called technical).

Second year college I went in for fencing, another thing besides chess that brought Franklin MacKnight and me closer together, and then after we'd known each other a few months he was visited for a few days by a friend, Harry Fischer, who was going to the University of Louisville, and whom Mac had built up to me as being most clever and strange. Although this Harry was rather toward the opposite end of the size range than mine, he had a dramatic, almost stylized way of speaking and holding himself, of lifting his eyebrows and looking sidewise and then straight at you—his movements were rapid and precise, he had large expressive hands and mobile features—that appealed to my sense of the theater. And I imagine Mac had been building me up to Harry, too; anyway we seemed to like each other and hit it off from the start: on our first long walk together in Jackson Park—it was chilly as I recall, on the verge of snowing—I got caught up in Harry's imagining of us as two tramps, Chicago Fritz and Louisville Hal, who were sim-mering mulligan stew at a small fire in a secret bivouac down by the lake. He talked brilliantly about books, too, and over a wider range than the weird and science-fiction ones Mac and I shared, stirring my curiosity. Ultimately through Harry I came to read the Norse eddas and sagas, Jacob Wassermann's fascinating *Mauritzius Case* (where Etzel Andergast is a character rather like the one Harry played), Richard Aldington's *All Men Are Enemies,* Webster's sin-ister *Duchess of Malfi* that is the real forebear of the Gothic novel, Cabell's *Jurgen* and *Cream of the Jest,* Eddison's *Worm Ouroboros,* and many another strange, curious, and richly thought-embellished volume.

Thereafter Harry and I kept up a correspondence that didn't slacken for decades and still goes on, and met just often enough—

Fritz Leiber and Harry Fischer caricatured by Tim Kirk as an older Fafhrd and Gray Mouser for Robert P. Barger's one-shot zine The Silver Eel.

once or twice a year, about—to maintain what I think of as a romantic friendship: one in which you build and share continuing fantasies, including heroic and refreshingly sinister ones about each other, usually come to your rare meetings rested up and sometimes with things to do and say rehearsed beforehand, and never are together long enough to become disillusioned, or have your relationship dinged by the wear and tear of daily life. It's a relationship very close to heterosexual romantic love as conceived in medieval times, I believe. You wear each other's colors.

Well now. I was at the point in my brief running (and skipping) account of my life where I was working for Consolidated Book Publishers in Chicago and living on Fifty-fourth Street with my wife and infant son (the time being early 1939), and had just sold the Fafhrd and Mouser story, "Two Sought Adventure," later re-titled "The Jewels in the Forest" for book publication. By the time it came out in *Unknown*, Hitler was launching his world war in Europe. After a bit Jonquil got increasingly into various pro-British endeavors such as "Bundles for Britain," while I stubbornly maintained my isolationist and pacifist attitudes, and did so, inside the fortress of my own mind at least, up to the war's end almost, until the incontrovertible revelations of the death camps. This produced little or no friction between myself and Jonquil; we accepted it as a matter of differing backgrounds, differing behavior; her parentage was upper class British, I belonged to the tribe of actors, a species of observers to my way of thinking, and that was that.

America was a long time getting into the war. I registered for the draft along with almost everyone else; I wasn't going to make any waves with my pacifism unless I had to. I wrote and sold a few stories, such as "Smoke Ghost" and "The Howling Tower." There were no raises at Consolidated and the work was getting dull. We'd finished *The University of Knowledge,* done a partial revision and rewrite of *The Standard American Encyclopedia,* and were into writing a series of books on self-improvement that never did get published and were at the time almost a joke: we a bunch of young writers with varied talents and no great experience, many of us prime neurotics, telling other people how to improve themselves while outside our editorial womb normal people were getting more and more uneasy and across the sea the world was going to hell!

My father picked this time (early 1941) to launch his last stratagem to get me (and his daughter-in-law and especially his beloved grandson) back to the Coast where to his way of thinking (and that of most sensible people, I must admit) I'd have a better chance of earning myself a decent living. And it was a sound stratagem, one that didn't attempt or risk too much, as were all of that truly gentle man's operations. It's impossible now to say exactly how much of it was consciously planned (the reader must know by now I have my paranoid tendencies), how much fortuitous, but it's safe to say both elements were there.

It worked this way. In the intervals between his movie jobs (he was always an independent; he never signed a studio contract), he directed and played the title role in a production of Ibsen's *The Master Builder* put on by the speech and drama department of Occidental College, Eagle Rock (another part of the city of Los Angeles, but one near Pasadena, at the opposite end of the city from Pacific Palisades; truly, Los Angeles has been called the largest suburb in the world). I'd have dearly liked to have seen that production; I've always been nuts about Ibsen and his spiritual successors, Strindberg and Ingmar Bergman; I put on a not-so-hot show of *Rosmersholm* myself in my senior year at U. of C. But anyway my father made friends at Occidental, and pretty soon I got an invitation from Dr. Lindsey, the head of the speech department, to be an instructor there at $1800 a year, about the same as I was getting from Consolidated, and for just two semesters' work, my summers free.

It was an offer that I just couldn't turn down, what with the stupid and unpromising way things were going at Consolidated, and so although I felt I was making the wrong decision and somehow surrendering again to Hollywood, June found me and Jonquil and Justin headed back for the Coast, just about the time Hitler was invading Russia. One of the things I felt the sorriest about abandoning then was a set of the Eighth Edition of *Encyclopedia Britannica* Jonquil had picked up inexpensively, the same edition Oswald Spengler had researched his *Decline of the West* from.

That short summer we spent at my father's new house in Pacific Palisades waiting for the fall term at Occidental to get started was just about the most miserable one I went through in my life. I didn't feel I was qualified to teach speech, a required freshman course at Occidental along with English, and I tried in a hurried yet desultory way to learn something about the academic side of it. I drove over to Occidental with my father and got introduced to Dr. Lindsey and President Bird of Occidental, the latter a hulking, blandly smiling man who tweetled something to his speech department head about how they were getting "two for the price of one," meaning my father as well as me, and then, a strange vacant look coming into his eyes, went on to announce to all of us, "I have just had an inspiration. We have had Youth conferences here at Occidental. And we have had Music conferences. Why not a Youth Music conference?" with all the air of Newton discovering the Law of

Gravitation. I tried to come to grips with what I'd gotten myself into, without success. Meanwhile my own writing seemed to have gone to hell. I don't recall getting any fiction done or even started that summer, but more than once passionately wishing I'd break a leg so that I wouldn't have to go through with my academic commitments that fall. I don't know why I thought I wouldn't be able to teach speech from a wheelchair.

Well, anyway, somehow the summer got lived through, and Jonquil and I found a court apartment a few blocks from the College, the other side of a steep hill, and I managed to fake my way through the first sessions of my freshman speech sections, while walking up and down that hill four times a day (I came home for lunch) began to get me into real good physical shape. I found I was actually enjoying a small class in history of the theater, where there was a textbook in which I could keep a chapter ahead of the class and pick my favorite plays for collateral reading, and not feeling too incompetent directing the fall play, *Kind Lady,* a good melodrama based on the Hugh Walpole story, "The Silver Mask," where we had a wonderful student actress, Charlotte Clary, in the title role (she later became a drama coach at MGM), while the villain was George Nader, who did achieve some success on screen and TV. We got a little into the social life of the faculty. I remember being relieved to find we wouldn't be expected to chaperon student house parties and trips, as all the other young instructors and their wives were, because I had all that work with student plays. And Jonquil had the dean's wife to tea, just the two of them, and got gently bawled out for this by Mrs. Lindsey, who felt she should have been invited; Jonquil's crime was clearly a case of going over the head of the wife of your husband's department head. While to my considerable satisfaction and guarded encouragement, a group of students decided they wanted to put on Irwin Shaw's pacifist play, *Bury the Dead,* and were getting signatures on a student petition to enforce that aim. But best of all, I was writing short stories again, selling some weird ones, trying to sell some science fictions, while larger literary projects were stirring inside me.

XIV: Black Pearl Sunday. We Become Tansy And Norman Saylor. *Gather, Darkness* In Santa Monica Canyon. I Surrender To The War. *Roots Of Drasil* Chopped.

And then came Black Pearl Sunday. Blackouts began and we and the chemistry instructor and his wife next door sat on the hillside steps outside our court apartments and criticized their omissions. An as-yet undetermined number of people hurriedly left the Coast for relatively or at least temporarily safer areas of the U.S.A., while my own sleep was troubled by nightmares in which Japanese bombers pursued the blacked-out train in which we were fleeing across the Mohave. People looked up over their shoulders at airplane sounds. The *Bury the Dead* petition was itself quietly buried. The dean with a knife edge in his voice changed "Peace on earth, Good will to men" to "And on earth peace to men of good will" in his chapel prayers, and numerous faculty members audibly expressed their satisfaction with faint warrior-growls. The price of real estate fell. Jonquil seemed happier. While I found myself growing happier, and it wasn't just a matter of contagious war-excitement or even vampiristic feeding on danger and catastrophe. No, I found myself possessed with a new concern compared to which worries like "Which job would best keep me from being drafted?" were relatively trivial. Rather suddenly the fact of war had produced a "now or never" mood in me and all my vague thoughts about Occidental and its queerly structured faculty life and about Jonquil and myself and women and their husbands generally and about safety and dangers and fancied security and undreamed perils were coming together and I was writing a novel titled *Conjure Wife* in which Occidental became Hempnell College and moved to New England so as to be in the heartland of American witchcraft—and also nearer Atlantic Highlands, where I planned to set a scene—and in which the dean's lady and a couple of other faculty wives, and Jonquil too, had secretly become witches and I was a cocksure anthropology professor named Norman Saylor intent on promoting the scientific outlook and eradicating superstition from the world, yet dumb enough to go poking around inquisitively in my wife Tansy's bedroom one idle Sunday morning, where the ivory-hued dressing table persisted in looking like the one in my Aunt Marie's bedroom. (It seemed Tansy kept little bottles of graveyard dirt there.)

The Occidental library had a book by a Professor Puckett called *Folklore of the Southern Negro.* This, along with a one-volume edition of Frazier's *The Golden Bough,* provided all the printed background I needed.

I remember that that Christmas Jonquil gave me a brand new copy of *Webster's Unabridged,* Second Edition. It was the best writer's gift this writer has ever got, and I still consult it daily and oftener.

One curious thing about Occidental and Hempnell. While there I discovered that before my time Aldous Huxley had spoken at the dedication of the then new Speech Building, Thorn Hall. It had been a blazing summer day, and all the professors and instructors in their heavy academic gowns had envied Huxley in his tropical weave white suit. Ever since hearing that, I've firmly believed that Occidental is also the original of Tarzana College in *After Many a Summer Dies the Swan* and Tarzana's festival-minded president Dr. Mudge a copy of Oxy's amiable and oratorical Dr. Bird.

I finished the first four chapters of *Conjure Wife* and sent them to Campbell, and he encouraged me to finish it for *Unknown* and gave me some good advice on keeping it simple. And when the spring term ended at Oxy, I abandoned the job that was supposed to keep me from getting drafted, junking my plans for starting a fall-semester fencing class (in which the girl students were more interested than the boys, who understandably were preoccupied with the prospect of having to learn the use of more modern weapons) and ending my career as a speech teacher once and for all, and Jonquil and I returned with kindergartener Justin to the seaward end of Los Angeles, doubly determined to make our living by writing.

We rented a small house with a fireplace a couple of blocks from the blacked-out beach in tree-thick Santa Monica Canyon, a section of Los Angeles lying between Pacific Palisades and the independent city of Santa Monica. The value of real estate had dropped a little further still, in part because California had decided to reward its citizens of Japanese extraction for staying conspicuously loyal during the first months of World War II by relocating them all in prison camps, which generally forced them to sell their own real estate holdings. War offers many business opportunities.

I finished *Conjure Wife* in a couple of weeks and Campbell bought it for *Unknown* and was after me to do a science fiction serial for *Astounding*. I was still in my "now or never" mood, and the preparations for war around me and for making money out of war, the blacked-out night-patrolled beach, a fascination with witchcraft from *Conjure Wife* and with the Jesuit order, and my irrational feeling that the war was a dark ritual in which both sides looked for and found devils on the other, all crystalized into the 90,000-word *Gather, Darkness!* which I managed to finish by Christmas. It ran as a three-part serial.

But then I began to run into writing difficulties. I produced a batch of short stories, but I hurried some of them too much, with

Jonquil and Justin on the beach in Santa Monica.

the result that as many of them didn't sell as did. Without an on-
going novel to sustain me, my worries about my draft status revived.
I went through a short period of indecision and anxiety and some-

what heavier drinking (it was at this time that I had my session with Thomas Mann, which I described at the start of this essay), and in the end I "surrendered," the way I looked at it, and went for a war job as a precision inspector at Douglas Aircraft, their Santa Monica plant.

This involved beginning with a six-week cram course at the University of Southern California, and I guess the university atmosphere must have agreed with me, for there I wrote and sold two stories to *Unknown,* "Don't Look Back" and "The Velvet Duchess." And when I started to work at Douglas on the 4 P.M. to midnight swing shift, which at least left my mornings free for writing, I was inspired to start a new novel, *You're All Alone,* for the same magazine.

At Douglas I worked mostly at magnetic inspection, a method for detecting flaws in steel forgings by magnetizing them and simultaneously sloshing them with iron oxide powder carried in kerosene, which made invisible hairline cracks stand out as if blackly inked.

With four or five chapters done of *You're All Alone,* about one fourth of the novel, word came from Campbell that *Unknown* had folded without even being able to publish the last two stories I'd sold it. (By a series of accidents and of oversights and omissions on my part, the manuscripts and originals of "Don't" and "Duchess" were both lost without seeing the light of print; both tales are gone beyond recovery.)

I laid aside *You're All Alone* and continued to work stubbornly, though more slowly, at science fiction short stories, most of them ironic tales about pacifism such as "Business of Killing" and "Wanted—An Enemy," while slowly planning and plotting what was to be a satisfyingly *long* novel in the same genre about three parallel worlds, one fascist, one pacifist, and one reverted to primitivism after an atomic holocaust, the whole story titled from the Elder Edda *Roots of Yggdrasil.*

The Douglas job was never too bad, only extremely boring. For a time I worked the graveyard shift, the one that started at midnight, and rather enjoyed the company of the quiet, reserved people who made up its crew. By comparison the swing shifters were jigging jabberers! I never did find out what the day shift people were like. I discovered I could just about complete one sonnet in my head during the full course of a shift, and I wrote a few that way, or else thought thoughts, mostly gloomy.

Life in the Canyon was fun, especially if you had a few drinks to make it go. We became good friends with Baron Paul Wrangell, who did movie research at MGM and entertained foreign celebrities for them, and his wife Nina (their son Pavlich was the same age as Justin and became his closest playmate, while Paul and I were a good match at chess), and with the explorer and writer Victor Wolfgang von Hagen, with whom I sawed up and split sycamore logs for firewood that made beautiful long blazes in our large fireplace, and with detective story writer Craig Rice and her fourth husband, Larry Lipton, who were bright and funny and (especially Craig) whimsical.

Perhaps the best week for Jonquil and me was one we spent on vacation in San Francisco. Using the excellent WPA guidebook, we explored and fell in love with the city. The first morning we went to see a big old downtown warehouse that was one of the two or three oldest buildings in the city and found it had fallen down the day before, and was just one big heap of pale yellow individual bricks that overlapped the sidewalk. I took off one day to bus up to Auburn (while Jonquil visited the de Young Museum) and meet Clark Ashton Smith, the lonely poet and author of matchless necrotic fantasies. "Death sets his icy hand on kings!"—and also on Clark Ashton Smith stories.

D Day came that week too, and it wasn't many more months before I was calculating how soon it would be safe to quit my war job. Back in Chicago, Consolidated Book Publishers were planning to start work on a new *Encyclopedia, The American People's,* soon (which was a good sign, because they'd never start work on it until they figured the end of the war was in sight), and they'd offered me a job, if and when, at a decent advance in salary, and I was planning to take my family back there. But I'd need money for the trip and getting settled, so I started writing *Roots of Yggdrasil* fast as I could.

But here two complications arose. One, we lost our nice little place in Santa Monica Canyon. Our landlord, who lived in the house next door, took a violent dislike to us and our little boy (who'd urinated on his lawn, or something), so violent that, since he couldn't evict us because occupancies and rents were frozen for the duration and I was a war worker, he sold the place to strangers to get rid of us. New owners *could* evict even war workers. (He got his comeuppance, poor frenzied soul. The new owners, who were from the hills of Tennessee, had *three* little children they'd never told him about.)

But by now the real estate and housing situations had changed completely. Because of the big influx of war workers in the aircraft plants and shipyards, and also due to what amounted to a freeze on new building, prices were way up and rentals almost impossible to find. Which meant in our case that we moved in with my parents again. Which grated on me and made me the more eager to get back East.

Two, Campbell had become terribly reluctant to take serials. Overseas soldiers had cried out against them, on the understandable and moving grounds that they could never be sure they'd get the next issue. Whether one soldier wrote in, or twenty, I don't know. Anyway, Campbell said he'd take a two-part serial but not three or more. This wasn't especially logical, but I had nowhere else to go. I'd sold no science fiction except to *Astounding,* which was supposed to be the best and pay the highest rate, a cent a word, and the one-half-cent-a-word rag *Future,* where I'd had to threaten a lawsuit to get even that (my story, "They Never Come Back," was admittedly feeble; see *Foundation* #17 for more on it). So, since I wanted a lump sum of money as soon as possible, I steeled myself and ruthlessly slashed the outline of *Roots* from what would have made five or six parts to what I hoped I could get into two, cutting out half the characters, including, alas, all the women.

XV: Potrero Canyon. Places And Patterns. Chicago Once More. A Fateful Surprise Party.

By now I'd got reckless and quit my Douglas job. I didn't feel able to write at my parents' place, so I borrowed a tiny outside room from a neighbor of theirs, George Barker, a retired painter and art teacher, who had a big house in the old Spanish style. The room lacked all amenities save electricity. I kept the door open while I typed and used a radiant electric heater when the sun wasn't shining in. It was around in back and admirably quiet and lonely. It looked out immediately on a very precipitous, deep, narrow, completely wild canyon called Potrero that ran like a secret knife slash through Pacific Palisades down to the sea. Mr. Barker told me there were black foxes in it and, he guessed, raccoons and opossums. Years later I found a couple of places where I could climb down into it and I discovered a family of mule deer too. I didn't know then, you see, that I would write not only *Roots of Yggdrasil* here but, twenty years later, most of my long novel, *The Wanderer,* too, when Jonquil and I were trying to live with, or at least near, my mother.

Pause a minute. What was happening here? Why, my life was developing *patterns* and *places,* too, holes and lairs, and would develop more, of course. Santa Monica Canyon would have become such a place, I fancy, except the rents were mostly too high. We'd been lucky to get in cheap that once during the Big Japanese Scare. That other time, twenty years later, when Jonquil and I were hunting for a place close to my mother's, we tried the Canyon, but had to settle for the next best thing to it, something next door in Santa Monica itself, a small apartment over an old stable turned garage (and so repeating the Mews pattern).

Or consider. This was the third time now I'd come out to the Coast and then found myself working to get away from it. Of course the first two times that had just involved working myself up (once when unmarried, once when married) to ask my father for money, but the *pattern* was the same. My life was beginning to repeat itself.

Which also means, I think, that we're getting to know something about the habits of the chief animal under discussion here, namely me, his ways of fighting and avoiding fighting, how he selects his den and marks his territory and gets his food, his courtship antics, the sort of compromises he generally ends up with. Now you could get just a flash of me and instantly say, "Yes, that's him all right. That's his behavior pattern, you can't miss it."

Which was what I was hoping for when I began to write this autobiography.

Which is a good thing, too, for now I've done what I set out to do in the first place, told the story of how I came to be a writer and not an actor, or minister, or scientist, or teacher, or magnetic inspector (or bank president or janitor), and it's time I stopped. But there are a few things I'd like to round off or mention, including other stories in this collection, if you'll allow me.

Moreover, there's another and final reason I have to break off at this point. I simply wouldn't be able to use the honest intimate style any longer. I've only been able to carry it this far by using devices such as our old friends the Psychology girl and the Poli-Sci girl and someone's plump charming young wife and a gay I knew, and I only risked those because it's so very long ago and I've lost touch; devices like that wouldn't work on more recent stuff, they'd become at least unbearably coy. So. But there is, as I've said, a little winding up.

Well, I finished the lopped-down *Roots of Yggdrasil* while sitting some eight feet from the waist-high wire fence and drop-off into Potrero Canyon, and Campbell paid me a cent and a half a word, which was nice, and it saw print as *Destiny Times Three*. And Jonquil and Justin and I hied ourselves to Chicago, where we found—surprise!—the same wartime housing and rentals shortage as had troubled us in Los Angeles. So we stayed with our friends Georg and Downing Mann (it had been Aunt Marie the time before) in the suburban town of Wheaton, and I commuted to my new job at old Consolidated.

Then came an unexpected repeat of pattern. For the past three years Georg had been associate editor of *Science Digest,* but now he was moving into a better job, with *The Book of Knowledge,* I believe. But with this inside track and his recommendations I had no trouble stepping into the job he was vacating at *Science Digest,* which was in turn a step up for me. It was to be a job I held for the next twelve years.

Animals develop characteristic behavior patterns, and sometimes they help each other.

Meanwhile Jonquil scurried around and found us a house for sale within our means on a quiet block-long street in our old University of Chicago neighborhood, just as she'd found the apartment on Fifty-fourth Street when I first worked at Consolidated. In fact the two places were barely two blocks apart. More pattern-repeating. Also, one is tempted to make remarks which might be interpreted as sexist about the female animal's natural talent for home-making, her proper sphere, nest-building, etc.

Well, if it was a matter of female instincts, all I can say is they were pretty darn subtle and with a fine eye for incidental advantages. For within a year, solely by her own efforts and thoughtful maneuvering, she got our son Justin transferred from Public School to the nearby University of Chicago Laboratory School, which turned out to be exactly the right place for him, and he became more thoroughly a product of the University of Chicago than I am.

You've already been inside our new house at 5447 Ridgewood Court. It was where, some twelve years later, I wrote "Deskful" and "Springers" and Jonquil boarded University girls. (It was nice for me, having girls around, and for my son too, when he came visiting; he met his first wife that way.)

We also had a roomer the first few years we owned it, to help swing things financially. We'd had to borrow money, you see, to make the down payment, from my father and Jonquil's cousin or "aunt," with whom a reconciliation had been worked, but by this time I was making enough money from *Science Digest* and my writing to pay back both loans with careful managing. (Those years, fiction writing supplied anywhere from a tenth to a fifth of my income.)

Jonquil and I had the following division of labor: I did my *Science Digest* job and my writing (averaging about 60,000 words a year); she took responsibility for everything else, including our son and our social life, mostly with the help of a Black maid and an old Scot who took care of the furnace until we switched from coal to oil, back in those bad old days of cheap ethnic labor. (And in *her* spare time she'd work at her writing, about which a lot could be said, but that's another story; there's something about it, and some of her poetry, in my biographical sketch of her in *Sonnets to Jonquil and All.*)

Those days I'd get home from *Science Digest,* have dinner, write fiction for two or three hours, and then relax with a few drinks. And write more on weekends, of course. I never went in for cocktails then, or thought of having a drink before the day's writing stint was ended. Which turned out to be a very good thing for me. I never "looked for inspiration in the bottle"; I always knew you could not find it there.

But a routine like that, held to for month after month, became pretty grueling, especially when I was selling only four or five short stories a year, nothing like my early wartime production. Although I was doing exactly what I wanted to do, I acquired a mild permanent depression and became habitually edgy and uptight. I think I can pinpoint the moment of transition from that state. We'd got settled in comfortably at 5447 and my routine was working efficiently, a little too well, in fact, as I've told you, when Jonquil threw a surprise party for me, a mix of old friends and new neighbors, on the sufficient occasion of my selling a story or something, and I *almost,* but not quite—I caught myself in time—blew up and threw a temper fit at Jonquil for lousing up my evening dinner-and-writing routine without warning me in advance.

But as the party went on that night and I soon began really to enjoy myself, it hit me hard how close I'd come to spoiling everything with a nasty explosion. I really was going to have to do something about myself, I thought. I was getting altogether too rigid or serious, or something. Blowing up about Thomas Mann was one thing, but doing it about this party would have been quite irrational. This was one of the good things of life, to be enjoyed.

That gave me my cue. When something like that happened I'd just play up to it, take heavier drinks, show off a bit, let go, play up to the other women who attracted me—for although Jonquil and I loved each other, and had worked up a pretty good sex life with the help of alcohol, the gnawing legacy of my superslow development in that area, my years-long comedy of ignorance and inhibition, was the feeling that I'd missed a lot. Well, now I'd just drink up and play around a bit, not seriously, of course, or offensively, whenever the situation seemed to call for it.

That was the beginning, perhaps, of the twelve-year-long drinking party our occupancy of 5447 became, a drinking party that went very well for years and years, and then got out of hand.

XVI: "Gonna Roll The Bones".
A Twelve-Year Drinking Party.

And that brings me right into the midst of alcoholism and the next story I'm due to discuss, "Gonna Roll the Bones." And right away we get into some trouble with time and some pattern repeats too. For that story was written in 1967, after I'd drunk for twelve years and then been off alcohol for eight years with the help of Alcoholics Anonymous, and then drunk for two or three years again, and then once more off it for a matter of several months with the help of AA again. And—pattern repeat—I was on the Coast for the fourth time, with Jonquil, and living in Santa Monica (and later Venice, yet another Los Angeles beach section) so as to be near my mother Bronnie, having gone out there in 1958, two years after my first recovery from alcoholism and almost ten years after my father's death in October 1949. But this time I have not returned East, but played the game out on the Coast. Certainly my mother, my wife, and I do seem to have been the originals, no matter how fantastically distorted, of the low-life gin-guzzling trio in "Bones." I sobered up from my second "test of strength" with alcohol (You never win!) with the thought in my mind that I'd been playing dice with Death again in order to liven up my life—and with the following dreary little ditty going round and round in my aching head: "Gonna roll the bones, Gonna roll the bones again, Gonna roll the bones with Death!" and I used it as the lead into a short story which ended itself in about a dozen pages without having had any suspense in it at all, and I set it aside. About six sober months later Harlan Ellison reminded me that I'd promised him a story for *Dangerous Visions* and now the deadline was at hand. So I read through the dice story again and at last grasped the simple point that there couldn't be any suspense about the outcome of the dice game if you knew in advance the identity of the adversary. So I rewrote the tale with that in mind, suppressing the ditty, and my subconscious must have been working on it in the interim, because it exfoliated to about three times its original size.

Joe Slattermill ends up in the story determined to go home the long way, around the world. Myself, as his distant prototype, have never got farther than England, the SF world-con of 1979, by which time the other two character-prototypes, regrettably, had been dead eight and ten years.

And although the story didn't make me a devotee of craps, it made me something of a dice freak, so that now I'm as devoted to backgammon as I am to chess. Backgammon is closer to real life because the player has to follow a compromise path between, on the one hand, his desires and plans and, on the other, the blows and gifts of chance—or fate.

XVII: "Coming Attraction". *New Purposes.* I Discover The Science Fiction Community At The Convention.

"Coming Attraction" is the only real science fiction story in this collection, and its speculations are in sociology rather than the hard sciences. James Gunn uses it to illustrate a chapter he calls "The Social Side" in his remarkable three-volume historical anthology, *The Road to Science Fiction,* the best history of science fiction to date. I would describe "Black Glass" as science fantasy and likewise, marginally, "A Deskful of Girls."

I wrote "Coming Attraction" in 1951 when the McCarthy Era was getting into full swing and when atomic war was a chief matter for speculation and warning. My story was one more such.

Four influences were pushing me in the direction of science fiction writing in those days and some of them also helping equip me for writing it. First there was my job at *Science Digest,* where I read all the popularized science that came along in search of articles and book sections we could purchase for our magazine. It kept me thinking in the direction of new inventions and technical advances. It scanted pure science and the philosophy of science, to be sure, but made it a bit easier for me to delve into those things on my own.

Second there were the new magazines that were being launched, *The Magazine of Fantasy and Science Fiction,* which did much to raise literary standards in the field, and *Galaxy,* which was strong on the sociological side and breathed the "in the know" spirit of New York City.

Third there was Campbell, who was once more encouraging me, even providing ideas, as for "The Lion and the Lamb." He was, by all odds, the best editor I've ever known at getting a writer going, if he chose to do so.

And fourth, there were the other science fiction editors, writers, and enthusiasts, fans, whom I got to know with a rush at the 1949 World Science Fiction Convention, the Seventh, the "Cinvention." The year 1949 was a very active one for me. In January I began issuing my personal duplicated semimonthly magazine, *New Purposes,* in which I let loose with both my idealistic and sardonic sides. I did most of the work myself; it was a lone wolf job. Jonquil cut stencils. Friends helped collate. The print run never reached one hundred. There was much talk in it by me of breaking down the walls confining us, especially the wall of inhibition, or Taboo Wall, as I called it, and of replacing the trinity of Truth, Beauty, and Goodness with that of Wisdom, Ecstasy, and Adventure. I'm afraid that that one was to a considerable degree a plea for free love, for which, even fortified by alcohol, I was hardly the fittest prophet or practitioner. Perhaps the notion should be filed among Philosophical and Psychological Oddities along with my earlier concept of Emotional Crimes. But at the time it was heady stuff. (And there *were* some good things in the rag: bitter sardonic essays by Robert Bloch and Georg Mann, Harold Meig's cartoon series "Civilization on Trial," and my choppy beginning of a search-for-truth novel, *Casper Scatterday's Quest,* which later, given a science-fiction setting, became *The Green Millennium* and "The Big Holiday.")

And for the first time I had a literary agent, Frederik Pohl, whom I'd acquired by mail and who'd been very successful selling stories of mine I hadn't been able to, "Let Freedom Ring," "Martians, Keep Out!" and "You're All Alone," which I'd been writing for *Unknown Worlds* when it folded, and was now encouraged by Fred to finish; I also did a long version hoping for book publication, and it finally saw print as *The Sinful Ones;* it was a book I wasted a lot of time on.

The opportunity to meet Fred in the flesh was one of my motives for attending the Cinvention, along with the hungry hope of finding a lot of new subscribers to *New Purposes.* The trip itself provided an example of the amount of drinking and work I was able to combine in those days. I traveled in an almost empty night coach, judiciously sipping blackberry brandy and writing two book reviews for the *Chicago Tribune,* a somewhat reactionary newspaper which had the still uncommon virtue of paying cash money for such items. The convention was for me a revelation—I just hadn't guessed how many people there were in this thing called science fiction—and a dizzying mixture of lost weekend and getting-acquainted party. I met Fred, of course, and his wife Judith Merril, Lester del Rey, Horace Gold, a very young Poul Anderson, an engineer-author who was a lush like me and told me how he banished hangovers with hot-cold showers, even a "Miss Science Fiction of 1949," and any number of editors and publishers, especially editors and publishers soon-to-be. Nor was I too drunk to engage in and appreciate enough conversations about the fascination and exciting possibilities of science that told me I was really with my sort of people. I also found out that about half of them had got out little magazines of their own that sounded rather like *New Purposes,* though emphasizing science more, but even *that* was encouraging in a way! I got a tremendous shot in the arm that weekend and met a not inconsiderable fraction of my lifelong friends-and-colleagues.

A month later my father died swiftly of a second coronary, shortly after completing the film *Devil's Doorway* in Aspen, Colorado, where he played an old Indian chief and took mountain snapshots from the ski lift and died (in the film) and was ceremoniously buried by being slid down a bottomless pit into a cave, a nice synchronicity. I recall seeing him in his coffin and being somewhat surprised to feel chiefly a fierce surge of pride.

I phased out *New Purposes* after sixteen issues and set to writing science fiction with a new seriousness and new and professional friends to impress. I switched my habits around and took to doing my fiction writing early in the mornings, in part because my drinking had begun to muddle my evening writing, but also because I wanted my mind at its freshest for fiction. (Even when I began taking barbiturates, tuinal chiefly, to cut the night's drinking short, I valued most the fuzzy tranquility they gave my morning thoughts while still permitting creativity...for a while.) I'd get up and catch the 5 A.M. Illinois Central train to the Loop, marvelling to see the same identical people in the same seats every morning, and walk to my office from there and get in three hours work on my stories before *Science Digest* began its day's work, producing in that way "A Pail of Air," "Poor Superman," "The Moon Is Green," and "Coming Attraction."

XVIII: San Francisco. Sobriety & Astronomy.
"Black Glass". Wonderful Roof-Worlds.
Ever Fresh Fantasy.

Upon my wife's death in Venice in 1969, I moved to San Francisco and there conducted and terminated the three-year spell of drinking which her death precipitated. This final (thus far) separation from alcohol was accomplished at Garden Sullivan Hospital in the three-week rehabilitation program of Dr. O'Briant, pioneer of this manner of therapy, which depends on AA ideas a lot. I have given my own recovery a shape which reinforces my habit of early morning writing. I begin each day an hour or two before dawn with calls to Time-of-Day and Weather, to re-establish, you might say, my place in the time stream and my relation to the city and area around me. This is followed at once by a trip to the roof to reorient myself with regard to the stars and the orderly wandering planets and phase-changing moon; I become in tune, figuratively, with the universe around me, its great rhythms and cycles. Then the day's work, its creations and occupations, may begin clear-eyed and -thoughted and -emotioned, without confusion and muddle. This regimen has led me to a passionate interest in field astronomy and meteorology, astronomy's sister science, so that I try to learn a little more of the pattern of the stars each night and look forward with ever-increasing interest to the return of Halley's Comet in 1986 and, a year or so after that, the farthest northing and southing of the moon in the culmination of her nineteen-year cycle. Surely if Mystery be the Goddess of Cosmos, then Luna is her most familiar manifestation, at once loving and sinister, worthy of our close attention and closer devotions. (I write a little more about Time in relation to this configuration of interests in my essay *The Mystery of the Japanese Clock*, introduction by my son Justin, the philosopher and my fellow cognitive psychologist, published by Montgolfier Press; while I am at work on a lunar calendar further calling attention to these matters.)

I feel that in these activities I am somewhat belatedly paying the devoirs of a science-fiction writer to pure science and its sister-study mathematics, which are the ultimate inspirers of all of us.

For my first seven years in San Francisco, I lived in a fifth-floor one-room apartment in a six-story apartment building that had once been a hotel (the Rhodena, later the San Carlos).

I first used 811 Geary as the chief set in my novel *Our Lady of Darkness*, begun in 1974 and finished in its short first form, *The*

On the town in San Francisco with Margo Skinner, early 1970s.

Pale Brown Thing, in March 1975, and it was from the window of my fifth-floor room there that I first glimpsed and then became very familiar with the red-flashing TV tower on Sutro Crest, with jaggedy Corona Heights just below it, and the occasional star that traveled slanting down beyond it. But, oh, the sense of thrilling liberation I enjoyed when I first discovered that I could mount from there past the sixth floor and through a small penthouse housing the electric motor and relays of the building's elevator and gain the freedom of the roof. More people should get out on roofs, despite what happened to Jonquil's father; astronomy's nowhere near as dangerous as roof-hopping, though I have to admit I'm regularly tempted to lean out over an edge, and then lean out a little farther, in hopes of spotting some planet I suspect of hiding behind an inconveniently placed skyscraper.

Anyway, it was as if I'd finally penetrated to the sinister yet darkly glorious secret world I'd first glimpsed from Chicago's el trains as I first traveled down and up that smoky city between 4353½ and the U. of C. And now I saw the cityscape spread all around, the Stonehenge of San Francisco's high-rises, and even before I got my telescope observed in the late spring of 1975 the blood-red moon eclipsed in Scorpius and in the early fall glimpsed on its first night Nova Cygnus '75 making the Northern Cross crooked for a few days. And a year later with my telescope devoted seven weeks to studying the moon, learning some of the goddess' secret lineaments, from Tycho past Bulliardus Crater and the Straight Wall on the shores of Mare Nubium to Lacus Mortis and its Crater Bürg, and from Mare Crisium past rayed Copernicus and Kepler to distant dim Grimaldi.

And just this morning (January 13, 1982) at six o'clock, an hour and some odd minutes before dawn, the sky being superclear in the wake of last week's killer rainstorm, I glimpsed in my binoculars from the south edge of my roof the third magnitude star Zeta Centauri hanging due south just above the San Bruno hills that bound San Francisco from the lower peninsula. That happens to be the farthest south star I've ever seen from San Francisco, forty-seven degrees below the Celestial Equator and in the lucky (for me, this morning) thirteenth hour of right ascension. I could see the little triangle of stars making the Centaur's face, brighter Theta and Iota marking his shoulders, and then, way down, Zeta, about where his human belly button would be and where his human body becomes horse body, the latter being all hid below the horizon, including our old friend and neighbor, Alpha Centauri, where a fore hoof would be, and the Southern Cross hanging just below his horse belly. And this I saw, mind you, despite the sky being paled by the glare of the waning gibbous moon only four days past full riding high in the west. While lying along the Equator high above the Centaur were the three naked-eye outer planets Mars, Saturn, and Jupiter, forming with the bright star Spica a temporary spectacular constellation I call the Spindle pointing straight at the moon.

And last evening just after sunset I saw the two inner planets Venus and Mercury low in the west trying to hide behind the Hamilton Hotel, Mercury perceptibly higher than he'd been the previous evening and Venus much lower, as though she were riding a fast down elevator or being fairly yanked down out of the sky, so that by the end of the month I'd be able to see her in the morning except there are high-rises just east of me I know will intervene. Busy times for the planets!

"Black Glass" was written in the early autumn of 1977 almost immediately after I moved from 811 three blocks east to 565 Geary, where I've dwelt since, occupying a roomier sixth and top floor apartment with even easier access to the roof. My place at 811 had become cramping to me, permanently overheated, and far too noisy, and the new novelette was written partly to celebrate my honeymoon with my new apartment, which pleased me mightily, and partly in response to an invitation, conveyed by Peter Weston, to be the American guest of honor at the Seacon in Brighton in 1979. Peter was hunting stories for his third *Andromeda* anthology, and I was happy to oblige with "Black Glass."

But the special impetus for this particular story seems to go back to the Christmas holidays of 1972–73 which I celebrated in New York at the West Village apartment on Horatio Street of my son Justin, then an associate professor of philosophy at Lehman College in the Bronx. Being in New York again for the first time in about five years, and some walks during which I saw the Empire State Building from afar, and memories of the film *King Kong* and a renewed interest in the great dirigibles and their disasters, and my son's presence as a professor in the city all combined to give me the idea for a short story, "Catch That Zeppelin!" which I wrote upon my return to San Francisco. Writing this story in turn increased my interest in high-rises and skyscrapers, of which I was already making a sort of study in San Francisco, my modern Stonehenge viewed from two different observation posts at 811 and 565 Geary and also visited afoot, sniffing out the monoliths at their bases, you might say, and when I next visited my son in New York City I made a point of seeking out the World Trade Center and taking the express elevator to the observation floor of Tower Two and from there by escalator to the catwalked roof; I also took a walk crosstown by way of Forty-second Street and up Fifth Avenue as far as Radio City, accumulating from both some dozen pages of notes in my daybook, and it was these that formed the basis of the rambling walk that makes up the first half of "Black Glass."

As for the young woman in green whom the narrator pursues with desultory and then ever-quickening interest, she unquestionably springs from my own evergreen addiction to and dependence upon romance to make my life go round and keep my thoughts and emotions fresh and sweet. My own lifespan has overlooked considerable changes and increases, to say the least, in ways and means of communication and communion between people and in resources available to the friendseeker, even if basic relations between people seldom change quite as much as they seem to. Yet what's to know ever grows more, the powers be thanked! And new horizons *are* there for the unveiling-effort. So I am attracted to youth, I'm happy to say, though that's not all of me, and aim to have something to offer it, such as this true tale of olden times, perhaps. (I must say I find a few of my age-mates rather overprepared, brr, for death. My old uncle-in-law William liked to say, "The old must die, and the young *may* die." That's more like it, fighting back.)

I was pleased and surprised when I wrote the end of the story to find that old adventure-arena of my earliest childhood, my kindergarten *querencia,* the primitive suspension bridge, turning up. And I'm happy to say that I don't yet know, though I wonder, what shapes swim, other than alligators, in the inky waters (?) below it.

For there will be a sequel or sequels, I'm confident. Next Chicago, where the Sears Tower whets my appetite. Then maybe Los Angeles. And certainly San Francisco.

That's really why I have to break off here. Also while I was writing the last twenty pages I got from a friend for Christmas two wonderful new cat books, *Great Cats* and *Great Comic Cats,* and from another the marvellous annual cat calendar, *A Pride of Cats* by Jean Moss. They remind me I've for some time had in mind a Gummitch story I simply must write. New fiction calls! And from yet another friend a charming little night light with green and blue panes. Charming, yes. But last night late I looked at it and then turned it off. A shiver had crept up my neck and then into my skull, I guess, for something new was growing there. A green and blue night light keeps off the dark, admittedly, a little. But it might also summon something. Why green and blue? The drowned are blue and the decayed and rotten may turn green. Some of the most charming things. . . . New fantasy!

FRITZ LEIBER writes, "I was born December 24, 1910 in Chicago and mostly educated there: four years at the University of Chicago (third year Phi Beta Kappa) leading to the degree of Bachelor of Philosophy in the biological sciences; one year at the General Theological Seminary, NYC; one year graduate studies at Chicago.

"My parents were Shakespearean actors, touring their own company 1920–35. I acted with them for two seasons.

"I was regularly employed for nineteen years: one year instructor in speech and dramatics, Occidental College, Los Angeles; four years writer-editor for Consolidated Book Publishers, Chicago; two years inspector at Douglas Aircraft, Santa Monica; twelve years associate editor of *Science Digest* magazine. More recently I taught at the Clarion Science Fiction Writing Workshop during its first three summers.

"Four persons influenced me greatly: Jonquil Stephens, British poet and writer, our marriage lasting 33 years; our son Justin, professor of philosophy at the University of Houston and author of the scientific romance *Beyond Rejection*; H.P. Lovecraft, with whom I corresponded intensively for three months before his death; and Harry Fischer, the friend who invented the characters of Fafhrd and the Gray Mouser, heroes of my Swords Saga.

"My chief and some of my minor concerns in writing fiction, mostly involving science and the weird-supernatural, but in general following the fantasy trail that curves and zigzags between imagination and fancy are: wars; other catastrophes; social conflict and growth; the monstrous and thrillingly terrifying in big industrial cities; weaponry and swordly adventures; sex; alcohol; Shakespeare and the Jacobean dramatists; cats, our lovely and elegant fellow travelers; chess (at which I've been rated Expert), the most elegant, mysterious, and merciless of games; and spiders, those most elegant and horrifying of arthropods; astronomy; and our mistress the moon.

"My novels include: *Gather Darkness, The Big Time, The Wanderer, The Night of the Wolf, Conjure Wife, Our Lady of Darkness, Tarzan and the Valley of Gold*; and *Swords against Wizardry*.

"My novels and shorter fictions have luckily won awards: nine Hugos, four Nebulas; four Lovecrafts; two British Fantasy; one Balrog; and one Second Stage Lensman at Moscon."

BYRON PREISS VISUAL PUBLICATIONS, INC. is the award-winning producer of numerous illustrated volumes of science fiction and fantasy literature, including editions by Ray Bradbury, Samuel R. Delany, Harlan Ellison and Roger Zelazny. Their monograph on the work of Leo and Diane Dillon, the two-time Caldecott Award-winning artists, was displayed at the Metropolitan Museum of Art in 1981. They recently produced the book, *The Words of Gandhi*, in collaboration with Richard Attenborough, director of the Oscar award-winning film. This Masterworks Edition is the second in a series of volumes to be produced by them for Berkley Books.